MAGGIE HOLT
A Nurse
At War

arrow books

Published by Arrow Books in 2011

9 10 8

Copyright © Maggie Bennett 2005

Maggie Holt has asserted her right under the Copyright, Designs and
Patents Act, 1988 to be identified as the author of this work

First published in Great Britain in 2005 by
Century as *For Love of Lily* by Maggie Bennett

Arrow Books
Random House, 20 Vauxhall Bridge Road,
London SW1V 2SA

www.randomhouse.co.uk

Addresses for companies within The Random House Group Limited can
be found at: www.randomhouse.co.uk/offices.htm

The Random House Group Limited Reg. No. 954009

A CIP catalogue record for this book
is available from the British Library

ISBN 9780099564829

Penguin Random House is committed to a sustainable future for
our business, our readers and our planet. This book is made from
Forest Stewardship Council® certified paper.

MIX
Paper from
responsible sources
FSC® C018179

Typeset by SX Composing DTP, Rayleigh, Essex
Printed and bound in Great Britain by Clays Ltd, St Ives plc

A Nurse
At War

Maggie Holt was born in Farnborough, Hampshire, in 1931. She worked as a nurse and midwife for many years before marrying and moving to Manchester where her two daughters were born. Having been an avid reader and scribbler all her life she took a correspondence course in creative writing after her husband's death in 1983, and won the Romantic Novelists' Association New Writers' Award in 1992. Writing as Maggie Bennett, she is also the author of *A Child's Voice Calling*, *A Child at the Door*, *A Carriage for the Midwife* and *A Child of Her Time*, all available from Arrow. *A Nurse at War* was previously published as *For Love of Lily* under the Maggie Bennett name.

Also available in Arrow by Maggie Bennett

Acknowledgements

My thanks are due:
– to my sister Jenny Taylor for her reading, and valuable criticism of my script at every stage, and to my friend Maureen Delaney Hotham for her patient listening.

– to my friend Lin Wright for her unerring choice of book or cassette, and her generosity in presenting me with exactly what I needed for research.

– to my friend Pauline Wilding for so willingly and vividly sharing her memories of training to be a nurse during the Second World War.

– and as always, to my agent Judith Murdoch for her constant help and encouragement.

Part I

The Fiery Trial

Beloved, think it not strange concerning the fiery trial
which is to try you . . .

1 Peter, chapter 4, verse 12

Prologue

1924

Lily Knowles the Doctor's daughter stood firm on her sturdy legs, facing the jeering circle of Pinehurst children who attended the Church school at Belhampton. She was wearing a smart new frock in a tartan material, box-pleated like a miniature gymslip, with white sleeves, and frills at the neck and wrists.

'Cor, yer don't 'alf look posh, Lily!' breathed little Beryl Penney, in contrast to the jibes of the others in their washed-out, much-mended schoolwear.

'Ain't she sweet! See 'er walkin' dahn the street!' they taunted, and Polly Dawes stuck out her tongue, which encouraged Jimmy Watson, not the brightest of boys, to cross his eyes and whistle through his teeth.

Lily went as scarlet as the bow in her fair hair. Auntie Daisy had gently suggested that it might be best to save the new frock for church on Sunday, but Lily had wanted to wear it straight away. What was the good of having nice new clothes if they were only worn on Sundays? The pretty frock, like the new green winter coat with its fur collar, had arrived in a flat cardboard box for her seventh birthday, and there was a card with it saying, 'To our darling Lilian, from her loving Grandfather and Grandmama.'

'I want to wear it *today!*' she'd insisted, and Auntie Daisy had given way, as she usually did – but nobody had said how nice Lily looked in it – only

3

Beryl Penney, who didn't count because she was a *waif* who'd say anything to be liked. That was the trouble with the Pinehurst children – they were all *Waifs and Strays* who didn't know any better.

'You're all ignorant and stupid!' Lily cried, tears pricking the greenish-gold eyes that could look so appealing when somebody praised her. 'I'm going to tell my daddy of you!'

'Telltale tit! Yer tongue shall be slit!' chanted the mob, and Polly tossed her head.

'Tell 'im all yer like, 'e don't never take no notice o' yer. 'E's got better fings to do!'

Now that really hurt, because it was true that the busy Doctor seldom took Lily's part in her fallings-out with the other children; he either passed on her complaints to Mabel, or told her to be a big girl and take no notice of petty squabbles. It was her place to set a good example, he said – but how could she do that when they did nothing but make fun of her?

'Hey, what's goin' on over there?' came a familiar voice through the railings, and Lily's tormentors at once looked around for something else to occupy their attention. Tim Baxter was in the Big School overlooking the Infants, a strong thirteen-year-old lad who'd been one of Mabel's first admissions to Pinehurst, before her marriage to the Doctor. He'd been a *stray* who'd run away from a foster home, and Mabel had taken him in and become his adored mum. He remembered the day that the Doctor had arrived at Pinehurst, holding a bewildered three-year-old Lily by the hand, and he'd always looked upon her as his special little sister.

Now he came out of the gate of the Big School, and into the Infants' playground. 'What's up then, Lily? Are they upsettin' yer?' He looked around at the

4

scattered group. ''Cause they better not, that's all!' he announced loudly enough for them all to hear. He turned back to smile at her and Beryl. 'See yer later, then, girls. We got cherry-cake for tea today – that'll be nice, won't it?'

'Oh, ain't 'e good an' kind, Lily!' said Beryl. 'I never knew such a nice boy as 'im, did you?'

And Lily could only agree that Tim Baxter was different from the other horrible rough boys. Not that Mabel thought them horrible, of course. She was the Matron of Pinehurst, who had been Miss Court until Lily's father had married her and turned her into Mrs Knowles. The Society kept her supplied with a dozen Waifs and Strays, and amazingly she loved them all, no matter where they came from. They were often distrustful when they arrived, spoke rude words and had dirty habits, but Mrs Knowles was never shocked, and never threatened to send them back, however badly they behaved. They discovered that at Pinehurst they were safe, and in the course of time, which varied from one to another, they succumbed to Mabel's special secret treatment: love. It was something they had usually never known before, and when they got used to it, they called her 'Mum' or 'Mummy', and settled in. They did not turn into angels, and many of them never lost the scars of their earlier lives, but carried them into adulthood; but Pinehurst gave them a new chance, and the security of a family life.

Except for Lily. She was neither a waif nor a stray, but could just remember having a real mother of her own, who had died, and soon after that, the Doctor had taken her away from her grandparents' Northampton home, and brought her to Pinehurst where, for reasons best known to himself, he had

5

married Mabel, who continued to run her children's home while he practised as a local GP, visiting patients, delivering babies, running his surgery from the home of old Dr Forsyth, and giving the anaesthetics on operating days at Belhampton War Memorial Hospital. Lily did not see as much of him as she did of Mabel and Auntie Daisy, who was the deputy matron, Mabel's youngest sister, a dark-eyed, lively girl of twenty. They had another sister, Mrs Westhouse, Aunt Alice, who lived in a fine big house in Belhampton Park, and did a lot of fund-raising for the hospital and other good causes like – of course! – the Society for the Provision of Homes for Waifs and Strays. Lily shared the life at Pinehurst with these twelve others, so could be nobody's favourite, though she liked to sit on her daddy's knee when the opportunity arose, and claim his undivided attention. She refused to call Mabel 'Mummy', though the Doctor said it was disrespectful for a young child just to say Mabel.

'Can't you call her "Auntie Mabel"?' he asked.

'She's not my auntie, either. She's just Mabel,' replied Lily, pouting.

'Oh, for goodness' sake, Stephen, what does it matter?' asked Mrs Knowles with a laugh. 'I've been called worse'n that in my time!' And she gave Lily a broad wink, which for some reason made the cross little girl feel that her stepmother had scored a point over her.

Auntie Daisy was different altogether, easy to tell things to, and best of all, she sometimes sought out Lily's company.

'Come to evensong with me on Sunday, Lily, just you and me together, showing off our nice new dresses, shall we?'

Lily brightened at once, for it was just this sort of special attention that she craved. On Sunday mornings the whole of Pinehurst trooped off to attend matins at the parish church and listen to the vicar's sermon. In the evenings it was a smaller congregation, and Mr Wingate, the curate, usually took the service and preached a much livelier sermon that made Daisy laugh, especially when he looked straight at her. He had a young wife who had stopped attending church after the birth of their baby and, because she was finding it difficult to cope, had gone to stay with her mother at Basingstoke until she felt better able to look after it. Mr Wingate stood outside the church after evensong, chatting to a circle of sympathetic ladies, and he remarked on Lily's pretty dress, which made her blush with pleasure. So did Auntie Daisy, for these were the post-war years when able-bodied young men were in short supply after the terrible carnage of the Great War.

The dream of going to visit her mother's parents was one that the little girl frequently indulged in, but it met with little enthusiasm from her father.

'It isn't convenient for you to travel all that way, Lily. You'll have to wait until you are older,' he said with a frown, though that might have been because of the pain in his war wound.

'But they looked after me when I was little, didn't they, Daddy?'

'Yes, but I didn't see much of you, and after your mother died I didn't want you to be brought up by grandparents. That's why I brought you here with me.'

'To be brought up by Mabel?'

'Yes, by Mabel and myself – and your Aunt Daisy, of course.'

7

'Aren't Grandfather and Grandmama lonely without me, Daddy?'

'I expect they may be, sometimes – but they're old people, and lead a quiet life; they don't really want children around.' Knowles spoke awkwardly, for this was not a favourite topic.

'They send me lovely presents and dresses and things, don't they, Daddy?'

'Yes, they've been very generous.'

'Grandmama sends me cards and letters, "to our darling Lilian", so they must want to see me, mustn't they?'

'Oh, Lily, we've been through all this before. You can go to see them when you're older.'

For Dr Knowles was sometimes troubled by his conscience, as well as his war wound.

Daisy had helped Lily to write a thank you letter to Mr and Mrs Rawlings, correcting her spelling with a dictionary.

Dear Grandfather and Grandmama,

Thank you very much for the new dress which is Scottish tartan, and I look very nice in church. You are kind to me and I wish I could see you, but it is a very long way to Northampton on the train. When I am older I shall come to your house when there is somebody to come with me. Daddy cannot come because he is very busy, and so is Auntie Daisy who is Daddy's wife's sister and looks after me. She is very kind.

With love from your granddaughter,
Lily Knowles (You call me Lilian, but they call me Lily here.)

And thus were sown the seeds of so much future pain.

Chapter 1

1938

The longcase clock in the hall had just struck eight, the usual twelve seconds before the one on the parish church tower boomed out its strokes. Tim Baxter, standing on the kitchen doorstep, could hear the voices of Mum and the Doctor drifting on the evening air, and caught their note of seriousness; they were either discussing Lily again, or the latest rantings from the Fascist leaders in Europe. He grimaced, and brushed the war rumours from his thoughts, for this was his favourite time of day, when the children were in bed, and the house was quiet at last. If only Lily were here to share this sunset hour, instead of wasting her lovely smiles on that twerp Geoffrey Westhouse ...

A sudden howl of indignation from the open window of the boys' dormitory sent him indoors and upstairs to investigate. He found the two youngest sleeping, or pretending to, and the other four perched on one bed, playing cards. They looked up at him, half sheepish, half pleading.

'Now then, what's goin' on? Time you lot were settlin' down to sleep,' he said with as much sternness as he thought necessary, deftly sweeping up the cards to a chorus of protest.

'It wasn't us, Mr Tim, it's 'im, Charlie Samms, 'e's bin cheatin'!'

'Too blinkin' early to go to sleep, anyway,' growled the accused.

'Aw, go on, Mr Tim, give us 'em back agen. We won't make anuvver sahnd, honest!'

Tim wanted to smile, but kept his face straight before these London urchins, transported from grime and neglect to clean and healthful rural Hampshire; it was his job to watch their behaviour.

'Come on, ye've been playin' outside all day –'

'We ain't bin playin', we bin *workin*'! Mum told us to 'elp ol' Mr Cheale in the garden, an' 'e didn't 'alf keep us at it, cuttin' the 'edge an' sweepin' up till we got blisters on our 'ands – look!'

'An' anyway, the girls ain't sleepin', neiver,' put in Charlie. 'Miss Beryl's readin' to 'em abaht that ol' Christopher Robin. It's ever so rude!'

There was a yelp of laughter. 'Yeah! The boy 'oo shits hisself!'

'*What* did you say?'

' 'S right, we 'eard 'er readin' it to 'em – "wherever 'e goes, there's always Pooh!" Yeah, that's wot she said – *pooh*!' There was another explosion of mirth and holding of noses.

'Right, that's enough from you, Charlie – and you too, Jack. Get back to yer own beds this minute, or there'll be trouble, d'ye hear me? Not another word from any of yer!'

There was a scuffle as each returned to his bed, followed by silence.

'That's more like it.' Tim paused, looking round the room. 'All right, then. Good night, boys.'

'G'night, Mr Tim.'

' 'Ere, can we go to the pitchers in Bel'ampton one aft'noon?' asked the boy called Jack. 'See ol' Charlie Chaplin – an' them Seven Dwarfs?'

'Not if yer don't pipe down, yer won't. Not another word, didn't yer hear me?'

Silence again, and then a muffled, 'Sorry, Mr Tim.'

'That's better.' After three or four minutes spent adjusting the curtains and watching them out of the corner of his eye, Tim nodded and quietly murmured, 'G' night, boys. Be good.'

Outside the door, he stood in the wide corridor that separated the two domitories, and listened. Yes, there were murmurings from the girls' room, though they were happy sounds: one rather stumbling reader accompanied by breathy oohs and aahs. Tim hesitated for a moment, then tapped softly on the door. He heard a collective gasp, and there was a shuffling sound. The door opened, and Beryl Penney's timid face appeared around it.

'What's goin' on, Miss Beryl? Why aren't they asleep?'

'Er – the trouble is, Mr Tim, they can't settle 'cause it's too light,' she faltered, coming out and closing the door behind her. 'I came up an' told 'em to stop talkin', but they asked me to read to 'em – in fact they begged me – so I thought just for a few minutes maybe, Mother don't really mind when it's holiday time, an' they asked for *Winnie-the-Pooh*, y'see –'

'Ye're too quick to give in to 'em, Beryl,' said Tim, dropping the 'Miss' as they were out of the children's hearing. 'Yer got to be firm about bedtimes, same as mealtimes.'

'Beggin' yer pardon, Mr Tim, but readin' 'em a story 'elps 'em to settle, though I can't read as good as Miss Lily can – and it's a nice way to end the day.'

Her earnest little face was as persuasive as her words, and Tim softened, as he invariably did. 'Well, all right – but yer must say goodnight now, and tell 'em to go to sleep.'

'Please, Mr Tim, can I just finish the chapter? It's only another page an' a half – *please!*'

'Just another five minutes, then, but after that ye're to come down.'

'Oh, *thank* yer, Mr Tim!' Beryl beamed as she scurried back into the girls' room and closed the door. Tim was not allowed in there, just as she was not allowed into the boys' room; only Mother and her deputy, Miss Styles, had entry to every part of the house – and, of course, the Doctor.

Tim descended the stairs, satisfied that he had done his duty. A place like Pinehurst needed a good disciplinarian, he thought, seeing that the Doctor had his practice to attend to, and Mum wasn't as energetic as she'd been when the Home was opened in 1919. At twenty-seven Tim was now her secretary, book-keeper and general factotum, happy to stoke up the boiler, bring in the coal, chop wood and keep order among the boys – no light responsibility during these August days of the school summer holidays. Tim took great pride in being Mum's right-hand man; this was home to him in every sense of the word, and he had a secret dream that one day, when Mum and the Doctor retired, he and Lily would run Pinehurst together, as man and wife – even though he knew in his heart that it was never likely to happen. Lily had changed from the pretty child he had always thought of as his special little sister, into a discontented young woman who seemed to prefer hobnobbing with the Westhouses up at Cherry Trees.

Seated behind the sprawling, thorny tangle of the blackberry bushes, Dr and Mrs Knowles were having a private conversation. They were not finding it easy.

'I suppose she's at the Westhouses again?' he said,

and when his wife nodded he frowned. 'Do you think she's getting overfriendly with young Geoffrey?'

She smiled and shrugged. 'She's a pretty girl, and he's a well-set-up young man, so o' course there's bound to be some interest. Stands to reason.'

Mrs Knowles had never made any effort to lose her London accent, though twenty years of country living had softened it a little; she still spoke the language of most of the children in her care. She had no affectations, and it was one of the qualities that Stephen Knowles had always loved about her, ever since those days at the East London children's hospital where, during the war, he had found himself able to talk to her about certain nightmarish experiences he could confide in no other. How different she was from her sister Alice, who as Mrs Westhouse of Cherry Trees in Belhampton Park had become a member of Belhampton society, on the Board of Governors for the War Memorial Hospital and tireless fund-raiser for Mabel's Waifs and Strays. The doctor's mouth tightened: he did not care to see his wife patronised, nor for his daughter, Lily, to mix with social climbers like the Westhouses – and their son.

As if reading his thoughts, Mabel remarked that Alice had been a good wife to her husband, Gerald, badly scarred and half-blinded in the war. 'She helped him cut down on the drinkin', an' got him back into his father's office – and never said a word against him.'

'Hm. Nor, as far as we know, did he against her,' grunted Knowles. 'I just wish that Lily spent less time at Cherry Trees and more at giving you a hand here at Pinehurst.'

'I've got willing help enough, Stephen, an' don't need anybody to be forced into it.' She hesitated, choosing her words carefully, so as not to appear critical. 'I can see it isn't easy for Lily, brought up without a mother –'

'My dear Mabel, you've been –'

'*No*, Stephen, I'm *not* her mother, though I've tried to be fair and treat her the same as the others, but the fact is she's not the same as them – she's your daughter. Most o' mine never knew their parents, or have bad memories o' them, but Lily had a mother who loved her, and I can't ever take her place.' She smiled and touched her husband's arm. 'We haven't done so badly, have we? Lily may not have had a normal home life, but then neither have you!'

He gave her an affectionate look, for it was true. He had accepted their unconventional marriage, simply because he loved her and had needed her. He had got used to coming home to a houseful of children who were often disturbed and difficult, knowing that Mabel loved them all and had a healing touch, even with the most recalcitrant. He'd known from the start that he'd have to share her, just as he accepted his war wounds, the almost constant pain in his right buttock and thigh. It didn't improve with time, and now that arthritis was setting in, he had to use a stick for walking. But he'd survived, and three-quarters of a million of his countrymen had not.

'So what are we going to do about Lily?' he asked point-blank. 'You've been wonderful with her, Mabel, but she'll be twenty-one next month, and it's time she took herself in hand. I ask you, what has she done since she left school? A year at Houghton Ladies' College, a few months at poor Miss Drew's

14

teashop, then the Commercial College at Winchester, and now the Westhouses' office, where she spends her time powdering her nose and making eyes at young Geoffrey.' He sighed deeply.

'Well, at least she got over her idea o' goin' out to Spain an' joinin' the International Brigade or whatever it was,' Mabel pointed out.

'Yes, thank God – she had me worried for a while with her silly ideas, but the horrors of Guernica last year made a lot of crack-brained idealists think again. Huh!'

'I reckon she just wants to show that she's got a mind of her own.' Mabel suppressed a sigh, for Stephen's grown-up daughter had always been more of a trial to her than any of the children sent by the Society, though she would not have dreamed of saying so; nor did she voice her opinion – her wish? – that her stepdaughter should leave Pinehurst and stand on her own feet.

'Couldn't you possibly have a word with her, Mabel – you know, talk some sense into her, woman to woman?'

Oh, Stephen, Stephen, she thought silently – can't you see that I'm the one person who *can't* talk to her? She resents me enough as it is.

Shaking her head slowly, she ventured, 'What about her grandparents in Northampton? She seems to set a lot o' store by what Grandmama tells her.'

He frowned. 'Hm. I don't like her going there. Too much harping on about the past – it isn't healthy.' And they poison her mind against me, he added to himself.

'But if she needs to talk about her mother, there's surely nobody better to confide in than her grandparents,' said Mrs Knowles gently, fully aware that

15

there was no love lost between her husband and his former in-laws, and that there were faults on both sides. 'Just think, it must've broken their hearts when yer took Lily away from them,' she went on, remembering the motherless three-year-old clutching her father's hand. 'Why not send her to them for a visit, say a couple o' weeks, let her have a change o' scene, open her heart to them? Yer never know, they might persuade her to follow in her mother's footsteps an' take up nursin'!'

'Hm, I'm not sure that she'd be up to the hard work and long hours – but perhaps you're right, you usually are. I'll write to them, and suggest she goes to stay – ask if they can help her make up her mind what she wants to do with her life – use a little soft soap.' He gave a mirthless laugh. 'Whatever I say will enrage them. They'll never forgive me.'

Nor me, thought Mabel Knowles as he drew himself up stiffly to a standing position, and grasped his stick.

'Come on, my love,' Stephen said. 'Let's see what the excellent Tim's been up to.'

She put her arm in his and they made their way back to the house. Tim had just reached the foot of the stairs.

'Everythin' all right, Tim?' Mabel asked with a smile.

'Sure thing, Mum. Just a bit o' fidgetin' up there 'cause it's so light. They've quietened down now.' Tim said nothing about the cards or *Winnie-the-Pooh*.

'Is Miss Beryl around?'

'Just comin' down.'

'D'you want to listen to the wireless? We're havin' it on tonight for a nice concert from the D'Oyly Carte Opera. They're doin' *The Yeomen o' the Guard*, so

16

that'll be jolly good. I see Miss Styles's already taken a seat with her knittin'!'

'Thanks, Mum, but I'd better swot up on astronomy for Church Lads' Brigade tomorrow evenin'. Mr Perryman's givin' us a talk an' lettin' us look through his telescope, so I want to have a rough idea o' what he's talkin' about! But I'll tell Beryl, shall I?'

'Thanks, Tim. Don't know what I'd do without yer, and that's a fact! I'll make a pot o' tea for us all before it starts, an' take it in on a tray – let's be posh!'

'Right oh, Mum. I'll take mine up to me room,' grinned Tim, thinking that he might be able to waylay Lily as she came in, and maybe have a little chat – try to find out what was bothering her these days, and let her know that she was still special to him, no matter how much she teased him. Or snubbed him, which was rather hurtful, though he tried not to show it.

Miss Lilian Mary Knowles had eagerly accepted the invitation to tea at Cherry Trees with the West-houses. Aunt Alice had always treated her as a niece, a cousin to Geoffrey, Geraldine and Amelia, though she was related only by marriage, not by blood. It was such a relief to exchange the constant clamour and lack of privacy at Pinehurst for the leisurely comforts of Cherry Trees that her cousins took for granted. Geraldine was a pretty girl of eighteen and Amelia three years younger, but the real attraction was, of course, Geoffrey, born a few months before Lily in 1917, which made them both war babies. He had grown into a presentable young man with his mother's good looks, though he was fair and she was dark, and it was difficult to trace any family resemblance to Gerald Westhouse, whose face had been badly disfigured by burns and who wore a black eye-patch, a legacy from his service as a flyer in the war. Lily was a little in awe of Uncle Gerald whose temper could blaze suddenly, and Geoffrey admitted to a similar wariness of Pa's abrupt changes of mood. They had all passed a pleasant evening on this occasion, but Lily knew that the best part was yet to come, when Geoffrey would escort her back to Pinehurst; both of them waited in pleasurable anticipation for that evening stroll together in the summer dusk.

Cherry Trees stood halfway up a steeply curving crescent of spacious detached houses in Belhampton's best residential area, known as the Park. Tall hedges and wrought-iron gates screened their gardens from the public gaze, and tradesmen used separate entrances that led round to side doors. Professional men drove out each day from the Park to their offices and consulting rooms, while their wives decided what to wear, went shopping and met each other in The Spinning Wheel, Miss Drew's genteel tearooms, where their talk was often about the difficulty of getting reliable domestic staff these days.

Lily listened to Aunt Alice's stories of cheeky housemaids and sullen cooks who muttered about giving notice and getting better places; Alice managed to make it sound amusing, and she always looked so charming in her well-cut suits and day dresses, the blouses with frilly sleeves and frothy lace collars; she was the perfect hostess.

So different from her sister, thought Lily, for Mrs Knowles never seemed to bother about her appearance, and spoke just like the rough children who rampaged around Pinehurst. 'Such a pity to see a gracious family home turned into a bear garden,' Aunt Alice had once remarked, though Lily had learned not to criticise her stepmother in front of Uncle Gerald; when he'd heard Geraldine comparing her Aunt Mabel to the Old Woman who lived in a Shoe – the one with all the children – and Lily had giggled, he had suddenly rounded on them both in fury.

'If you two foolish girls grow up to be half as good as Mabel, you'll do very well – but it's not likely, because I've never met a woman to match her. Knowles is damned lucky!'

They had sat in abashed silence with eyes downcast, though Lily was mystified that any man could think her father *lucky* to live in a children's home with scratched paintwork and worn carpets, not to mention the pervading odour of washing soap and carbolic that never quite overpowered the smell of a dozen children's bodies. It was hardly a place to bring friends home to, however much Mabel might insist that at Pinehurst the door was always open and visitors welcomed. Just imagine taking Geraldine up to her room, which she shared with poor Beryl Penney; Lily could just hear her apologising: 'Oh, sorry, Miss Lily, beg yer pardon, I didn't know yer was in!' Geraldine would be sure to giggle, and Lily would have to tell Beryl that it didn't matter. It simply wasn't worth it.

More and more Lily wanted to get away from Pinehurst. But how? She quite enjoyed her job at Westhouse and Westhouse, especially with Geoffrey there.

'Y'know, I'm frightfully pleased to have you in our office, Lily,' he was saying. 'You really brighten the place up. Trouble is, Pa wants me to go up to London and get experience as an articled clerk with a larger firm, and there are frightful examinations to be sat. I can't say that I'm all that keen.' He could have added that Pa was counting on him to become an equal partner in the Belhampton solicitors' office within a year or two. His grandfather was now in his seventies, and Pa's unpredictable temper had lost them more than one client; Geoffrey was only too well aware of the expectations they had of him.

Lily's eyes brightened at hearing this. If Geoffrey went to work in London, so could she!

'Oh, you should take the opportunity, and go, Geoffrey. I'd be off like a shot if I were you!' she said with feeling.

'I say, would you really, Lily? I wouldn't mind if you could find your way up to town sometime – it would be too marvellous!' He spoke eagerly, and Lily remembered her grandparents' suggestion that she should train to be a nurse, as her mother had done. Her father had studied for his medical degree at the London Hospital in Whitechapel Road, but up until now Lily had had mixed feelings about nursing, and certainly no wish to work in a poor area. Mabel sometimes came out with stories about her own training at an awful-sounding Poor Law infirmary, before she moved to the East London children's hospital where she and Dad had met during the war while she, Lily, had been a baby living with her mother at her grandparents' home in Northampton – until her poor mother had died in the postwar influenza epidemic, and he'd lost no time in marrying Mabel. Lily's mouth hardened. Everybody in Belhampton thought Mabel was so marvellous – but not at Northampton. It was Grandmama and

Grandfather Rawlings whose significant hints in recent years had made her look at her stepmother with an increasingly critical eye.

Perhaps she should think again about nursing. If the training could be endured, there might be opportunities for private nursing with well-to-do patients in pleasant surroundings. And if Geoffrey was going to be in London . . .

He had taken her hand as they walked down the hill, and by now they had reached the old turnpike road that led southwards across the common to the village of Beversley and then on to Petersfield and Portsmouth. He stopped walking and rather awkwardly drew her towards him, looking into her face.

'I say, Lily, you really have got the loveliest eyes, y'know – such an unusual colour, almost green in this light, with golden flecks. Quite beautiful, actually.'

She wondered if he was about to kiss her. It would not be her first kiss, but it might be better than the tentative attempts that other fellows had made. Her heart gave a little thud, for she was not quite sure how to react. Should she respond – or would it give a better impression to refuse?

Geoffrey Westhouse hesitated, for his previous experience with young women was not as extensive as he liked the world to think. Lily had accepted his compliment, but did she expect him to follow it up with a kiss? Standing here with her in the fading light, it seemed the natural thing to do.

It was Lily who made the decision to break away and continue walking. She needed a little more time. 'It's a lovely evening,' she said lightly as they rounded the church and the cluster of cottages before the corner on which Pinehurst stood. In the glow of the sunset the solid Victorian mansion appeared better proportioned than Cherry Trees; it had been built by Mabel's grandfather and left to his three daughters, the youngest of which had been Mabel's mother. During the war it had been used as a convalescent home for wounded servicemen, and now it was Mabel's property, which she allowed the Waifs and Strays Society to use as one of their 'cottage homes', with herself as matron.

And Dad and I have to share it with her and all that mob, thought Lily with a now familiar stab of resentment – and vexation, because young Westhouse knew of her position.

'Thank you for seeing me this far, Geoffrey,' she said politely. 'I can walk the rest of the way myself now.' She didn't want him to be seen by Mabel or one of the others, and perhaps asked in: it would be too embarrassing.

But young Westhouse was not to be so easily dismissed.

'I – I was rather hoping that we could say good night,' he pleaded, taking her hand again. 'I do think you're a – a lovely girl, Lily!'

So he *was* going to kiss her, and all right, it was up to him. She would neither encourage nor discourage, but just stand still on the path, the last rays of sunlight outlining her fair head like a nimbus. Keeping hold of her hand, he drew her towards him; she felt his lips touch her cheek and then settle firmly upon her lips. It was a very pleasant sensation, and she instinctively closed her eyes . . .

And then suddenly she drew away, remembering that they might be seen from Pinehurst by anybody looking out of a window facing north-east. He had to release her just as he was getting into his stride, and wondered whether he should apologise – or persuade her to stay and finish the kiss – if it was possible to resume an unfinished kiss.

'I think I heard somebody calling,' she muttered. 'Maybe not – but in any case I must go now, Geoffrey. Thank you for . . . er . . . good night!'

'I didn't hear anything. But good night, er, Lily. When can we see each other ag—'

But she was already hurrying along the path that led round to the back door, and entered the house through the kitchen. In the hall she stopped to listen: behind the closed door of what Mabel called the Quiet Room she heard a sound of music, so they must all be in there, listening to the wireless – Dad, Mabel, Miss Styles with her knitting, Tim Baxter sitting with a rapt expression on his face, and Beryl worshipping him with her sheep's eyes. None of them would have seen her and Geoffrey, Lily thought, impatient with herself at behaving so childishly.

She tiptoed up the stairs to the first floor, past the children's dormitories, and was about to climb the second flight to her own room when she was startled by Tim Baxter's voice calling to her softly from his doorway, next to the boys' dormitory. He and Miss Styles had rooms on the first floor so as to be on hand during the night for both boys and girls.

'Had a good evenin', Lily?'

'Oh, hello. It was all right,' she said coolly, wondering if he'd been looking out of his window.

'They're all listenin' to a concert on the wireless,' he said, smiling. 'Why don't yer go an' join 'em, Lily?'

'Why don't *you*?' she countered

'I would've done, only I've got to prepare for CLB tomorrow.'

'Oh, yes, of course, Captain Indispensable! I'm afraid it's not *my* idea of an evening's entertainment to sit and watch Miss Styles dropping her knitting needles and counting her stitches. Good night, Tim.'

'Lily, wait –' But she hurried up the stairs before he could say anything more. The days when he had played with her and defended her against the others were long gone, yet he still seemed to think he was some kind of elder brother, and she didn't care to be ordered around by Tim Baxter in his rolled-up shirtsleeves and Fair Isle pullover that Miss Styles had knitted; you could see the mistakes in it where she'd used the wrong colour all along a row, poor old thing. She was kind enough, and well-meaning, but no substitute for lovely Auntie Daisy, who had been sent away from Belhampton in disgrace after that silly business with Mr Wingate . . .

Yet at the same time Lily was cross with herself for speaking to Tim as she had, and for behaving in a way that could only be called horrid. Oh, life was trying! The sooner she got away from here, the better.

Tim Baxter wished that he had not spoken. It was difficult to know how to approach Lily these days. She was so impatient, and snapped at his well-meant suggestions; when would he learn to keep his big mouth shut? He blamed himself for his clumsiness, and felt no anger towards her; he knew that she was not happy, and it bothered him. Worse still, he could see that it bothered Mum too.

'I've had a letter from your grandparents, Lily,' said Dr Knowles at breakfast a few days later. 'They've

24

asked if you'd like to visit them for a week or maybe two, if you can get the time off from Westhouses.'

'Yes, I know, Dad. I had a letter from Grandmama yesterday.'

'Oh, did you? So how do you feel about it?'

'I'd quite like to see them again. I need to talk to them about my future. As a matter of fact, I've told Uncle Gerald, and he says it will be all right for me to take the last week in August.'

'Hm. You didn't see fit to mention your plans to us. Still, I think it would be a good idea for you to see – er – your Rawlings relations, and have a bit of a change before the summer's over. You'll need to travel up to London and go on to Northampton from King's Cross.'

'From Euston, actually. I've been there before, you may remember.'

He finished his coffee, and set down the cup. 'Of course, Lily. I'll let you have some extra cash today.'

'There's really no need, Dad. Grandfather has sent me a cheque for my train fare.'

'Has he? Very good of him, I'm sure.'

There seemed to be nothing further to say, and as usual Knowles felt at a loss when talking to his only child, especially when her only grandparents were the subject. He wondered what she would say to the old couple about life at Pinehurst, about himself and Mabel. He really shouldn't mind, because they had at least taken up his suggestion, and said they appreciated this opportunity to help and advise their granddaughter. Would they persuade her to follow in her mother's footsteps and train to be a nurse? This was what he had hoped for her, but now he felt less sure, especially about the London Hospital – or any hospital in London. It was impossible to ignore the

25

storm clouds gathering over Europe as the threats of Fascist leaders grew louder. Mussolini in Rome seemed less heroic now that he'd allied himself with that strutting nobody in Germany – what was his name, Hitler – and Franco was the worst of the lot, seizing power in Spain amid scenes of brutality reminiscent of the war, and setting himself up as a dictator. Would the other two press on with their demands for more territory? And this frightening persecution of Jews who were getting out of Germany to escape from – what . . .? Stephen Knowles shuddered. Surely it could not happen all over again, a mere two decades after the most terrible of all wars . . .

But if it did, London would not be a good place for his daughter to be. Perhaps she should train at Winchester instead, though a provincial hospital hadn't the same prestige. He decided to keep his own counsel and wait to hear what the Rawlingses advised – and back them up.

But when Lily returned to Pinehurst after her stay in Northampton, defiant, defensive and ready for a battle of wills, not even Mabel's attempts at peacemaking could cool her husband's fury. It wasn't just a case of accepting the Rawlingses' opinion, but rather their pronouncement on Lily's future, which had been decided and settled.

'St Mildred's? Did I hear you right? That antiquated bastion of the rich and privileged? *St Mildred's*? An anachronism in the twentieth century? You're not going *there*.'

'Yes, Dad, I *am* going there, just as my mother did.'

'Then you realise you'll have to pay for your tuition, your board and lodging, your uniform, your—'

'My grandfather is paying for me.'

'*What*?' he roared.

'Grandfather's paying for everything, just as he did for my mother when *she* trained at St Mildred's,' Lily replied with a quiet firmness unusual for her and in marked contrast to her father's shouting.

'Stop talking about your mother! She trained nearly thirty years ago, before State Registration. I wonder the General Nursing Council hasn't withdrawn approval as a training school from that outdated place – it can't possibly have a sufficient number of beds. I'm telling you, Lily, you won't go there with my consent, and I'll be bitterly disappointed in you if you do.'

Lily's face was pale, and her mouth a tense, straight line. Before she could answer, Mabel Knowles intervened on her behalf.

'That's quite enough, Stephen. Lily's a grown woman, and must make her own way. It's only natural for Mr and Mrs Rawlings to want to give her a helpin' hand, so no more shoutin', if yer don't mind. It'll upset the children, and I won't have that.'

Dr Knowles relapsed into angry silence, and Mabel turned to his daughter with a smile.

'We'll leave well alone for the time bein', Lily, and talk about it again when yer dad's calmed down. Let's have a nice cup o' tea, shall we?'

Lily's self-control suddenly snapped, and all her resentment and jealousy against Mabel boiled over into a fatal outburst, overheard not only by Tim Baxter and Miss Styles, but also the cook who had come to enquire about the grocer's delivery that day.

'I don't want your tea. I'm sick and tired of living in your house with all your precious children who mustn't be upset, no matter what happens – and I'm not even allowed to mention my poor mother's name!' she cried. 'My father puts up with it – and serve him right, after the way he treated her – but *I'm* not going to, not any longer. I'm going back to my mother's parents!'

With these words she turned and ran upstairs to her room, where she locked the door and threw herself on the bed in an agony of sobs.

Tim Baxter stood helplessly staring at the shock on Mum's face and the outrage on the Doctor's, but Miss Styles quickly beckoned him and the cook away with her to the kitchen. It was left to Mabel Knowles to stop her husband from going after his daughter and demanding that she apologise.

'Let her be, Stephen. I reckon she'll come to regret what she said in time – but for now just leave her alone, for everybody's sake.'

And let her go to St Mildred's if that's what she wants to do, she pleaded silently to Heaven. For she was tired of the tension between father and daughter, and the way it permeated the atmosphere of her beloved Pinehurst.

And not only that. Tim Baxter had grown too fond of Lily, and Mabel had no wish to see him hurt, the boy she had always looked upon like a real son, having borne no children of her own.

Chapter 2

'Don't let the sun go down on wrath, Lily,' warned Miss Styles kindly, and Mabel Knowles gave her husband much the same advice in the course of a wakeful night. Both father and daughter would have welcomed a flag of truce from the other, but as neither was willing to make the first move, they remained unreconciled when the taxi arrived the following morning to take Lily to the station. An early call to a sick patient took Dr Knowles away from the house before Lily left, and Tim Baxter stowed her trunk in the boot of the taxi. He then got in beside her, in spite of her insistence that she could manage without him.

'Don't part from the Doctor in anger, Miss Lily,' he told her. 'He's only ever done what he thought best for yer.'

'What *he* wants for me, you mean,' she muttered, forcing back tears as the taxi turned out of the lane, away from Pinehurst. 'And now he won't even say goodbye.'

'But he's been called out, Lily. Look, there's Mum wavin' to yer – give her a wave back! It's hard on her too, seein' yer go off like this, without even a kiss. She thinks the world o' yer.'

'Oh, yes, I'm second only to you and a dozen Waifs and Strays,' she answered bitterly, staring straight ahead, and wishing that he'd sat with the driver, a local man that everybody knew, and left her alone.

'That's not true, Lily. She thinks the same o' you as she does o' the rest of us.'

'But she's not my mother. I had a real mother who loved me, but she died.'

'I know, Lily,' he said gently. 'Which is why yer father brought yer to Pinehurst to be looked after by Mum.'

'And because he wanted to marry her as soon as my mother was dead.' Suddenly she rounded on him in fury. 'Oh, shut *up*, Tim Baxter. It's nothing you can understand. You've never known anything better than Pinehurst!'

The taxi driver coughed to remind them of his presence.

After a pause Tim answered very quietly, 'Ye're right, Lily. I've never known anythin' better'n Pinehurst, but I'll tell yer what, I've known a jolly sight worse, before they sent me there at eight years old. I must've had a mother at some time, but I never knew her. The only mother I've got is the one who took me in an' brought me up like a son – and I wouldn't change her for diamonds.'

Lily did not reply, and after a minute he went on, 'I hope ye'll write an' tell yer dad how yer get on, 'cause they'll both want to know. And so will I, Lily. Ah, here we are – ye're in good time for yer train.'

'There's no need for you to wait,' she said as she paid the driver and looked around for a porter. Tim picked up the trunk and carried it on his shoulder.

'I said there's no need to wait.'

'I'm puttin' this trunk in the luggage van, Miss Lily, so I'm waitin' for the train.'

He tried to shake her hand when she got into a compartment, but she turned away to hide her tears, and slammed the door shut. Tim was left standing on

30

the platform watching the train depart in a cloud of steam.

Mr and Mrs Rawlings eagerly received their grand-daughter back into their pleasant redbrick four-storey home on the outskirts of Northampton, indignant at her father's treatment of her.

'It's the influence of that woman, James,' Mrs Rawlings confided to her husband. 'When I think how we gave her up to him at such a tender age, poor little mite, to be brought up in a children's home – and now *this*! Well, she's twenty-one soon and can please herself. *This* is her home now.' Her mouth curved upwards in a triumphant smile. 'It's like having our poor darling Dilly back again. Lilian looks *so* much like her at that age.'

Mr Rawlings agreed, but pointed out that their granddaughter would soon be leaving them for London and St Mildred's Hospital.

'Yes, yes, that's something we've been able to do for her,' answered the old lady with satisfaction. 'I'll go with her to her interview, just as I did with Dilly all those years ago, and take her to be measured for her uniform at Garrould's. I'll enjoy seeing St Mildred's again.'

'She'll have to give her father's name as next of kin,' said Mr Rawlings, a tall, white-haired man in his seventies. 'After all, it's because she's a doctor's daughter that she's been accepted.'

'*And* because her mother trained there – that's an even more important point,' answered his wife. 'Certainly she can give Knowles's name as her father, and Pinehurst as his address, but I'll have a quiet word with this Miss Russell, and tell her the circum-stances. Apart from Knowles, we're her closest

31

relatives, and she will give our address as her own.'
She turned to her husband in an untypical flurry of
emotion. 'Oh, James, I haven't felt so pleased and
happy for years! I feel that we've got her back again,
not just for a few occasional visits, but for good. She
need never go back to Belhampton again!'

On a bright, sunny morning in early September Mrs
Rawlings and her granddaughter boarded the
London train. They were booked to stay for two
nights at a small, select businesswomen's club in
Holborn.

'It's where I used to stay when I came up to visit
your mother,' said Mrs Rawlings, who seemed to
have acquired a new lease of life following Lily's
arrival. She held herself upright, a commanding
figure in her late sixties, dressed in a well-cut, light-
coloured summerweight coat with a matching hat
planted firmly on her grey curls. Lily thought she
resembled Queen Mary, the Queen Mother, who
now had to guide the new King and his wife in the
role thrust upon them by the abdication of his elder
brother. Lily wondered how the two young
princesses addressed Queen Mary: surely not as
'Grandma'? It was surprising what a difference the
addition of an extra *ma* made, turning it into
Grandmama, which had a ring to it, an old-fashioned
dignity that exactly suited Mrs Rawlings.

London was full of new and exciting impressions,
and Lily found the Cavendish Ladies' Club to be the
last word in elegance, with a deferential receptionist
who called you 'madam', and who summoned a
maidservant who asked you to step this way, please,
and whisked you up to the next floor in a clanking
lift, which deposited you in a carpeted corridor, and

32

so to a charming, well-furnished room with two beds and a balcony overlooking the street below.

'Will madam be dining at the Cavendish this evening?' asked the maid.

'Yes, dinner for two at seven,' Grandmama replied. 'And we'll have a tray of tea now, please, in our room. And perhaps a little refreshment – do you still do those delicious chicken sandwiches? Good, we'll have those.'

Having refreshed themselves, they set out to explore the area in which Lily would be living.

'Look up at St Paul's Cathedral, Lilian – you'll be living almost in its shadow! And so close to Cheapside, which has some very attractive shops. After your interview tomorrow, we'll take a taxi-cab to the West End and order your uniform – and find you some nice new dresses and a winter coat. We'll try Marshall and Snelgrove – and we can't come to London without shopping at Harrods!'

Lily was lost for words: her future seemed to stretch before her like a golden road.

From the outside, St Mildred's Hospital in Bread Street looked rather like a church: one of those graceful Wren churches in which the City abounded, and deceptively spacious; once inside its narrow arched portal, that space was used to good effect. A bronze bust of each of the founders stood on either side of the entrance hall, near to Matron's office. She was waiting to greet them, an imposing lady in a dark maroon dress topped with an elaborate lace cap with an attached veil that hung down her back and floated with her movements. She introduced herself as Miss Russell, her preferred title.

'One of the older members on my staff remembers

Sister Rawlings,' she said with a slight inclination of her head, 'and I'm very happy to welcome her daughter to our hospital as a probationer nurse. Your grandmother will have no doubt told you, Miss Knowles, that St Mildred's is a very ancient foundation, once a medieval hospice devoted to nursing the sick. The present building dates from the late seventeenth century, endowed by the Earl and Countess of Suffolk – you can see their bronzes in the hall – and the present Dowager Countess is our president and patroness. She takes an active interest in our work, especially the selection of nurses for training, which is so vitally important, isn't it?'

She paused long enough for Mrs Rawlings to say she was in complete agreement.

'Our patients include royalty and the nobility, so we must have young women from suitable backgrounds. Our nurses sit the examinations for the State Register, but our own St Mildred's Hospital certificate is far more prestigious, together with our silver badge and buckle. A St Mildred's-trained nursing sister is uniquely equipped to take a responsible post in charge of others anywhere in the world.' She smiled with complacent pride. 'I will now take you to see the wards. Princess Louise and Lady Margaret are our two wards for ladies, and the children are in Princess May. I hear that your mother loved looking after the little ones, Miss Knowles.'

As they followed her from ward to ward, up and down marble stairways and across mosaic floors, Lily was quite overawed. The women's wards each had eight beds, the one for men had twelve, and the children's ten. Miss Russell proudly showed them the new six-bedded unit for ophthalmic cases, presented by the Silversmiths' Livery Company and opened the previous year by the Princess Royal. It had its own small theatre, and six separate rooms, so men, women and children could be accommodated.

Lily had only distant glimpses of patients who were mainly in single or double rooms, but she caught a familiar odour: a blend of antiseptic, beeswax and brass polish – and something else, the smell of the human body, of skin and scalp, of exudations. It carried an indefinable tang of sickness, and was exactly the same smell as in Belhampton War Memorial Hospital, which for some reason surprised her. Everything looked neat and clean, and the nurses wore pretty lace caps with short gauzy veils at the back; but that whiff of humanity proved the patients to be no different from sick people in any other hospital.

'Some of the top specialists in the country have patients here,' Miss Russell told the visitors, 'and you will have first-class lectures, Miss Knowles, both from them and from our Sister Tutor. The classroom is in the nurses' home, St Mildred's House, which is further up the street. I'll take you to see it when I've shown you the theatre suite and the chapel which –' she lowered her voice – 'which has a crypt used as a mortuary chapel, and is all that remains of the medieval foundation.'

St Mildred's House was agreed by Lily and her grandmother to be satisfactory in every way. Each nurse had a room of her own with a full-length mirror – 'the Countess insists that every nurse needs one' – and a wardrobe and dressing table on which she could arrange her own possessions. There was a light, airy dining room and a spacious sitting room with a small library attached, for nurses to use as a study. Original portraits of past patrons looked down from the walls, and vases of fresh flowers on well-polished tables added up to an all-pervading atmosphere of good order.

Lily returned Miss Russell's cordial handshake in happy anticipation of her return in three weeks' time, with two other new probationers.

Once away from St Mildred's Mrs Rawlings led her granddaughter straight to a select little tearoom nestling between a jeweller's and a haberdasher's in Cheapside. Seated at a table by the window, she put her gloved hand over Lily's on the embroidered cloth.

'I can't tell you how happy it makes me, Lilian, to see you following in your dear mother's footsteps,' she said, unconsciously echoing Dr and Mrs Knowles's words.

'I just can't believe I'm going to be a nurse at St Mildred's,' answered Lily with shining eyes. 'It's too marvellous!'

'Yes, my dear, you'll learn about so many things there, and be much better equipped for life than poor Dilly. Oh, what a tragedy it was for her, with that dreadful war spoiling everything –' Mrs Rawlings broke off, and Lily's curiosity prompted her to ask a question.

'Why did she go to that East End children's hospital, Grandmama?'

'Ah, my dear, you may well ask. She said she wanted to specialise in sick children, but it may have been because Knowles was there.' The old lady sighed. 'When he and Dilly were engaged to be married he seemed so lively and charming – and handsome! – and she looked such a picture in her wedding dress. But he went off to France with the

RAMC, and it changed him. He saw terrible sights, and his hair turned grey within a year. Dilly had two miscarriages, poor darling, and came home to live with us, but he was wounded and went back to the children's hospital where he met – that woman.'

Mrs Rawlings now made no attempt to hide her hostility against the woman who had brought up her granddaughter, and Lily felt a certain awkwardness.

'Mabel's very well spoken of in Belhampton, Grandmama.' She felt that this needed to be said, but Mrs Rawlings pursed her lips.

'So she may be, but she's a nobody, whereas Dilly was a little *lady*, Lilian, a lady to her fingertips.'

'Did you always call her Dilly?'

'Yes, the dear little soul called herself Phylly-dilly as soon as she could say her first words, so we called her Dilly from then on, though *he* always said Phyllis.' Grandmama's face clouded as she continued, 'When she came home to live with us, I could see that something was very wrong. She just seemed to withdraw into herself and took no interest in anything. He so seldom came to see her – he was back at the East London by then, and the bombing had started. He said he couldn't take leave at such a time.'

There was a pause while she toyed with her spoon, and seemed to hesitate.

'Go on, Grandmama. Do you mean that my father was already in love with – with Mabel?'

'Oh, I don't know, dear, and perhaps I shouldn't talk about such things now. He *did* come to visit Dilly at Christmas in 1916, and that was when you were . . . I mean we were so glad and happy when she told us that a dear baby was on the way, but your father went back to the hospital, and there was a ghastly incident there that year – some school was bombed, and he and this Nurse Court, as she was called, worked together on the injured children. She'd trained at some dreadful Poor Law infirmary, and came from a very unstable family – the mother had drowned herself, we heard, and Mabel was engaged to a Salvation Army captain who was shell-shocked and died. And then she came into money for some reason, and opened up this – this children's home after the war. Meanwhile your mother died . . .' Mrs Rawlings' voice broke, and she lowered her eyes. 'She died of a broken heart.'

'But I thought she died in the influenza epidemic after the war.'

'She succumbed to the flu, certainly, because she was in a weakened condition due to her melancholy state of mind. She'd sit and look out of the window, day after day, and I had to engage a nursemaid to help me care for you.'

'Oh, Grandmama, how dreadful!' breathed Lily. 'And all this time he – my father was away?'

'For much of the time, yes. I'm sorry, Lilian dear. I shouldn't be saying all this, especially now that you're starting out on your nursing career. You've got all your life before you, and you remind me so much of dear Dilly. I know you're going to be a credit to us – and to her.'

'I'll try to, Grandmama – oh, I promise you I'll do my best!'

Lily's eyes were now fixed upon her goal of becoming a St Mildred's nursing sister, able to give first-rate care with the right degree of courtesy and confidence. On their way back to the Cavendish Club and for the rest of their London visit, she scarcely saw the newspaper headlines about the Cabinet's delib-erations on the situation in Europe, the mobilisation of the armed services, the calling-up of reserves. Grandmama said nothing about the rumours, but if Lily had questioned her and looked closely into her eyes, she would have seen the old lady's unexpressed fear that what had happened a quarter of a century ago could – oh, heaven forbid it! – happen all over again.

'Happy birthday, Lilian dear! Twenty-one, and you've got the key of the door!' smiled Mrs Rawlings on the morning of 17 September. They were sitting at breakfast, and the post had just arrived.

'There are three letters for you from Belhampton, Lilian,' said her grandfather, 'and half a dozen cards – and these are from both of us, my dear.'

These turned out to be two packages, one containing a smart and cosy woollen dressing gown in navy blue, from Grandmama; the other, from Grandfather, was a cut-glass dressing-table set, complete with a silver-backed brush and comb.

'Oh, how lovely – thank you both!' she said with a smile, though her heart had plummeted as soon as she recognised her father's handwriting on one of the letters from Belhampton. The other two were from her Aunt Alice and Geoffrey Westhouse, as well as cards from Tim Baxter, Miss Styles, Beryl Penney and the Westhouse girls. Three of the Pinehurst children had also sent her cards they had made themselves, which made her feel oddly guilty.

'If you'd prefer to take them to your room and read them in private, please do so, dear,' said her grandmother with commendable tact, for she was naturally curious as to what Knowles had written to his daughter.

Lily decided to open her father's letter there and

then; after all, she thought, she had thrown in her lot with her grandparents, who had been extremely generous and had surely earned their right to be in her confidence. She sliced open the envelope, and out fell a postal order for twenty-five pounds. She skimmed through the short letter in silence.

It was very much to be regretted that you left us in the way you did, and I am sorry for my contribution to it. It is also unfortunate that there has always been ill feeling between your mother's relations and myself, and I have to take my share of responsibility for this also. Your grandparents have been very generous, but do not forget that Mabel has loved and cared for you for eighteen years, and does not deserve the cruel and untrue things you said. However, we both wish you happiness in your training at St Mildred's, and I am sending the enclosed for you to get yourself anything you may need.

I also send my love, as does Mabel, who wants me to remind you that the door is always open here.

Lily stared down at the single sheet of paper while her grandparents waited discreetly.

'He says he's sorry about the – the difference of opinion,' she said briefly.

'Well, I'm sure we're glad to hear that,' said Mrs Rawlings without much warmth. 'And I see that he's sent you some money.'

'Yes, twenty-five pounds.' Lily placed the postal order on the table.

'You'll have to write and thank him, dear.'

'Yes, of course. I'll write today,' replied Lily, making up her mind to be brief and not to mention Mabel. She would keep in touch with her father at intervals, but she wanted no further contact with the woman who had caused her mother's death – for that was how she now saw her father's wife. She never wanted to see her again. Or Pinehurst.

She opened the cards with their conventional birthday greetings, and said she would read the letters from Cherry Trees later.

'Mrs Westhouse is your stepmother's sister, isn't she?' said Mrs Rawlings. 'Isn't her husband a solicitor?'

'Yes, and they've always been very kind. Geoffrey will become a junior partner when he's had more experience.' Lily spoke rather self-consciously, knowing that they would see Geoffrey as Mabel's nephew and therefore not to be encouraged. And when she opened his letter there was little doubt about his feelings.

Life's jolly dull around here without you, Lily. I hear that you're going to London to be a nurse. If so, will you write and let me know which hospital you'll be at? I've agreed with Pa that I'm to transfer to a London firm in the new year. I miss you terribly. Do you miss me just a little bit?

Aunt Alice had sent five pounds and cautious sympathy, inviting her to keep in touch – which might be difficult, thought Lily, not sure whether she should write to the Westhouses now that she had escaped from Pinehurst. In the end she penned a short thank-you note to Aunt Alice, saying that at present she was very busy getting ready to go to St Mildred's, and asking that her kind regards be passed on to Geoffrey, Geraldine and Amelia.

Grandmama complimented her on her discretion and good sense. 'Once you start your training you'll have so much on your mind that you'll forget all about these associations,' she said with a knowing nod.

Friday, the last day of September, was memorable indeed, on two important counts: the first was Lily's departure for London and her arrival at St Mildred's House to take up residence before starting work on the wards on Monday. The second was the arrival of the Prime Minister, Mr Neville Chamberlain, at Heston Airport at a quarter to two in the morning. He had flown back from a twelve-hour conference in Munich where he had personally discussed the European situation with Herr Hitler, the German Chancellor, and Signor Mussolini, the Italian Premier. Monsieur Daladier had represented France, but it had been Mr Chamberlain's adroit diplomacy and passionate dedication to peace that had secured an agreement, an Anglo-German pact by which Herr Hitler undertook to make no further demands on Czechoslovakian territory. It was peace with honour, and the Prime Minister was greeted by cheering crowds, later appearing on the balcony of Buckingham Palace with the King and Queen. The threat of war was banished like an evil dream, and relief swept across the nation.

'Oh, Lilian dear, you couldn't have better news at the start of your nursing career!' cried Grandmama. 'I haven't let you know how desperately worried your grandfather and I have been, but now it's all over, thanks to our wonderful Prime Minister. Thank God for him!'

It was an auspicious day to arrive in London, and the jubilant atmosphere pervaded St Mildred's House as the three new probationers sat down to dinner that evening. One introduced herself as the Honourable Miss Henrietta Tarrant.

'Only do call me Hetty. Isn't it simply marvellous to be here at last? I intend to have lots of fun in London – how about you two?'

Lily hesitated, and the other girl, round-faced and rosy-cheeked, spoke up. 'I'm Beatrice Massey. My father's a Justice of the Peace in Wiltshire and loves working on the estate. They call him Farmer Jack, so I'm the farmer's daughter!' She smiled. 'My sisters were débutantes and found themselves husbands, but I didn't want all that, and in the end Father and Mother agreed to let me come here.'

'Good for you,' said the Honourable Hetty, and turned to Lily. 'Now let's hear from you!'

'I'm Lily Knowles and – er – from Hampshire, but I live at my grandparents' home in Northampton,' she said, aware of Hetty's keen look. 'My father married again after my mother died, and I – I live with my mother's parents.'

'Oh, what jolly rotten luck, Lily! And the old step-mother's worse than Cinderella's, I'll bet!' Hetty's tone was sympathetic, but Lily felt that she had been less than honest. However, it seemed a good start, and Hetty declared she was sure that the three of them would become the best of friends.

In the sitting room after dinner they met Sister Tutor who told them that they would each have a 'mentor', a second-year probationer to give them friendly help and guidance on all aspects of life at St

Mildred's. Lily's mentor was there and waiting to meet her.

'Nurse Knowles, let me introduce Nurse Blumfeldt,' said the sister, and Lily was confronted with a solemn face framed in dark hair. Sombre brown eyes regarded her from under thick brows, and a hand reached out to take hers in a formal clasp.

'Good evening, Nurse Knowles. I am pleased to meet you.' The guttural German accent was a surprise: a German at St Mildred's? The sister smiled and turned away, leaving them to get to know each other.

'You will be working on Suffolk ward with me. It is for men,' said the girl. 'I will tell you what you need to know, but you will learn most by watching.' Her heavy features softened when she smiled, which Lily discovered was not often. 'My name is Hanna when I am off duty.'

'And mine's Lily. Thank you – Hanna.'

'Where is your home, Lily?'

That awkward question again: Lily gave a similar answer to the one she had given Hetty. 'And where do your parents live, Hanna?'

At once she was aware of tension, a sense of unease, almost of fear. The girl shook her head and frowned.

'My father is a biochemist, and is working in a laboratory at St Mary's Hospital,' she said. 'He and my mother decided we should come to England last year, but Mother has since gone back to see her parents and bring them over here also – but they are old, and do not want to leave their home. It would be better to have them over here – it is very difficult for our nation in Germany at this time.'

Lily hardly knew what to make of this. Did it mean

44

that the Blumfeldts were German Jews who had left their homeland because of the persecution she had vaguely heard about? She hardly liked to ask, but felt that she ought to say something hopeful.

'Now that there's no danger of war, things will surely be easier for your family, Hanna.'

Nurse Blumfeldt shook her head gloomily, her dark eyes bleak. 'It will never be easy for us.'

From across the room Lily heard Hetty Tarrant's upper-class tones ring out. 'Don't look now, girls, but I think Lily's finding her mentor rather uphill work!'

On Monday morning the new probationers attended a lecture from Sister Tutor, and were given instructions on what their attitude to the patients and other grades of staff should be. Lily made a big effort to remember it all when she reported on duty that afternoon on Suffolk ward in her blue and white striped dress, snowy apron and lacy cap. The only male ward at St Mildred's took both surgical and medical cases, and the ward sister was known as Sister Suffolk, presiding over two staff nurses, three probationers in their first, second and third years respectively, and three green-clad nursing orderlies, one of whom was a man, Webster, ex-RAMC and very good at his job, Lily was told. At the bottom of this hierarchy were the wardmaids in brown overalls and turban caps, who did all the cleaning – sweeping, dusting, polishing of brass plaques, sluicing of soiled linen, scrubbing of bedpans and urinal bottles; the nurses did not have to do these menial tasks at St Mildred's, which set them apart from probationers at most other hospitals, municipal and voluntary. As a first-year probationer, from the very start Lily accompanied Sister and the nursing team on doctors' rounds, dressing rounds and medicine rounds; as an assistant she learned by watching how to change dressings and prepare and give injections, enemas, fomentations, inhalations and all other essential treatments; she soon knew who should be doing what at any hour of the day on Suffolk ward.

There were many new impressions during that first week, including having close contact with parts of the adult male body in a necessary degree of intimacy. Sister Tutor's words of wisdom echoed in her head: 'That is why ward protocol is so important, Nurses. Your formality preserves the patient's dignity.' Nothing had been said about the patients' attitude, their openly admiring looks and smiles in the direction of the new probationer, but Lily soon realised that the same rule applied: a cool formality was the best response. Nevertheless, there were patients whom she felt deserved an answering smile, such as the old brigadier in his single room where he lay gazing vacantly out of the window or idly turning the pages of his newspaper. He suffered from something called a general systemic disorder, Sister said, and only Webster attended to his daily treatments. He would look up and smile hopefully at the nurses who took him his meals on a tray or gave him his medicines, and Lily smiled back into a ravaged, once handsome face with blue eyes that seemed to be remembering a time of past happiness, now lost. He had had a distinguished military career in the war, Lily learned, and it seemed so sad that he had come to this infirmity of body and mind.

Lily's mentor, Nurse Blumfeldt gave her some useful, if somewhat surprising advice. 'You can learn much by watching the nursing orderlies and helping them with their work whenever you have time to spare. You will understand that they do the actual nursing of the patients.'

This did not quite reflect what Sister Tutor had said. 'Avoid familiarity with the nursing orderlies who should be kept in their place. They must address you as "Nurse", while you call them simply by their surnames – Smith, Brown and so on. Treat them fairly by all means, and show your appreciation of work well done, but always keep your distance. And your dignity.'

Lily decided that it was possible to follow both guidelines, and duly avoided familiarity while helping the orderlies to give out meals, attend to toilet needs and make beds, a never-ending routine. The other activity each morning and evening was the 'back round'. Two nurses, or a nurse and an orderly, went from bed to bed with the 'back trolley', carrying clean linen, soap and water, surgical spirit and talcum powder. Behind drawn screens they turned the patient over, washed his back and buttocks, dried the skin and rubbed it with surgical spirit before dusting with powder. In cases of very thin old men this treatment was extended to hips, elbows and heels, anywhere there was a bony prominence: the aim was to prevent the formation of pressure sores – 'bedsores', a dreaded complication in bed-bound patients and very difficult to treat once it had occurred, so a great deal of nursing effort went into prevention, especially when patients lay for weeks with a long illness or recovering from an operation. Patients either responded to treatment and recovered, or failed to respond and either died or became chronic cases that had to be sent home or transferred to long-stay hospitals suited to their needs. It was only when the poor brigadier's family decided to remove him to a mental hospital in Surrey that Lily discovered he was in the final stages of tertiary syphilis; and that far from being an old man, he was only fifty-one. She was told to look the condition up in her nurses' medical dictionary, and not to discuss it on any account. Sister Tutor would explain all in due course . . .

Meanwhile there were off-duty activities, and Hetty Tarrant led the way to London's theatreland where the musicals of Ivor Novello and Noel Coward seemed likely to go on for ever without losing their popularity.

'Let's go and see Lupino Lane in *Me and My Girl*!' she enthused. 'I've heard it's wonderfully vulgar! Who's off on Saturday? What about you, Hanna? You always look so deadly serious! Why don't you get away from St Mildred's once in a while? It might cheer you up a bit.'

Hanna shook her dark head mournfully, and Lily felt uneasy about her, as she frequently did. The girl was clearly living with a shadow of fear hanging over her, and discouraged questions, as if by expressing her fears, she might give them real and terrible shape. The concept of anti-Semitism was a mystery to Lily: both the words 'German' and 'Jew' had unfortunate overtones, embarrassing even to mention. There were those who still thought Germany a threat to Europe, but what *was* it about Jews that had made them outcasts throughout history? Lily could not understand it at all, but did her best to show support for the lonely girl. She managed to persuade her to come out to tea one afternoon at the little café where she and Grandmama had gone after the interview with Miss Russell.

'Is your mother expected back in England soon, Hanna?' she enquired discreetly, and the dark eyes brightened a little.

'She hopes to sail some time next week, but nothing is certain,' came the careful reply. 'And it sounds as if she will be leaving her parents behind. They do not want to leave their family home, and do not understand the importance of getting out. If they hold her back, I shall not find it easy to forgive them,' she added, and Lily could think of nothing better to say than that she hoped all would go well.

But then, at the beginning of November, the blow fell. News came through on the wireless of a violent uprising in towns throughout Germany, a purge directed against all Jews; their houses were attacked, their shops smashed and looted, and hundreds of synagogues were burned down. This night of terror became known as 'Crystal Night' because of the piles of broken glass left lying in the streets afterwards.

On hearing about this, Lily went looking for Nurse Blumfeldt, but the girl had gone to see her father in his laboratory at St Mary's Hospital. When she returned late that night she was called to see Miss Russell, who offered sympathy but told her she must continue carrying out her duties, just as Professor Blumfeldt was doing. The unanswered questions were how had her mother and grandparents fared in the night of terror, and how soon would they now be able to get out of Germany?

Some of Hanna's fellow probationers found it hard to show sympathy for her, for she did not invite it. She seemed strangely alone in her trouble, her white face grimly set, her eyes full of pain – and anger.

'Many lies have been told about my people,' she said in her deep, flat voice. 'All Hitler's henchmen are liars, like the detestable Dr Goebbels, who has done this to us.' She turned her gaze upon them, almost as if in accusation. 'And you and your poor fool Chamberlain have swallowed the lies and will pay for it.'

'I say, I'm not listening to *that* sort of talk in my own country!' protested Hetty indignantly, while Beatrice and Lily exchanged significant looks and shrugged.

Hanna turned her back on them and went to her room, locking the door behind her. In the weeks that followed the news of the persecutions continued. The nurses heard that Jews were turned out of colleges, forced to pay exorbitant taxes, insulted and spat upon wherever they went. And there was no news of Hanna's mother.

'I shall never see her again,' she said with a chilling finality that sent a shiver down Lily's spine. That was when Lily began to lose her belief in Mr Chamberlain's 'peace in our time'. Something unspeakable was happening, and nobody was denouncing it. The world was looking the other way, just as her friends looked uneasily away from Hanna the German Jewess.

Halfway through November there was a change of wards for the probationers. Beatrice Massey came to Suffolk, and Lily was directed to Princess Louise, one of the two women's wards. It was for surgical cases, mainly gynaecological, and the patients were there for repair of the damage done by childbirth: torn and overstretched pelvic floors resulting in prolapse of the womb and bladder. Actual removal of the womb was performed only for cancer and fibroid growths. Many of the patients were anaemic due to excessive blood loss, and had poor bladder control; the thought crossed Lily's mind that if the rich and privileged suffered this much with 'women's trouble', how did poor mothers of large families cope with it?

Ward protocol was as strict as on Suffolk; most of the women were middle-aged and extremely shy about having their private parts exposed and examined, their pubic hair shaved off, rubber catheters passed to drain urine from the bladder and bigger ones to douche the vagina, so a respectful formality had to be observed by the nurse carrying out these procedures. And as on Suffolk, cleanliness was constantly emphasised, as the greatest danger from operative surgery was the risk of infection invading the body; a 'septic appendix' could result in a patient needing months to recover, and so becoming prone to the dreaded bedsores. Lily learned to be ever vigilant in the unending battle against infection.

'At least you haven't got to put up with that dismal mentor of yours, Lily!' remarked Hetty, to which Lily made no reply, for she had come to feel protective towards Hanna, and preferred her to be close at hand.

With the approach of Christmas, all the talk was of a ball to be held at St Mildred's House on Friday, 16 December. This was an annual event presided over by Miss Russell, and attended by their president and patroness, the Dowager Countess of Suffolk. The nursing staff were invited to hand in the names and addresses of partners, either gentlemen friends or relatives such as brothers, to whom official invitations would then be sent. Lily's face fell, as did some of the others who had no partner to invite, but they brightened when Hetty announced that she could supply at least three suitable gentlemen.

'There's my brother – he's obsessed with fox-hunting, but he'll do for you, Lily – and a couple of his friends, one for me and one going spare – any takers? Ah, I saw your eyes light up, Beatrice, so are you interested? Going – going – *gone*! That's us settled!'

'Oh, thank you, Hetty, but what abour poor Hanna?'

'I don't suppose she'll want to come, do you?'

But it seemed that Professor Blumfeldt had told Miss Russell that he would like to come and meet his daughter's friends, so he was sent an invitation. Lily began to feel apprehensive about being landed with a young aristocrat who might expect her to know all about fox-hunting, and when a letter arrived out of the blue from Geoffrey Westhouse, she seized on it eagerly.

'Mother told me you were at St Mildred's,' he wrote. 'I'm starting at Badger, Badger and Crangle on Kingsway in March, which will be rather jolly, as I'll be able to see you and take you out. I do miss you, Lily. It's fearfully dull in the office with the old biddy who's taken your place. I wish you'd write to me . . .'

It was like a gift from above. Somebody else could have Hetty's fox-hunting brother, and Lily gave Miss Russell the name of a partner who was both suitable and eager.

On the night of the ball Lily was seized with an attack of nervousness, although Beatrice assured her that she looked stunning in her pale green silk dress that clung to her figure and flared out into dark green fullness just below her hips. She tried taking deep breaths to steady the wobbly sensation in her stomach as the probationers trooped down the staircase. Would Geoffrey be there? Would her friends like him? Oh, please, God, don't let the evening be a complete disaster!

St Mildred's House had been transformed into a blaze of light, music and colour. A glittering Christmas tree stood in one corner of the sitting room and a three-piece band was in place on the opposite side; in the adjoining library a bar had been set up, and a lavish buffet had been prepared in the dining room. Miss Russell, in a dark blue velvet gown, stood beside the Dowager Countess, a spirited old lady in silvery grey, waiting for the guests to be introduced to them both. Lily recognised a consultant physician and an anaesthetist who regularly attended St Mildred's, but before she could take in the scene any further a knot of younger gentlemen in evening dress surged forward, and one made straight for her, all smiles.

'*Lily!* I say, you look absolutely ravishing!'

'Geoffrey, how nice to see you,' she murmured in relief as he took her hand. Her heart was thudding, and she had to remind herself to stay cool and dignified.

'Can I get you a drink from the bar, Lily?'

'Not until I've introduced you to Miss Russell and the Dowager Countess.'

'My word, they look frightfully grand – but you're the most beautiful girl in the room, Lily.'

This was pleasing to hear from a presentable young man, and she smiled as they took their place in the line of couples waiting to meet the two hostesses. They shook hands with Miss Russell while

Lily murmured, 'Mr Westhouse, who has come from Belhampton,' and then curtsied to the Dowager, and Geoffrey made a formal little bow. That done, there were other less formal introductions to be made, to the Honourable Miss Henrietta Tarrant and Miss Beatrice Massey and their partners; Lily was pleased with Geoffrey, who struck just the right note with the company, and made no secret of his admiration for her.

She turned to find Hanna at her side. 'Miss Knowles, I would like you to meet my father, Professor Heinrich Blumfeldt. He is an old friend of the Countess.'

Lily looked up into the serious, bearded face of a grey-haired man who bowed politely and said he wished to thank her for the friendship she had shown to his daughter. His eyes were dark like Hanna's, and like her he gave an impression of carrying a constant burden of anxiety. Lily was rather at a loss for words, knowing the desperate situation of his wife – or rather, not knowing it, for Hanna's mother had still not arrived in England. She told him about the help that Hanna had given her as a mentor, and introduced him to Geoffrey, who shook his hand.

The fact that the Blumfeldts were acquaintances of the Dowager Countess went some way towards explaining why the professor's daughter had chosen St Mildred's as a training school. In the next few minutes Hanna told Lily that the old lady – 'only she wasn't an old lady then' – had met her father many years ago while on holiday in the Alps, and more recently had advised him to transfer the bulk of his capital to a London bank.

'He was not sure that it was a good thing to do, but

now we are so thankful, Lily – at least they can't get their dirty hands on my father's money, whatever else they take from us.'

The band struck up with a lively quickstep, and Geoffrey came to ask Lily to dance.

'I'm to tell you that they're missing you at Pinehurst and hope you haven't forgotten them altogether,' he said as they matched their steps. 'Actually, Mabel's a jolly decent sort, and it seems a pity not to keep in touch – doesn't it?'

'I've sent cards to most of them at Pinehurst this Christmas, and don't forget I also owe a lot to my grandparents,' she replied with the familiar stab of unease whenever Pinehurst was mentioned; she had no intention of visiting the place over the Christmas period.

'Oh, yes, of course, quite,' he said quickly. 'I say, we dance awfully well together, don't we? I just can't believe my luck, being here with you!'

He took her into supper, and when they had piled their plates with smoked salmon and salad, he asked her about her new friends.

'That old chap you introduced me to, with the daughter – are they Jews? I'm sure he's frightfully clever, but I wouldn't have expected to meet those sort of people here.'

This struck a discordant note with Lily, and after supper she talked again with the Blumfeldts while Geoffrey was seized by a couple of third-years, curious to know more about Nurse Knowles's admirer.

The Dowager came over and asked Lily if she was enjoying her training.

'I remember your dear mother, Miss Knowles, and I'm sure she would have been proud of you!' She then talked long and earnestly with the professor and his daughter.

The hours flew by, and Geoffrey became emboldened by the wine he had drunk; Lily limited herself to two glasses. All too soon it was midnight, and Miss Russell thanked everybody for coming, after which the band played for the last dance, 'The Way You Look Tonight'.

'It's just the way *you* look tonight, Lily – so adorable,' whispered Geoffrey, holding her close as they circled the floor. 'I could just wrap my arms around you like this and make love to you tonight.' His lips brushed her forehead, and his breath was hot against her right ear. Lily knew that he was not just talking about kissing her, though there had been no opportunity even for that. Miss Russell's safe-guarding of her nurses was unobtrusively effective, and they had all been constantly under her surveillance. Now it was time to say good night, and end the evening with a rousing farewell chorus of 'We wish you a Merry Christmas'.

It was only after Geoffrey had gone off in a taxi-cab to his hotel that Lily discovered what he had told the third-years about her, and they lost no time in spreading it – that Nurse Knowles had been brought up in a *children's home* – yes, honestly, one of those cottage homes run by the Waifs and Strays Society!

'He seemed to think we already knew. Her father's a GP married to the matron of this home – isn't it unbelievable? Of course she's got these grand-parents, and there must be money there, but does Miss Russell know about *this*? I ask you!'

Lily burned with humiliation, and not just because her background was now common knowledge. The fact that she had tried to conceal it was somehow even more shameful, and made her appear to be an ungrateful snob. For how could anybody possibly understand the way she felt about her mother and father – and her stepmother?

Chapter 3

Cheapside was dark and almost deserted as Lily and Beatrice hurried to attend the first Holy Communion of Christmas Day at St Mary-le-Bow. It was five minutes to seven, and the interior of the church was bathed in a glow of candles, though Lily shivered as she knelt down with the other early worshippers. This old city church, with its graceful arches and Corinthian columns, was conveniently near to St Mildred's, and Lily hoped that the atmosphere of the place would envelop her in its peace and calm; but almost at once her thoughts wandered back to the Christmas ball, the sensation of Geoffrey's arms around her as they danced, his warm whispers in her ear – and then he had gone and made that revelation about Pinehurst.

Her first-year probationer friends had liked him and thought him a pleasant enough young man up from the country, and she liked him too, though if their attachment continued and developed into something closer – as he clearly hoped it would when he came to London – she would inevitably be drawn back to Belhampton. It was a troubling thought, and not the only one: there were the amused looks cast in her direction by the third-years, and the remarks being made about the girl from a children's home.

Hetty had already quizzed her about it, in her direct way.

'What on earth did your Mr Westhouse say to

those chatterboxes, Lily? You weren't really brought up in a children's home, were you? I'd got the impression that you lived with your grandparents.'

'I do *now*,' Lily had answered, colouring. 'After my mother died, my father married the matron of a home for children under the care of –' she had drawn a breath – 'the Church of England Incorporated Society for the Provision of Homes for – for Waifs and Strays.'

'How incredible! He must have been desperate for her! Forgive me, Lily, but did you actually grow up with all those little ragamuffins?'

'For part of the time, when I was much younger,' Lily answered evasively. 'But I've been spending more and more time with my mother's parents in recent years – Grandfather and Grandmama in Northampton.' Her faltering tones sounded less than convincing, even to her own ears, but Hetty seemed sympathetic.

'Take my advice and ignore the cat scratches, then. The fact that Miss Russell accepted you is proof enough of your credentials. But why on earth did he *say* it?'

'Goodness only knows. They must have wormed it out of him,' Lily had said unhappily, for she was not even sure that Miss Russell *did* know that Pinehurst was a children's home. It had not been mentioned at the interview, as Grandmama said it was unnecessary. But now it would surely reach the ears of the matron and patroness, and she would be questioned. Oh, it was all too vexing . . .

A bell sounded, announcing that the service was about to begin. Lily suddenly thought of Hanna and her desperate anxiety for her mother and grandparents. Bowing her head again she prayed for the

59

Blumfeldts and all their persecuted race, even though they were not Christians, ending with a fervent plea for peace in Europe. Oh Lord, let Mr Chamberlain's promise be kept!

Christmas was not a busy time at St Mildred's. There were no booked admissions or operations over the festive season, and the only patients were those too ill to go home. As there would be only twenty or so of the forty-four beds occupied between Christmas and New Year, staff were granted extra time off during that week. Lily was free from five o'clock on the Tuesday evening until Thursday afternoon at two.

'I've sent my grandparents a telegram to say I'll be able to see them tomorrow!' she said at supper-time.

Hanna Blumfeldt raised her mournful eyes. 'Do you never go to see your father and his wife?' she asked with disconcerting frankness.

'No, I prefer to stay with my mother's parents,' Lily replied, aware of glances around the table.

'You dislike your father's wife, Lily?'

If anybody else had asked such a question, Lily would have told her to mind her own business. As it was, she answered briefly, 'Not really, it's just that I'd rather stay away. I'm much closer to Grandmama and Grandfather.' She felt herself blushing, but Hanna persisted.

'How old were you when your mother died?'

'About three.'

'Then you cannot remember her.'

'I can remember her, actually, and Grandmama has told me everything about her.' Lily frowned and shook her head to show her annoyance. Everybody within earshot was listening.

'To show dislike to your father's wife will not bring your mother back, Lily.'

By now there were murmurs of protest, and Hetty Tarrant spoke up indignantly.

'That remark is completely uncalled for, Nurse Blumfeldt, and you should apologise to Nurse Knowles! Of all the *nerve!*'

There was silence. Hanna Blumfeldt said no more, and Lily lowered her eyes and burning cheeks – because she knew that Hanna had only spoken the truth, however tactlessly, and because she knew that she ought to go to Pinehurst and be reconciled with them all. But the thought of having to listen to her father castigating St Mildred's, and the awkwardness of facing Mabel . . . No! She told herself it would only reopen wounds and cause more trouble.

'It's like Christmas all over again, having you with us, Lilian dear!' exclaimed Mrs Rawlings. 'We want to hear all about your meeting with the Countess of Suffolk. Did she speak to you? What did she say? Did she remember your mother?'

After enthusing over Lily's highly satisfactory answers, the old lady asked archly, 'And were there some nice young gentlemen there for the dancing?'

'Er, yes, Mr Westhouse was invited as my partner for the evening, Grandmama. That's Geoffrey Westhouse, you know, Aunt Alice's son.'

'Oh.' This was less welcome news. 'Your step-mother's nephew?'

'Yes, Grandmama. He's coming to London in February to get more experience with a firm of solicitors in Kingsway.'

'Mm. I see. Well, I'm sure he's a nice enough young fellow, Lilian, but it's a great pity about the connection. There must be plenty of eligible young gentlemen in London, and I think you'd be most unwise to get involved with this one.'

Mrs Rawlings frowned, and Lily replied rather lamely, 'I do see what you mean, Grandmama.'

'Good. Now, tell us about this unfortunate friend of yours with the very German-sounding name. Did you say that her father is acquainted with the Countess?'

Lily repeated what she knew of the Dowager's former encounter with the professor, and the wise financial advice she had given him.

'That explains why this girl's at St Mildred's instead of a Jewish hospital,' nodded Mrs Rawlings with a certain reservation in her tone. 'And what about the Honourable Miss Tarrant and the other girl – did you say her name was Massey? Your grandfather thinks that he knows the family.'

Lily was happy to talk about life at St Mildred's, but could not bring herself to ask her grandmother if Miss Russell knew about Pinehurst, much as she longed to know.

Although she had had short notice, Mrs Rawlings managed to arrange a small dinner party on Wednesday evening, inviting a couple who were near neighbours and the local GP, a Dr Wardley, with his wife and son Dennis, an agreeable young man in his twenties who was studying medicine at St Bartholomew's Hospital. Lily was seated next to him at dinner, and he asked her about St Mildred's, what sort of patients went there, and the conditions treated. When she told him that its patroness was the Dowager Countess of Suffolk, he laughed out loud, but checked himself and apologised when he saw her unsmiling face.

'Our patients are under the care of some of the top specialists in the country,' she informed him coldly, and named one of St Bartholomew's own distinguished surgeons. 'And our standard of nursing is second to none.'

He nodded, suitably rebuked, and she forgave him; after all, he really seemed to like her.

After dinner Mrs Rawlings led the party into the drawing room where two card tables were prepared for a rubber of bridge. Lily confessed with embarrassment that she could not play, and so one table was given over to whist, at which she partnered young Wardley against the neighbours, an obliging couple who said they would prefer the simpler game. Fortunately Lily and Mr Wardley won two games out of three.

'Perhaps I may arrange to meet you in town some time, Lilian?' he suggested when he left with his parents.

She smiled and said that she didn't see why not, and although no definite arrangement was made, her grandparents exchanged little smiles.

Back at St Mildred's, the Hon. Miss Henrietta Tarrant decided that it was time to expand their social life.

'Here we are in the capital city, with every kind of entertainment on our doorstep, and yet we're not getting out to sample it! Well, I'm off to a *thé dansant* on Thursday afternoon at the Queen's Theatre in Shaftesbury Avenue. So who's coming with me? We can get a taxi-cab down High Holborn and be there by half-past two.'

It was all very well for her, thought Lily, who would have loved to go; her grandfather gave her a generous dress allowance, but she didn't think he would approve of it being spent on dashing off in a taxi to an afternoon tea-dance when she ought to be writing up her lecture notes on the functions of the liver.

Hetty saw her hesitation. 'Oh, *good*, Lily, I knew I could count on you! Any other takers?' She raised a pencilled eyebrow at the second-year who was walking up Bread Street with them to St Mildred's House. 'What about you, Nurse Grey? Are you free then?'

'Yes, all right – only we could get a bus there and have a taxi to bring us back by five,' answered the girl, at which Lily brightened. Sharing a taxi between three for one way only wouldn't be so extravagant.

The Queen's Theatre was known for its 'tango teas', where couples danced to a band that played popular tunes of the day and well-dressed ladies took afternoon tea among potted palms. The three girls sat down at a table, and Hetty ordered tea. Lily looked around with interest, secretly wishing for a gentleman partner to lead her on to the little dance floor, while Hetty poured out the tea in bone-china cups and speculated about the patrons seated nearby.

'Do you think those two are married, Cicely?' she asked Nurse Grey. 'If so, I think she's made a mistake, don't you? He looks a fearful bore! Now that couple over there are certainly married, but not to each other – oh-ho I spy an *affaire de coeur*!'

'What about those?' asked Lily, indicating two ladies sitting together, and Hetty's eyes narrowed as she considered them. 'I'd say mother and daughter, and the mother's getting absolutely desperate to find a husband for the poor overweight creature. Just look at her legs, they're like tree-trunks – but oh! look, girls, over there – do you see what's just strolled in?'

Two young gentlemen were eyeing the company and then, by mutual consent, made their way to the table nearest the girls.

'Don't look now,' whispered Hetty, giving her companions a surreptitious wink. Then holding up the teapot, she raised her voice. 'Is anybody ready for another cup, ladies?' she trilled in her splendidly upper-class accent. 'Or a top-up of hot water? Add your own milk and sugar to taste!'

Lily could not repress a smile at the clear, carrying tones aimed more at the adjoining table than at their own. Sure enough, as soon as the cups were replenished, the two young men got up and stood beside them.

'Good afternoon, ladies,' said one of them politely. 'May we ask if you are here to dance?' He looked at Hetty. 'Because if so, I'd very much like to have the pleasure . . .' His words tailed off and his pleasant open features broadened into a smile as Hetty graciously rose and took his hand. His companion looked at Lily enquiringly.

'And may I also have – er . . .?'

That left Cicely sitting on her own for a while, but Lily was jubilant. Her partner introduced himself as Johnny Marshall, and was a far better dancer than herself; he led her skilfully into a lively quickstep to the tune 'A Nice Cup of Tea' – which she remarked was quite appropriate.

When they sat down again the men drew up their chairs and handed out cigarettes. Having taken one – not her first – Lily allowed Johnny to light it for her and felt immensely sophisticated.

The other young man's name was Ned Carter, and they explained that they were volunteer reservists called for training in the Royal Air Force in preparation for active service if needed.

'We're off on a flying course down in Wiltshire tomorrow,' said Ned.

'You mean if – in case there's a war?' Lily asked, wide-eyed. 'Even though Mr Chamberlain says the danger's over?'

Johnny grinned. 'I wouldn't bank on our friend Herr Hitler. We'd be idiots not to be prepared,' he said, adding with all the eager anticipation of youth, 'Can't wait to get into the cockpit of a Tiger Moth. They're our training craft – great little aeroplane – oh, boy!'

When the band struck up with 'Cheek to Cheek', he got up at once and held out his hand to Lily. Ned was about to ask Hetty, but she tipped him an almost imperceptible wink in Cicely's direction, and he got the message. The next hour and a half passed delightfully, talking over tea, dancing and smoking. The men, or rather boys, for they were both under twenty, were sorry when the girls insisted on calling a taxi, which returned them to St Mildred's House in time to change and report for the evening shift on their wards. Lily was exhilarated by this taste of London life, but Hetty reminded her that they'd been lucky in running into Johnny and Ned.

'You won't always be able to count on a good pick-up!' she laughed, and seeing Lily's face, added, 'Don't look so shocked – you don't get *that* sort of pick-up at the Queen's in daylight!'

But it was a start, an appetiser for the sort of future Lily Knowles dreamed about.

Princess Louise ward had a run of major operations in February and March: wombs, gall bladders and grumbling appendices were removed, and there were a couple of mastectomies for breast cancer. Operation days were busy for all ward staff, and Lily hurried from bed to bed with the staff nurse in charge of preparing the patients for operation.The women varied enormously in their reactions, some admitting their fear, while others were stoical; others spoke of their religious faith. Lily endeavoured to adjust her attitude accordingly, and hid her own fears of inadequacy behind a reassuring smile.

The consultant surgeon smiled and spoke encouragingly to his post-operative patients, though when he looked grave and called a woman 'my dear' instead of Your Ladyship or Mrs So-and-so, it sometimes meant that the outlook was less than hopeful. Lily was saddened by the case of a thirty-six-year-old wife and mother who was found to have inoperable cancer of the pancreas, a death sentence that no amount of wealth or privilege could prevent.

'What do you say to relatives when they're about to lose the person they love the most?' she asked her companions in the dining room later that day.

'Nobody can answer that, Lily, because everybody's different in the way they take the news,' Beatrice Massey said thoughtfully. 'Some may want to talk or cry – others just want to be left alone.'

'Actually it's not our job – we're nurses, not ministers of religion,' said Hetty with a slight shrug. 'Send for the clergy, that's all we can do. And tell an orderly to brew quarts of tea.'

Lily thought these answers unsatisfactory. 'You know that Hanna thinks she'll never see her mother or grandparents again, don't you?' she said seriously.

The others looked uneasy. 'Yes, poor Hanna goes around looking like a week of wet Sundays, so people keep away from her,' said Hetty. 'It isn't as if it's our fault, is it? Can't she go to her . . . what do they call the men who run synagogues?'

'Rabbis.' Lily frowned. 'Hanna's been a good mentor to me, and I must do something for her. Maybe I'll ask her out to tea or the pictures, and try to get her to talk about her feelings.'

'They have very good concerts at the Wigmore Hall, so I've heard,' said Hetty, who always seemed to know what entertainments were on offer. 'Why not take her to one of those?'

'I could try.' Hanna's pale, unsmiling face was a constant reminder to Lily of what was still going on in Europe. Hitler had continued to send troops into Czechoslovakia, and Czech Jews added to the stream of fleeing refugees: refugees whom it seemed nobody wanted, for there were protests from some quarters about the trainloads of Jewish children regularly arriving in England, sent by their despairing parents to take their chance among strangers.

And this unwelcoming attitude was soon brought home to Hanna Blumfeldt in no uncertain terms. Miss Russell sent for her to say that she was to be transferred immediately to another ward, because a patient in Suffolk had complained that she had been both neglectful and rude. His relatives seized the opportunity to make their feelings known.

'I must say, Miss Russell, that in a hospital of this distinction one would expect to find decent, well-educated *English* nurses,' the patient's wife told the matron. 'Certainly not Jews or Irish or suchlike immigrants. I'm astonished that this person was ever appointed, and the wretched girl is not to be allowed near my husband again. Do I make myself clear?'

Miss Russell had expressed her great regret, and a

letter of apology was sent to the family. The Dowager Countess of Suffolk, when informed of this unfortunate matter, also wrote a letter of regret, but pointed out that the nurse's father was a distinguished scientist living in London and engaged on work of national importance, adding that the family had been tragically divided by recent events in Germany. Nurse Blumfeldt was reprimanded and transferred to Princess May ward, but no further action was taken.

'Just because I told him he must wait his turn for the barber who was shaving another man,' Hanna told Lily bitterly. 'All they think about is themselves, these people – they care not a penny for the troubles of others. They are utterly selfish.'

Lily listened patiently until Hanna had vented her anger, and then changed the subject by asking her if she would like to go to a concert. Hanna looked surprised, but agreed to attend, as long as there was no Wagner. They had a shared half-day in the last week of March, and Lily got the tickets from an agency in Fleet Street, where she learned that Mendelssohn's sacred oratorio *Elijah* was to be performed at the Wigmore Hall on that day.

'Oh, very suitable!' remarked Hetty. 'An Old Testament figure – I mean, you couldn't very well take her to *Messiah*, could you?'

And then . . .

Two notes arrived on the same day for Nurse Knowles. One was headed St Bartholomew's Hospital, which Lily had discovered was quite near, in Smithfield, and it contained a polite request from Mr Dennis Wardley that he might call on Miss Lilian Knowles at a convenient date and time, and take her out for an evening. Was there any play or film she would like to see, or maybe a concert? He was very much looking forward to meeting her again, he said.

Lily clucked her tongue in annoyance, having arranged to go out with Hanna on her last free half-day in March. It would have been bliss to go to *Elijah* with Dennis, but she was bound to keep her commitment – and could hardly invite him to join them! Would it be all right to name another time in April, she wondered. If she put him off now, he might not ask again.

And then she opened the other letter, which was from Geoffrey Westhouse. He was arriving in London almost immediately to take up his position at Badger, Badger and Crangle, and would be living in lodgings in Parker Street; could he possibly meet Lily at the weekend?

Oh dear, thought Lily. Geoffrey Westhouse. There would be time enough to meet him later, and she did not want to appear too eager. Since the Christmas ball she had realised that young Mr Westhouse, whilst making a good enough impression in Belhampton, was by no means the only fish in the big pond that was London. The place was full of young men about town, just as presentable as Geoffrey and without what Grandmama called 'his unfortunate connection'. She frowned at the thought of Pinehurst and her father's last letter, more or less pleading with her to visit them, as they all missed her, so he said. He also mentioned that it might not be safe for her to remain in London now that the European situation was worsening.

'What's up, Lily? You look very pensive,' said Hetty, taking a seat beside her in the nurses' sitting room. 'Too many clashing invitations?'

'You may think you're joking, Hetty, but in fact

you're not far wrong.' And Lily explained her dilemma. Hetty was intrigued.

'Geoffrey seemed all right to me, and I saw several pairs of envious female eyes looking in your direction that evening,' she said, her own eyes twinkling with amusement. 'But you can't afford to throw away a Bart's man. Mm, I can see you've got a problem, old thing.'

'Dennis is only a medical student as yet, Hetty.'

'Yes, but he'll be a Bart's man one day, and you don't want to lose him to a Bart's nurse, do you? While you're dithering around, one of them's probably getting her dainty little claws into him as we speak!'

'Well, don't ask me to let Hanna down, because I'm not going to,' said Lily stoutly.

'Right, then, in that case the solution seems to me to be obvious. Get two more tickets and ask both these fellows to join you in a foursome with Hanna at the Wigmore Hall. And if they're half decent, they'll pay for the lot and take you out to supper afterwards at one of those Soho clubs. Ooh, you're in for a good time!'

'I suppose I could suggest it to them,' mused Lily, hoping that Dennis would not mind, and not caring much whether Geoffrey minded or not. 'Only do you think *Elijah* might be a bit heavy? I've just heard bits of it on the wireless at Pine—' She checked herself quickly, but Hetty did not appear to notice.

'They'll jump at it, mark my words, if they're that keen! Only make sure that Hanna doesn't bore them stiff with Blumfeldt family history. Better have a word with her.'

Lily wrote back to both students, the one of medicine, the other of law, and both accepted the offer with a show of good grace, each hoping that he would sit beside Lily. She was determined to sit beside Hanna, with Dennis on her other side, and the trick was to make it look accidental. In this she succeeded, and Geoffrey Westhouse found himself marooned between Miss Blumfeldt and a stranger. He hid his disappointment well, making valiant but not very successful attempts at conversation with the solemn-faced girl.

It turned out to be an unexpectedly memorable evening. Lily noticed that all three of her companions were involved through the power of the music with the drama of the story as it unfolded. Dennis specially praised the soprano in the scene where Elijah's thrice-repeated prayer raises the widow's son from apparent death: her ecstatic cry, 'My son reviveth!' was met by sighs from the audience, and Lily's eyes filled with tears, which gave Dennis an opportunity to take hold of her hand, though at the end of the scene she gently withdrew it, not wanting the others to notice. In the interval the men were full of praise for the performance, dispelling Lily's fears that this deeply religious work would be boring or, worse still, comical to them; they had after all paid her for the tickets.

In the second and more meditative part of the oratorio, Lily was unprepared for Hanna's intense concentration when a chorus of angelic voices sang the words of the psalm, 'He, watching over Israel, slumbers not nor sleeps.'

Israel, the chosen nation. Israel, the hated race. It was at this point that Lily instinctively put out her hand to Hanna, who seized it in a firm grasp, and for the rest of the performance the two girls sat holding hands between the two young men. Lily did not feel self-conscious about it, for she knew that Hanna Blumfeldt needed a true friend, someone willing to put up with her lack of humour and tiresome tactlessness; and when they ended the evening in a small coffee house on Ludgate Hill before the girls returned to St Mildred's, Dennis said he looked forward to taking Lily, as he now called her, to a Promenade concert at the Queen's Hall later in the year – at which she smiled and felt well rewarded.

But Geoffrey Westhouse was not to be dismissed as a mere country bumpkin, and turned his inexperience to his own advantage.

'I say, Lily, we ought to explore London and see something of the sights, don't you think?' he said with boyish eagerness. 'I'll be with this firm for a year or two, and you've got your training, too – so let's go on a few expeditions!'

Lily could only admire his good humour, and as the days lengthened into spring they met for occasional walks when they could snatch an hour or two, tramping around the Inns of Court and strolling along the Embankment, gazing on the constant traffic of the river. Fleet Street held endless fascination, and Lily thought she could actually smell the printer's ink drifting up from the presses that ran all night to produce the morning papers. They liked visiting the time-honoured pubs where journalists, reporters and photographers thronged, though there was an awkward moment when, having ordered a drink and sandwich in a little smoke-filled café, Geoffrey bumped heavily into a pert, pretty blonde at the counter, who looked up and gave him a cheeky wink. He was soon warned off, none too ceremoniously.

''Ere, mate, 'oo d'ye fink yer lookin' at? Take yer

smarmy eyes orf my gal,' growled a voice, and Geoffrey stared back into the sun-starved face and red-rimmed eyes of a printer who had been working till the crack of dawn.

'I beg your pardon, I didn't even notice the young lady until she –'

'Yes, 'e did, Billy, 'e pushed up aginst me an' pinched me backside!' said the girl, to the glee of the bystanders, who sensed a confrontation.

'Wot yer mean, yer didn't notice my Sal? Yer better watch yer step, mate,' said Billy, moving closer with a menacing air.

'I say, look here, you can't just threaten a complete stranger like –'

'Better leave 'im alone, Billy. 'E's just some blue-nosed toff in the wrong place, 'im an' 'is fancy piece,' interposed the girl called Sal, at which Lily took the opportunity to seize Geoffrey firmly by the arm and steer him out of the door and into the street.

'Actually that awful girl was right – we *were* in the wrong place,' she said, wondering what Miss Russell would say if she could see one of her nurses almost involved in a Fleet Street brawl. 'That's where the roughs go, the likes of Billy and Sal – so let's leave them to it.'

'I'm frightfully sorry, Lily, I honestly didn't –'

'I know, never mind – but we'll be more careful in future. Weren't they ghastly?'

'The original Me and My Gal!'

'Yes – my gal Sal!' She tried to laugh off the indignity of being put at a disadvantage by the lower orders. 'Come on, let's go down to the river!'

Standing on Southwark Bridge in the late afternoon sun that glittered upon the water flowing endlessly eastwards, Lily's spirits quickly rose.

Holding her hat on with one hand against the stiff up-river breeze, she sniffed appreciatively, closing her eyes.

'Oh, just breathe it in, Geoffrey, that delicious tang from the docks!' she sighed. 'Tea, coffee – and can you smell rum? And all sorts of spices – mm-mm!'

Westhouse could not share her enthusiasm, and privately thought the river smelled more of rotting marine matter and tar. The humiliating encounter with Billy and Sal had unnerved him, and set him thinking about home comforts and the little Hampshire market town where he knew everybody, and his family was held in respect. He was dismayed by Lily's continued refusal to go back there, even on a short visit, and had given up trying to persuade her, as it only caused them to disagree.

For at twenty-one years of age Lily Knowles had fallen in love with London, and revelled in being a part of its teeming life. With work that was both exciting and challenging, the prospect of becoming a St Mildred's nursing sister in less than three years' time, and her friendships and flirtations – ah! There was nowhere else in the world she would rather be.

'I suppose that one day you'll want to . . . well, to marry some lucky fellow and have a family of your own, Lily?' said poor Geoffrey, tentatively putting his arm around her.

'I suppose I will *one* day, but not yet. I simply can't imagine anything better than this,' she said truthfully, for every day brought something new in this wonderful life.

And she had not yet met a man for whom she was willing to give it all up.

75

Chapter 4

Spring – and the grass was green again in the squares, the daffodils bloomed and the London trees once more put on their tender new foliage. Another generation of sparrows chattered high up in the branches, and Lily Knowles discovered that London could be as beautiful as the country in spring, to those who knew and loved it. Dappled sunlight filtered down to the pavements, and found its way into ancient courts and alleyways off the main thoroughfares. It struck the roofs of city churches and passed through their windows in shafts of light and colour; it gleamed on the great dome of St Paul's Cathedral, crowned with its cross of gold – and while looking up at it, Lily almost collided with Dennis Wardley, hurrying through St Paul's churchyard on a clear May morning.

'Lily! It seems ages since I saw you – what have you been doing?'

There had been nothing to stop him from sending her a note, she thought, and replied, 'I could ask the same of you.'

'Oh, Lily, it's all such a fearful nuisance, this constant talk of war!' he groaned. 'We've had to attend endless extra lectures on first aid and what to do in the event of an air raid – poison gas and firebombs – and there's talk of Bart's being evacuated to somewhere in Hertfordshire. We could be conscripted into the armed services – my God, it's all too much to take in!'

Lily noticed that his eyes looked tired and strained. 'And we've still got our regular lectures and practice to get through,' he continued. 'I've just been ticked off because my hair's too long, and that's because I haven't even had time to go to the barber's!' He gave a short laugh. 'And I've missed you, Lily! Where are you going now?'

'I've got a morning off, nine till one, and I've come out for a breath of air – it's such a beautiful day. Where are *you* going?'

'To get my hair cut, and I haven't got much time. But listen, Lily, let me take you out somewhere when we've both got a free half-day. We could go up to Hampstead Heath and have a picnic or something – and they have open-air concerts at Ken Wood. I'll send you a note as soon as I can suggest a day, because I really do want to keep in touch with you, Lily.' His eyes softened as he looked down at her. 'Especially with things being as they are.'

'All right, Dennis, that sounds lovely. I'll look forward to it,' she said smiling, pleased by his interest but somewhat disturbed by the inference of his words, and his troubled thoughts.

'Right, Mrs Redfern, Nurse Knowles and I are now going to get you ready for your operation,' said the staff nurse, and Lily smiled down at the rather formidable lady in her sixties who had endured the discomforts and embarrassments of uterine prolapse for several years. It was on her husband's insistence that she had at last agreed to surgical repair of the pelvic floor and vaginal wall, including amputation of the eroded cervix.

'I had hoped that the bladder leakage would be better after the change of life,' she told the nurses.

77

'But now I hardly dare leave the house. My grandson does so enjoy taking me out for drives, and I'm hoping that he'll be able to do so again, after this. But, oh dear, what one has to go through! Last night I was shaved – er – down there, and then came that *dreadful* enema! By the time it was finished, I didn't want any supper, but that was my last chance to eat. Oh, how I'd love a cup of tea and a round of toast now! But I suppose there's no chance of it.'

No chance whatever. Together they removed her nightdress and replaced it with a flannelette operation gown, which tied with tapes at the back; wool socks were put on her feet, and a triangular cotton cap, tied turban-style, covered her hair. The whole of the shaved area had to be painted with a pink antiseptic dye, and while she lay with parted legs the staff nurse passed a catheter into her bladder. She gasped and grimaced while this was done – 'Oh, my goodness, what women have to endure – oh, oh, *oh*!'

Lily took hold of her hand, murmuring, 'All right, Mrs Redfern, all right, well done.' Finally an injection of a sedative was given into her arm, rendering her mercifully drowsy by the time the theatre orderly arrived with the stretcher trolley.

Lily then had to make up the bed ready for the return of the unconscious patient with her dressings, drains and drip. An electric blanket was plugged in, and wooden bed-blocks were on hand to raise the foot if there were signs of shock. An oxygen cylinder was brought to the bedside, and on the locker Lily set a tray with a vomit-bowl, tongue forceps, gauze swabs and a chart for recording the pulse and observations.

By midday Mrs Redfern was recovering from the

anaesthetic. Lily gently removed the rubber airway from her mouth, and told her that she was back in Princess Louise ward, her operation successfully performed.

'Oh, Hanna, what is it? What's happened?' cried Lily when she saw her mentor's stricken face.

'My father has a letter. It has come through the Red Cross,' answered Hanna, her voice a hoarse whisper.

'A *letter*? You mean you've got news of your mother? What – I mean, when –'

'There is no news of her coming, only that she asks us to send food parcels. She is in a transition camp, and they have not enough to eat. The message begs us to send all we can. It is not like my mother to beg.'

'Oh, Hanna dear, we'll take a collection straight away, and I'll go out shopping this afternoon,' promised Lily, thankful at least that there was something she could do. The others contributed generously, and that afternoon Lily and three other off-duty probationers went out to buy tinned goods ham, salmon, sardines, fruit, vegetables and evaporated milk. Hetty Tarrant added bars of chocolate and a Stilton cheese, and on the following day two stout cardboard parcels were sent off from the post office in Cheapside to the Blumfeldt family, care of the Red Cross in Germany. Hanna's father also sent two parcels, and Lily prayed that they would all reach their destination – and that Frau Blumfeldt and her parents would get out of the transition camp and across the English Channel before it was too late . . .

'Nurse – excuse me, Nurse, but I think Grannie needs your attention.'

The evening visitors had arrived, and Lily was in

the sluice room, arranging flowers in vases. When she turned round, she saw the apologetic face of a young man in a well-cut suit. He had the sort of looks that Hetty would have called 'stop-dead-in-your-tracks'. Wide-spaced blue eyes regarded her from under long, straight brows, and when he saw her face he opened them a little wider, as if in pleased surprise at encountering such a pretty girl.

'I'm so sorry to trouble you, Nurse, but Grannie says she needs – the lavatory, actually, and Grampy and I aren't quite sure . . . I mean, does she need the bedpan or whatever it's called?'

'Which lady is your, er, grannie, sir?' Lily asked, quickly wiping her hands on a towel.

'It's Mrs Redfern in room number four, if you wouldn't mind, Nurse. Thank you so much.'

Mrs Redfern's husband rose from his chair when Lily entered the room.

'She's very agitated, Nurse, because she needs to – er, make water,' he said, and Lily patiently explained that his wife had a tube in her bladder, so did not need to pass it in the usual way. She asked the two men to step outside the room while she checked that the catheter was not blocked, and told Mrs Redfern that she would tell Sister, who was in charge that evening.

Sister Louise turned down her mouth. 'Let's just hope it's not the start of a urinary infection, Nurse Knowles, but in any case she'd better have another injection of morphia for her pain – it'll help to settle her down. And we'll give her a dose of potassium citrate.'

The injection was duly checked and given; Mrs Redfern screwed up her face in disgust at the taste of the medicine, and the two gentlemen sat with her another ten minutes, by which time she had fallen into a doze.

'We're going now, Nurse – but we'll be here again tomorrow evening,' said the grandson with his charming smile. 'We're very grateful for all you're doing for Grannie. Thank you!'

Lily nodded and smiled, knowing that she was already looking forward to seeing him again. Looking up the case-notes, she saw that the Redferns lived in St John's Wood, and wondered if their grandson lived with them, as they obviously had a close relationship – though surely he had parents? Grampy and Grannie! What warm, friendly titles compared to Grandfather and Grandmama! Yes, he was nice . . .

But disappointment struck. Owing to staff sickness, Lily was moved the following day to Princess May, the children's ward, where she had to get used to a completely different atmosphere, and had no time to speculate about Mrs Redfern's delightful grandson, though she did not stop thinking about him.

Princess May had six single rooms and two doubles for children aged from a few weeks old to a thin nine-year-old girl with an unexplained digestive disorder. Inevitably Lily thought of the Pinehurst children, those rough-and-ready urchins who sometimes hid their fears under a defiant, distrustful attitude, and who often arrived with infestations of head lice, fleas and threadworms. The children admitted to Princess May did not have those kind of problems; cared for by nannies, they transferred naturally to Nanny May, as they called Sister May, a reassuringly motherly figure who treated their parents with just the right blend of deference and

'Nanny Knows Best' to calm their fears. However, Lily soon learned two important facts about sick children. First, however well they were cared for by Sister May and her staff, neither she nor the most illustrious child specialist – nor any amount of money or influence – could guarantee a cure for certain progressive conditions; and secondly, when a frightened child had to be prepared for an operation or have its body thrust into some unfamiliar appliance, he or she behaved in much the same way as any waif or stray, and whined, screamed and struggled. The apparent informality of the ward, where even consultants talked like jovial uncles, concealed a very strict regime. As ever, infection was the great bogeyman: post-operative sepsis was a disaster that could prove fatal, and could only be combated by rest, cleanliness and nourishment, for there was no other specific treatment. And *Nanny* May might be a soft and cuddly figure to the children, but to nurses who failed to maintain her high standards, *Sister* May was a dragon, as Hanna Blumfeldt warned. Hanna was still on Princess May, but on night duty, so she and Lily met only at the change-over times, when Hanna had little or nothing to say, and merely shook her head in response to enquiries about her relatives and whether or not they had received the food parcels. She had heard no more, she said. It was as if she averted her eyes from terrible possibilities.

'Take a look at that breathtaking view, Dennis! Hampstead and Highgate in a heat haze – and we're up here under these shady old trees – mm-mm, isn't it heavenly?'

Lily had taken off her hat and thrown it on the

grass. It was her second visit to Ken Wood, for she had been so enchanted by her introduction to the stately house and its tree-shaded park sweeping down to the lake, that she had begged to come again on a day when there was an open-air concert. The orchestra was tuning up under a white awning, and the audience was settling down to listen from across the water. The atmosphere was magical.

Dennis lay on his back, a Sunday newspaper shielding his face from the sun and hiding his troubled eyes – the fears, the question mark that hung over his life, his future. How could he court a girl when he had nothing but uncertainty to offer her? In another year he could be a qualified doctor, and thrust into the army as a medical officer, facing danger and death . . . Here he was, alone with the girl he was falling in love with, on a perfect summer's day, and he could think of nothing to say to her, for he could not share his gloomy thoughts.

'How's life on the children's ward these days?' he ventured, turning towards where she sat smiling against the wide sweep of Highgate and London's immensity shimmering below them.

'Oh, I'm feeling my way carefully, and keeping on the right side of Sister!' she answered, thinking of the parents who had thanked her for the care she had given to their daughter – the thin little nine-year-old, now diagnosed as diabetic. The girl had screamed at the very sight of an insulin syringe, and Lily had gritted her teeth and injected herself with a couple of minims of sterile water into her left arm, to show how it could be done with a smile – 'even though it stung like hell,' she told Hetty later.

'Come over and sit down here, Lily,' he said, patting the grass beside him as the air filled with the

strains of the 'Intermezzo' from the *Karelia* suite by
Sibelius.

Lily listened entranced as the music wove a
powerful picture, growing louder and more insistent
– and suddenly she caught sight of a pair of blue eyes
fixed intently upon her. Good heavens above, it was
Mrs Redfern's grandson! And he was sharing the
excitement of the music in a way that made her
unable to look away – until the triumphant crash of
the climax made her shiver with pleasure, conscious
of those eyes upon her. As the music slowed and
quietened, they exchanged a long, long look, as if to
see into each other's very heart.

He was one of a group of Royal Air Force officers
in their blue uniforms, and two of them waved to her;
she recognised Johnny Marshall and Ned Carter,
looking so much more mature than the two boys at
the tea-dance. But Redfern! So he was an officer in the
RAF.

As soon as the piece ended and the applause was
fading, they got up and came over. Dennis reluctantly submitted to being introduced, and Johnny was
clearly delighted to see Lily again.

'It's Lily, isn't it? Are your friends around, that
marvellous Hetty and the other girl?' He indicated
the other two officers. 'You've met Ned Carter – and
this is Flight Lieutenant Redfern who's been giving
us the low-down on piloting a Tiger Moth – and he's
some flyer!'

Redfern held out his hand. 'I've been watching you
for some time, Lily. You like Sibelius?'

'I certainly liked *that*,' she replied, thankful that
nobody could know how her heart was racing. He
looked even better in uniform, if that were possible.

'We're FOs now, with nine hours of flying and

ready for the off!' grinned Ned. 'Sandy Redfern's boys'll be more than a match for the Luftwaffe, Lily.'

The *what*? she wondered, guessing it to be something German and hostile. She turned to Redfern. 'I was very sorry to be transferred from Princess Louise ward so soon after Mrs Redfern's operation.'

'So was I, Lily. I enquired about you. We all missed your kindness.'

'How is Mrs Redfern now?'

At this point Dennis cut in firmly. 'The orchestra's about to begin again, Lily, and I suggest we all settle down to listen to it. Nice to have met you,' he said to the officers in a distinctly dismissive tone, and they glanced at each other with some amusement as they sauntered off, saying that they hoped to see Lily again some time.

But Flight Lieutenant Redfern turned back and looked her straight in the eyes, raising his hand in a way that said quite clearly, *I shall certainly see you again*.

Feeding baby Simon Dersingham with his special teat, Lily reflected on what a shock he must have given his parents by being born with a hideous hare lip and cleft palate; having to cancel the photographer and put a carefully worded notice in the Births column of *The Times*, announcing the gift of a son to his lordship and her ladyship, and in a separate small news item, making it known that he was for an early corrective operation.

'Good boy, Simon. Let's try changing your position and give it another go,' she said as poor Simon hiccuped and spluttered, then tried to fasten his divided lip on to the teat again.

'You handle him very well, Nurse Knowles,' said

an approving female voice, and Lily looked up to see Miss Russell on her ward round. 'Don't get up, Nurse, just carry on.'

'Thank you, Miss Russell. Yes, he's for operation tomorrow.'

'His poor parents are dreadfully upset, of course,' said the matron, 'though it must have been so much worse in days gone by, when there were no operations. Let's hope that this can be reasonably repaired.' She smiled and added, 'You have an advantage over the other probationers on this ward, Nurse, because of your experience with the children at Pinehurst.'

Lily gasped, a quick intake of breath. So Miss Russell had heard: what was coming next?

'Your grandmother was quite frank about it, Nurse, but I could see for myself that you were your mother's daughter, and able to put your previous knowledge to good use. Good morning!'

She moved on, leaving Lily feeling both relieved and grateful. And perhaps a little foolish too.

'Miss Lily Knowles! Are you just coming off the ward or going on?' asked the RAF officer who knew perfectly well that she was just coming off, because he had been hanging around in Bread Street waiting for the nurses' lunch-time.

'Oh! Hello – er . . .' Lily gazed up in blank amazement, her heart lurching at the sight of the uniformed figure.

'Call me Sandy. And I'm off to far-flung Wales this afternoon for more training – but before I go, Lily, I want to show you London!'

'B-but there's no time! I've only got forty-five minutes for lunch,' she protested, conscious of curious glances from other nurses passing them.

'We only need forty-five minutes,' he smiled back, although there was a certain urgency in his manner. 'I mean to show you London from the very best vantage point – from up there.' He waved his arm towards St Paul's. 'Are you game to give up your lunch, Lily?'

'I – er – yes, all right!'

'Good, come on, then.' He held out his hand and hurried her down Cannon Street and up to St Paul's churchyard. They entered the cathedral by the west front, up the broad staircase to the huge stone columns upholding the double portico. He almost pulled her along the nave and under the dome resting upon its eight arches. The stairs up to it began on the south side.

'This way, Lily – it's only five hundred and sixty steps!'

Up and up and up and up – to the Whispering Gallery and further up to the inner Golden Gallery and then the outer. Flushed and breathless, she found herself at last looking out on to the panoramic view to be seen on a fine, clear day such as this.

'Look down there to the south, Lily, you can see the Surrey hills – and to the east, there's Greenwich and the Observatory, do you see? And Tilbury docks further down.' He flung an arm across her shoulders. 'Let's walk round – you're not scared of heights, are you?'

'Oh, no – not at all.' Was she dreaming?

'There's Highgate to the north, and the Heath, near where we met at Ken Wood, and you were with that surly fellow! And over there to the west you should be able to make out Wimbledon Common – and beyond. It's some sight, isn't it, Lily, eh?'

He was regarding her intently, and she could only gaze and marvel at the prospect below and around her, under an arching July sky. Still breathing rapidly after her marathon climb, some wordless emotion stirred deep within her at the sight of the city – *her* city and its environs. It was an almost mystical sensation, and when Redfern came and stood behind her, encircling her in his arms, clasping his hands just below her breasts, she stayed quite still. A line from a poem she had once heard came into her mind.

'London, thou art the flower of cities all.' She had spoken the words aloud without realising it.

'Yes,' he said, chuckling softly. 'And I have a variation. "Lily, thou fairest one of flowers all".'

And then he turned her round in his arms and kissed her. She had somehow known that he would, and willingly gave herself up to the touch of his lips upon hers, the warmth of his skin, the pressure of his body against her, even the texture of his blue uniform jacket. She lifted her arms and put her hands on his shoulders; she thought she could hear his heart thudding beneath his ribs – or was it her own? High up here alone in the Golden Gallery of Wren's great cathedral, with a man she did not know, Lily Knowles first truly experienced the intoxication of a kiss between a man and a woman. It took her breath away, and she trembled in his arms. He held her closer, and bent his head to kiss her again.

But time was rapidly passing, and her lunch hour was nearly up. She drew back from him.

'I must go – you must let me go,' she breathed, though every part of her longed to stay.

'Oh my God, yes, I know.' He hesitated just for a moment before releasing her, then went in front of her to lead the way back down all the stairs, descending to the echoing vastness of the nave. Organ music drifted on the air, and Lily felt an overwhelming compulsion to stop, kneel down and say a quick prayer before leaving.

'Sandy – excuse me – wait a moment.'

He stood beside her, his hand on her shoulder as she silently prayed that even now England might be spared from war; that Hanna Blumfeldt's mother and grandparents might yet be saved; and she asked forgiveness for using God's house to exchange a kiss with a stranger. And then confusedly gave thanks for what had just happened.

They parted on the steps with a brief hand-clasp.

'Lily – there's going to be war, you know, and soon,' was all he said, and she hurried back to Princess May, just in time for the afternoon shift.

What had happened? She felt herself changed in some way: something that had been sleeping within her was now awakened, and it was all so sudden. Was this what it felt like to be in love? Lily was not sure; she only knew that her heart was full of a singing exultation, reliving again and again a moment she would remember as long as she lived. And in the same way she knew, without a doubt, that her future would be linked with this man's, whatever disaster might be about to fall.

Trains had been taking children out of London, but this train from Harwich drew in to Liverpool Street Station and deposited its burden of weary, frightened children and two adults, a man and a woman, on to the platform. It was the last *Kindertransport* of Jewish children from Germany, Austria, Czechoslovakia and Poland. Worried-looking officials moved among them with clipboards and lists, checking names and ascertaining their destinations. A few of them were being met by volunteer foster parents, also looking apprehensive at what they were taking on, but others would have to go to a special children's centre until billets could be found for them. Meanwhile they huddled together, child refugees from their homeland, clinging to the vain hope that one day they would see their parents again.

They had been escorted on the trains and cross-Channel steamer by the man and the woman whose duties were now ended. They were pale and shabby, and the woman seemed almost too weak to walk. The man could speak a little English, and accosted a station official to ask if the woman might make a telephone call; she had no money, he said, and all she possessed were the clothes she stood up in.

'Isn't there anybody here to meet you?' asked the official, eyeing the woman doubtfully. 'Because if there isn't, you'll both have to go to an internment camp. And the sooner the better for her,' he added, for the poor soul did not look long for this world.

'No – please – she speaks to her husband by the telephone, and he comes here to take her,' pleaded the man, producing a crumpled piece of paper with two numbers written on it.

The official frowned, looked at the woman's haggard face and said, 'Better come to the office, then. Bring her along.'

He picked up the office telephone and dialled the first number. He was put through to a switchboard, and gave the second number, which was an extension. There was a pause, and he asked the couple for a name to give to whoever answered.

'Blumfeldt,' replied the man, and the woman closed her eyes.

'Quick, sit her down on a chair,' said the official. 'Hello? Is there somebody called Blumfeldt there? Yes, somebody to speak to him. Yes, tell him it's urgent. All right. Hello? Blumfeldt? There you are, m'dear.' He handed the receiver to the woman who put it to her ear.

A man's voice said, 'Hello. Hello? Who is this?'

The woman's sunken eyes lit up and she gave a sob.

'Who is this?' repeated Blumfeldt with sudden fearful urgency. *'Wer ist das? Wer spricht eigentlich?'*

She cleared her throat and whispered, *'Heinrich . . . Ich bin Minna. Ich bin in London.'*

Within the hour Frau Blumfeldt was reunited with her husband, and a telephone call was put through to St Mildred's, to fetch their daughter from her daytime sleep.

Nurse Knowles, coming off duty and on her way to the dining room, was seized around the waist by her mentor, laughing and crying and repeating over and over again, 'She's here, she's *here* – my mother's in London – she's safe, Lily, she's *safe!*'

Never before had anybody seen this girl so animated, so alive.

It was only just in time. A month later Germany invaded Poland and Britain declared war, just twenty-one years after the end of the Great War, which would now become known as the First World War.

The Second World War was just beginning.

Chapter 5

The rejoicing over the eleventh-hour arrival of Frau Blumfeldt in London was inevitably overshadowed by the realisation that her parents and an aunt and uncle had not escaped with her, but had gone to a destination from where there was to be no more news, not even a plea for food parcels. Darkness descended upon the Jews left in Nazi Germany, forgotten by the rest of the world.

'Mutti says the conditions in the transition camp were terrible,' Hanna told Lily. 'They were like animals, starving and dirty – and then one day they were rounded up and told they were going to another camp at a place called Bergen-Belsen. While they were being marched to the railway station, a guard got hold of my mother and said, "You, woman – come with me, and you can go on a train to look after children!" She did not understand, and of course she said no, she would not leave her elderly parents.'

Hanna's dark eyes stared into nothingness for a moment, picturing that desperate scene. 'But the guard told her not to be a fool, he was giving her a way out, and he pulled her very roughly by the arm, away from the others – and pushed her into some kind of hut, and said she was to go on a train carrying refugees into Holland. She was crying for her poor mother and father, and she cries for them still, but that man saved her, and only God knows why. My father is grateful to him, and so am I.'

Frau Blumfeldt had been put on the *Kindertransport* train with a doctor who, like her, had been given this last chance of escape. Looking after the needs of the distressed children kept them occupied on the journey by land and sea, which ended at Liverpool Street Station. The professor had come to claim his wife, and took her travelling companion with them to his flat near to St Mary's Hospital.

'Mutti knows she will never see them again, because they are old and will not survive the winter in that camp,' said Hanna. 'Many will not live to see the end of this war.'

And how long would that be? This was the question everybody was asking. A year? Five years? Ten? Nobody knew, and Lily Knowles, now twenty-two and a second-year, braced herself in anticipation of whatever challenges lay ahead.

Overnight the war changed everything. Theatres were closed, and air-raid shelters appeared in public places; buildings were sandbagged against blast damage, and grotesque-looking gas masks were issued to every man, woman, child and baby, in preparation for German aeroplanes spraying clouds of deadly poison gas to clog the lungs and burn the skin. And at night London became plunged into darkness: no streetlamps or shop displays were allowed, and air-raid wardens patrolled the streets to check that there were no chinks of light showing between curtains, for fear of being seen by enemy aircraft. The resulting confusion was called the black-out, and was the cause of many road accidents.

At St Mildred's life went on much the same as usual, though with the evacuation of children to safer areas in the country or across the Atlantic to Canada and America, there were rarely any child patients in

Princess May. The Countess ordered the ward to be converted to receive air-raid victims, though the only casualties to arrive were those involved in blackout incidents, which gave the nurses new experience in dealing with injuries to various parts of the body. The probationers were required to attend a course on first aid and bandaging, and how to treat victims of the different kinds of poison gas.

The weeks went by without anything much happening, though there was grave news of naval losses due to the dreaded German submarines, the U-boats, a word that was to become horribly familiar. The country was shocked to hear of the sinking of the battleship *Royal Oak* in her home base of Scapa Flow, and at the same time an enormous number of British troops set out across the Channel to join up with the French, aided by RAF reconnaissance flights over the German 'Siegfried Line'.

Was Sandy Redfern involved in these sorties? Lily did not know. She received occasional postcards from him, with pictures of flowers and film stars, and brief messages like 'Thinking of you' and 'Remember St Paul's?' – as if she ever could forget! – and signed 'Sandy'.

'He can't tell you anything, because it's all top secret,' said Hetty, having discovered that Lily had met a dashing RAF officer who outshone all previous romantic attachments. 'Just be thankful to hear anything at all! How's the Westhouse boy bearing up, by the way?'

'He's had to register and be put on reserve,' answered Lily with a regretful shake of her head, because poor Geoffrey was bewildered and upset by this turn of events, and had begged her to agree to an unofficial engagement before he was conscripted.

'Only you and I need know about it, dearest Lily,' he had pleaded. 'You could break it off at any time if you changed your mind. It would make such a difference to me if – when I'm called up. Couldn't you even consider it?'

And the answer, of course, was that she couldn't, now that she had met Redfern and experienced that awakening kiss . . .

'Nurse Knowles! There are two gentlemen to see you. I've asked them to wait in the library,' said the receptionist at St Mildred's House, and Lily's heart leaped. Sandy Redfern? But there were two of them. Johnny and Ned? Dennis? Geoffrey?

But when she saw Dr Knowles standing stiffly in the middle of the carpet, his left hand grasping his stick, her jaw literally dropped, just for a moment.

'Dad.' The old familiar name came straight to her lips. He was looking at her in astonishment and – was it admiration?

'Lily. You look so grown up in that uniform. Oh, Lily, my girl.' He held out his right hand, and she went to him; he dropped the stick and put both arms around her in a wordless hug.

'It's been such a long time,' she said shakily, realising how much she had missed him.

'It was your choice, Lily. We asked you to come and see us every time we wrote.'

And at once there was that rasp of irritation at hearing him say 'we', for himself and Mabel. It was never Dad on his own. Mabel's name always had to be dragged in, while Lily's mother's name was never mentioned. She released herself from his arms, and turned to look at his companion, who was wearing naval uniform.

'*Tim*! Oh, Tim, I didn't recognise you – and you're a – a sailor! Oh, *no*.' The sight of Tim Baxter brought back years of memories, of summers and winters at Pinehurst as a child growing up among a dozen other children. She saw the kitchen with its range oven and scrubbed deal table, the Quiet Room with the wireless, the longcase clock in the hall chiming the hours, the sounds of children's voices on the stairs. And she had been such a naughty little girl, always able to get her own way with this young man who adored her . . .

'Yeah, that's right, Lily, Able Seaman Baxter, ready to embark next week on HMS *Defiant* – though I shouldn't even say that much. I asked the doctor if I could come up with him to say goodbye before I go. Oh, Lily, it's so good to see yer again at last!'

Lily had a terrifying thought of the *Royal Oak*, sunk in home waters. '*Must* you go, Tim? Can't you wait till they call you up? How on earth will they manage without you at Pinehurst?'

He grinned wryly. 'Dunno. Remember how yer called me Captain Indispensable?'

'Oh, don't say it, don't remind me – I was so *horrid*! I didn't mean it, really I didn't, Tim!'

'I had to sign on, Lily,' he said gently. 'Some o' the lads who were in the CLB have been called up, so I couldn't very well stay behind. A couple o' them are old boys from Pinehurst, and they've chosen the navy, so I thought I'd go for that too.'

'You're as bad as Mabel, Lily,' Dr Knowles cut in. 'She's been inconsolable ever since he signed up.' He smiled at Baxter. 'We'll all miss him, no doubt about that. Cheale has agreed to extend his gardening to include odd jobs and seeing to the boiler, but he won't be able to guide those boys as Tim has done. I suppose I shall have to do a bit more in that line myself.'

'And what about the book-keeping?' asked Lily.

'Ah. Your Aunt Daisy's coming back to us, and that'll be one of her jobs.'

'Aunt Daisy?' Lily stared. 'Wasn't she sent away because of some affair with a married –'

Dr Knowles coughed. 'Daisy was not sent away. She went of her own accord, though admittedly she hadn't much choice, with all the gossip and cold-shouldering at church. Anyway, Mabel now feels that enough time has passed since the, er, trouble, and now that people are so taken up with the war – she feels there's not likely to be a problem.'

Lily's memories of Auntie Daisy had been happy until that dreadful night when she had heard her sobbing in her room, and Mabel had looked very grave. It turned out that Daisy had become involved with the married Revd Mr Wingate, and had left Belhampton under a cloud in the mid-1920s. The grown-ups had spoken about it in whispers, and the general impression had been that Daisy had been sent away from Pinehurst in disgrace.

'Didn't she get married after that – to somebody up north?'

Knowles nodded. 'Yes, but apparently he was a bounder, and deserted her – or she left him. She's known as Mrs Baldock, and must be thirty-five or six by now. And that fool of a cleric left Belhampton, so . . .' he hesitated, then went on, 'It's all a long time ago. And it'll be nice for Mabel to have her back again, not to mention the extra help.'

'I liked her,' said Tim. 'Always so full o' life.'

The two men exchanged a nod.

'I'll be off now, then, Doctor,' said Tim on cue, 'and

maybe see yer later, say about an hour. I'll get meself a pie or somethin' – an' will I see you again, Lily?' he asked with a longing look.

'Oh, yes, Tim. I'm not due back on the ward until five,' she said quickly, guessing that her father wanted a serious private talk with her. 'And I *do* want to see you before you go.'

'Can I take you out to lunch somewhere, Lily?' her father asked as soon as Tim had left.

Lily steeled herself for a confrontation. 'You could, Dad, but I feel that we might as well say what we've got to say *now*, or we'll only be thinking about it while we're eating. I suppose you're going to ask me to come back to Pinehurst.'

'Not necessarily, Lily,' he replied, returning her direct look. 'I want you to leave London, certainly, for your own safety, and as you seem to have decided that your permanent home now is at Northampton, I'll settle for you going there to complete your training. As soon as the bombing starts, London will be the prime target, and you can't possibly stay here right in the heart of the city. We wouldn't have a minute's peace.'

Part of Lily's mind acknowledged her father's generosity in conceding that she might prefer to go to her grandparents, but another little voice in her head whispered that Mabel had influenced him, because Mabel didn't want her at Pinehurst.

Her voice was very quiet but very determined. 'I shan't be going anywhere, Dad, because I'm staying here at St Mildred's, whatever happens. I've already said the same to Grandfather and Grandmama, because they want me out of London too. But I'm not going, and that's that.'

'Oh.' He sighed, knowing that any further argument or attempt to persuade her would be useless. She was as stubborn as he was. 'Then I might as well save my breath.' He sat down rather heavily on a small armchair, wincing as he put his stick aside. She noticed how much he had aged during the past year, and made up her mind that this meeting must be a happy one.

'We won't go out to lunch, Dad. I'll get us some sandwiches and tea from the kitchen.'

'That sounds like a good idea, Lily. Thank you.'

She bustled off to beg from the cook, who was used to supplying refreshments for *bona fide* visitors like parents.

'But you'll have to cut them yourself, Nurse – we're in the middle of serving lunches. There's fresh bread in the bin, and ham in the fridge. And a bit o' cake in the staff tin.'

Lily smiled as she carried in the tray. 'Here we are, Dad! I'll pull up a chair and we'll have a nice little lunch here on our own.' She lifted the teapot, and poured out two cups. This would be a very special hour, she thought, just the two of them, father and daughter alone and uninterrupted by Mabel or Miss Styles or the Pinehurst children with their constant demands.

So how did it all go so wrong? Which one started it? Whose fault was it, or had it been inevitable? Looking back in bitter regret, Lily could never decide.

'Well, Lily, you seem to be doing very well, I have to say – better than I ever expected.'

'Thank you, Dad. Yes, I'm very happy here, I suppose because my grandparents always believed in me, and wanted me to follow in Mother's footsteps. And of course I think of how she was here, working on these same wards, training as a St Mildred's nursing sister – and I want to be a credit to her, naturally.'

'Of course.' Knowles helped himself to a sandwich, remembering his own scornful remarks about St Mildred's, a mistake that he must not repeat. 'So which ward are you on now, Lily?'

'Actually I've just started on theatre. We don't get sent there until we're in our second year, and if we don't take to it, we soon get sent back to the wards. But I'm really enjoying the challenge of learning all the different surgeons' likes and dislikes, and the theatre sisters are so efficient. We're getting a lot of accident cases in now, because of the blackout, and some of them are dreadfully injured, like nothing I've ever seen before – but we're taught never to be put off by the sight of the victims, but to decide what needs to be done first, in order of priority.'

She smiled in her eagerness, and Knowles thought of some of the terrible sights he had encountered as a doctor at a casualty clearing station in what he still called the Great War.

'And don't you ever get time off to enjoy yourself, Lily?' he asked, returning her smile.

'Oh, yes!' she enthused. 'I just love going to the pictures, and everybody's talking about *Gone With the Wind*! It's the greatest film ever made, Dad, much better than *Wuthering Heights*! Has it been on in Belhampton?'

'Yes, all the women are flocking to see it, just as crazy as you and your friends,' he teased. 'And I believe that some of the theatres are reopening?'

'Yes, my friend Hetty Tarrant has been to see *Me and My Girl* three times. Oh, Dad, I do love London! I don't think I shall ever live anywhere else. I just feel as if I'm part of it – St Paul's, the river, and everything.'

Her greenish-gold eyes sparkled, and Knowles felt that the time was right to ask a question. He cleared his throat. 'Lily, there's something Tim wants to know, and I wonder if I might ask you on his behalf.'

'Go on, Dad. What is it?'

'He's got it into his head that you're engaged to young Westhouse. Are you?'

'Good heavens, no! Whatever gave him that idea?'

'Well, you've been seeing him, haven't you? We get the news from Cherry Trees.'

'I'm surprised that you should gossip about me behind my back, Dad. I haven't seen any more of Geoffrey than of – others. Some of my friends here have met RAF officers,' she added by way of explanation, while deciding that she was not obliged to reveal any more about innocent social acquaintances. Nevertheless, she felt her face colouring, and he noticed.

'So he's not the reason that you're determined to stay here?'

'I've told you that I'm not engaged to Geoffrey Westhouse, and that should be sufficient.' Her eyes flashed as she set down her cup, but Knowles did not heed the signs of rising anger.

'He seems to think that you are, Lily.'

Her face flamed. 'And you'd rather take his word than mine, obviously. Well, let me assure you, Father, that I wouldn't dream of marrying Westhouse – or any relative of – of Mabel's.'

'Lily!' It was his turn to flush with anger. 'Why on earth do you persist in this ridiculous prejudice against Mabel? She gave you as much love and care as any mother could. She –'

'She was never my mother! You married her after my mother died of a broken heart because you deserted her!' Lily burst into tears, and rose from her chair. 'Oh, I know all about it – the way Grandmama had to stand by and watch her looking out of the window, day after day, hoping that you'd come back – and all the time you were – you were carrying on at that East End hospital with – with that woman! Oh, how could you? How *could* you?'

Knowles turned very pale, and also rose. 'Oh, Lily. Oh my God, you've been listening to the Rawlingses, and they've poisoned your mind against us, as I knew they would.'

'I won't listen to you. Grandmama has told me the truth about it!'

The floodgates were open, and Knowles was unexpectedly filled with pity for his daughter. He made an attempt to reach out to her, to calm her by trying to explain the circumstances of the past.

'Ssh, ssh, my dear, please, don't let this come between us. I swear I never intended harm to your mother, but it was wartime, and she had this melancholic state of mind – not her fault, poor girl, but there was nobody I could turn to – not even my own father could understand what I'd seen in France – what I'd done – what I'd had to do . . .'

'Don't tell me – you turned to Mabel instead of your wife!' Lily spoke with scorn, overtaken by her pent-up grief and rage. 'Go away! Just go away! I never want to see either of you again!'

There was a tap at the door, and the home sister looked in. 'Excuse me, is something the matter? Are you not well, Nurse Knowles?' She glanced at the doctor. 'Only we can't have scenes like this in St Mildred's House, you know.'

Knowles picked up his stick. 'It's all right, Sister, I'm leaving now. Please look after my daughter, because she won't listen to me.'

His voice shook, and the home sister looked helplessly from one to the other. As Knowles reached the door, he turned and faced the girl's accusing eyes.

'I only hope that you are never in the same situation as we were, Lily – but if you ever are, then maybe you might understand – and forgive. Goodbye.'

Lily stood and watched as he limped from the library and out of St Mildred's House, his back slightly bowed in spite of his efforts to stand tall and upright. When he was out of her sight she sank down on the chair and sobbed uncontrollably. The home sister went to her side.

'I don't know what your trouble is, Nurse Knowles,' she said tentatively, 'but try to think kindly of your father, whatever he may have done. None of us are without blame, and perhaps you should pray about – whatever it is that's come between you.'

Lily thought wretchedly of Miss Styles and her warning not to let the sun go down on wrath. How could anybody else understand? Her tears continued to flow, and she did not notice that somebody had silently returned to the library: Able Seaman Baxter stared in consternation at this display of grief, so unlike the Lily Knowles he knew.

'Lily, what on earth's happened between you and yer dad?' he demanded. 'I've just met him outside, and he says ye've told him to go away. He looks worse'n I've ever seen him.'

She raised tear-stained eyes. 'Don't call him Dad to me. Not after the way he treated my . . .'

And to the home sister's astonishment, she got up and went towards the sailor, who at once held out his arms to her, just as her father had done on his arrival.

'Oh, Tim, Tim!' she wept, clinging like the little girl who had once turned naturally to him for comfort when she got into trouble at Pinehurst. And he did not fail her now; much as he loved his mum, much as he deplored Lily's misguided rejection of her, he could not resist seizing this opportunity to show his devotion to the girl he adored, before going away to face danger at sea.

'All right, little Lily, I've got yer,' he whispered, enfolding her in his arms. 'Yer ol' Tim's here, just like always, so don't cry – don't cry, me own darlin' Lily.'

And although she could hardly approve, the home sister tactfully turned away from the young seaman taking his leave of the girl he loved. This was obviously the explanation of the angry scene, the father's understandable disapproval of Nurse Knowles's choice; but surely one has to make allowances in time of war, she decided, closing the door behind her.

When Mrs Knowles saw her husband's haggard face, and heard about the bitter words that had been spoken, she consoled him as well as she could, but was privately thankful that she had not got to face his daughter, or her patience might have given out.

'She says she never wants to see either of us again, Mabel.'

'Never's a long time, Stephen, and maybe she'll have some hard lessons to learn before this lot's over. There's nothin' else yer can do. C'mon, let's have some tea, and rest yer legs. Yer look all in.'

And Mabel Knowles suppressed a sigh, reflecting that the two men she loved most in life were both troubled by their love for a girl who had been taught to hate her.

Very little happened in St Mildred's House that went unobserved, and the receptionist was not the only one to note Nurse Knowles's visitors. Although the home sister kept her own counsel, there was much speculation on what had happened between Lily and her father, also the young sailor – quite nice-looking but definitely not an officer – who had come and gone and then reappeared to comfort Lily in her distress. Who was he? Her closest friends knew something of the ill-feeling between Lily and her stepmother, and her preference for her maternal grandparents, but she had never mentioned a brother or half-brother; judging by the sailor's affectionate leave-taking with the distraught girl on the steps of St Mildred's House, he was clearly of importance in her complicated background – but was he *family*? Or some kind of lower class childhood sweetheart?

While Beatrice and Hanna hesitated to intrude on their friend's emotional problems, the Honourable Miss Henrietta Tarrant was not prepared to let these questions go unanswered.

'But who *is* he, Lily? You haven't got a brother, have you? Is he from Belhampton? How many more lovelorn swains have you got hidden away, unbeknown to us?'

Confused by the turmoil in her heart, Lily was not inclined to dismiss Tim Baxter as being nobody of significance, as she might have done before the dreadful scene with her father.

'He's part of my childhood, Hetty, so of course I'm fond of him, and I'll worry about him all the time he's at sea. It was my father who upset me, and – er – Mr Baxter understood how I felt, that's all it was.'

'Hm, that doesn't sound like the story I heard. You're a bit of a *femme fatale*, Lily! Poor Mr Westhouse was mooning around here last weekend, and Mr Wardley's going into a decline, by the looks of him – and *I* know that you'd give up both of them just for a scrawled postcard from a certain RAF officer. And now here's a jolly Jack Tar bobbing up and taking you in his arms, whispering sweet nothings in your ear –'

'Oh, I've no time for your nonsense, Hetty – and I'm due back in theatre. Excuse me.'

The challenges of the operating theatre, so eagerly recounted to her father, were a welcome diversion for Lily's troubled thoughts, the memory of the wounding words she had thrown at him whose concern for her safety had brought him to St Mildred's. She saw again his bowed back as he left the library, leaning on his stick and turning to face her at the door.

I only hope that you are never in the same situation as we were.

What exactly had he meant? Her mother had been dead nearly twenty years, and Lily had to admit to herself that she had not thought about her very much during her childhood years. It was Grandmama who had described the sad end of Phyllis Knowles's life, deserted by her husband and falling an easy victim to the fatal infection that had swept the country after the Great War. Was Stephen Knowles haunted by that memory, and was that why he never spoke of her? Lily could not tell, and as Hanna had observed in her solemn way, showing dislike for her stepmother could do no good to her mother, so long finished with the sorrows of this world. The more she thought about it, the more angry and confused Lily became.

And Tim? Ah, that was something else. He was Mabel's special favourite, looked upon as a son, and like a brother to Lily – except that when he had held her in his arms and called her his 'darlin' Lily', he had not sounded at all like a brother. She now realised that he loved her in the same way that Geoffrey and Dennis did, and was going to face the perils of the sea in wartime, possibly to lose his life. Like Sandy Redfern, and all the young men going to war . . . poor Tim!

'Nurse Knowles, where are the suture needles? Haven't you even got them threaded?' The sharp note of impatience in the theatre sister's voice broke in on Lily's wandering thoughts, and she sprung to attention with a muttered apology.

'We're goin' to hang out the washing on the Siegfried Line!' sang the Dame at practically every pantomime that Christmas, and indeed the war seemed to have become almost an anti-climax, with not much happening on the home front, while in France the combined British Expeditionary Force and the French troops were making advances eastwards. Then came wonderful news of the sinking of the German battleship the *Graf Spee*, bottled up by British warships at the mouth of the River Plate in Uruguay, and choosing to scuttle herself with all hands on board rather than surrender. It was like a Christmas present for the Allies, and brought new predictions of an early victory.

For Lily there was another exciting present, when a note arrived from Sandy Redfern. He was in

London on forty-eight hours' mid-week leave, staying with his grandparents in St John's Wood – and coming to see her! It could hardly have been better timing, for Lily had the same two free days before Christmas, 20 and 21 December. She had arranged to go to Northampton on the same train as an exuberant Dennis Wardley, also bound for home. His disappointment when Lily cancelled the visit at the last minute was painful to witness.

'But why, Lily, *why*? Your grandparents are expecting you – and I had such plans for us!' he groaned in his incredulity. 'Why on earth would you rather stay here at St Mildred's when you could – oh – unless – oh, Lily, tell me it's not that RAF type, the one who strolled over to us at Ken Wood. It's not him, is it?'

Lily could not deny that Flight Lieutenant Redfern was on leave, and that it was for his sake that she had changed her plans.

'I see.' Wardley's face reflected his utter dejection. She had deliberately chosen to spend this precious time with another man, and he could no longer hope that he came first in her affections. He had difficulty in wishing her well.

'I'm sorry, Dennis.'

'It's all right, Lily. He's lucky, and I'm not, that's all. I just hope that he's half worthy of you.'

Worthy or not, Sandy whirled her off her feet when he presented himself at St Mildred's House.

'Lily, thou fairest one of flowers all, dress yourself up in your glad rags – we're going to the Café de Paris!'

Everything else was immediately forgotten: Pinehurst, her father, Mabel, Tim, Geoffrey and Dennis – all were dispatched to the back of Lily's

mind as she stepped in and out of taxi-cabs in her
figure-hugging evening gown in two shades of green
– and danced in the arms of the handsomest RAF
officer in town, listened to his eager talk of his flying
exploits, gazed at him across the supper table,
walked arm in arm with him under the night sky –
and exchanged a lingering kiss under cover of
darkness . . .

'Tomorrow you're coming to dinner with Grannie
and Grampy and the family, Lily, my lovely,' he told
her, assuming that she would accept as a matter of
course, untroubled by any shyness or feelings of
inadequacy. 'We'll go for a drive somewhere for
lunch, and I'll get you back to St Mildred's in good
time for you to change and gild the Lily!' He
laughed delightedly at her wide-eyed, open-
mouthed expression. 'I'll call for you tomorrow
morning at ten – OK?'

Lily had to hide her apprehension, and told herself
that at least she had met the Redferns in Princess
Louise ward, where she had presumably made a
good enough impression for them to agree to
meeting her again. But to be their dinner guest,
presented to them by their beloved grandson – oh,
my! That was a different matter altogether.

The following day was very cold, and Sandy
arrived in his Ford 8, of which he was extremely
proud.

'Present for my twenty-first, from the grandparents,' he said, and when Lily casually asked what
date that had been, and was told 30 March that year,
she silently registered that he was six months
younger than herself.

'I thought we might go to Dorking and take a walk
up Box Hill if you feel like braving the elements,' he

109

said. 'Have you got your winter woollies on under-neath? It'll be a bit breezy!'

'I'd love a good, brisk walk,' she assured him, rather amused at his mention of underwear, but not inclined to go into details about her own.

'I suppose flyers get a bit obsessed about keeping warm, only you can get frostbite up there in an open cockpit, and it's pretty parky even with it closed,' he went on. 'You should see what I wear! Vest, under-pants, shirt, two pullovers, long johns, jacket, sheepskin, helmet, trousers and two pairs of socks – and we still get chilled to the marrow.'

Lily shuddered. 'Oh, Sandy, however can you do it – taking off all on your own and flying up there into the sky? I just can't imagine it.'

'Ah, and I can't describe it to you, Lily – seeing the earth spread out below me, the fields and woods and then the density of the towns on their rivers. They look so small from that height, but I'm like a bird in flight, free and far above the rest of humanity, toiling away down there – aah!'

He gave a long, contented sigh as he turned a sharp corner at Leatherhead on to the Dorking Road, and simultaneously Lily gave a scream. He braked and swerved violently, sending her forward and hitting her forehead against the dashboard. Only by inches did they avoid a head-on collision with a delivery van coming from Fetcham, and both drivers were badly shaken. Sandy drew up at the side of the road, and took the trembling girl in his arms.

'Oh, Lily, I'm sorry, I'm sorry – are you all right? Did you hit your head?' he asked anxiously, relieved to find her conscious.

'I certainly saw stars,' she muttered, rubbing her forehead. 'What happened?'

'We were both going too fast,' he admitted. 'Thank God for these brakes.' He gently tipped back her head to look at her face. 'You'll have a bruise there, Lily. Oh, I'm so sorry. We'd be safer up in the sky – no roads, no corners!' He kissed her. 'Are you all right to go on?'

She nodded, and the pain gradually subsided, though the impact left her with a slight headache and enormous relief that it had been no worse. She had seen enough of the results of serious road accidents in the theatre.

For a while Sandy drove more slowly, and Box Hill came into view to their left, a grey outline under the December sky.

'A bit further on, the road crosses over the Mole at Burford Bridge,' he said. 'There's a rather splendid old inn nearby where we can park the Ford and later we'll come back and have lunch there. We don't have to get to the top of the hill, Lily – do you think you feel up to it?'

Of course Lily replied that she was more than able, though privately she hoped she wouldn't be too tired before the evening engagement. Being alone with Sandy, whether seated beside him in the car or walking with him up a hill through leafless trees, was bliss indeed, but she was not really looking forward to dinner at the Redferns' St John's Wood villa, especially if sporting an unsightly bruise on her forehead. But she showed none of this self-doubt to Sandy, thankful that her training had taught her to hide her true feelings under a calm exterior. And to their mutual satisfaction, they did in fact reach the summit.

'Well done, Lily! Not as good as the view from St Paul's on a day like this, but it'll do for me.'

He turned and held out his arms to her. She felt herself drawn close to his heart, safe from the cold wind sweeping around them on the chalky eminence. His cap and her woolly hat touched as he laid his face against hers; his lips were warm, and she closed her eyes; the war was a very long way from this brief winter idyll, and for a long minute neither of them spoke, for fear of breaking the spell.

At length he drew apart from her. 'Lunch!' And they both smiled.

The ancient inn was dark and cosy, and a wood fire gave out a satisfying heat as they settled themselves on a bench seat. An aproned waiter offered them rabbit pie with ale, served with boiled potatoes and onions. Lily thought she had never tasted anything so delicious, but Sandy seemed a little preoccupied, and at length he put down his fork and spoke almost apologetically.

'Lily, there's something I'd better say,' he began, and her heart sank. She wanted to hear nothing that would put any kind of limit on their happiness. As if he read her thoughts, he went on, 'It's about this evening.'

'Yes? Go on.' What on earth was she to hear?

'It's just that we never talk about my parents, you see. It upsets Grannie. And I don't wear my uniform at home, because she doesn't like it.'

Lily nodded, though not understanding.

'My father was in the Royal Flying Corps in the Great War, and he was shot down and killed before I was even born,' he said, and Lily gasped at the horror conveyed in the quiet words. 'And I'm not sure what happened about my mother, or who she was – I only know that Grannie and Grampy were left holding the baby, if you see what I mean.'

'Oh, Sandy.' Instinctively she reached out a hand and touched his arm.

'They say I'm the image of my father, so it isn't as if she fobbed them off with some other chap's little basket – and I've sort of assumed that she died. So if you could remember not to mention parents, Lily, it's a non-subject at home.'

Lily's eyes reflected the range of mixed emotions stirred by this story.

'Oh, Sandy, that's so sad, but it's a funny thing – no, not funny at all, of course, but such a coincidence – you see, I've got only grandparents too. They're my mother's parents, and they live at Northampton.'

'*Lily!*' He turned to look into her face. 'Isn't that stange! I understood that you had no mother, but I don't know any more than that. Did she die?'

'Yes, when I was only three, so I don't remember much about her, but Grandmama has told me a lot. Mother trained at St Mildred's, which is why I'm there. And – and my father married again, and we don't actually get on, so . . .' Lily blushed and floundered a little, having told this story before and knowing it to be less than the whole truth; but she decided that it was true enough in essence, and if Sandy Redfern were ever to meet her grandparents, they would willingly – gladly, in fact – corroborate this version of her history. She no longer acknowledged her father, who now occupied a similar position to Sandy's mother, whoever she was.

'Isn't that amazing? We're both the children of grandparents, as it were,' marvelled Sandy. 'It's another thing that bonds us together. Don't you feel that, too, Lily?'

She nodded with happy conviction, and a warm

glow of mutual understanding enveloped them as they finished their meal.

Hetty did the best she could with the purple bruise on Lily's forehead, about half of which was visible below the hairline.

'It's lucky you haven't got a black eye,' she said, gently rubbing in vanishing cream, and powdering liberally over it. 'I'll draw your hair forward to help cover it. Don't touch it, will you?'

Lily studied herself in the mirror. The bruise had been well camouflaged, and the rest of her face was all right, she thought with satisfaction: bright eyes, glowing cheeks and just enough lipstick to emphasise a pretty mouth.

'Are you going to wear your green gown again, Lily?'

'Yes, I've only got the one,' she confessed.

'You can borrow my stripey one if you like – we're just about the same size.'

'Oh, Hetty, you don't mean your Molyneux gown from Paris? I'd be terrified of spilling something on it!'

'Of course you won't. It'll give you that bit of extra confidence. Come on, let's try it on now!'

The model gown looked stunning on Lily. Beautifully designed and cut, it was in black silk with a pattern of short crisscrossing lines in silver and gold, 'like flashes of lightning,' said Hetty. Lily could only stare at her reflection, knowing that she would be the equal of any other lady guest at the Redferns'.

'I just can't thank you enough, Hetty.'

'Don't try. Just go in there and dazzle them, kid!'

Mr and Mrs Redfern graciously welcomed Lily into

their handsome villa, Elmgrove, in Hamilton Terrace. Sandy led her into the drawing room, offered her a cocktail and introduced her to his cousin James, a couple of years older than himself, and also in the RAF, and James's wife, Mary. There were two other guests, a handsome, moustached man in his forties, in RAF uniform, introduced as Air Commodore Palmer-Bourne, and his wife, Daphne. Lily reckoned Mrs Palmer-Bourne to be about fifteen years younger than her husband, a beautiful woman who seemed to be completely at her ease. She wore a semi-transparent gown in a floral pattern of blues and mauves that left her shoulders bare and floated around her as she moved. When she smiled at Lily and offered her a cigarette, Lily declined in case Mrs Redfern disapproved, and Mrs Palmer-Bourne lit one for herself, placing it in a long silver and black holder.

'Such a pity that James and Sandy have to wear white ties and full evening paraphernalia when they look so much better in uniform,' she observed. 'Mrs Redfern hates to see air-force blue: it's a constant reminder of Sandy's father. But tell me about yourself, Lily. I believe you're a nurse – how very noble!'

Her smile was so charmingly intimate that Lily found herself chatting about her work, though when Mrs Redfern came up to them, she refrained from asking about the old lady's health in the present company, the operation having been of a delicate nature. They exchanged pleasantries and complimented each other on their appearance.

'I believe there was a slight accident in Alex's car this morning, Miss Knowles? I do hope that you are fully recovered. He's usually such a careful driver.'

Lily assured her that there had been no ill effects,

grateful for Hetty's ministrations, and the fact that nobody could know about her residual headache.

'Careful driver my foot,' murmured Daphne Palmer-Bourne. 'He's a maniac behind a wheel.'

Lily smiled, though she was a little confused by the use of the name Alex. Daphne explained that his name was Alexander, and his grandparents always called him Alex, while to his fellow officers he was Sandy.

'His father was Alex, and got killed in 1918 – before he was born, you know. Dreadfully sad.'

When they went in to dinner, Lily was seated between Sandy and his cousin James. The meal was served by two maids, the main dish being roast goose with apple sauce and redcurrant jelly, with vegetables handed round in silver tureens. They ate by candlelight, reflected softly in the polished mahogany, and wine was served with each course. Lily politely declined to have her glass refilled, and also refused the dessert; she had after all had a very good lunch that day.

When brandy and port were produced at the end of the meal for the gentlemen, Mrs Redfern withdrew with the ladies to the drawing room, where she dominated the conversation.

'Let the men talk about this horrible war,' she said. 'We women have much better, wiser things to occupy our minds. Families, our homes and our children and grandchildren, our charitable work for good causes, and our various skills. Miss Knowles is training to be a nurse at St Mildred's, and I'm sure she will be a very good one.' She smiled at Lily who felt she should make some sort of response, but could think of nothing. James's young wife, Mrs Mary Redfern, ventured a remark.

'But surely, Grannie, we have to use our skills as necessary in a time of war? Miss Knowles may well be nursing the wounded in another month or two, and women may be called upon to do jobs that only men have done up until now, because of so many men being called up. James and I think that –'

Mrs Redfern flushed. 'I thought I'd made it clear, Mary, that I want no talk of war between us here. Remember that I have already lived through the most terrible of wars, and lost my younger son. I simply cannot bear to contemplate losing a grandson, either my darling Alex or your James, so we will change the subject. What arrangements have we all made for Christmas this year?'

Sadly it had to be admitted that both Alex – or Sandy – and James would be away serving with the air force over the festive season, and it was simply not possible to pretend that there was no war. Daphne Palmer-Bourne stepped in to give what she said was her husband's opinion, that the war with Germany would be short but sharp, and fought largely in the air. She then pointedly asked Lily where she had found such a striking dress, and asked if she was correct in guessing that it had come from a Paris fashion house?

Lily smiled and confirmed that it had, but she felt chilled by the atmosphere. There was something about old Mrs Redfern's refusal to face reality that was both tragic and curiously off-putting, especially the fact that her two grandsons were not allowed to wear their uniform with pride, simply because it filled her with fear. Lily found herself wondering about Sandy's mother, how she had felt when she realised that she was expecting Alex's child. Did she or he tell the Redferns? And what happened when

Alex was killed? Did his parents stand by her and support her through the birth of their grandson? And did she then abandon the baby? It was hard to imagine such a thing. Or did she die having him? Lily felt that she would like to know what had really happened at that terrible time, but Sandy had warned her never to mention it, and she had no right to know another family's secrets. Her head was throbbing and she felt tired by the time the gentlemen joined them, and after some amusing exchanges of wit, largely between the two cousins and the Palmer-Bournes, the party broke up soon after eleven.

'I've had a fair bit to drink, Lily, my lovely, so I've ordered a taxi-cab to take you back to St Mildred's,' Sandy told her, kissing her cheek. 'Grampy thinks you're the most delicious creature he's set eyes on since – well, presumably since he first set eyes on Grannie, and that's going back a bit. And the air commodore's complimented me as well. Yes, Lily, you're the fairest one of flowers all – but I told 'em I saw you first, darling. And I'm coming with you in that taxi.'

How could she object when he so openly and obviously admired her? And was going back to whatever awaited him and his fellow air crews, officers and men, getting ready for a short, sharp war in the skies? So of course they kissed, and he fondled her on the all-too-brief journey.

'Lily, my lovely – you will wait for me, won't you?'

'Oh, yes, yes . . .' She closed her eyes as he kissed her again and put his hand down the front of the Molyneux dress.

'Makes a hell of a difference, knowing you're there, waiting. You won't go off with that dreary medical

118

type, will you?'

'No, no – I'll be waiting for you, darling Sandy.'

More kisses, more bold explorations as the taxi stood outside St Mildred's House. The driver coughed.

'Bastard's telling us we've got to part. Oh, Lily, kiss me again. This bloody war's going to hot up, Lily – it's going to hot up like hell, and God only knows when I'll see you again.'

That was when she first knew that he was afraid, and she would have done anything for him, given him anything he asked her for; but his leave was over, and they had to say goodbye.

Chapter 6

As soon as the Countess announced that the annual Christmas ball at St Mildred's would be held on Saturday, 23 December, both Geoffrey Westhouse and Dennis Wardley made it clear to Lily that they expected an invitation. Having just reluctantly parted from Sandy Redfern, she had little interest in the ball, but Hetty Tarrant said that of course she must go.

'Ask Miss Russell to invite them *both*,' she advised. 'There'll be a shortage of men anyway this year, and an extra one would be a gift to somebody like poor Cicely Grey. Is Hanna bringing the professor again?'

'I believe both her parents are coming, and the doctor who came over with Frau Blumfeldt,' replied Lily.

'Well, there you are. Miss Russell wants to keep up the numbers at all costs, so she'll be only too pleased to ask both your fellows, though you'll have to warn them beforehand that they'll be half of a pair, like two china dogs.'

The two invitations were sent, but the young men were taken aback, to say the least, on hearing that they would have to share the girl they both adored.

'You won't *have* to share me. There'll be plenty of nice girls there without a partner, and you'll be in big demand!' she told each of them in turn, though without much real enthusiasm, for all her thoughts were of the glorious two days she had spent with

Sandy Redfern. Still, she would just have to do her best for, as Hetty remarked, things were different in a time of war: the usual conventions were relaxed when young men might be called up at any time, and girls had to be kinder, less critical, more willing to smile and talk and listen. And generous with kisses.

'We have to hide our boredom, Lily, and give the boys a good time,' Hetty declared, which was all very well, but how could a girl (who was in love with somebody else anyway) give two fellows a good time simultaneously when they were at daggers drawn with each other?

Sighing, Lily began to dress for the ball, turning down Hetty's offer to lend her the Molyneux gown again; the green one would do.

And then in an instant the whole evening was changed. A nursing orderly came running up Bread Street to St Mildred's House.

'The theatre nurses are to report for duty straight away,' she gasped to the receptionist. 'A bad case has just been brought in, a woman with both legs broken and glass in her face – and the driver o' the car that ran over her, he's come in as well!'

Lily hardly knew whether to feel relieved or sorry to be so peremptorily called away from the ball, leaving her two partners to sink or swim among a chattering crowd of nurses, about half of whom were unpartnered. In actual fact Mr Wardley quickly returned to St Bartholomew's, where he asked permission to offer his services at St Mildred's, while Geoffrey was seized by an eager second-year who monopolised him for the evening; after a few gin cocktails he resigned himself to his fate.

*

'Nasty one here,' pronounced Dr Carruthers, the RMO on call for emergencies. 'An office cleaner on her way home in the blackout, stepped into the path of an MG saloon going much too fast. There's glass all over the place, so she must have been tossed up on the bonnet and smashed the windscreen. Both tibs and fibs broken, and God knows what facial injuries, it's just a blob of blood, and I think there's glass in her right eye, poor woman. She'll be a case for Moorfield's, I'd think, but an ophthalmic surgeon's coming over from Bart's to assess her.'

Lily and a nursing orderly set about carefully cutting off the woman's clothes. Her face was a mask of congealed blood, and she moaned feebly, scarcely conscious. Carruthers had straightened her legs and immobilised them with sandbags on either side.

'What's the staff situation for theatre?' he asked.

'A bit thin, Doctor,' replied Sister Reeves, the one and only theatre sister. 'One staff nurse has left at her parents' insistence, and a senior sister is in sick bay with influenza, so there's myself, two probationers and an orderly.'

'We'll have to manage, then. Nurse Knowles, you start cleaning that face under running saline, and get her into an op gown and socks. The legs will have to wait until this eye man's given his verdict.' He muttered under his breath about the relative merits of sight and mobility, and Lily began to pour a slow, thin stream of saline solution over the woman's face from an irrigator, while he dabbed it with tiny gauze swabs held between forceps; the orderly held a receiving dish under the patient's head. All three of them gasped as the injuries were revealed: torn eyelids, upper and lower, a distortion of the right eyeball, a split nostril and multiple skin lacerations.

Lily swallowed and braced herself: she had always recoiled from any injury to the eye, that amazing part of the human anatomy, so small and vulnerable, but so essential to normal life – and appearance. Poor, poor woman. Her name was Mrs Young, and she was about fifty.

The specialist from St Bartholomew's arrived, accompanied by none other than fifth-year medical student Dennis Wardley. He returned Lily's look of astonishment with a triumphant smile, as if to say, Look, Miss Knowles, I am not to be trifled with – or so easily got rid of!

But his smile vanished when he saw Mrs Young's condition, and the Bart's surgeon shook his head.

'Hm. Not good. You've got an ophthalmic theatre here, haven't you, for squints and things? We're going to need it. Have I got an experienced nurse to assist me?'

'Yes, sir, myself,' replied Sister Reeves. 'Nurse Knowles, you'll be runner, and perhaps the student from St Bart—'

Lily saw Dennis Wardley turn deathly pale and grip the nearest firm object, a low shelf of dressing drums.

The surgeon turned and spoke sharply to him. 'You'd better not pass out, young man, because I need all the help I can get. Buck up!'

'I – I'm sorry, sir. I'm all right,' replied Wardley, taking a couple of deep breaths.

'Don't worry, I've met quite a few doctors who're squeamish about eyes. I'm the same with gynaecology – all those rank, dripping caverns, I was never drawn to pot-holing. What you've got to do is ask yourself what this patient needs. Can you tell me?'

Poor Dennis opened his mouth and closed it again. The surgeon turned to Lily.

123

'Can *you* tell him, Nurse?' he asked, and she realised he was testing her.

'Attend to the patient's safety and comfort. Primary observation, pain relief if indicated. Clean with normal saline, examine and assess – sir.' All but the last word was a recitation from memory of a lecture on ophthalmology.

'Yes, good. And we've got fractured limbs here too, haven't we?'

'Control haemorrhage, treat shock, immobilise with splints – with sandbags, sir,' she quoted from the first aid manual.

'And the priority is . . . ?'

'Her eyes, sir. After you've controlled haemorrhage, which there doesn't seem to be, sir.'

'Correct. So let's get her to the eye theatre and under a general anaesthetic, which won't be easy. She'll have to be very carefully intubated, and then I can examine her and decide what to do for the best, assisted by Mr Wardley and your good selves. Dr Carruthers can see the other casualty, and if it's just concussion, he can stay on the men's ward. Otherwise we may have to send to Bart's for more help.'

As it turned out, the driver of the MG had no worse injury than mild concussion, some superficial skin lacerations and great regret for the accident. It was past midnight when Mrs Young's facial injuries had been minutely sutured with horsehair and fine catgut; Lily had been fascinated by the delicate instruments and tiny curved needles in their holders, the miniature dressings called 'dabs', the headlamp and magnifier that the surgeon wore to perform his intricate task, especially the removal of a shard of glass from the right eyeball.

'I think she could lose that eye, but we'll give it

124

time and pray that it doesn't get infected. The other should be OK,' he muttered, pulling off his face mask and rubber gloves. 'We'll have to see about her legs tomorrow. Meanwhile the complete immobilisation will be good for the eyes. Well, thank you, that's it for now. Is there a kettle on somewhere?'

'You did marvellously well, Lily,' said Wardley, similarly divesting himself of theatre gear. 'You shamed me into action.'

'You were very brave, Dennis, and I admire you,' she told him truthfully, then smiled and added, 'We certainly went to a ball tonight, didn't we?'

'I should jolly well say we did!'

'Pity we missed the last waltz!'

'But we don't have to miss saying good night, Lily.'

And he kissed her, there in the corridor outside the little ophthalmic theatre. She remembered what Hetty Tarrant had said, and let him press his lips against hers, even though he wasn't Sandy Redfern. After all, it was Christmas – and there was a war on.

'My word, Lily, your stock has certainly risen! And is it true that young Wardley actually came to join you in the theatre for that ghastly eye operation?'

The Honourable Miss Tarrant was clearly bowled over by the dramatic turn of events that had whisked a theatre sister, Lily and another probationer away from the ball.

'Poor Mr Westhouse was practically eaten alive by that creature with the buck teeth, though he was completely blotto by the end of the evening, and they had to get a porter to help bundle him into a taxi. I don't think Miss Russell was too impressed, actually.'

'Oh dear, poor Geoffrey. And what about the

Blumfeldts? Was it – er – did they enjoy the ball?' asked Lily.

'My dear, didn't they just! *Much* jollier than last year, and I had quite a chat with the little Frau who's really rather sweet in a humourless sort of way. But that Herr Doktor was a big surprise, you know, the one they brought with them – the one that came over with the Frau. They've obviously fattened him up, and I saw one or two calculating females glance in his direction!'

'Really?' Lily was amused. 'And did he return any of their glances?'

'Oh, no, he was too busy attending to our friend Hanna, actually dancing with her, and taking her in to supper – and she had stars in her eyes I've never seen before. She looked positively blooming! You must ask her to tell you all about him. I gather his name's Johannes, and apparently the professor's found him a job at Queen Adelaide's.'

A smiling Hanna was shyly willing to confide in Lily, up to a point.

'I have not spoken of this before, because nothing was certain. Dr Edlinger was nearly sent away to an alien's internment camp in the north of England, but my father arranged for him to take a post as a junior doctor at Queen Adelaide's Hospital for Women in Marylebone. And you know, Lily, I think that I too will apply to take training there as a midwife when I finish here in June. Mutti says that a woman in the pains of childbirth does not ask for a nurse with an English name and English way of speaking. She wants only to give birth to her child.'

Lily smiled. 'Yes, I'm sure that's true, Hanna, but can't you tell me more about this Johannes Ed— what did you say his name was?'

'Dr Johannes Edlinger. He is highly qualified and very clever, but he is a Jew, so is a nobody, and was on his way to a concentration camp like my mother – but a friend risked his own position to put Johannes on the *Kindertransport* at the last minute, again like my mother. She had never met him before, but now we are all close friends!'

And likely to become closer, by what I hear, thought Lily affectionately, and although she refrained from asking any more questions at that juncture, she casually put out an invitation.

'Dennis Wardley's talking of going to a concert, and maybe you and this Johannes would like to join us, and make up a quartet? I don't know if he's musically minded, but it would be nice!'

Hanna shook her head and said she could not answer for the doctor's taste in music, nor did she know when he would be free. Nevertheless, Lily noticed the gleam in the girl's dark eyes, and was quite hopeful. The fact was that she did not want to refuse poor Mr Wardley the pleasure of a musical evening, but she preferred not to be alone with him, as it were. An outing with friends would be much easier.

The war really came home to Geoffrey Westhouse on New Year's Day, when his call-up papers arrived, and he was dispatched to Catterick on an army training course, from which he would emerge later as a non-commissioned officer. He had demanded and got his own farewell kiss from Lily before setting out for Yorkshire on a bitterly cold January day in a train with no heating, and only a dim blue light after dark. And one kiss, however freely given, was hardly a feast, unaccompanied as it was by any fond promises from the girl he left behind. Since this damnable war had begun, thought poor Geoffrey, his life seemed to have fallen apart.

Lily felt that another connection with Belhampton had gone with his departure, and thought there was now little point in keeping contact with Aunt Alice and the family at Cherry Trees, who were in touch with Pinehurst. She knew that Uncle Gerald would sympathise entirely with Mabel against herself, and would say so in no uncertain terms – and it was impossible to keep up her friendship with Geraldine, now nineteen and, according to Geoffrey, clamouring to join the Women's Auxiliary Air Force. It was a part of Lily's life that was over . . .

Until she remembered that other and much closer connection with Pinehurst: Tim Baxter. His letters arrived at irregular intervals, forwarded from a postal depot at Portsmouth. They were discreetly written, in that they contained no dates, no names of ships, locations or destinations; he described his thoughts about his life at sea, his mates and their histories. His work with the Church Lads' Brigade had come in useful when dealing with young seamen away from home for the first time, he told her. He also wrote about his memories of Pinehurst, the Hampshire countryside, the children – and of herself as a little girl. Never a word of reproach, nor any criticism of her present rebellion against the woman who had brought her up. And yet the very kindness of the letters was a reproach to her, and she dutifully wrote back, taking her cue from him and not mentioning the rift. She told him about her work, her friendships among her fellow probationers and her meeting with several RAF officers, and of Flight Lieutenant Redfern in particular. It seemed right and natural to confide in him, though of course her letters to Sandy were quite different, being largely reminiscences of the time that they had spent together, and how much she missed him. She eagerly looked out for his brief postcards from various RAF bases, and slept with them under her pillow.

She also wrote to her grandparents, who had been so disappointed by the cancellation of her pre-Christmas visit, and told them honestly about her new attachment – at this stage she could call it nothing more than that – and of the cordial welcome she had been given at Elmgrove.

'Like myself, he has only grandparents, his father's father and mother,' she wrote. 'And also like me, he is devoted to them. I look forward to introducing you both to Mr and Mrs Redfern at some time, perhaps when this horrible war is over.'

Grandmama wrote back at once, saying how happy they would be to meet this courageous young man whenever it was convenient – and to meet his grandparents too. Her letter brought a sparkle to Lily's eyes: oh, let it happen soon, please, Lord – sooner rather than later!

The war now began to make itself felt at home. The weather turned very cold, and the Thames actually froze over. At the same time, food rationing was introduced, and although hospitals were kept well supplied, householders had to register with their local butcher and grocer, and ration books had to be produced for some essential items like sugar, butter and bacon. In the bitter weather, housewives formed queues outside the shops before they opened, quite often with babies in prams. It was to become a depressingly familiar sight, and a reminder that

Britain was dependent upon imports, mainly from across the Atlantic, and the convoys bringing these vital supplies were under constant attack by the German U-boats – who in turn were hunted by RAF patrols. The long Battle of the Atlantic had begun, and Lily's thoughts were never far from Sandy and Tim, in their different areas of danger. She found it almost impossible to imagine how Sandy must feel, crammed into the cockpit of a small aircraft thousands of feet up in the air. It was somehow easier to picture life on a cruiser or destroyer, ploughing through the grey expanse of water, on patrol or in a convoy, escorting merchant ships carrying essential supplies of food and equipment. She realised that Tim told her only about the lighter side of life on board, the jokes and the mateyness, particularly a London boy called Billy Webb, whom he had taken under his wing; he said nothing of the monotony, the cramped conditions below, the constant tension of knowing the U-boats were always on their track. Did he ever feel terrified? Was his faith still strong in the face of danger? She could not help wondering what he wrote to Pinehurst – and to Beryl Penney. And what sort of things did *she* tell him in her letters?

Lily remained on theatre, both general and ophthalmic, simply because she was needed there. Listening to exchanges between surgeons and anaesthetists, it seemed that the war in Europe was not going as well as was generally believed at home. She supposed that doctors heard things through a medical grapevine that were not broadcast on the wireless, and there were lowered voices and head-shakings, mutterings about 'the same shambles as in 'fourteen–'eighteen.'

There was official news of Russia attacking

Finland, and terrible conditions for both armies in the winter snows. Russia had made a non-aggression pact with Hitler shortly before the outbreak of war, so this was seen as a bad sign. The wireless became an important part of everyday life, and the nurses gathered to listen to the set in the sitting room, though gradually most of them acquired a set for themselves, and Lily joined her friends to listen in to the BBC news, talks, concerts and comedy shows like *Band Wagon* and *Much Binding in the Marsh*. Less welcome was the nasal drawl of the English Fascist William Joyce, whose broadcasts from Germany had the effect of spreading doubt and undermining morale.

'Personally I think he's a scream,' laughed Hetty, and she seemed to voice the majority opinion, for the British nicknamed him 'Lord Haw-Haw', and treated him as a joke. Yet his prophecies of bombing raids that were about to descend on Britain were undoubtedly unnerving to those who feared the might of Germany, and Joyce's English accent gave weight to his words. Lily had no doubt whatever of eventual victory, but she had to admit that Haw-Haw sent a shiver down her spine.

The iron grip of winter slackened at last, and sunshine returned to a city that seemed strangely distanced from the war. A vigorous anti-rumour campaign warned from walls, buses and railway stations that 'Careless Talk Costs Lives', and a result of this was a news blackout. The navy seemed to be shouldering the worst of the fighting, but in Europe there were stories of troops playing cards while waiting to attack the enemy, while the RAF was dropping nothing heavier than leaflets behind the German line.

'Lily! Lily, I see you are off on Friday evening, so would you like to come with your – a friend to a concert at the Queen's Hall?' asked Hanna eagerly. 'They are playing Brahms's First Symphony, and Johannes says he can go. Would you like to?'

'Yes, that would be lovely,' smiled Lily, pleased that her idea was being taken up. 'I'll ask if Dennis is free on Friday, otherwise I may have to ask one of the girls, if that's all right!'

But someone else claimed Lily that Friday evening. As soon as Sandy Redfern appeared at the door of St Mildred's House, all else was forgotten.

'I've only got this evening until ten, Lily, thanks to a chum at Hen— at the sector station, who's covering for me – and I drove straight here.' He was smiling, but his mouth was tense, and there were signs of strain in the blue eyes.

'Oh, Sandy, Sandy – just to see you again!' she breathed, though words quickly deserted her, and she forgot all the things she had intended to say when next they met. Seated beside him in the Ford, she trembled in his arms, and he pulled her head down on to his shoulder.

'Let's drive to some quiet spot, Lily, my lovely, and let me make love to you. Oh, don't worry, I shan't take any chances – you can trust me. I just want to hold you close. The news isn't good, darling, and it's going to get a lot worse. Oh, Lily, I need you!'

She knew that he meant the sudden, unexpected invasion of Norway and Denmark by German troops, but neither of them had any wish to discuss what this might imply. They only wanted to be alone together for a few short precious hours on a chilly April evening, and as soon as possible. He drove northwards into Essex, in the direction of Waltham

Abbey, and found a quiet lane leading towards a farm. Halfway along he turned off down a narrow track towards a dense coppice of alder, bumping the car along it, and coming to a halt close to the sheltering bushes, just beginning to show their green leaf-buds. Beyond was a field with black and white cows grazing.

'Will you come into the back seat with me, Lily?'

She obeyed without hesitation, and lay passively in his arms, giving herself up to his hands as he touched her, his lips as he kissed her, sighing over her, calling her his beautiful girl, his lovely Lily. As if in a dream she let him gently remove her clothes, and gasped with sheer pleasure when she felt him holding her breasts, smoothing her shoulders, her back, her belly, her thighs, while murmuring of his delight in every part of her. She was overcome by the sheer amazement of it, the warmth of his hands, his face, his lips – and the incredible moment when he took her right hand and put into it the proof of his passion, firm and erect, while his own hand discovered her own mounting desire. And then his fingers were probing her, and she gave a low cry.

'It's all right, my lovely, my fairest of flowers all, you're safe with me,' he whispered, then with sudden urgency he was begging her, imploring her, 'Lily! Oh, darling, hold me, I'm here with you – oh, my God! Here – here's a handkerchief . . .'

It was so sudden, so strange, the sensation that seized her at almost the same time; he was a few seconds earlier to reach his climax, and was able to guide her through the completely new experience of her own, reassuring her, soothing her, telling her it was all right and that she was his own beautiful girl. Afterwards she lay in his arms while they regained their breath, and he reached for cigarettes and matches from his jacket. He wound down the window, and lit one for them both.

'Lily, my lovely.'

Her voice was a shaky whisper. 'I've never had anything like – like that in my life.'

'I know, darling, I know. And I've never had anything better.'

'Sandy, do your grandparents know that you're off duty this evening?'

'No. There isn't time to visit them. I had to see *you*. Oh, Lily, there's so little time.'

'Yes, I know, Sandy. I wish I could – I – I'm glad you've come to see me,' she said, feeling that she was gabbling incoherently, wanting him to be able to confide in her. 'Try to talk to me.'

'Dearest Lily, there's going to be trouble, and none of us can guess what the next few weeks are going to bring, but if I know that you're here waiting for me –'

'And I *am*, Sandy, I *am*!'

'Well, then, that's all I need to know.'

And they kissed again, and she had to dress, and he put away the handkerchief. Now I am truly committed to him, she thought, and rejoiced in spite of her secret, unmentioned fears.

By the end of April Norway had been overrun, and Holland and Belgium were next to see the German jackboot marching on their land. At St Mildred's the nurses' work went on as usual, as did their off-duty activities, though Lily felt oddly detached from everyday life; part of her mind was constantly reliving each moment of that magical evening. It was as if Redfern was always present with her wherever she was, as when she joined Beatrice and Flying

Officer Ned Carter with Hanna and Dr Johannes Edlinger to attend a concert at the Queen's Hall, with the London Symphony Orchestra playing Elgar's Violin Concerto. Lily was thankful to close her eyes and wrap herself up in the music, imagining Sandy's arms around her, and when they went for tea afterwards at a Lyon's Corner House, she remained in a dream-world of her own while the others talked about the situation in Scandinavia and the Netherlands.

'Holland was supposed to be a neutral country, surely?' said Beatrice.

'What notice does the Führer take of any country's neutrality?' replied the doctor. 'And isn't it obvious why he's pushing his men and tanks through the Low Countries?'

Ned looked very grave. 'Yes,' he muttered. 'This is where it starts warming up.'

The others fell silent, and Lily remembered Sandy's words. *As hot as hell.*

His next postcard simply bore the words 'Churchill Good News', referring to the appointment of the belligerent Mr Winston Churchill as Prime Minister in place of Chamberlain, now a sick and broken man – but this was swiftly followed by bad news: the German armoured divisions had broken through into France via Holland and Belgium, and were rapidly heading towards Paris, though not until the end of May did it become generally known at home that the British Expeditionary Force was fighting a desperate rearguard action, and retreating to the beaches of Dunkirk. Suddenly the news was of an overwhelming defeat, a rout, a complete failure of the British and French armies to keep the enemy at bay, and now hundreds of men, some sick and wounded, all hungry and tired, were trapped on the other side of the Channel.

There it all was on the Gaumont British News and Pathé News at the cinemas, in jerky black-and-white pictures: the crowded beaches, the crowded sea, the aircraft overhead, RAF and Luftwaffe, strafing and bombing whichever was the enemy. All sorts of stories now began to be told of a miraculous rescue, an evacuation on a grand scale by Royal Navy destroyers, by cruisers, by pleasure steamers and cockle-boats, of journeys back and forth across the sea. It was called Operation Dynamo, and although many men were lost, over three hundred thousand British and French troops were ferried to safety. The 'Dunkirk spirit' became a byword for courage in the face of overwhelming odds, and a thankful nation rejoiced.

'I'll join in the celebrations as soon as I know that Sandy and Tim are all right,' Lily told her friends. 'I don't even know if either of them took part in it.'

Once assured of their safety – Sandy had been one of many flyers defending the evacuation, and Tim had not been involved – her relief was reflected in her shining eyes and buoyant steps; Miss Russell personally congratulated every member of her staff who'd had a relative or gentleman friend in the Dunkirk operation.

One dissident note was struck by Webster, the male nursing orderly on Suffolk ward, the ex-RAMC man who had fought in the Great War. He was heard to remark that wars were not won by evacuations, and the poor sods who'd been rescued would have to fight again and most likely die in other battles before this show was over. When Miss Russell heard this, she summoned Webster to her office and reprimanded him severely for his lack of patriotism.

'The most charitable interpretation I can put on your behaviour, Webster, is that you must have had too much to drink,' she told him. 'If I hear a word of such defeatist talk again, I shall have no choice but to dismiss you from St Mildred's – because we believe in nothing less than total victory here, and I won't allow any of my staff to spread alarm and despondency!'

Webster's was not the only despondent voice, however, and Lily was worried by Dennis Wardley's attitude as the time neared for his qualification as a doctor, a Bart's man, a graduate of the oldest hospital in London. His name would be placed on the Register of the General Medical Council, yet he seemed to take no pride or pleasure in his status.

'This hideous war has spoiled everything, Lily. I had such hopes, such plans for the future, for . . .' He turned away, not wanting her to see the pain in his eyes.

'But, Dennis, you're still the same man that you were when you first came to Bart's to study medicine,' she pointed out. 'The war affects us all – you and your friends are all in the same boat. We must look to the future, and do as Mr Churchill says,' she added, not knowing how to deal with what seemed to be his self-pitying frame of mind.

'Are you so sure that there's going to *be* a future, Lily? We haven't made much of a showing so far, have we? Norway, Denmark, Holland, Belgium and now France, all gone under. And we're next! Even Churchill's telling us to brace ourselves for an invasion.'

'Yes, and he says we shall *never surrender*,' replied Lily promptly. 'We shall defend our island –'

'What, with a rabble of old Local Defence Volunteers armed with spades and pitchforks? Come off it, Lily, that's just a pipe dream to keep people's spirits up!'

'Which is what we're all supposed to do as part of our duty!' countered Lily, raising her voice. 'You'd better stop talking like that, Dennis, or you'll be in trouble. Miss Russell threatened a male orderly with instant dismissal only the other day for being a – for being defeatist.'

'And would you report *me* for defeatism, Lily?' he demanded, turning round and facing her.

'No, Dennis, it's not my place to report you to your superiors, but I shall rebuke you myself if you say one more word about defeat – and then I'll stop talking to you. So come on, buck up!'

'I'm sorry, Lily, I didn't mean to annoy you. It's just that I'd hoped that you . . . oh, put it down to the war.' He paused, and then remarked with a mirthless laugh, 'Poor old Westhouse, I never had a lot of time for him, but I've got some sympathy for him now. Have you heard how he's getting on at Catterick?'

'Seems to be all right, square-bashing and learning how to fire a – yes, I think he's doing very well,' replied Lily, though Geoffrey's gloomy letters were depressingly similar to Dennis's dubious patriotism.

And she knew that both young men could be instantly encouraged by a few kind words from her, and a promise that she would wait for them . . .

Chapter 7

'Shall we go to see that silent double bill on at Leicester Square, Lily?' asked Beatrice Massey eagerly. 'Everybody's saying how fascinating it is to see the great beauties of the early twenties!'

Lily was doubtful. With Sandy Redfern in London and likely to turn up at any time, she did not want to be out at the cinema or anywhere else if he called and, in any case, she would rather have spent her afternoon off resting. She had now been allocated to Lady Margaret, the ward for women with mainly medical conditions, which often meant incurable, and she was not sleeping well, being troubled by dreams in which she watched helplessly as Sandy Redfern fell like a stone, down and down into a terrifying abyss.

'Shall we go to see it, Lily?'

'What? Oh, I don't know. Is Greta Garbo in it?'

'No, no, these are two silent films made before her time. One's *The Sheikh*, with Rudolph Valentino – he was the great lover of the silent screen – and the other was made at the same time, 1921 or thereabouts, with the actress Maud Ling and some heart-throb called Reginald Thane. My mother said you could tell that they were lovers, off screen as well as on!'

'But they didn't make the change-over to talkies, like Garbo?'

'No, I think Maud Ling died young, and Thane just disappeared, I suppose because he couldn't go on without her. I'd really like to see what my mother swooned over when she was my age – so come on, Lily, let's go and see for ourselves!'

Lily hesitated. The name Maud Ling rang a distant bell at the back of her mind. Auntie Daisy had loved the cinema, particularly romances, and had talked a lot about the beautiful actress. And even Mabel, who hardly ever went to the pictures, had actually gone with Daisy to a matinée showing at Belhampton's one and only cinema at the time, when one of Maud Ling's films was on. A memory stirred.

'Didn't she make a picture called *On Wings of Love*?'

'Yes, that's it, that's the one that's on with *The Sheikh* – so let's go and see it!'

Beatrice was an enthusiastic picturegoer, but Lily thought it a pity to spend a gloriously sunny afternoon in a dark cinema, just to see an old silent film with subtitles. The spring had been beautiful this year, and June looked set to follow with perfect summer weather. A light mist over the river each morning lifted as the sun rose, and London basked in a noonday blaze; hot afternoons cooled to evenings of lengthening purple shadows, just right for sitting out on the balcony at the back of St Mildred's House – and at night the sky was thick with stars because of the blackout. It was holiday weather, and Lily found herself remembering the shimmering Hampshire fields around Pinehurst; she knew that Tim on his ship would also be dreaming of the one place he called home.

Her thoughts turned as ever to Sandy. He was now a squadron leader at twenty-two, a young leader of men, highly trained and skilled in the intricacies of piloting a fighter aircraft, a Spitfire or a Hurricane.

After training courses in Wales and the north of England, he was now based at one of a ring of sector stations around London, ready and poised for the expected invasion. It meant that he and Lily could meet for brief, snatched afternoon and evening meetings: glorious hours with no past or future, for they dared not think about tomorrow.

'All right, Beatrice, let's go,' she agreed. 'It'll be a change of subject, at least.'

There were impending changes at St Mildred's, as the third-years took their final State examinations, and talked of little else. Hanna Blumfeldt and Cicely Grey were about to become fully trained St Mildred's nurses with the coveted badge and buckle. A further two years as a staff nurse would earn them the certificate of a St Mildred's Nursing Sister, able to apply for a prestigious position anywhere in the world; Cicely was happy to stay on to obtain this, but Hanna could hardly wait to commence her midwifery training at Queen Adelaide's, and work alongside Johannes. She had confided in her closest friends that he had been married and had a daughter; he would have to wait for another three years before he was free to marry again.

'His wife was – is – a Roman Catholic, and they married without really thinking what the consequences would be,' Hanna said. 'When the persecution of the Jews began, they decided to have an annulment of marriage, for her sake and the child. The Catholic Church was only too happy to declare the marriage annulled, and said it had never existed, but there are legal difficulties to be settled before he . . .' She shrugged, and nobody liked to ask her if Johannes had actually spoken of marriage; Lily wondered if his feelings were as strong towards

Hanna as hers clearly were for him, and Hetty advised the solemn girl to stay on at St Mildred's.

'She could always leave to get married, but if he doesn't pop the question she'll be glad of her certificate,' observed the practical Miss Tarrant.

Seated in the cinema, Lily and Beatrice were struck by the enormous changes that had taken place in film-making over less than twenty years.

'Don't you think the great Valentino was a little overrated?' whispered Beatrice. 'Those long, slow, smouldering looks at that girl with the ringlets and all the make-up round her eyes!'

'Yes, just compare *The Sheikh* with *Gone With the Wind*,' laughed Lily.

'No comparison. Even the horses are better-looking now!'

Lily giggled, causing irritated whispers from adjoining seats. At the end of *The Sheikh*, Lily felt a tap on her shoulder.

'I thought I recognised that laugh.'

'*Sandy!*'

He had come to the cinema with Ned Carter; a hasty moving of seats was accepted by the cinema-goers nearby, as nobody now complained about men in service uniform. Once he was seated beside her, Redfern put his arm around Lily's shoulders.

'Any chance of seeing you later this evening, fair flower? I've got till seven.'

'Oh, sorry, Sandy, I'm on at five.'

'Then we must make the most of this.' He kissed her lips and nose. 'Ned said this was a good double bill, but I didn't think much of the passionate sheikh, did you? Bet he blew his nose through his fingers! If this other one's no better, we'll decamp and go for tea in Cheapside.'

But *On Wings of Love* turned out to be quite compelling, and hand in hand they watched the two bygone stars of the silent screen. It was about the early days of flying, with Reginald Thane as a daredevil aviator piloting a damaged sticks-and-string biplane across the Channel, home to the airfield where Maud Ling waited, alternately wringing her hands and praying for his safety. When the tailplane fell off and he made a bumpy landing in a ploughed field, smoke billowing all around, Maud rushed forward as the subtitle appeared, 'Darling, are you hurt?' Instead of evoking a derisive laugh from the audience, they remained oddly silent as Thane climbed out of the cockpit, took off his goggles and embraced the lady, gazing down into her huge eyes while the subtitle spelled out, 'My only love.' When the picture faded on their tender kiss, Sandy turned to the girl beside him and said, 'Wasn't she sweet? I wonder where she is now?'

'She's nowhere, Sandy. She died quite young, so Beatrice told me.'

'Oh, what a shame. For my money she's as beautiful as Vivien Leigh. Have we got time for a quick drink before you have to report back?'

There wasn't time, and the two young officers escorted the nurses back to Bread Street.

'Grannie wants you to come to tea, Lily – says they haven't seen you for much too long. What about Sunday? It won't be anything starchy. Just put on that heavenly blue dress, and in this weather we can sit out in the garden – mm-mm, bliss!'

But although the warm weather held, the atmosphere was darkening for England. The wail of the air-raid siren began to be heard more and more frequently, and sporadic bombing raids over major towns and cities sent the population scurrying to the shelters. Gas masks relegated to cupboards were brought out again, and some of the children who had returned from the quiet boredom of the country were re-evacuated. And everyone everywhere gathered round their wireless sets to listen to Mr Churchill's sonorous phrases.

'I do not at all underrate the severity of the ordeal which lies before us, but I believe our countrymen will show themselves capable of standing up to it . . . I expect that the Battle of Britain is about to begin . . .'

The Battle of Britain – by which of course he meant an invasion of the British Isles, now standing alone against the German enemy, and there was both anxiety and defiance in the air as the country braced itself for the inevitable. How would she react, Lily wondered, if the sky was suddenly full of German aircraft and parachutists descending? If invasion barges crammed with German troops appeared along the southern coast? If helmeted, booted forces marched in columns through London as they already had through Paris?

It was in this atmosphere of poised expectancy that Lily took Sunday tea with the Redferns in their garden at Elmgrove. As usual when at home, Sandy did not wear his uniform, and Lily called him 'Alex', as his grandparents did. She wondered what they would find to talk about, as the war was to be avoided, but she managed a few harmlessly amusing anecdotes about St Mildred's, and Sandy mentioned their visit to the cinema and the silent screen double bill.

'The films themselves were a bit creaky, but there was this beautiful girl called Maud Ling, Grannie,' he said. 'Lily tells me she's dead now, though she can't have been that old. And her partner just disappeared as well. Where did you find out about her, Lily?'

'Er – it was Beatrice Massey who told me,' Lily replied, though the image of her Auntie Daisy came vividly to her mind – Mabel's sister, Daisy, who had so much admired the actress. But these people did not even know of Daisy's existence, or Mabel's – though one day they would have to be told, if she ever married their grandson. Her father and his wife could hardly be left out of such a momentous event. The knowledge came to her in sudden realisation – why had she not seen it before? – and she wondered if her thoughts showed on her face, because a most peculiar silence fell upon the four of them. Mrs Redfern's face seemed to close up, and at length her husband remarked that they had never cared much for the cinema: the live theatre was much more to their liking, and would Miss Knowles care for another cup of tea?

On the way back to St Mildred's, Sandy apologised for the atmosphere

'It was nothing to do with you, Lily darling. They've got the jitters about this latest turn in the war, and Grannie's half beside herself with worry.'

'I don't think your grandmother likes me,' Lily said unhappily.

'That's not true, Lily. They both like you very much, and they're looking forward to meeting *your* grandparents when times are more settled. Honestly, Lily, that's the truth. Kiss me!'

Lily obeyed and kissed him, but could not shake off her disquiet. It wasn't what Mrs Redfern felt about her that was the problem, it was her own instinctive dislike of the woman that troubled her, because it was so important that they should be

145

friends, for Sandy's sake. They loved him, and so did she, and if – oh, please, God! – he survived the war, they would be her family as well as his. She would not be able to break with them as she had broken with her father and Mabel.

'I say, Lily, *Doctor* Wardley was round this afternoon,' reported Hetty Tarrant. 'He was asking for you, but had to make do with me. I took him into the sitting room and gave him some tea.'

'Oh, dear. Thanks for that, anyway.' Lily sighed. 'I just couldn't cope with Dennis right now. How was he?'

'Absolutely whacked out, poor chap. Since he got his MD you know he's taken up a junior housemanship at Bart's, because they're frightfully short of doctors. It was either that or go for an immediate commission as an MO in one of the services, which I don't think he fancies. Now he seems to be permanently on call, with hardly time to eat, let alone sleep. Actually, Lily, I felt desperately sorry for him. He's slogging himself to death.'

'I'm sorry, Het, but I'm not in love with Dennis Wardley, and you wouldn't want me to pretend that I am, surely? They say that work is a great cure for disappointments in love, so perhaps this slogging will help him to get over it.'

'Well, if it clobbers him into a state of sleep-walking insensibility, I suppose it will, but quite frankly I think you've treated him badly, Lily. You were keen enough on him at first, when poor Westhouse had *his* nose put out of joint, and then along comes this Brylcreem boy Redfern –'

'I wish you wouldn't say that, Hetty.'

'It's what everybody calls them, these glamorous

fighter pilots. They can get any girl they fancy by beckoning with their little finger. Look at how he picked *you*!'

'That's not true!'

'So you say, but I'm not so sure that you're being sensible – or careful enough. Anyway, I'm letting you know that I gave the poor fellow some tea and advised him to forget you.'

Lily's cheeks were blazing, but she replied quietly, 'All right. Thank you for telling me.'

'To hell with your thanks, madam, you've behaved like a bitch. Excuse me, I'm due on duty.'

It was the first time that Lily had quarrelled with one of her fellow probationers, and she found it deeply upsetting. For some reason she thought of her father, and what he would have said about her changes of heart. After all, he should know something about that . . .

June gave way to July, and still there was no invasion, though the war in the air stepped up, with Hurricanes on patrol over convoys in the Channel, chasing off and shooting down German fighters and bombers about to attack the ships. At the same time the bombing of towns became heavier, and at St Mildred's they were told to stay in the nurses' home if an air-raid warning was sounded. Miss Russell announced a curfew for all staff, though this was not always adhered to, and the medieval crypt was cleared to make room for the patients on the second floor of the hospital. Huge barrage balloons hovered over London and across the country, ready to hamper low-level attacks from the sky, and anti-aircraft units were set up, manned by RAF and Civil Defence crews.

But not only the Luftwaffe's Messerschmitts and Heinkels were being shot down: the losses of Spitfire and Hurricane fighters and their pilots also began to mount with the almost daily grapplings in the skies over London and the south-east, and people stood and stared up at these daylight 'dogfights' as if they were sporting events. 'Thirty-eight Jerries gone, to twenty-two of ours!' the news-vendors would report, and cheers rose as stricken enemy planes fell out of the sky, to crash in fields or suburbs where they were likely to cause damage to life and property, or to disappear into the sea. It became a daily spectacle, and Lily lived breathlessly from hour to hour, sharing her hopes and fears with Staff Nurse Cicely Grey who had become unofficially engaged to Johnny Marshall, while Beatrice secretly dreamed of Ned Carter.

A letter arrived from Geoffrey Westhouse who was on embarkation leave and spending it at Belhampton with his parents and sisters. He was being posted to the Mediterranean, he wrote, with an instalment of troops to guard Egypt and the Sudan against the Italians who had entered the war against the Allies. It would be a long journey, all the way round the Cape and up to the Red Sea, where they would be joined by Indian and Australian troops.

'I shan't be able to write as freely as this again, Lily, because of censorship, and Heaven only knows when we shall meet again, but I wish you happiness with Redfern, and hope you will be able to spare me some thoughts from London.'

Poor Geoffrey, Lily thought guiltily, I've treated you as badly as Dennis. Hetty's absolutely right, but I can't help being in love with Sandy Redfern, and everything's so much worse because of the war.

As soon as her final examination results came through, Hanna Blumfeldt packed her few belongings and went in a taxi to Queen Adelaide's Hospital in Marylebone, much to Miss Russell's disappointment at what she saw as ingratitude. All that Lily had received from Hanna was a brief note in her gothic writing to say that the work was very hard and the hours long.

'I did not understand that other hospitals have no nursing orderlies,' she wrote. 'We pupils have to do all the domestic work as well as the nursing and learning to be midwives, which I find very difficult.'

'Hm. Doesn't sound as if she's seeing much of the Herr Doktor,' commented Nurse Tarrant, who had decided to speak to Nurse Knowles again. There wasn't time for falling-out when the air-raid siren went, she said, though in fact she was concerned by Lily's pallor and the dark circles under her eyes, because she knew that the girl lived in a constant state of tension, waiting endlessly to hear that Squadron Leader Redfern had safely returned from his latest combat with the enemy in the sky.

He sometimes called at St Mildred's, quite late in the evening, and they talked on the balcony behind the nurses' home.

'I love flying, Lily. I took it up because I love the sensation of piloting a craft – the exhilaration of being at the controls, up there above the earth and sea. It's like nothing else in the world.'

He was talking to her, he was telling her, and she must listen and understand.

'But I never wanted to fight with other pilots, Lily, I never wanted to kill other chaps like myself, and I still don't. But now I've got to play my part in defending this country against invasion, and so every time I take off, each time I go up there again, I know that death may be only a couple of minutes away. That's when I think of you, Lily. That's when I get my extra surge of – of whatever it is, to get me back to base. Back to earth. Back to you.'

'Yes, Sandy, I know, I know. And I know that you *will* come back to me. Every single time.'

She had to sound certain. She had to hide her terror from him.

'Every split second counts, Lily. You have to have razor-sharp reflexes, absolutely ruthless precision. I can do as tight a turn as any in the squadron, attacking from below, where he won't see me – I open fire from just the right angle, and swoop away before he knows what got him.'

He turned and took hold of her hand. The sky was clear, with high, feathery cirrus clouds strung out across the west. 'And do you know what I do when I get back to base, Lily? I light a cigarette and stretch out on my back, there on the grass, and I say, "I'm back, Lily." And maybe in half an hour I've got to go up again.'

She suppressed her sharp intake of breath, and smiled up at him; her voice was calm. 'And I'm there with you, Sandy, however many times they send you up again. I'll always be there. You're never far away from me.'

'Lily, thou fairest one of flowers all . . .' He was smiling, but she saw that there were tears in his eyes, and he did not hide them from her. 'You're the difference between life and death.'

An awesome responsibility indeed. He needed her that much, he believed that her faith and love were essential to his very survival, upholding him in her heart at all times.

'I'll always be there,' she said again, holding up her face to be kissed.

And still there was no invasion, only rumours that Hitler was waiting for the right tides and weather. In the second week of August the skies turned cloudy, with drizzly rain, and a consequent lull in attacks. Redfern had hinted to Lily that the RAF had a unique advantage over the Luftwaffe in this respect, a highly secret defence system spread across southern England, which could pinpoint enemy planes when they were still some considerable distance away. It was known as RADAR, and Lily had cause to be thankful for it, though night bombing raids continued, attacking aircraft factories in the Midlands, and as far north as South Shields. Portsmouth was also bombed, though there were retaliatory raids on Berlin. It was a war of nerves, and the staff of St Mildred's were typical of the public in general, in that their resolution became stronger: at no time did Lily ever doubt that this war would end in victory.

It was a relief to share her feelings and fears with Cicely Grey, and the two girls grew closer.

'Johnny says that they can be scared to death three or four times in a day, and yet end up drinking in a pub before closing time on a summer evening,' said Cicely. 'And you know, Lily, I don't think that anybody else can understand what their true thoughts and feelings are, only the other boys in the squadron, the ones that share and know. They're like brothers, in it together.'

'But another chap can't satisfy the need for a woman,' replied Lily, remembering what Sandy had said. 'After all, there are some things that only a woman can give.'

The two girls fell silent, both thinking the same thing.

'And we can't deny them, Cicely, not at a time like this, not when they're risking their lives every day. How can we?'

Cicely lowered her eyes. She was a sensible girl whose aim had always been to become a St Mildred's Nursing Sister.

'It's very difficult sometimes,' was all the answer she gave.

It was as inevitable as nightfall. Lily should have been off duty at five, but stayed on until past six o'clock that evening because of a death on St Margaret's. Sandy came for her in the Ford, and she put on the blue cotton dress that he liked. He drove fast along the almost deserted road to Waltham Abbey, and they arrived at their secluded destination within half an hour. The coppice by the lane was now in full leaf, and it offered them a sheltered bed.

'We won't use the back seat this time, Lily. It's too much like being bunged into a cockpit. The grass is dry, and I've got Grannie's old picnic blanket. Come here, darling.'

They spread the tartan blanket between the car and the dense thicket of alder; above them a low ash tree spread its branches like a canopy. There was no sound but the subdued evening chirping of sparrows in the leaves and the rustlings of the small mammals – fieldmice and shrews that had made their home in the coppice.

'I love you,' he said. 'Let me show you how much.'

The blue dress was unbuttoned and pulled off over her head; the rest of her clothes simply seemed to melt away, and he removed most of his. She shivered.

'Are you cold, Lily? Let me warm you. Put your arms around me.'

Obediently she put her arms around his shoulders as he pushed her back on to the blanket. She felt his weight upon her, the warmth of his body between her thighs.

'Hold me, Lily – hold me as tightly as you can.'

She clung to him, clasping him within her arms and legs. She knew that he was going to enter her, and tightened her legs around his hips as she received him deep inside her. It all happened very quickly, and was over in a matter of moments. He thrust hard into her and groaned as he reached his climax, while she winced in discomfort and clenched her teeth to stop herself from crying out. And then to her amazement an exquisite sensation swept over her: there was a moist warmth between her legs, and she seemed to catch his excitement. She arched her back and moaned with sheer pleasure, halfway between tears and laughter, and time stood still for their enjoyment of each other. At last she relaxed and her legs fell back, spread out wide as he lay between them, no longer within her but smothering her with kisses and murmuring reassurances.

'You didn't mind?'

'No, it was wonderful.'

'Did I hurt you when I . . . ?'

'No, it's all right.'

'You're so lovely, Lily.'

'Have I made you happy?'

'Yes – oh yes, so very happy, my darling!'

'That makes me happy too.'

How sweet was their lovers' talk as they lay together – though after a while the evening breeze began to cool their skin and reminded them that neither had eaten for several hours.

'We'll find a nice country pub and ask them to make us some sandwiches. Oh, Lily, my lovely, are you sure that you're all right? Ought I to be sorry?'

'No, no, don't worry, dearest Sandy – don't say another word.'

For she had let him make love to her. He had not forced her, nor even cajoled or persuaded her. She had been as willing as he, and would cling gratefully to the memory of that summer evening of love.

Many changes were to take place before they met again.

The enemy's attacks took on a new fury. There was no need to read the papers or listen to the wireless now, for it was all happening up in the skies above the home counties and beyond. Again and again weary young air crews had to put on the flying gear they had just taken off – or had not even removed when they fell asleep on returning to base – and get into their fighter planes to take off yet again to repel the wave upon wave of bombers coming in from France and the Low Countries. As they neared the limits of physical endurance, the death toll rose.

'Never in the field of human conflict was so much owed by so many to so few,' thundered Mr Churchill, leading the country's praise of their young saviours – and Lily's days on St Margaret passed in a waking dream, carrying out her duties to the patients while her mind was hourly engaged with Sandy Redfern and his squadron.

And then the news: the dreaded message relayed to St Margaret ward by a nursing orderly, the blank faces, the silence in the dining room. Flight

Lieutenant John Marshall had been shot down over the Channel, and his craft had nose-dived straight down to the sea, killing pilot and navigator. Miss Russell sent for Staff Nurse Cicely Grey, and said that the Flight Lieutenant had given his life in the defence of his country, and would always be remembered by a grateful nation as one of the Few. Even though Cicely's engagement had not been officially announced, she was offered two days off.

'You could go to visit his parents if that is what you would like to do, Staff Nurse.'

But the white-faced, dry-eyed girl had declined.

'I told her that he'd died doing his duty, and that I'd carry on doing mine,' she reported to Lily who could think of nothing to say, because she was so thankful that it was not Sandy who had 'bought it', to use the irreverent RAF slang. She hesitated to put her arms around Cicely, who was senior to her, but she awkwardly clasped the girl's hand while her own tears flowed.

'I was so angry with myself for crying,' she told Beatrice, whose thoughts were with Ned Carter, who, like Sandy, had escaped so far.

'Sometimes there's nothing left to say or do but weep with those who mourn,' her friend gently replied. 'It's like when a patient dies, and you don't know what to say to the relatives because everybody's different in the way they react. Cicely's never had a lot to say, but she'll be grateful for your sharing. Oh my God, Lily, who will it be tomorrow?'

Lily now faced another thought, a possibility that she could not share with anybody else. Suppose Sandy *was* lost like Johnny and those other casualties among the Few, and suppose that she was carrying his child? The disgrace of illegitimacy would surely be outweighed by such a legacy of himself – and surely too his grandparents would help and support her? Once again she thought about his mother, whoever she was, and wondered if she had really abandoned her baby son. Lily knew that she herself could never do such a thing, but her circumstances were different: Sandy was still very much alive, and she dreaded the thought of having to tell him such news: she knew she would be very thankful to see her next period.

During the first week of September all she got from him was a postcard on which was scrawled, 'Flat out. Catching up on a spot of zizz at home. Bad show about Johnny.'

She could just picture Grannie and Grampy fussing over their exhausted hero, making him stay in bed or sit in a garden chair, taking him meals on trays, pouring him drinks: a brief respite before returning to gamble with death in the air. But she wished he would come to see her, especially after what had passed between them. Didn't he miss her as much as she missed him? She began to have doubts: had she been mistaken in giving herself so freely?

The first Saturday that month was another sunny day. Londoners were strolling and shopping, planning to go out or spend a quiet evening at home; there was cricket at the Oval and football at West Ham, as well as a greyhound meeting at New Cross. In the crowded homes of the East End, women stood at their doors chatting with their neighbours, and the City was relatively quiet, though the usual knot of sightseers hung around St Paul's. Lily had an evening off, and had made up her mind to go to St

John's Wood and find out if Sandy was still at Elmgrove; another hour on duty, and then she would be free.

It was tea-time on Lady Margaret, and the air-raid siren had just begun its up-and-down wail. This always unsettled the patients, several of whom needed help with feeding, like Miss Gifford, propped up on her pillows, blue-faced and wheezing with cardiac asthma – and Lady Granger whose diabetes seemed impossible to stabilise, and who complained about everything, from the three times daily injections of insulin, to the mysterious pains and cramps in her legs, the sudden paralysis that would seize her when the nurses tried to get her out of bed. The consultant physician had confided to Sister his suspicions that Lady Granger might be a secret drinker, and was debating whether to confront her with this and prescribe a small daily intake of sherry, adjusting the insulin dosage accordingly.

'Nurse Knowles! *Nurse Knowles*, I'm speaking to you!' called Lady Granger from her room. 'When you've finished dancing attendance on that woman opposite, I need assistance – why am I always so neglected?'

Lily could not remember what she replied, or what exactly happened next; before the siren had finished sounding its warning, the approaching hum of bombers was heard, and from a window they saw a V-shaped formation of aircraft coming in from the south-west. Already there were defiant Spitfires preparing to engage with them, but the next thing they heard was a ground-shaking thud, followed by several more thuds, uncomfortably close, it seemed. Down in the street people were running for shelter, and there were shouts of, 'They're here! It's them, get down!' Ack-ack guns fired, the ground shook and doors and windows rattled in the blast of exploding bombs. The drone of the bombers was deafening.

The nurses' first duty was to their patients, and the staff nurse in charge of Lady Margaret that afternoon ordered that the serving of tea should go ahead, for they still had to eat. The evacuation of second-floor wards to the windowless crypt had not yet taken place, in the hope that it would not be necessary, and could not be done at this moment. In spite of Lady Granger's screams and demands that her husband be sent for, the others of the half-dozen patients kept their nerve fairly well. Nurses who were off duty in St Mildred's House at once returned to their wards to give all the assistance they could, and somehow or other the routine work continued – of meals, toilet rounds, medicine rounds and the usual general nursing care of the very ill, like Miss Gifford – 'Is it safe to use this oxygen cylinder during the raid, Nurse?' – and the young woman dying of leukaemia who was past human aid and beyond fear. Her mother and sister sat by her bed.

The air attack was directed at the docks, and the first bombs hit the huge Royal Victoria Dock, followed by the East and West India Docks. The oil installations along the Thames and the Royal Arsenal at Woolwich were also bombed, and so were the homes of the East Enders; streets of houses were demolished, and whole families killed or injured. After dark Lily stared out of the windows at the lurid glow of the sky, against which the dome of St Paul's serenely rode. To the south the Thames was a lake of fire, with burning barges drifting everywhere, sending up dense clouds of smoke. When the raid ended shortly after midnight, London had been under aerial siege for nearly eight hours.

Miss Russell, a tall figure in her maroon dress and lacy cap, visited all the wards in turn, and spoke to every patient and every member of staff.

'We shall evacuate the two second-floor wards to the crypt tomorrow, and all unoccupied beds will be available for air-raid casualties from now on,' she announced.

Lady Granger turned despondently to her husband, now seated at her side.

'It's the end of the world,' she moaned.

But it wasn't the end of the world. It was the beginning of the Blitz.

Chapter 8

'It's that man again, it's that man again, it's that Tommy Handley is here . . .'

The wireless churned out the familiar signature tune, and eyes brightened; the ward fell silent except for Mr Handley's snappy exchanges with his circle of grotesque characters, especially the favourite, Mrs Mopp, and her weekly opening line of 'Can I do you now, sir?' – followed by a roar of laughter.

'It must come a close second to Churchill's speeches,' remarked Dr Carruthers. 'Anybody who's not actually dead or deeply unconscious sits up and chortles when *ITMA* comes on. Gives me a chance to go and snatch a half-hour on the bunk. God, I could sleep for a week, given the chance.'

Everybody agreed that sleeplessness was the worst part of the Blitz – or rather, the noise that banished sleep, night after night. The sound of bombs exploding, guns firing, masonry falling and glass breaking, added to the shouts of air-raid wardens, firemen, police and ambulance crews on their various errands of mercy – all these took their toll of Londoners' nerves, as did the sight of the fires, the smoke and flames, the wreckage and the carnage. But it was the accumulated tiredness from chronic lack of rest, the constantly interrupted snatches of sleep, that in the end overcame even fear.

'Show me a bed of nails, and I'll sleep on it,' groaned Hetty Tarrant. 'Actually, it's best to be on night duty now – you get a better chance of sleep in the daytime.'

The rest of the staff wearily agreed. Day or night, they had never worked so hard or under such chaotic conditions. Within days of that first heavy raid on the docks, St Mildred's had turned from a small, select private hospital for the rich and privileged to an overcrowded refuge for all sorts and conditions of men and women – and a few children, for air-raid casualties could be anybody. They were brought in on stretchers, covered with dust and soot, blood-stained blankets over their broken bones and bleeding wounds, every kind of injury. Suffolk ward became a clearing station for new admissions, who were assessed on morning rounds by Dr Carruthers and visiting specialists; women were then trans-ferred to Lady Margaret ward, now crowded into the crypt, men to Princess Louise on the first floor, and theatre cases of either sex to the six former ophthalmic beds. The ten beds of Princess May were used for such private patients who still chose to be treated in St Mildred's, though any empty single or double rooms were soon taken for the injured.

'I hear that Nanny May has taken herself off to a children's hospital out in the country somewhere,' Nurse Massey reported. 'Otherwise everybody seems to be staying put. One thing's for sure: we haven't got time to feel sorry for ourselves, have we? Just looking around here, have you ever see anything like it?'

Nurse Knowles shook her head, because she hadn't. After a night of raids the wards would be full of the clothing and possessions brought in by the injured, or their relatives and neighbours; the pathetic belongings might be all that was salvaged from the wreckage of their homes. An old man tenaciously held on to a birdcage with a chirruping canary, begging for somebody to go and buy birdseed for it; a woman with a fractured arm wept bitterly for her lost cat, and two grubby little children, a brother and sister, sat shaking and clinging to each other in silent terror, apparently the only survivors of a family. Injuries varied from a middle-aged woman who had lost both legs, to a mother badly scalded when a kettle of boiling water tipped over as a wall of her house caved in. And the routine work had to go on: the mealtimes, toilet rounds, medicines and dressings. Probationers and nursing orderlies worked more closely together than formerly, and both felt morally obliged to hide their own fears, tiredness and any personal problems for the sake of the patients. Lily tried to strike a balance between sympathy and a positive attitude of hope, and found that it wasn't easy.

That first daylight air raid on the docks had been followed two days later by another, and halfway through September a huge armada of bombers had come over to destroy London. This time the Royal Air Force was ready for them, and a great battle was fought in the sky with many more losses to the Luftwaffe than to the RAF, which emerged undefeated and forever to be remembered. From then on Hitler turned his attention to Britain's centres of industry, the aircraft and munitions factories: the civilian population was now facing a terrible bombardment.

'It's not only us who're getting it, though,' said male nursing orderly Webster with a grim smile. 'Did you hear on the news this morning that our boys had gone in and blown up their invasion barges waiting to sail from the Meuse and the Schelde – ha! That's taken care of *them*!'

Miss Russell on her morning rounds gave him an approving smile, as if to say, 'That's better!' In the changed circumstances, patients naturally addressed her as 'Matron', and she accepted the title for convenience. On her three-times-daily rounds of the hospital, the last one being late at night, she lifted the spirits of patients and staff alike. Her tall, slender figure in her tailored dress with lace-edged collar and cuffs, and her splendid lace cap with its gauzy veil embodied the spirit of St Mildred's, and when accompanied by the Dowager Countess of Suffolk, who visited the hospital at least once a week, patients would stare at the gracious ladies in awe.

'We're safe 'ere, 'cause ol' Jerry wouldn't dare drop a bomb on them two!' they joked.

'Not exactly practical,' murmured a second-year when Matron donned a large white apron with a bib, to give assistance with nursing care.

'I don't agree,' snapped Hetty Tarrant. 'A matron's image is important. Imagine her slouching through the ward in an overall, with a scarf tied round her head in a turban, like a domestic. It wouldn't be at all the same!'

Lily's thoughts were elsewhere. The previous evening she had received a message from the receptionist at St Mildred's House that three RAF officers were there to see her. Strictly speaking, she should not have left the ward while on duty, but so great was her longing to see Sandy Redfern that she took a chance, and a nursing orderly promised to try to cover up for her, as long as she didn't take longer than five minutes. Breathlessly she arrived at the reception desk, and found that Sandy Redfern was

163

indeed there, sprawled in one of the two armchairs and smoking a cigarette. She gasped at the sight of an angry-looking, jagged scar down the left side of his face: black silk stitches were still in place for all to see, and the surrounding area was inflamed and slightly swollen. Two fellow officers stood beside him and gave Lily a questioning look, as if half-expecting her to remonstrate with them.

'Er – good afternoon, Nurse Knowles,' said one of them apologetically. 'Squadron Leader Redfern insisted that we – er . . .'

The sentence was left unfinished, and Lily had to sum up the situation quickly. Sandy was smiling at her, waving the cigarette in her direction. He had obviously been drinking, and though by no means drunk, was clearly in a belligerent mood, expecting to get his own way.

'There she is, the flower of cities all – no, lilies all. Darling, I've come to take you to a party.'

Lily stared at him, at the scar, at the proprietorial look in the blue eyes. 'Where did you get that?' she began, and one of the other officers answered.

'It was in that big show on the fifteenth, when the Jerries lost fifty-odd of their crates – the great invasion that was supposed to knock out the RAF. Sandy must have seen off half a dozen. It's been a hell of a time, Nurse, er, Lily.'

Sandy rose from the chair, stubbing out his cigarette in a flower-pot. 'Come on, Lily, my lovely, change into your party frock. We're going to dance till dawn at the Palmer-Bournes', and I told Daphne I'd bring you with me. Don's taking us in his car.'

'But, Sandy, I can't, not tonight. I'm working – I'm sorry, but with all these air-raid casualties coming in –'

'Oh, come *on*, Lily, tell 'em you've been asked out by one of the chaps who sent the Jerries packing – nobody refuses a fighter pilot! Go on, go and get changed, darling.'

'But, Sandy, I *can't*. I shouldn't even be here talking to you now. I should be on the ward, and I'll get into trouble if I stay here any longer,' she pleaded, glancing at the others. Sandy frowned and stuck out his bottom lip like a cross little boy who'd been denied a treat.

If only I could have two minutes alone with him, she thought desperately – I'd kiss him and tell him I love him more than ever, and how much we all owe to him, and that I'll see him again as soon as I can; but the five minutes were ticking away, and if her absence was discovered from Lady Margaret . . .

'Sandy, I must go – I *must*. I'll come out with you another day, I promise.'

'There might not be another day, Lily,' he growled. 'The next one might get me. I'll tell Daphne and Peter that you wouldn't come. Very ungrateful of you. Very inhosh – inhospitable.'

She gave a despairing look towards the other two, then went up to Sandy and kissed him on his right cheek. 'I'm more sorry than I can say, Sandy darling,' she whispered. 'Just so sorry.'

He turned away from her, and the other men grinned.

'Sorry, Lily, we did what he asked us, and now you can get back to your duties and we'll go on to the party. Better luck next time. Come on, Sandy, old son.'

And taking him by the arms, they left the nurses' home and Lily returned to Lady Margaret with a sinking heart. And more than that, a secret anxiety, for her September period was now eight or nine days overdue. What on earth would she do if . . . ? It didn't bear thinking about.

Letters arrived from Auntie Daisy at Pinehurst, written on behalf of them all, and from her grandparents in Northampton, all entreating Lily to change her mind and leave London. There was a postcard from Geoffrey, a picture of the Pyramids with the message that he missed her. A little note from Hanna said how difficult life was in what she called the *Blitzkrieg*, and hoping that her friends at St Mildred's were safe. Delivering babies was frightening enough, without having to do it with bombs falling all around, she reported. She did not mention Dr Edlinger, and Lily assumed that, like herself, Hanna was not finding much time for romance.

Hetty agreed. 'She'd have been far better off staying here with us, instead of chasing a man with a lot of personal stuff to sort out, and at a time like this. Er – how's the squadron leader these days, Lily? That last big battle in the air must have taken its toll.'

'Yes, it has, Hetty. He's not at all himself. He took part in that battle on the fifteenth, and got hurt in the face, a laceration all down the left side. He's got stitches and looks – terrible.' Lily's voice shook, and Hetty at once put a hand on her shoulder.

'Oh, hell – did it catch his eye?'

'No, though it could easily have done. And it's affected him. I mean, he wanted me to leave the ward there and then and go to a party with him and two friends. He was quite put out when I said I couldn't possibly do that. You know what it's like on Lady Margaret now.'

'Yes, the same as on Princess Louise-in-Boots –

absolute pandemonium. But how rotten for you, Lily. Was he unreasonable about you not going?'

'He wasn't very pleased, but luckily he had these friends with him, and they yanked him away, but I felt utterly wretched. I *wanted* to go, of course, but . . .'

For a moment Lily wondered if she could confide her fears to Hetty. Of all the nurses at St Mildred's she felt that the Hon. Miss Henrietta would be the least shocked by such a revelation, and might even be able to make a recommendation as to what could be done if those fears were confirmed. But she decided to wait until her October period was due, in the hope that her cycle had been affected by the air raids and general strain of the changed regime.

And if October brought no reassuring flow of menstrual blood, then something would have to be decided. But what? Lily knew that 'abortion' was a word scarcely to be mentioned, and was against the law, a criminal offence. Sister Tutor had told them in the gynaecology lectures that a doctor could be sent to prison for performing such an illegal operation, and had mentioned that there were certain women, sometimes midwives, who did it for payment, but that it was dangerous and could result in death or disability, or end a woman's chances of having children in the future. There had been whispers among the nurses of cases they had heard about, of knitting needles and crochet-hooks (Lily shuddered), of douching with hot soapy water and drinking neat gin (ugh, she would be sick), jumping from the top to the bottom of the stairs (she might break her neck or at least an arm or leg), and taking preparations like slippery elm bark, whatever that was. Lily found herself confronting the desperation that women have suffered through the ages; and the alternative, to admit to her condition – if she was indeed in early pregnancy – and have the child and give it up for adoption, would mean the public disgrace of everybody knowing. It would be the end of her career and any vestige of self-esteem.

A chill settled over Lily's heart and mind as she faced the facts: the change in her attitude since she had first considered the possibility of bearing Redfern's child – how she had thought she would bravely face the world and cherish it! Ah, but that was if he had been killed, which he had not. And now that she had seen him in a very different mood, demanding and petulant, her earlier thoughts seemed less noble, and more like unrealistic sentiment. He had gone off to dance until dawn, and perhaps console himself with a more available girl, for there was no shortage of girls for the Brylcreem boys. Suppose she *was* expecting, how would she tell him, and what would he say? Would he be happy to marry her, or would he ask humiliating questions? What would that haughty Mrs Redfern say? And her grandparents? Her father and Mabel? Matron Russell? She could see nothing but their blank, incredulous stares. And what about Tim? At the thought of him she covered her face, for she now saw pregnancy as an unmitigated disaster. Panic rose in her throat: she remembered stories she had heard of desperate girls who had taken their own lives.

'Oh, dear God, forgive me, and don't let it happen,' she prayed. 'Let me see my period, and I'll never give way to temptation again – *never* – I'll *never* let it happen again.'

But the days went by with only the pattern of work and weariness to mark the passing of September into October. News came of bomb damage to St

168

Bartholomew's Hospital, but with mercifully very light casualties, as many of the nursing and medical staff had been evacuated to Hill End Hospital at St Albans in Hertfordshire. A note arrived from Dennis Wardley saying that he too would be leaving Bart's shortly, and would like to see her before he went. What would he say if *he* knew? Lily did not welcome the strain of a conversation in which she would have to hide her true thoughts, but none the less agreed to meet him at the Cheapside teashop where she and Grandmama had gone after her interview, two and a half years ago, when poor Mr Chamberlain had brought back the message of 'Peace in our Time'.

'Yes, that was another world,' said Dennis, stirring his tea and looking at her haggard face with concern. 'But, Lily dear, you're obviously not well. They're overworking you!'

'I'm no more overworked than any of the others,' she replied with a little forced smile, knowing that she would never know a minute's peace of mind until the blessed sight of blood, for if it did not appear by the end of the week she would have to confide in Hetty. 'Life at St Mildred's is very different now, and it's opened my eyes to the real world, in a way. Some of the patients we get now are in a pretty awful state – verminous and, er – smelly, you know – but I've never seen such courage.'

'Well, when you think of their background, Lily – living in cramped, crowded little houses with no baths, no hot water, sharing lavatories – it's no wonder that their hygiene isn't up to much by our standards. But we're the lucky ones, remember. I think this war's going to pull down a lot of the old class barriers, and that can only be a good thing.'

For some reason Lily thought of Mabel and the

Pinehurst children; she said nothing, and Dennis went on, 'Have you seen them going down to the air-raid shelters with all their bits and pieces, poor devils? And now the government has had to give way over the underground stations. They're all crowding down there with sleeping-bags and blankets, to settle themselves on the hard platforms all night. My God, just imagine it!'

'And none of us knows where the next bomb's going to fall, do we?' Lily said dully, wondering if in her heart she wished for annihilation as a solution to the now constant dread hanging over her head. 'You've caught it at Bart's, haven't you?'

'Yes, that was a close call, but fortunately it was the medical college that got it rather than the wards that are still open for air-raid casualties, like yours. They got the old laboratory and lecture theatre, along with the photographic department, which means that an awful lot of valuable material has gone. London's going to look very different after this lot – you wonder how much is going to be left still standing. Are you sure you're right to stay, Lily?' He was looking at her intently as he spoke. 'Doesn't it worry you, honestly?'

'Let's just say that there's nowhere else I'd rather be.'

'I have to admit that I'll be glad to be out of it, though there are better chaps than I who are staying on.' He sighed. 'Lily, I think I know the reason you're staying put. It's Redfern, isn't it? He lives in St John's Wood, doesn't he? Churchill was right, you know – we'll never be able to repay the debt we owe to the Few.'

Lily simply could not speak, and lowered her eyes. He put his hand over hers on the table.

'I hope that things will all work out well for you, Lily – and for him. No hard feelings, eh?'

She nodded, and wiped her eyes on the back of her hand. 'Thank you, Dennis. I hope it works out for you, too. Life's too short . . .' She realised what she had said, and gave a little shrug. 'I'd better be getting back.'

'Me too. But promise me you'll take care of yourself, Lily.'

They parted with a brief kiss, and she wondered if she would ever see him again. He would have made a good husband, she thought, if she could have fallen in love with him.

'Nurse Tarrant! Hetty, wait a minute! Can we talk later today? There's something I've simply got to – to discuss with you. When are you off today?'

'This evening, if I ever get away. Why, what's up, Lily, old thing?'

'May I come to your room after supper – say about half-past eight?'

'Of course you can. If there's anything I can do . . .'

'There might be. Tonight, then, in your room – unless you'd rather come to mine?'

'Either way. My dear Lily, you're in a right old state, aren't you? What's the –'

'Not now. And don't ask anybody else, will you?'

'No, of course not.' She lowered her voice. 'You know you can trust me, Lily.'

'Thanks, Het. Heavens, I'm late. Byee!'

Lady Margaret presented the usual morning shambles after another night of bombing. New admissions lay on beds or mattresses on the stone floor of the crypt, some already due for discharge after treatment for relatively minor injuries.

'You're needed in theatre this morning, Nurse Knowles,' said Sister, looking up from her dressing trolley. 'There's a bad case from Princess Louise going up for abdominal repair straight away, and Sister Reeves is on her own with an orderly.'

' 'Is guts was all over the place, Nurse,' murmured a woman awaiting a dressing. 'Policeman – big bloke, ever so nice, but I reckon 'e's 'ad 'is chips nah.'

Lily's head swam momentarily. The last thing she wanted just now was a long session in the operating theatre, at the beck and call of surgeon, theatre sister and anaesthetist – especially if the patient died at the end of it. Bracing herself, she climbed the stairs to the theatre, to find the anaesthetist, Dr Freeman, holding a rubber mask over the face of an enormous man lying on a theatre trolley, dressed in operation gown and socks. An intravenous saline drip was running into a vein in his left arm.

'Who can help me lift him on to the table?' asked Freeman, looking round impatiently. The surgeon and Sister Reeves were already scrubbing up, and the orderly was nowhere to be seen. 'Come on, Nurse, you'll do. Take the poles at the head end, and I'll take the feet.'

He pushed the trolley into the theatre, alongside the operating table. Lily took hold of the two wooden poles slotted through the canvas stretcher-cover, and waited for Freeman, a somewhat undersized, weedy individual, to lift them at the other end.

'Can you manage, Nurse? He's a fair old weight, must be all of sixteen stone or more. Here we go – oof! – mind the drip – up he comes – oof! – and over he goes,' he panted, while Lily heaved at the poles for all she was worth.

The surgeon looked up from the washbasin. 'Good

heavens, couldn't you find a porter?' he asked sharply. 'That's my theatre nurse whose arms you're trying to dislocate, Freeman.'

'Well, I did ask for assistance, and got no response,' replied the anaesthetist, and nothing more was said. Sterile towels were spread over the abdomen, and the dressing removed, revealing a large, jagged-edged wound through which loops of intestine could be seen.

'Right, have we got the sucker at hand, Nurse? First we'll need to irrigate and have a good look round while we're inside.' The surgeon plunged his gloved hands into the abdominal cavity. 'Stomach – liver – spleen – pancreas – uh-uh – give me something wet and warm to wrap round these guts, they're stone-cold. Diaphragm seems to be intact – uh-huh – can't see any bits of metal or anything – so let's irrigate again, sprinkle everywhere with stardust, and get on with sewing him up.'

The nursing orderly was then sent to help in the ophthalmic theatre, and Lily as 'runner' was left to wait on every order, fetching and carrying, wheeling the aspirator and irrigator on their stands as required, uncapping bottles of normal saline and pouring them into the twin bowls for rinsing instruments, fetching more sterile towels, gauze swabs, large and medium, counting them all, and likewise counting the soiled ones thrown into the pails, using forceps to pick up those that landed on the floor. She carefully opened the glass container of sulphonamide powder, the 'stardust' that the surgeon lightly sprinkled into the peritoneal cavity before beginning the closure. Its amazing ability to halt the spread of certain bacteria was being hailed as a medical miracle.

'I'll want another pair of gloves, Nurse – size eight!' he barked.

'And we'll need chromicised catgut as well as plain,' added Sister Reeves.

'Another airway, Nurse, and a length of cotton bandage – and bring in that second cylinder of nitrous oxide.' Dr Freeman's requests always followed straight after those of the other two, and Lily felt like a ball being bounced between them. Layer by layer the man's abdomen was stitched together; first the delicate membrane lining the abdominal cavity, then the deep and superficial muscle, and finally the skin.

'Better stick a couple of drains in, one north, one south. Can you fetch me a corrugated one, Nurse? How's he looking, Freeman? Well, we've done the best we can for him. He'll have a paralytic ileus after all that manhandling, I shouldn't wonder, and the whole lot could get infected and carry him off with septicaemia.' The surgeon pulled off his gloves and mask. 'Any tea going, Nurse?'

It was over, and the theatre seemed to be lurching sideways, causing Lily to sway. She opened her mouth, but no sound came out. All she could think was that the operation had been completed, the swab count was correct, so it wouldn't really matter if she couldn't do whatever it was he'd just asked her – what was it? Trying to gather her thoughts together, she gripped the side of the operating table with the unconscious man lying on it.

'Are you all right, Nurse?' asked Freeman. 'Quick, somebody come and grab her, don't just leave everything to me – quick, she's falling!'

Lily's thoughts slithered away from her: she fell down after them into darkness and silence.

When her eyes fluttered open, she found herself lying on a bed; sounds floated back into her head. Somebody – was it Sister Reeves? – was looking down at her and speaking.

'Are you feeling better now, Nurse Knowles? You fainted at the end of that operation, and we've popped you into Princess May. Here, take a sip of water.'

Lily tried to pull herself up, but a wave of nausea seized her, and she retched. Ugh!

'Do you want to be sick? Here's a bowl.' Lily groaned, aware of a pain in her back and deep down in her belly. She retched over the bowl, and brought up a little dribble of bile-stained fluid. She lay back on the pillow, and heard the sister speaking to somebody else.

'That wretched Dr Freeman made her lift a very heavy unconcious patient on to the operating table, Dr Carruthers. I think she may have strained something.'

'Let me just take a look at you, Nurse Knowles – easy does it, stay flat on your back and let me feel your tummy. Aha – now can you sit up for me?'

Lily heaved herself up into a sitting position, and a sharp, cramp-like pain seized her tummy – while at the same time she felt a familiar warmth and wet ness. Instinctively she put her hands down between her legs, and discovered that her secret ordeal was over. *Blood*!

'Oh dear, we'll need a sanitary pad, Sister. Her period's started, probably brought on by all this. Mm, it seems quite heavy, her underwear's soaking. If you'd just see to that, I'll examine her when you've finished. When were you next due, Nurse Knowles?'

Lily fell limply back on the bed. Nauseated, giddy, racked by backache and the cramps in her lower abdomen, she collapsed into tears of sheer, incredulous thankfulness. Her prayers had been answered at last, and the agony was at an end!

'When were you next due, Nurse Knowles?' Sister Reeves repeated the question as she removed the blood-soaked knickers. 'Has it come on early this time?'

Lily knew that she had to answer carefully. 'Yes, Sister,' she whispered. 'It's a week early.' Tears fell weakly from the corners of her eyes and ran down into the pillow.

'Don't upset yourself, Nurse. I'm sure you'll be quite all right after a rest. We're all working under a strain these days.'

She proceeded to take Lily's temperature, pulse and respiration rate. Dr Carruthers checked her blood pressure, which he said was rather low.

'Better keep her in bed and under observation for today, and let her sleep if Jerry gives her a chance. She's a bit run-down like the rest of us, poor girl.'

And because the hospital was busy and the staff under pressure, Lily was saved from any further investigation. She spent the rest of the day on her own in the cubicle, getting herself to the lavatory and changing her pads as the clots came away and disappeared down the pan. By evening the pain was subsiding, and so was the loss. She gratefully drank a cup of tea.

And she had a visitor, Hetty Tarrant.

'Lily! We've heard all sorts of wild rumours about you – that you'd strained your back, broken your neck, passed out in the middle of an operation – my God, you look positively ashen!' She sat down on the side of the bed, which was against the rules. 'Come on, tell Auntie Hetty what really happened.'

'Oh, Hetty, it's all right. I just fainted after lifting a big, heavy policeman, that's all.'

'Yes, we've got him on the ward. But we heard you'd practically broken your back in half.'

'I'm all right.' The sight of her friend and the sound of her voice had the effect of releasing Lily's pent-up emotions, and she began to sob. 'Oh, Hetty, I've been at my wits' end. I've been desperate, but now I – I'm pretty sure I've had a – a miscarriage, and nobody knows.'

'Ah.' Hetty nodded. 'You mean they just think that your curse has come on?'

'Don't call it a curse, Hetty – it's the greatest blessing I could wish for. It means I'm all right.'

'Let off the hook, eh? Thank God – or whoever it is we have to thank – that big, heavy policeman, perhaps? He's pretty groggy, poor chap, but he may come through.' She lowered her voice. 'I've had my suspicions for a week or two, old thing, and then when you said that this morning, I guessed, and I honestly didn't know what I was going to say to you, Lily – only that I'd stand by you and go on being your friend. Will you tell – him?'

'No. There's no need to tell anybody now, because I shall never, ever take such a risk again, Hetty. 'Never!'

'Mm-mm. As long as you remember that if *you* won't, there'll be others who will, Lily. Don't forget he's a Battle of Britain hero who's survived intact with his good looks, which means he'll be much sought-after for parties, dances, night clubs – anything where the champagne flows and girls gather round. You'll have to understand that, old thing.'

177

'I do, you needn't worry. Oh, Hetty, bless you – thank you for being so good to me!'

Hetty said nothing more, but held her close while she sobbed her relief and thankfulness.

The almost nightly bombing continued, and one by one the familiar London landmarks suffered damage. The Tower of London was hit, though not badly; Madame Tussaud's was in ruins, with waxwork arms and legs scattered, faces chipped and every exhibit covered with black dust. The BBC was hit several times, the worst incident killing six people as the news was being read; Regent's Park Zoo was hit several times, though not seriously, and among the West End shops, John Lewis was gutted, Bourne and Hollingsworth badly damaged, and Selfridges and Peter Robinson temporarily closed; yet within four days most of them were open again.

The plight of the bombed-out homeless was wretched. People were wandering dazedly around their devastated streets, and the rest centres that had been hastily set up in church halls and schools were often woefully inadequate, with pails to serve as lavatories, no way of heating water and hurricane lamps for lighting. As the weather grew colder and the days darkened, nerves began to crack under the strain, and by November the traditional Cockney humour had reached a low ebb, though it was by no means extinguished. The big policeman, now recovering in Princess Louise, was keeping up the spirits of the other men with his stories of goings-on in the shelters and the resourcefulness of prostitutes during air raids.

St Mildred's now had only two or three private patients of the kind that had previously paid for its running costs, and when the Countess asked for assistance from the Ministry of Health for the care of casualties, she was told that the hospital should close, which angered her.

'As long as Matron Russell and her staff are willing to stay, the hospital will remain open,' she declared, and although no new probationers came forward for training, most of the existing staff stood by their intention to stay with the old flagship.

Lily's initial euphoria soon gave way to a curious lassitude, a fatalistic outlook combined with a dogged determination to see the bombardment through to the end, whatever that end might be. Life consisted of work and short periods of rest, enlivened by afternoon visits to the cinema with whoever else was off duty. If the air-raid siren went, they all stayed in their seats and the film went on. She and Beatrice emerged red-eyed from *Good-bye, Mr Chips* with Robert Donat and Greer Garson, and met Hanna Blumfeldt at a showing of *Fantasia*, Walt Disney's full-length animated cartoon based on pieces of classical music. Hanna dismissed it contemptuously.

'The cartoons may be clever, but they are silly and trivial, not how I think of Tchaikovsky or Mussorgsky,' she said. 'However, I am glad I came, Lily. How are you all at St Mildred's?'

'We're bearing up,' Lily replied with a half-smile. She would have liked to enquire about Dr Edlinger, but did not want to embarrass Hanna, nor did she feel inclined to field enquiries about Redfern. 'What about Queen Adelaide's? How many babies have you delivered?'

'I think it is seventeen so far. We have them all down in the basement for safety. In the new year I shall be going out with a midwife to deliver women in their homes – if there are any homes left. It is not a good time to bring children into the world,' said Hanna gloomily.

'I hope you don't say that to the mothers! And how are your parents?'

'My father is very busy with research, and Dr Edlinger has gone to assist him. It is very secret, and I cannot reveal what it is about. And my mother cries every day for her parents.'

'What a little ray of sunshine she is,' sighed Beatrice when she had left them. 'You can't really wonder that he's made off!'

But Lily felt sad for the girl who had seemed to bloom in the warmth of a man's attentions, and had followed him only to lose him, by the sound of it.

And then, suddenly, like a Jack-in-the-box, there was Sandy Redfern on the doorstep of St Mildred's House again, all smiles and wearing his scar like a badge of honour.

'And how's my fairest of flowers all? Oh, darling, I've missed you so much! Can you come out for tea or something? Kiss me, Lily – there's nobody about!'

Of course she was overjoyed to see him, and was able to take half an hour to walk with him to a café in Cannon Street, listening eagerly to all that he had to tell her about his experiences during the past two months.

'Don't get the impression that the Blitz is all one way, Lily. Our chaps have been giving Berlin and Hamburg a fair old pounding!' he told her. 'No doubt about it, when the Luftwaffe turned its attention on London, it took the heat off Fighter Command, and gave us a breathing space – for a start they'd destroyed so many air bases – not to mention a hell of a lot of crates and good chaps like Johnny Marshall.' For a moment his face took on a sombre look, but he quickly turned to her and smiled.

'Heaven to see you again, Lily, but you look a little bit pale and – what's the word? – wan. You need a good evening out! Listen, what about the Café de Paris tonight? Don't tell me you can't make it. Swap with somebody – go on, Lily, be nice to a fighter pilot who's still around!'

And that was his argument, his stratagem for getting his own way. Hetty had been right: Sandy Redfern was now a hero, and enjoying it. 'Apart from these air raids, it's a damned good life! Only I *have* missed you.' He leaned close to her ear. 'And you know why, darling. You know what I've missed the most. Have you missed it too?'

'I think I can manage the Café de Paris tonight, Sandy – I should be off at nine – but I'll have to be back by eleven.'

'You didn't answer my question.'

She smiled up at him. 'I can't wait to dance in your arms again, Squadron Leader.'

He grinned. 'That'll do for the time being.'

Determined that it should be a memorable evening, she resolved not to think about tiredness, and as soon as she came off duty she put on the green evening gown and the pearls her grandparents had given her. She fluffed up her hair, which fell into waves framing her face, and applied discreet vanishing cream, powder and lipstick. He was in uniform, and told her she looked stunning. 'We're easily the handsomest couple here, my lovely Lily.'

The Café de Paris was for many the most sophisticated venue in London – and the safest, according to the manager, who boasted of twenty-five thousand bottles of champagne in stock, twenty feet below ground, in the basement of a cinema in Coventry Street. With uniforms and glamorous evening dresses mingling amidst laughter, chatter and a rising blue cloud of cigarette smoke, the revellers danced to the music of band-leader 'Snake-hips' Johnson, while bottles were uncorked and poured with a liberality unusual in these days of growing austerity.

Sandy drew Lily close to him, encircling her body in his arms, and she obediently clasped her hands together behind his neck. He deliberately held her against the hard erection beneath the layers of material between them.

'He wants you, darling – can't you feel him searching for you?' he whispered in her ear.

She could, but she did not answer. She much preferred the sensation of his face close to hers, the warmth of his cheek, his skin smooth and smelling deliciously of Yardley's aftershave. She closed her eyes and let herself enjoy these moments on the dance floor with other couples in the same close proximity as themselves.

This is all I can give him, she thought, and no doubt there'll be a little more intimacy in the taxi; but we musn't be alone together again, not as we were at Waltham. Caution would have to prevail over desire from now on, because she could never go through *that* again . . .

And as she had anticipated, Redfern argued unavailingly with her in the taxi to Bread Street.

'Listen, Lily, my lovely, I've got a treat planned for us – a whole weekend to ourselves alone! There's this little hotel just out of Bognor Regis, where we can have a glorious, uninterrupted night. You *must* get the time off, Lily. Oh, my darling, I've thought of nothing else but how sweet you were – and how much more we'll enjoy each other at Bognor. Ah, Lily . . .'

But she had to shake her head, sadly but implacably. 'No, Sandy. I can't do that again.'

'Lily! Why ever not? Didn't I make you happy?'

'Yes, but only for a moment, and afterwards I regretted it, because – well, because it was wrong,' she said lamely. He stared at her.

'I can't believe what you're saying! You *know* how I need you – how essential you are to me as a fighter pilot, risking my life every time I go up – and yet you refuse to allow me a brief weekend of happiness? You'd deny me – both of us – the right to those few short hours? I can't believe it!'

'Oh, Sandy, my love, Sandy, my darling, you'll *have* to believe that I love you as much as ever – but I honestly can't let that happen again.'

'You've come over all churchy and evangelical on me – is that it?'

'Sandy, please try to understand that it's much more serious for a woman. I can't cope with the – the aftermath of it. I'm sorry, but I'm not going to be led into temptation again.'

'Oh, wonderful! So I'm the evil tempter now – Sir Jasper, seducing the innocent maiden!'

'No, Sandy. I did it of my own free will, and realised later that it was a mistake. I'm not blaming you, but as I said, these things carry more dangers for a woman. Oh, don't be cross with me. I know how you must feel, but –'

His face was a study of surprised disappointment and anger. 'So you'll send me off up into the sky again, then, off on sorties over the Channel, over

France, with no promises to bring me back to you? All that stuff about how you'd always be there for me was just empty talk!'

'Oh, Sandy, *please* try to understand.' In desperation she decided to be more frank. 'Look, suppose I told you that I was expecting your child? What would your reaction be? Would you be willing to marry me? Would you even want to, as things are now?'

'Christ, you're not, are you?' His horrified embarrassment was answer enough.

'No, I'm not, thank God, but I – I might have been. And I can't risk that again, not even for you, Sandy. I've been through – well, a lot of worry, and I couldn't face it again.'

'But you're a woman, and a nurse – you must know what to do about these things, surely?'

'No, I don't. I'm no different from any other girl in that sort of – oh, Sandy, just *think* of the predicament I'd be in!'

He frowned. 'I see. So that's what's bothering you. Another time I'd bring French letters with me, not that I like the things, but if that would make you feel any better, I will.'

'No, I don't want to take even the slightest risk. Too much is at stake for me.' Her eyes filled with tears at this wretched ending to their evening. 'Kiss me, Sandy, and tell me you're not cross, and that you understand – *please*.'

The kiss was somewhat grudgingly given, but she clung to his lips and gently ran her forefinger down the line of the scar.

'I love you, Sandy, as much as I ever did.' Then she got out of the cab, waved to him and went up the steps to the entrance of St Mildred's House. The taxi drew away, and she stood irresolutely on the steps, outside the beautifully carved door. It suddenly opened, to reveal Matron Russell.

'It's two hours after curfew time, Nurse Knowles. How are you going to give of your best on the ward tomorrow if you keep these sort of hours?' She beckoned Lily in, and locked the door. 'Where have you been, Nurse?'

'I'm sorry, Matron. I've been to the Café de Paris.' Miss Russell stood silently waiting for her to say more, and she added, 'I was invited out by Squadron Leader Redfern.'

'Ah, yes.' Her tone softened. 'He's one of the Few, isn't he – the young airmen who saved us from invasion in the Battle of Britain. Flight Lieutenant Marshall was another, wasn't he?'

'Yes, Matron.'

'Thank heaven that the squadron leader has been spared. Very well, Nurse, go to your bed, and don't keep such late hours in the future. Good night, Nurse.'

'Good night, Matron. Thank you.'

Matron was letting her off lightly; but what would she have said if . . .? In spite of her regret over Sandy's vexation, Lily could only give thanks yet again for a disaster avoided. Poor Sandy! She had broken her promise always to be there for him in the way that he'd understood her to mean it; but she knew that a weekend at Bognor would have been just as disappointing.

It was all very well for men, she thought, climbing wearily into bed. By their very nature they could never understand women's pain, women's blood, women's fear and shame – and the shadow of lifelong heartbreak.

In mid-November, when it seemed that London could endure no more, the aerial raids took a new turn. Following the RAF's visits to major German cities, the Luftwaffe turned from the capital and attacked other centres of industry. A terrible raid on Coventry hit twenty-one factories and destroyed the beautiful medieval cathedral, as well as wrecking nearly a third of its houses. Hundreds of people were killed. Bristol was 'Coventrated' next, followed by Birmingham and Southampton; in December half a dozen more provincial cities suffered while London received a much-needed respite. Lily became anxious about her grandparents, not thirty miles from Coventry, but Grandmama wrote to say that Northampton's shoe factories had so far escaped the bombing. 'Your grandfather says that they're after aircraft production, not footwear!' she wrote with grim humour.

In view of the lull in raids over London, the Countess announced that the annual Christmas ball would be held as usual, as a statement of hope and defiance. The date was fixed for the Saturday before Christmas, and for the first time Lily tentatively invited Sandy Redfern; to her joy he accepted, and Beatrice asked Ned Carter. The numbers were down on previous years, but Matron Russell's open invitation to the RAF base camp at Hendon, a thing unheard of before the war, resulted in partners for all the nurses able to attend. The buffet was less lavish than formerly, but the Countess donated a good supply of bottles from her own cellar.

Dancing in Sandy's arms while the three-piece band played 'A Nightingale Sang in Berkeley Square', Lily let herself believe that their earlier happiness had been recaptured, and when he whispered that she was as lovely as ever, she dared to hope that he accepted her stance and perhaps even respected her for it. When he asked her to accompany him to a New Year party at the Palmer-Bournes' Maida Vale home, to be held actually on 29 December, a Sunday, as being more convenient than a weekday evening, she promised to make sure to be off duty. The ball ended with much delightful kissing under the mistletoe and a rendering of 'We Wish You a Merry Christmas' – followed by the National Anthem, at which everybody stood to attention.

But the party at the Palmer-Bournes' never took place, because on that night the enemy tried to burn the City of London to the ground. Ten thousand incendiary bombs were dropped, and for a time the fires raged out of control; all around St Paul's the flames blazed as one historic building after another collapsed. To Lily and her colleagues, dealing with an influx of victims, some with terrible burns, it was a scene from hell.

'The whole bloody world's on fire, Nurse!' gasped an ambulance attendant, bringing in another injured fireman to Suffolk. 'There won't be a stick left by morning!'

Horror-stricken, Lily turned to the man on the stretcher, his face streaked with blood and black dust. He opened one eye. 'Don't give up, Nurse,' he said hoarsely. 'There'll be somethin' o' London left, you'll see. It's like ol' Churchill said, we won't never surrender, Nurse!'

And when Lily raised her eyes to the fiery night sky, what did she see but the dome of St Paul's Cathedral, sailing above the flames and smoke like a great ship, its cross of gold a symbol of the people's endurance, in this second Great Fire of London.

Chapter 9

Everywhere there was work to be done. As the New Year of 1941 dawned on a devastated City where ruins still smouldered after three days and brown smoke blotted out the winter sun, the sheer numbers of injured were too great for St Mildred's forty-four beds to accommodate, and in any case it was too dangerous a place for the care of the sick and injured. It became partly a clearing station from which patients were sent to hospitals out of London, partly a treatment centre for facial and eye injuries in the ophthalmic theatre, and partly a terminal haven for the very badly injured who were lodged in the crypt.

'It was used as a chapel in medieval times, and as a mortuary before the war,' recalled the Dowager Countess, 'so it seems fitting that it's now a place of quietness where lives can ebb away in peace, devotedly cared for by our nurses.'

Dr Carruthers did not stint on morphia when the end was near, and no patient with extensive third-degree burns had to suffer pain that could be relieved.

Less badly damaged patients, like the fireman who had inspired Lily on the night of the great conflagration, were sometimes transferred to hospitals with special burns units, and a specialist from Bart's mentioned a place name familiar to Lily.

'That case should go to Park Prewitt,' he said to Dr Carruthers when they were doing the daily assessment round on Suffolk. Lily was surprised, for she associated the name with a large mental hospital near Basingstoke, and not too far from Belhampton. The Pinehurst children used the word in a derogatory way – 'Go back to Park Prewitt, they're out lookin' for yer!' – and she wondered why a courageous fireman who was perfectly sane should be sent to such a place. Sister Suffolk explained that there was a newly established centre there for 'plastic surgery'.

'Sir Harold Gillies is working on airmen whose hands and faces were burned in the Battle of Britain,' she said. 'He uses skin grafts from other parts of the body, like the thigh or buttock. He must be a highly skilled man – and brave, too. Imagine if the graft didn't take!'

Lily immediately thought of Uncle Gerald Westhouse, who'd had a skin graft from his leg to his face in the Great War, though he'd lost the sight of his left eye and wore a black patch over it; the left side of his face, neck and shoulder were badly scarred from burns sustained when he had bailed out of his blazing craft over France.

Thinking about him turned her thoughts towards his son, Geoffrey, somewhere out in the eastern Mediterranean. News reports came through of thousands of Italian prisoners taken in North Africa, and of a heavy RAF raid on Tripoli, followed by the capture of Benghazi. It all seemed an unimaginably long way off, so far removed from London and the horrors of the Blitz. It must be terribly hard on Aunt Alice and Uncle Gerald, she thought, and Geoffrey's sisters, Geraldine and Amelia; whatever must they think of her, knowing that she had fallen out of love when she met Dennis Wardley – and discarded *him* when Sandy Redfern came along and swept her off her feet; what sort of a girl was she? Would she have been so heartless if there had been no war? Yes, perhaps she would: the war hadn't started when she'd rejected her father and Mabel. For the first time ever, she began to wish that she could put the clock back and be friends again. But it was too late: unforgivable things had been said, and she had thrown in her lot with Grandfather and Grandmama.

Once again she turned to her work, the theatre skills that gave her something absorbing to do, something else to think about and concentrate on, especially in the ophthalmic department, where a surgeon from Moorfields Eye Hospital performed operations on one or two days a week. St Mildred's facility was used for relatively minor ophthalmic repairs, and Lily was becoming quite expert at assisting with the delicate suturing of eyelids and lacerated corneas. Severe damage to the eyeball was treated by irrigation, a gentle pad and transfer to Moorfields for more intricate surgery.

On the first Sunday of the new year Lily realised that in the week since the night of the fires she had stepped outside only for the short walk along Bread Street between the hospital and nurses' home. No wonder she looked pale and had headaches, and though the dust-laden air still smelled of burning, it was beginning to clear, thanks to a stiff easterly wind.

'Let's get up early and go to church, Beatrice,' she said on the Saturday evening.

'Where? They say all the City churches are flattened,' sighed Nurse Massey, unwilling to look on the scenes of desolation all around them.

'My dear Beattie, we can't stay holed up in here like moles. Let's walk round to St Mary-le-Bow, and give thanks for being alive.'

The beautiful Wren church was still there, though the steeple had collapsed, and part of the roof was open to the sky. Much of the rubble had been cleared away, and the shattered fragments of stained glass swept up; the door was open for Sunday services, and the two nurses joined a surprisingly large turn-out of worshippers at seven on that Sunday morning, to take Holy Communion. When the congregation stood to recite Psalm 57, a wave of emotion passed over all present as the first verse was spoken. '. . . in the shadow of thy wings will I make my refuge, until these calamities be overpast.'

Beatrice put out her hand to take Lily's as they stood side by side, exchanging a special bond of understanding: there was no need for any other words. Lily kneeled down and gave thanks for their survival, and of course she prayed for the safety of Sandy Redfern, Tim Baxter, Geoffrey Westhouse and all men serving in the armed forces. When she rose from her knees, she was glad they had made the effort.

Walking back along Cheapside, they faced their sadly changed city. A fair number of people were around at that hour: a milkman was delivering bottles from a horse-drawn cart, and a female figure carrying a black bag picked her way among the rubble and roped-off potholes, her unbecoming navy hat pulled down over her greying hair.

'Oh, Good Lord, there's Nurse Big-Mouth,' muttered Lily, for there was little love lost between the garrulous district nurse and the staff of St Mildred's; she had been heard to refer to them as 'stuck-up madams', while they considered her a gossip and irredeemably common.

But the night of the fire had changed everything, and she waved to them across Cheapside.

'Been to church, have yer?' she called. 'Don't it do yer good to see St Paul's still up there?'

'Good morning, Nurse – er . . .' Heavens, I don't even know her name, thought Lily. 'You're out early on your rounds.'

'Same time as usual, to give me diabetics their insulin before their breakfast,' the woman replied. 'Ha! Half o' them'll still be down the underground, and the other half gone to stay with relatives out o' London. I've just been to one house that had a note stuck on the door, "Gone to me sister's", but nothin' to say where her sister lives!'

Her easy-going cheerfulness was infectious, and they could only echo her praises of the dogged endurance of the people she served.

'Things are gettin' a bit better for 'em now that the councils have bucked their ideas up,' she said. 'They've got toilets and washbasins down the shelters, better'n what some of 'em had at home! Same with the underground. They smell a lot sweeter'n they did at first, and the army's given 'em no end o' blankets! They get hot food every day at rest centres, off the Londoners' Meals Service, and they make good use o' the WVS – don't know what they'd do without the women, eh?'

'I think you're all just marvellous,' said Beatrice, and Lily nodded.

The nurse grinned. 'Everybody's pullin' together and doin' their bit,' she said with modest pride. 'It's a cryin' shame to see so many lovely old buildin's gone, but to tell yer the truth, girls, I wouldn't've missed any o' this. I reckon I'll look back on it in me old age and say like old Churchill says, y' know, this was me finest hour! Well, better be gettin' on – nice seein' yer, girls!'

'Do you know, I think I understand what she means,' said Beatrice.

'Of course you do – we're all in the same boat, aren't we?' Lily replied. 'Didn't we all defy our families and say we'd stay in London?'

Beatrice nodded. 'Yes, I suppose we did.'

Neither of them voiced the possibility that they still might not survive.

After the great night of fire, London experienced two months of comparative lull, and Lily noticed that people had begun to lose the dead-tired, haunted look brought on by sleeplessness and constant strain. The days were beginning to lengthen, and Hetty suggested that they should get out and enjoy a little social life while they had the chance.

'I don't know about the rest of you, but I'm pining for a bit of glamour – dressing up and dancing again!' she said longingly. 'Let's go to a dance at Covent Garden, and check out these new arrivals coming into the country – these Polish chaps clicking their heels and kissing your hands, to say nothing of Czech airmen, Dutch, Norwegians. And, who knows, we might meet some of these gorgeous Canadians who are supposed to be so gallant with the ladies. It's up to us to be good hostesses when they've come over to fight for us!'

It was certainly a temptation. Dances had become all the rage, and Covent Garden Opera House was the most resplendent venue, having closed for operatic performances and reopened as a ballroom, drawing in all the servicemen on leave in London. Lily pictured herself dancing there in Sandy's arms, and wondered where he was now; so many things had to be kept secret for fear of informing the enemy.

Well, there was one way to find out: most of the buses and tube trains were running, and she would go up to St John's Wood on her next half-day, and ask his grandparents about him – and he might even be there! Her heart gave a little lurch at the thought of his blue eyes gazing into hers, even if he reproached her.

Maida Vale had caught some of the bombing, and St John's Wood had suffered blast damage; windows were boarded up in Hamilton Terrace, but Elmgrove was untouched. Lily walked up to the imposing front door, and rang the bell; she was confronted by a middle-aged maidservant.

'Mrs Redfern's not feelin' too well,' she was told before she could open her mouth. 'She isn't at home to visitors today.'

'I'm very sorry to hear that,' said Lily pleasantly, though her heart sank. 'I've come over from St Paul's, hoping to see her, as I wanted to enquire about Mr and Mrs Redfern after the bombing ' She broke off, feeling rather foolish, and the woman stared hard at her.

'You've been here before with Mr Alex, haven't you? Miss Knowles, if I remember right?'

'Yes, you're quite right, I am Miss Knowles,' said Lily with a smile and a nod that she hoped would get her over the threshold. 'I really would be grateful if I could see Mrs Redfern for just a few minutes, if you wouldn't mind telling her I'm here.'

'She said she wasn't seein' anybody,' repeated the maid, but with a hesitation that raised Lily's hopes. Domestic servants were in very short supply now, with women pouring into the factories, and those that remained had to be humoured. She waited, smiling.

'I'll just go and ask her,' the woman said, leaving Lily on the doorstep, and while she was gone, Mr Redfern came into the hall and saw her.

'Miss Knowles! I do beg your pardon. Er – come in, my dear,' he said apologetically. 'Mrs Redfern is resting, but I'm sure she'll be happy to see you. Come into the drawing room. Dear me, these are dark days, Miss Knowles – Lily. Very dark days for us – ah, yes.'

She followed him into the well-furnished room she had seen on previous visits to Elmgrove. A small fire burned in the large grate. The maid returned and said that Mrs Redfern would be down in a minute, and had asked her to make tea; she then disappeared off to the kitchen, and Mr Redfern shrugged.

'She's the only help we've got in the house now, Miss Knowles, apart from a charwoman who comes in once a week and goes to two other households.'

Lily smiled and made appropriate remarks in a polite and friendly manner, but she was conscious of an uneasiness in the atmosphere. When Mrs Redfern joined them, Lily was shocked at her appearance: she seemed to have aged ten years, a frail old lady with sunken eyes. Her thin lips made a wintry attempt at a smile, but Lily got the impression that her unexpected visit was causing them some embarrassment.

Mrs Redfern poured the tea, and offered Lily a biscuit. They spoke about the fearful raid on the night of 29 December, and remarked on the comparative lull of the past few weeks.

'Let's just hope that that dreadful man isn't planning anything worse for us,' said the old lady, and Lily replied stoutly that nobody believed that Hitler would ever conquer Britain.

'Yes, but you must understand that we live in

constant fear for Alex and James, and it's difficult to remain hopeful when one's nearest and dearest are risking their lives night and day.' There was a hint of reproach in her words, and Lily replied carefully.

'Yes, I'm sure it must be, Mrs Redfern. I can imagine what you're going through, both of you. And to be truthful, it's Sandy – Alex – that I've come to enquire about. I haven't heard from him for a week or two, and I wondered if you had any –'

'We can't give any information about him. It's absolutely top secret with the Air Ministry,' said Mrs Redfern.

And her husband added, 'It's hush-hush, you understand, my dear.'

'I can assure you that I have no ulterior motive. I'm not a spy!' smiled Lily, trying to sound light-hearted. 'To be honest, I'd hoped that I might see Alex and maybe have a talk – go for a walk, perhaps – but I certainly don't want to intrude upon you.' She rose to her feet, forcing yet another smile to hide her disappointment. 'If you see him, will you be kind enough just to let him know that I called, and give him my best wishes? Right, I'll be on my way, then. Thank you for the tea. Let's hope this respite continues, for all our sakes.'

She saw the old couple exchange glances, and for a moment she thought that Mr Redfern was going to say something further; but with an almost imperceptible shake of her head, his wife counselled silence. He stood up to show her out, and gave her hand a sympathetic squeeze on taking leave at the door.

'My dear Lily, I hope you don't feel that we're driving you away, but I'm sure you realise that the poor boy's going through a very difficult time, with

197

all the strain he's been under for so long. He's been promoted – so much responsibility – and of course he's so young, still only twenty-two, far too early to be making any – er – commitments in life, particularly with things as they are.' He hesitated and cleared his throat. 'We – we're only too glad that you're there to give him the friendship and support that only a – a young woman friend can give, but . . . well, we've all got to wait and see how this terrible war goes, before making any – er –'

'It's quite all right, Mr Redfern. You've made your point very clearly,' replied Lily, feeling her face reddening. 'All I ask is that you'll tell him I called. Good afternoon.'

She walked away quickly, without looking back. She had always thought Mrs Redfern cool towards her – and now they seemed to be actively discouraging any understanding with their grandson. What had he told them? Surely not about . . . *that*! But perhaps he had managed to convey his disappointment in her . . .

Lily smarted at the unfairness of it. What about her side of the story, the anxiety that *she* had endured? *Thank you, Mrs Redfern, but you need not worry. After being saved by a lucky miscarriage, I wouldn't dream of risking it again.* That would certainly make them stare!

She returned to St Mildred's in a fog of uncertainty that made her discourage questions for which she had no answers.

And still there was no word from Sandy.

There had been no casualties lately, and the hospital was quiet, so it was a fairly simple matter for Hetty Tarrant to organise an evening party of nurses to go to a dance at Covent Garden. Matron was surprisingly indulgent towards her nurses who had worked so hard during the worst of the air raids, and was willing to reward them now that things were easier.

'Let's make it this Friday. I'll order a taxi to take us there, and ask for the driver to return for us at half-past eleven,' said Hetty. 'Do you want to borrow my lightning-flash gown again, Lily? We might as well dazzle them while we've got the chance!'

Privately she asked Lily if she intended to invite Redfern, and after some thought Lily decided to send a note to Elmgrove telling him that she was going with a party of friends, and that if he was able to join them he'd be very welcome. She hoped that this informal invitation would strike the right note of friendliness without appearing too eager.

No answer was returned until the actual Friday morning, when a note was handed in at reception; it simply said, 'See you at the Garden. Sandy.'

She kissed the note and tucked it into the front of her dress. Here was her opportunity, in the presence of friends, to show him that her feelings were unchanged, in spite of the necessary limits she'd placed on their relationship. She'd make it an evening to remember – and could hardly wait to dance with him, to feel his arms around her again . . .

Wearing the Molyneux gown, she joined Hetty and a group of four other probationers and staff nurses, squeezed into a taxi-cab that took them to the magnificent Covent Garden ballroom, dancing to the RAF Squadronaires. As Hetty had predicted, the place was filled with uniformed men from all the Allied European countries, and a sprinkling of Canadians, some French-speaking, and all charmingly courteous and open-handed towards the delighted English girls. In fact Hetty said she was quite ashamed of the shameless little gold-diggers who crowded round the brand-new uniforms.

Lily anxiously looked out for Sandy, and heard his laughter before she caught sight of him in the centre of a group that included as many young women as men – and she noticed that the Palmer-Bournes were with them. Should she go up to him and make her presence known? Or wait for him to see her and make the first move? In their changed circumstances, she felt nervous and unsure. Her friends were not short of partners, and while she debated with herself, a smiling officer in Air Force uniform came up and asked in an attractive foreign accent for the pleasure of dancing with her. She let him lead her on to the huge floor, to dance a slow fox-trot to the tune 'Whispering Grass'. He turned out to be Polish, with enough English to compliment her on her lightness of step. She smiled, and asked how long he had been in the air force, wondering all the time if Sandy had seen her.

As soon as the dance ended she excused herself and returned to the group of nurses from St Mildred's, who all seemed to be enjoying themselves hugely. True to Hetty's expectations, there was no shortage of partners, and Lily found herself trying to fend them off while looking round for Sandy Redfern. She soon saw him drifting past with a WAAF officer in uniform, talking animatedly as they danced. Had he seen her yet? Surely he must have done!

A cheerful Canadian approached and asked her to join him in a lively quickstep to the tune 'Kiss Me Good-Night, Sergeant Major', which he sang with gusto as they danced. Out of the corner of her eye she saw Sandy again, now dancing with Daphne Palmer-Bourne; he was also singing the words, or a parody of them, and Daphne's peal of laughter rang out above the general chatter and swishing of feet across the floor. Lily's heart gave a downward lurch as the thought came to her that she was being deliberately ignored – passed over – stood up – oh, *no*, surely he wouldn't be so cruel! But perhaps he wanted to give her a taste of her own medicine, for rejecting his offer of a weekend at Bognor Regis; had he really been hurt that much?

The dance ended, and once again she excused herself and returned to her group, which had doubled in number, each nurse having got herself an attentive partner for the evening. Happy faces and sparkling eyes surrounded Lily wherever she looked, and when the next number was announced as a 'ladies' choice', she made up her mind to be bold and ask Sandy to dance. And having got him to herself, she would then insist on knowing whether he still wanted to continue their friendship. She was *not* going to be tamely shoved aside, not after all that had passed between them . . .

Having made her resolution, she marched straight towards him, and in front of his friends she faced him, flushed and slightly breathless.

'May I have the pleasure of this dance, Wing Commander Redfern?'

'Lily, how nice to see you. Of course, I'd be delighted.' And he led her out on to the crowded floor of the ballroom.

'You look ravishing in that dress, Lily.'

'Yes, so you've told me before,' she said, matching her steps to his in waltz time. The tune was 'Always', which could be a good omen or a mockery. 'Hetty Tarrant's lent it to me again.'

'It certainly suits you.'

'Half the women here seem to be in service uniform. I might as well have worn mine.'

After a short pause, he said, 'You seem to have had plenty of partners.'

So he had noticed. 'Yes, it's a positive League of Nations here,' she replied. 'But I was looking forward to dancing with you, Sandy, and I thought – well, I wasn't expecting you to arrive in a party.'

'Why not? *You've* come with a bevy of nurses, hellbent on having a good time!'

'Oh, for goodness' sake, I was hoping that we'd be able to *talk*, just as we did when you used to call at St Mildred's House last year, and when we –'

'And when we danced at your jolly Christmas ball under the watchful eye of the Matron and the old Dowager Duchess!' He was smiling, but there was unmistakable resentment in his sarcasm. 'And all that kissing under the mistletoe at the end – I wasn't sure how many I was expected to salute, the two grand ladies or – everybody present!' He grimaced, and the long scar appeared lividly red, giving his face an almost sinister look.

'You know perfectly well that you weren't under any such obligation, Sandy! You didn't have any objection to kissing *me*, did you?' she demanded, remembering how happy she had been.

'No, it was delightful, and I made the most of it, seeing that it was all I was allowed – and in front of the whole hospital staff!'

She could think of no answer to this, and they danced in silence for a while. She missed her step a couple of times, and said 'Sorry' as formally as if he had been a stranger. It was misery, and to break the tension, she mentioned her visit to Elmgrove.

'Did your grandparents tell you that I called?'

'Yes. They think a lot of you, Lily.'

For some reason she found this unbearably patronising. 'It's nice that they approve of me, Sandy, but I don't really care one way or the other. I only went there to enquire about *you*.'

'But they *like* you, honestly – and they'll be glad for you to keep in touch when I've failed to return from some deadly sortie over occupied Europe!'

She flinched at his bitterness – and all because of her broken promise to be always there for him – which for him meant giving all of herself. There was only one way to get him back, and that she could not and would not do. She lifted her eyes in a despairing look, but saw only scorn in his, and again they relapsed into silence.

The dance ended. 'Thank you, Lily, that was nice. Care to join the gang for a drink? Peter's over there at the bar, I see.'

Why not? All of Hetty's party had paired off for the evening. 'Thank you, that would be . . . nice.'

Daphne greeted her with a friendly smile, and the air commodore told her that she looked as pretty as a picture. 'We all think Alex is damned lucky to have found you, Lily, my dear,' he said in a low voice. 'You're good for him!'

How many more times was she to hear that dubious compliment? She accepted a gin and lime, and Palmer-Bourne then asked her for a dance.

'Actually our lot are leaving soon,' he told her. 'Going on to a club in Soho, more up Daphne's street! Would you care to come with us, Lily? I'm sure Alex would like you to.'

'Thank you, but I'm with a party of friends from St Mildred's, and we've got a taxi coming at half-past eleven,' she said, gritting her teeth to sound easy and casual. 'And I'm on duty in the morning, so . . .' She gave a meaningful shrug, and when they left she nodded to Redfern.

'Good night, Alex.'

''Night, Lily, my lovely – thanks for the memory!'

It was their farewell, and in the taxi going back to St Mildred's she could not check the tears. Hetty was tactfully sympathetic, and did not even remind Lily of her prediction.

'One day he may come back – you never know, old thing – and realise you were right.'

'And maybe he won't come back because he'll be *dead* – and I sent him away without giving him the one thing he wanted!' wept poor Lily. 'I've let him down, and he'll never forgive me.'

With spring on the way, the bombardment had started again, and the provinces were subjected to the kind of nightly visitation that London had suffered throughout the autumn, and now seemed set to endure again. On the morning following the dance at Covent Garden, Lily witnessed a telling incident involving Matron and a thin, shabby man who was brought into Suffolk smelling of whisky and muttering obscenities. He had been knocked into the gutter by an ambulance, which had then stopped to pick him up.

'Drunk as a rat, Sister,' said the ambulance attendant with a touch of contempt. 'Otherwise no serious injuries.'

Miss Russell was on her round, and stopped to speak to the man. 'I see your name's Mr Thompson,' she said. 'Well, this is a fine way to behave, I must say! We need these beds for genuine air-raid casualties.'

'Then chuck me back in the gutter, missis,' he muttered wearily. 'I never ars' to be brought in. I ain't got nuffink to live for no more.'

'Shame on you, Thompson! We've *all* got our country to live for, and our freedom. You're a Londoner, aren't you? Show some of the spirit of our King and Queen!'

'King an' Queen be buggered, missis. They still got each ovver an' the two kids. My missus an' kids was killed in a bloody filthy shelter, an' they was all I 'ad in the world. An' don't talk to me abaht ol' Churchill an' 'is blood an' tears an' sweat – *that* won't bring 'em back agin.'

Lily gasped, and wondered how on earth Matron would respond to such blasphemy, for so it sounded. After a longish pause, Miss Russell picked up one of the enamel mugs now used instead of glasses for drinks.

'Come on, Thompson, your mouth's dry. Take a sip of water. The orderlies will be round with tea soon.' She held the mug to his lips and he lapped at the water, then lay back on the pillow, closing his eyes. 'Fanks, missis.'

Miss Russell caught Lily's eye. 'His injuries may not be severe, Nurse Knowles, but it's his heart that's broken. And unless it mends, I doubt the poor man will survive.'

Lily shook her head, marvelling at the way Miss Russell had adapted her attitudes to the enormous changes that had taken place at St Mildred's during the past six months. Living through times of mortal danger and enormous challenges to the human spirit,

Lily supposed that Miss Russell's outlook was probably much the same as the garrulous district nurse who talked about her finest hour – and both women unconsciously influenced Lily to despise self-pity and personal considerations.

'Nurse Knowles! Nurse Knowles!' Home Sister was coming along the corridor, calling her name. Lily had just removed her uniform after coming off duty; it had been a long day, and she was planning to go straight to bed. She opened the door to Home Sister.

'I'm sorry, Nurse Knowles, but you're to go to the ophthalmic theatre straight away. The surgeon from Bart's has just come to operate, so Sister says can you come over? I'm really sorry, Nurse,' she added, seeing the girl's drawn features and tired eyes.

Lily closed her eyes momentarily, and swallowed. She felt giddy with fatigue, but had no choice but to pull her uniform dress back on, and pick up the shoes she had thankfully kicked off. It was nearly nine o'clock, a windy March night, and the air-raid siren had sounded. Of all the times to start a delicate operation! She hadn't even made a cup of tea. Wrapping her cloak around her, and taking a deep breath, she returned to the hospital and the ophthalmology department, where she found there had been a change of plan.

'I think he'd better go to Moorfields for surgery,' said the surgeon. 'Have we got anybody to send with him? He really ought to have a nurse escort.'

'Could you possibly go with him, Nurse Knowles?' asked the theatre sister. 'It's not that far. You'll be back within the hour.'

Lily thought she might as well oblige rather than send one of the hard-pressed night staff. The man was in some pain, so was given a morphine injection just before being settled in the ambulance.

'Will I lose the sight in my eye, Nurse? It's the thing I dread the most.'

'No, because you're going to be operated on by a highly qualified specialist, and that's why we're going on this trip, Mr – oh, that was a close one!' A ground-shaking thud made the vehicle lurch, and Lily took hold of the man's hand. 'Don't worry, we'll soon be there – we go up Moorgate to City Road, and then it's not much further. They'll be ready and waiting for you.' Always providing that it hasn't been hit by a bomb, she thought with a shudder. Lord Haw-Haw had been jibing again lately, saying that London was in for heavier bombing than ever. Having demolished much of the East End, the West End was next to be targeted, he'd drawled. Ugh, what a despicable traitor he was – but she would not let him frighten her, though the journey through the darkness, noise and sudden flashes of light resembled a surreal dream, and she kept hold of her patient's hand as he slipped into a morphine doze.

'They're gettin' it up West tonight, Nurse,' said the driver. 'Reckon that'll be me next call, soon as we've delivered this chap and taken yer back.'

To her annoyance, Lily found that she was trembling. Tiredness was taking its toll, as was the strain of air raids and her sadness at the loss of Sandy Redfern's love. But she must not think about him now.

The ambulance drew up outside the Royal London Ophthalmic Hospital, generally known as Moorfields.

'Ah, we're here now, and you'll be well looked after by the theatre staff,' she told her drowsy patient, adding to herself, 'Will you ever look back and remember the night you travelled through the Blitz?'

Having handed him over and seen him wheeled away on a trolley with his case-notes, she was urged by the driver to hurry.

'I got to get over to Leicester Square, Nurse. There's been a big explosion – two bombs on the Café de Paris, about half-past nine – blown it to bits, and full o' people dancin'!'

Lily felt the blood drain from her face; her legs went weak, and the driver had to help her up into the passenger seat beside him.

'You all right, Nurse?' he asked.

'I've been there,' she whispered, remembering dancing with Sandy, who had told her that it was the safest night-club in London. 'I might have been there tonight.'

'Just lay back in the seat an' close yer eyes, Nurse, an' I'll get yer back to St Mildred's as quick as I can.'

She did as she was told, trying not to let her imagination run riot. When the ambulance suddenly jerked to a halt, she was flung forward at the windscreen.

'Good grief, what on earth – why are you stopping here, driver? This isn't Bread Street. It's completely blocked – it's been bombed!'

'Oh, my Gawd,' muttered the driver. 'Oh, my Gawd.'

'What? Where are we?' Lily stared out of the window and gave a cry of horror at what she saw: it was a scene of utter chaos, a cloud of whirling dust in the darkness, heaps of fallen masonry and stonework, brick and marble blocking the narrow street. Oh, there was the beautiful carved wooden door of St Mildred's House – only it was lying horizontal, half-buried under a heap of rubble and broken glass.

She leaped out of the ambulance and started to clamber over the wreckage; in minutes her throat was full of choking dust, and there was a horrible, smoky, metallic smell of cordite. The driver was shouting after her, and other voices were telling her to keep out of the way, but she scarcely heard them. Tripping over a fallen beam, she fell headlong, but heaved herself up and stumbled on, looking for she knew not what.

And there was Miss Russell in her maroon dress with the lace collar, not standing but lying down like the door, next to somebody else – was it a man? – wearing something white. Lily stood looking down at them and – oh God, oh God! She froze in her tracks . . .

'Come back down *here*, Nurse!' shouted the driver.

Somebody was groaning and crying out like a madwoman. Who was it? Oh, it was *herself* making the noise – because of what she'd seen. Miss Russell's head was grotesquely twisted, and the body beside her had no head at all. This was a nightmare, full of the sound of voices calling out of a dreadful, eerie silence.

'Found any more?'

'Only two bodies so far, we think one's the matron. There must be dozens under this lot.'

'Same as at the Café de Paris, a direct hit.'

'Look, can somebody deal with that girl? She's half out of her mind.'

'Any o' the Salvation Army about?'

'They're all up West. They say there's thirty or forty dead and at least a hundred injured at the Café.'

And then there was another voice, a woman's, deep and foreign, but familiar.

'There is one that I know! You must help me take hold of her!'

'Who's that? Sounds like a bloody German.'

It was a voice she knew! And hands were touching her.

'Lily! Thank God you are alive. I am here, come with me, my poor friend.'

She felt arms being put around her, steadying her, guiding her through to firm ground.

'Are you taking charge of her, then, miss?'

'Yes, she is a friend of mine. I will take care of her.'

'Good – the sooner she's away from here, the better. There won't be many survivors out o' this lot.'

Part II

The Uphill Road

Does the road wind up-hill all the way?
Yes, to the very end.

from 'Up-hill' by Christina Rossetti

Chapter 10

Lapped by night and silence, Pinehurst stood solidly in the deep dark of the Hampshire countryside, now passing from winter into spring. A belt of low cloud hid moon and stars, and not a glimmer of light showed from the blacked-out windows. In the hall the longcase clock ticked away the hours: it was twenty-five minutes to midnight when the sudden ringing of the telephone in the Doctor's study shattered the stillness, intruding into the dreams of the sleepers upstairs. Children stirred and mumbled, Daisy moaned and then sat bolt upright, jolted into consciousness by the insistent ringing: why didn't Stephen answer it? Then she remembered that he was asleep with Mabel in their room on the third floor, and not on his divan in the study where he slept during his nights on call – three one week and four the next. He had retired to bed at nine, exhausted, leaving his junior partner in Belhampton to take the night calls.

Daisy decided that she'd better answer the telephone before it woke the whole house. Jumping out of the bed she occupied in Tim Baxter's room while he was away at sea, she grabbed her dressing gown from its hook on the door, which was always left ajar in case one of the boys needed her in the night, and pattered downstairs in her bare feet. In the study she quietly closed the door and took the receiver from its wall socket.

'Hello? Yes, this is Pinehurst Waifs and Strays, Mrs Baldock speaking. What? *Who?* Yes, Dr Knowles is here, but he's asleep – who wants to speak to him, please? Oh – *oh*, did you say *Lily?* Is she there with you? I shall have to go and wake Dr Knowles! May I take your number, Miss – er – so that he can ring you back? Why not? A *hospital?* All right, give me the message, then – Queen Adelaide's Hospital for Women, Lisson Grove, Marylebone – and you say she's all right? Not injured, then? Yes, yes, of course, I'll tell him straight away, and yes, he'll want to come as soon as he can. Thank you very much. Goodbye.'

She replaced the receiver in its socket, and came out into the hall to find the dim figure of Miss Styles standing on the stairs.

'What is it, Mrs Baldock? Does somebody specially need the doctor?'

'It's Miss *Lily!* She's been bombed out of St Mildred's, and taking shelter at another hospital overnight. Some woman with a German-sounding accent got this number from somewhere, and says the Doctor will have to go and fetch her.'

'Oh, my goodness! Did they say she was hurt?'

'She's not injured, the woman said, but very badly shaken. Oh, Miss Styles, now she'll *have* to come back to Pinehurst again!'

'Outside call for you, Dr Wardley.'

'Thanks, Nurse.' The weary-eyed houseman reached for the receiver. 'Hello?'

'Is that you, Wardley? Griffiths here, at Bart's.'

'Oh, good evening, Dr Griffiths.' Wardley was at once alerted. What on earth could this supercilious registrar want with him?

'Sorry to ring you at this hour, old chap, but I

thought you'd better know. We've had a hell of a raid here, and it's bad news, I'm afraid.'

It must be, if you're calling me 'old chap', thought Wardley, tensing. He was sitting in the office of the female medical ward at Hill End, writing up the case-notes of a new admission, an asthmatic whose constant anxiety for her soldier son was beyond his power to ease. The night nurse discreetly placed a cup of tea at his elbow. 'Ye-es?'

'In a word, the Café de Paris is no more, and neither is that nice little hospital you were so interested in, Wardley. Actually old Popeye had a lucky escape tonight. He went down to Mildred's at about nine to do a repair job on an eye, but changed his mind and sent it to Moorfields. Hello? Are you there?'

'Yes, go on, Dr Griffiths.' Wardley could feel his mouth drying as he held his breath. 'So . . . ?'

'So, he came back here, only just missing a direct hit. A little place like that, reduced to rubble in minutes, both hospital and home. Not much hope of survivors, I gather, only bodies recovered so far, both patients and staff. Death must have been instantane-ous for them.'

Wardley gripped the receiver and made an effort to speak normally. 'Oh. So St Mildred's has caught it.' His voice was calm to the point of dryness, and only a catch in his breathing betrayed his fear. 'Er, Griffiths, d'you know – have you heard – is there any news of – of a Nurse Knowles, Lily Knowles, a probationer, third year? Have you got any names so far?'

'No, that's the trouble. It's going to be difficult to sort them out because all the records have gone. Nobody knows how many people were actually in the building, so they'll have to wait until relatives start enquiring – and identifying. All I know for certain is that the matron's gone – dead, I mean – and they'll be digging them out through the night, just like at the Café de Paris – ghastly business. I'm on my way down there now to see if there's anything to be done, but I thought I'd ring you first.'

Wardley gave an involuntary groan, which brought the nurse back to hover at his side. He felt her tentative hand on his left shoulder.

'You all right, old chap?' Griffiths sounded concerned.

'Just see what you can find out, will you, Griffiths? Ask about Lily Knowles for me – if she's been found . . . if she's alive.'

'I'll do my best,' replied the registrar, now wondering if he should have made the call. 'Good night, old chap.'

Wardley then dialled the switchboard and asked to be put through to his parents in Northampton. They could decide how much they should tell the poor old Rawlingses, who had been begging their grand-daughter to leave London ever since the war began.

There was not much space to spare in the Durrants' little two-up, two-down off the Clerkenwell Road, and not much money coming in. Dad had been gassed in the Great War, and couldn't work, so the couple relied on the support of their daughter, May Terry, who hadn't seen her soldier husband since their hasty wedding at Christmas 1939. Little Betty was now nine months old, and slept every night with her gran in the Morrison shelter in the front room, and they never knew when May would be called out to a case. She'd trained as a midwife at Queen

Adelaide's, and now worked from home, cycling to confinements in basements, under staircases and even in an air-raid shelter on occasion, while Mrs Durrant kept busy at home, stretching the rations to put meals on the table and looking after Betty, too young to be evacuated to the country without her mother. Nurse Terry often said she followed the example of the Queen.

'When they ask her why she don't clear off to Canada with the princesses, she tells 'em she won't leave the King, an' he won't leave London, so there they are, and here *we* are!' she would boast with satisfaction, while reasoning that if they didn't survive the Blitz, at least they'd all go together – presumably including the pupil midwife she'd accepted from Queen Adelaide's for six months' district training, though it meant sharing her bedroom with the girl, because you could hardly expect Dad to give up his room, and they practically had to live in the kitchen, though the Morrison served as a table during the day, on which she could refill her bag, check her drugs and write up her case-notes and register. There was no bathroom or indoor lavatory, and Mrs Durrant carried hot water up to the washstand in May's room for the pupil to give herself a wash down every day; the rest of them used the kitchen sink. The extra income was welcome, and Mrs Durrant eagerly seized on another ration book, though they found Nurse Blumfeldt rather heavy going; she seldom smiled, and her deep, accented voice got on Dad's nerves.

'Yer wimmin won't like that 'orrible German way o' speakin',' he predicted, turning down his mouth. 'Wouldn't surprise me if some o' the 'usbands don't let 'er into their 'ouses!'

Nurse Terry pointed out that the girl was a good worker, and that a woman in the pain of childbirth doesn't care about the nationality, sex or social status of anybody who can relieve her agony. Besides, Nurse Blumfeldt had a sad history, she said, and it seemed that her father was a professor and very clever: he was working with a team of biochemists at St Mary's, under another professor called Fleming.

It was a patient's husband who told Nurse Terry and her pupil on that Saturday evening that St Mildred's Hospital had been flattened by a direct hit. Nurse Blumfeldt had just delivered the baby, but without another word she had rushed out of the house, grabbed her bike and cycled down to St Paul's. She always said later that the Lord of her people had directed her steps, or rather her pedals, for as soon as she arrived at that scene of chaos she saw Lily Knowles clambering over the rubble and calling out like somebody demented. Throwing aside her bicycle, Hanna seized Lily bodily and dragged her away from what was left of Bread Street, waving down one of the taxi-cabs acting as ambulances that night, to take them both to Queen Adelaide's Hospital. Nurse Knowles was seen by a doctor and given a sedative injection and a bed for the night, to be counted as an air-raid casualty; Nurse Blumfeldt was allowed to telephone a children's home at Belhampton where her friend's father lived, and ask that he come to collect her the next day. Nurse Terry was very cross about her pupil's precipitate disappearance, and the loss of her bicycle, which was never seen again.

The Sunday newspapers were full of the tragedy of the Café de Paris, 'London's safest restaurant'. The band under their leader 'Snake-hips' Johnson had just gone into 'Oh, Johnny, Oh, Johnny, How You Can Love!' when two bombs crashed through to the basement, killing Johnson and most of his musicians. The death total was thirty-four, with twice that number injured. A weeping bystander described the scene as officers in uniform carried out their dead or injured girlfriends whose trailing evening dresses seemed to add to the pathos. The incident caught the public imagination in much the same way as the sinking of the *Titanic* nearly thirty years earlier, when glamour and luxury had suddenly been turned to death and destruction. A humbler dance hall a mile away to the east was also hit, resulting in two hundred casualties, but this only got a few lines in the papers, and not until the Monday morning was 'a small private nursing home in the St Paul's district' mentioned as having been completely destroyed, with the loss of an estimated thirty patients and staff – and by that time a church and a hospital at St Pancras had been hit and become the latest news. The Dowager Countess of Suffolk, interviewed at her Bloomsbury home, told of her shock and sorrow at the loss of an ancient foundation under her patronage, the death of her dear friend Miss Russell and so many fine nurses. All records had perished with St Mildred's, and the bereaved relatives had confirmed the deaths of the Honourable Henrietta Tarrant and Miss Cicely Grey, among others; Miss Beatrice Massey had been injured and taken to a hospital near to her Wiltshire home, where it was feared she must lose a crushed leg. The theatre sister on duty that night had perished with the ophthalmology department, and the home sister was also dead.

On hearing about St Mildred's, Wing Commander Redfern contacted his grandparents, who got in touch with the Dowager Countess; she told them brokenly that she had received no word of Miss Lily Knowles, who was thought to have been in the building that night, either in the hospital or the home, and was therefore listed as 'missing', as her body had not been recovered. It was left to them to break the news to their grandson who nodded, swallowed, and buried his head in his hands. Mr Redfern poured him a stiff whisky and laid a hand on his shoulder; his grandmother shed a few tears but privately thanked God that it was the girl and not Alex who had been lost. After a while young Redfern left them to join his squadron, unable to endure sympathy for the loss of a girl he had never truly appreciated. Oh, this bloody war . . .

The Countess remained inconsolable, as Professor Blumfeldt found when he visited her.

'It was my foolish pride that insisted on keeping St Mildred's open, and now my life's work has gone, and taken those dear nurses with it,' said the lonely old lady, who had put her heart and soul into the hospital since the loss of her husband and son in the Great War.

The professor was able to give her the news of Nurse Knowles's lucky escape, to add to the very small number of survivors, though most of the staff were now believed to be dead.

'I shall arrange a memorial service for them in St Paul's Cathedral, because that is all I can do for them. I wish I had died with them. There's nothing left for me in life now,' she told him, unconsciously echoing the words of the man rebuked by Miss Russell.

The professor agreed that it was indeed a sad end to an ancient institution, for St Mildred's was one of the last of its kind, a relic of a bygone age and in any case not likely to survive as a training school for nurses. He did not say this to the poor Countess, but took hold of her trembling bejewelled hand.

'Do not add to my distress by losing hope, my dear Countess,' he begged, the stilted formality of the words softened by real affection. 'Many troubles have been inflicted upon our generation, but we must trust in . . .' He hesitated, and then continued, 'We must put our trust in Him who is Lord of us all, who will not let our enemies triumph over us for ever.'

She looked at him with tear-filled eyes as they stood together in her elegantly old-fashioned drawing room, two survivors of a former era, united in the fiery trial of another Great War. But she looks back to the past, and my work takes me into the future, thought Blumfeldt in pity for his old friend.

After a long, wordless minute, she withdrew her hand and gave a deep sigh. 'You are a very good friend to me, Heinrich,' she said. 'I am thankful that Minna got away in time.'

Dr Knowles and Mrs Baldock caught the first available train from Belhampton on that Sunday morning; he decided not to subject Mabel to what might be a difficult journey and an even more difficult interview with his daughter. Having telephoned Queen Adelaide's Hospital and been told that Miss Lilian Knowles was in a mixed surgical and casualty ward, he asked Daisy to put some suitable clothes into a suitcase, assuming that Lily had probably lost all of hers except for what she stood up in. Mabel got up to make tea and toast, and saw them off.

'Shouldn't you let the grandparents know?' she asked.

'Chances are they know already, from the same woman who telephoned here. If Lily prefers to go to them, it will be her choice – but I want to see for myself how she is. It's high time, anyway, Mabel,' he added, and she saw the self-reproach in his eyes.

Waterloo Station had been damaged, and the train terminated at Clapham Junction. Daisy's early memories of a south London childhood were rather sketchy, and she suggested getting buses across London to Marylebone, but Knowles hailed a taxi-cab, wanting to get to Queen Adelaide's as soon as possible.

In the cab Daisy surreptitiously studied her brother-in-law's drawn features and faded blue eyes. Not yet sixty, Dr Knowles had the look of a man who carried a continual burden, she thought. She knew that he was often in pain from his war wound, but she now suspected that the pressure of living in a children's home in addition to running a busy general practice was becoming more burdensome as time went by. He had always been dependent on Mabel's steadfastness, her calm commonsense, her inward serenity in the midst of daily difficulties; but Daisy now wondered if he had been more deeply affected by the rift with his daughter than even Mabel had realised. Daisy sighed; perhaps his conscience sometimes troubled him with memories of the past – but *then*, as now, it had been in a time of war, and who was to judge?

'Right, 'ere we are, guv'nor! Queen Adelaide's 'Ospital!'

'Thanks, driver – here you are – keep the change. Come on, Daisy.'

Mr and Mrs Rawlings both shed anguished tears

when their GP, Dr Wardley, and his wife called to tell them about St Mildred's, and of course they were desperate to find out what had happened to their granddaughter.

'She'd have got in touch with us if she possibly could,' wept the old lady. 'But she may be lying unconscious or – or injured under the wreckage.' She simply could not bring herself to utter the word 'dead'.

'Dennis will do all he can to find her,' said Mrs Wardley soothingly. 'Do you happen to know the names of any of her friends that he could contact?'

'Well, no, because they're her fellow probationers, and they could all be lying there with her,' replied Mrs Rawlings with a sob. 'There was Henrietta Tarrant and Beatrice Massey she used to mention a lot – and that strange German girl, a Jewish refugee – she left St Mildred's to take midwifery training somewhere, I think. Do you remember Lilian telling us about her, James? Something about her parents making a last-minute dash to get out of Germany?'

'Yes, the name was Blumfeldt,' replied Mr Rawlings. 'I remember it because we once had a client of that name.'

'I'll ask Dennis to find this girl if he can, to see if she knows anything,' said Mrs Wardley. 'Can you write the name down for me?'

Dennis Wardley at once remembered the dark, deep-voiced girl who had come to the Wigmore Hall with Lily, himself and that Westhouse chap to a performance of *Elijah*. And yes, he remembered Lily saying something about her leaving St Mildred's as soon as she got her Finals, and going to do midwifery at – where was it? Queen Charlotte's? No, Queen

Adelaide's, that was the one. He'd enquire there to ask if she was still on the staff – not that she'd be likely to throw any light on what had happened to Lily, he thought, but any contact was worth a try.

He duly telephoned, and was told that Hanna Blumfeldt was now out on the district in Clerkenwell for six months.

'But wait a minute,' said the switchboard operator, remembering an incident the previous night. 'Nurse Blumfeldt suddenly turned up here with a nurse from St Mildred's. It was bombed, you know –'

'Oh, what was her name? Please, you must tell me!' Wardley almost shouted.

'She was in a terrible state, poor girl, and was admitted to a ward. Let me look it up – yes, the name was Knowles, Lilian Knowles. Nurse Blumfeldt had to get back to her district, but this Miss Knowles is in Burney Ward, under sedation.'

It was enough. Dr Wardley immediately telephoned his parents with the news, begged and bribed a colleague to take over his weekend on call, and rushed for the London train.

Throughout a night of terrifying dreams, sudden awakenings and falling back into semi-consciousness, Lily struggled to reach the light of morning, while at the same time dreading what it might reveal. Memory had become something fearful, something to run away from, to disbelieve, for surely it could not be true – the thing that she had seen . . .

She was in a narrow bed with a rather lumpy mattress and a pillow with striped ticking showing through its cover. There were other beds with other restless sleepers, and a woman in a blue overall hurried between them at intervals.

'D'you want a cup of tea, dear?' she asked Lily at some point in the night. 'Help you to get back to sleep, maybe?'

'Where is this place, Nurse?' asked Lily hoarsely. 'Is it a hospital?'

'Yes, dear, it's Queen Adelaide's, women only,' came the reply from the hard-pressed night nurse who had not time to stop and talk. After a few minutes a cup of tepid tea was put down on the bedside locker, and Lily drank thirstily, for her mouth was dry. Her head whirled: she must have been given something strong, she thought, like Medinal.

'Nurse, where's Hanna? Hanna Blumfeldt who brought me in here?' she asked, but the nurse had disappeared, and Lily slid back into drugged sleep. When she woke again the lights were on and the other women were stirring. A trolley trundled past, and a weary-looking nurse took temperatures and pulses; Lily looked around at a bewildering mixture of gynaecological and accident cases. There were no babies to be seen or heard, and she remembered Hanna saying that the maternity ward and nursery were in the basement.

Screens were suddenly pulled round a bed at the end of the ward, and a whispered exchange took place between the nurse and a night sister who had been hastily summoned.

'I reckon that one's *gorn*,' said the woman in the bed next to Lily, and the words unlocked the terrible memory of what she had seen the night before. She began to shake violently, and burst into sobs. There were startled looks in her direction, and the sister came over to her.

'Now then, Miss – er – you're from St Mildred's

aren't you? You should be giving thanks for a very lucky escape, my dear! The best thing for you would be to get up and have a wash – freshen yourself up before your parents arrive to take you home.'

'Are my grandparents coming here, Sister?' gasped Lily. 'Has somebody told them?'

'Yes, they're on their way. Can you can get yourself to the washroom? It's over there by the lavatories. The nurses are very busy just now, but it will do you good to make the effort.'

'Yes, Sister, I'll try,' Lily answered with the habitual obedience of two and a half years of training, and proceeded to get out of bed and pad across the ward in her bare feet and a shapeless white hospital nightgown she could not remember putting on. There were three washbasins, each with a tablet of hard white soap and a communal roller towel. Lily had no face flannel, comb or toothbrush, and swayed slightly as she bent over a basin to splash her face and wash her hands. Compared to St Mildred's this place seemed poorly equipped and comfortless, but she did in fact feel refreshed. Padding back across the ward, she had to stand aside while a covered trolley was trundled by a porter towards the screened bed. There was a soft, sad murmuring from the patients as it was wheeled out of the door, and the bed stripped.

'D'you want some porridge, dear?' somebody asked her. 'Bread and marmalade? A nice cup o' tea?'

She accepted the tea, but nothing to eat. Lying back on her one pillow, she closed her eyes, willing sleep to return, but only succeeded in dozing intermittently while voices and footsteps blended into an indistinguishable background noise. What had the night sister said? Her parents, meaning grandparents of course, were coming to take her home, and were on their way! Her heart lurched at the thought of seeing dear Grandmama and Grandpapa, their faces full of loving anxiety . . . and then suddenly there was a rattling of screens and the sound of approaching footsteps. She heard the ward sister's voice.

'This way, Mr Knowles – Mrs Knowles – here she is!'

Lily opened her eyes and there was her father standing beside the bed, looking down at her with a love and thankfulness that showed in every feature. Tears stood in his eyes, and his mouth trembled.

'Lily, my dear.' And now he was bending over to kiss her, and she was putting her arms up to hug him and pull him down to sit on the bed. His stick fell to the floor with a clatter.

'Dad. Oh, Dad . . .' She buried her head against his shoulder. 'St Mildred's has gone, Dad. It's all gone – all my friends – only me left, because . . .' And she cried like a child, while he murmured to her, rocking her gently in his arms.

'I know, my dear, I know. But you're still here, my Lily – my little girl. Sssh-ssh, Daddy's here, ssh-ssh.'

Daisy silently produced a large white handkerchief from her handbag, and gave it to him.

'Listen, dear, Aunt Daisy and I have come to take you home. We've brought some clean clothes for you to put on, and then we'll call a taxi-cab and be on our way.'

'That's right, Lily. Your room's waiting for you at Pinehurst,' smiled his sister-in-law, and Lily looked up and noticed her for the first time.

'Auntie Daisy – *Auntie Daisy!* Oh, you've come too. Oh, it's been such a long, long time. But you look just the same as when – you haven't changed at all!'

So there were more hugs and kisses, more smiles

227

and tears, and gradually Lily felt her shattered life coming into focus again. *Dad* was here with Auntie Daisy, and they'd come to take her home – to Pinehurst, where she had been a child, and where she had grown up . . .

'All right, Mr Knowles? Mrs Knowles?' The ward sister's face appeared between the drawn screens. 'You must be feeling so relieved! We're all very thankful and happy for you!'

The doctor and Daisy smiled back at her, not bothering to correct her assumption.

'I'll get out of the way now, so that – er – Daisy can help her to dress,' said Knowles, slowly and painfully heaving himself up from the bed. Daisy handed him his stick, and he was about to emerge from the screens when the sister laid a restraining hand on his arm.

'I was about to say that Miss Knowles has another visitor,' she said. 'A Dr Wardley has just arrived. Shall I bring him in now, or ask him to wait until you're dressed?'

For a moment Lily stared blankly at her, as if not understanding. Then she clasped her hands together and said, 'Ah, do you mean Dennis Wardley, Sister?'

The sister noted the familiar use of a doctor's Christian name, and took it to indicate friendship, if not something closer.

'He didn't give his first name, but he's a very pleasant young man,' she replied archly. 'I'll ask him to wait while you make yourself look nice, shall I?'

'No! Yes, I mean – will you bring him in now, please, Sister, and I can tell him that I'm going home with my father?' And he'll be able to let my grandparents know, she thought.

Dennis Wardley strode in, with eyes only for her.

'*Lily!* Thank heaven! I've had such a time tracking you down – but now I've found you, and I've come to take you home – yes! Your grandparents have been nearly out of their minds with worry, and so have I. Oh, Lily, my dear, you're alive, you're safe, thank God!'

He impulsively leaned over to kiss her, and only then realised that they were not alone. The sister had said something about Lily's parents, but he had not really taken it in, so eager had he been to see her for himself; but now he became aware of a grave-faced middle-aged man leaning on a stick, and a dark-eyed woman who was dipping into a suitcase and spreading items of clothing on the bed. The ward sister remained inside the screens, intrigued by this somewhat confusing situation: it seemed that Miss Knowles had two homes to go to, and both were anxious to receive her. Which would she choose?

Lily now faced an embarrassing and potentially painful introduction. She sat up straight in the bed and smoothed back her uncombed hair.

'Dennis, dear, it's good of you to come for me, and – and I'm most grateful,' she stammered. 'But actually my father has come to take me home, to Belhampton.'

'Belhampton? But you're from Northampton! I thought – obviously I hadn't realised – I thought your parents were –' He broke off, puzzled, and turned to Daisy. 'Is this Mrs Knowles?'

'No, Dennis, this is my Aunt Daisy, and – this is Dr Knowles, my father. Dad, this is Dr Dennis Wardley of St Bartholomew's Hospital, a – he's a friend.'

Dr Knowles had been listening to this exchange, and on hearing the words 'grandparents' and

'Northampton', he had made a fairly accurate guess. He held out his right hand, smiling.

'I'm very pleased to meet you, Dr Wardley,' he said warmly. 'My daughter's family has been sadly divided in recent years, but after so nearly losing – after this I intend to bury the unhappy past, and I hope to meet you again very soon.' The two men shook hands, and Knowles added firmly, 'But meanwhile, Lily needs to rest, and I'm taking her home to Belhampton.'

There was a pause. Dennis Wardley glanced from one to the other, trying to work out these relationships he knew nothing about. He turned to address Lily directly.

'I've always understood that your home was now with Mr and Mrs James Rawlings, your grandparents at Northampton, Lily. They have been desperate for news of you. We thought you were dead. What am I to tell them now?'

Lily made an effort to stay composed. It would be all too easy to give way to tears, to use her terrible ordeal as an excuse to avoid facing her obligations to her grandparents and this man who had searched for her on their behalf. She had to be honest.

'You're so good, Dennis, and I – I'm sorry you've had so much trouble. P-please tell them I'll write and . . . and tell them I love them and . . . and I'll come to see them very soon, only . . . my father has come for me, and I must go with him.' Her voice shook, and she drew in a breath that turned to a sob in her throat. She held out a hand to Dennis, and he took it, not taking his eyes from her face.

'I *must* go to Pinehurst with Dad because it's been such a long, long—' She covered her face with her free hand, and Knowles broke in, speaking in a pleasant, professional manner as one doctor to another.

'I'll see that Mr and Mrs Rawlings are kept fully informed, and as soon as it is reasonably convenient, Lily will visit them at Northampton,' he said. 'You have my word on it, Dr Wardley, and I thank you for all the trouble you have taken to find her and get here.'

Wardley let go of Lily's hand and straightened himself up, remembering that other time in December 1939 – heavens, was it that long ago? – when he had eagerly looked forward to accompanying this girl to Northampton, and had been so bitterly disappointed when she changed her plans because that RAF type had turned up on leave.

'Very well, Lily, I'll give them your message. Like me, they'll be overjoyed to know that you're alive, and I hope you'll write to them soon. I'd better get out of your way now. Goodbye, Lily.'

He leaned over and kissed her cheek, nodded to Knowles and Daisy, murmured, 'Thank you, Sister,' and left them.

'What a very decent fellow,' commented Knowles with a slight frown, for he sensed that this decent fellow had taken a heavy blow at the hands of himself and his daughter. He would have to talk seriously with her at some point about young Dr Wardley, and find out how far her own feelings were involved.

Daisy Baldock kept her own counsel. She saw clearly enough that Lily was not in love, at least not with this young doctor who so obviously cared for her.

'Come on, Lily, off with that awful nightdress, and let's see what we've got here for you to put on,' she

231

said gently. 'And I've got a brush and comb, and a bottle of eau-de-Cologne!'

As the train steamed westward, Lily's pale face stared from a corner window at the built-up suburbs, gradually thinning out towards the Surrey pines and common land used for rifle practice, villages with their church spires, here and there a market town, some with barrage balloons hovering over them, and an air of sabbath quietness. They passed through the garrison town of Aldershot and its outlying barracks, and soon there were ploughed fields divided by hedgerows, the bare trees of woodlands and winding lanes – and then they were at Belhampton Station, where a porter grinned and greeted them.

'Yer car's where yer left it, Doctor!'

Lily sank into the back seat with Daisy for the half-mile drive along the Beversley Lane that led off the main road into Belhampton. She glimpsed through the hedge that rose above the ditch at the side of the lane, and saw wintry fields; here and there she caught the golden gleam of daffodils opening to the early spring sunshine, though there were as yet no primroses. In sudden emotion she turned and laid her head on Daisy's shoulder.

'It's all coming back to me, Auntie,' she whispered. 'I haven't forgotten anything.'

Daisy put a reassuring arm around her. 'Of course you haven't, dear, though you'll find there've been some changes. But Pinehurst hasn't changed – look there, straight ahead!'

And there it was, the gracious Victorian mansion standing on the corner where the lane turned southwards across the common to the village of Beversley. Knowles drove in through the double gate and up to the front door, which had opened to so many children, including Lily herself, over twenty years ago. It was open now, and standing on the step was Mabel Knowles, still wearing her Sunday hat and coat, having just returned from church with her twelve children. A shy young woman stood just behind her, and an older lady to one side: Beryl Penney and Miss Styles were smiling and exchanging excited glances.

Lily heaved herself out of the car, wondering what she should say. Mabel came straight towards her, and lightly kissed her on the cheek.

'Welcome home, Lily. Daisy'll look after yer, an' see to whatever yer need. Ye'll be her special charge,' she said.

Turning to her husband, she kissed him and smiled happily. 'Well done, Stephen!'

Chapter 11

Lily was home. The house she had left in such bitter anger now received her back into the years of her childhood, back to her own room on the third floor – except that instead of sharing it with Beryl Penney, it was Aunt Daisy who now occupied the other bed: Daisy who was there to comfort her when she had nightmares, to brew tea at all hours, to bring her the half-pint of stout last thing at night, ordered by the Doctor as a sedative. Beryl took over Tim's old room on the second floor, and she and Miss Styles shared the 'night watch' for both boys and girls.

Daisy's unobtrusive attentions continued around the clock. She brought Lily breakfast in bed, and other meals were taken together in some convenient nook, not in the dining room with the children, of whom Lily saw little in those first few days. She heard their distant clamour as they went off to school and came home; she heard their footsteps on the stairs and landings, their eager voices telling Mabel and Miss Styles what they had been doing. Far from being disturbed, she found them soothing, being in complete contrast to the sounds of air-raid sirens, the bangs and thuds of bombs, the bark of ack-ack guns.

'They sound so *normal*, Aunt Daisy,' she said as the two of them sat in the living room with the big work-basket, for there was always mending to be done, socks to be darned, sheets to be hemmed. Mabel spent her time in the kitchen or her office, sometimes in the Doctor's study while the children were at school, and after supper Lily and Daisy would retire to the Quiet Room to be joined later by Mabel, Miss Styles and Beryl – and the Doctor if he was in – to listen to the wireless. They all loved it, and each had their favourite programmes – *ITMA* and *In Town Tonight*, plays, concerts, church services and talks from the Radio Doctor and Mr J. B. Priestley, whose *Postscript* talks followed the nine o'clock news on Sunday evenings: all were avidly heard and talked over. The Doctor's favourite was a new panel programme in which three wise men of widely different areas of knowledge answered questions sent in by listeners. It was called the *Brains Trust*, and Professor Joad's high-pitched voice, Commander Campbell's tall stories and Mr Julian Huxley's vast knowledge of humans and other animals – he was director of the London Zoo – became familiar to the nation, to be praised or criticised, depending on whether you agreed or disagreed with them.

The wireless saved the Pinehurst residents from having to make conversation, for which Lily was grateful. She never found herself alone with Mabel, whose first consideration was, as always, the children, leaving Daisy to be Lily's confidante, if she needed one; and Daisy never pressed her to talk, though she gave the impression of being willing to listen if required to do so.

And there was Dad, of course. He made time for little chats with Lily in his study, and told her that he had sent a telegram to her grandparents and followed it up with a letter, because like many of their generation they had no telephone. He had now received a reply.

'Oh, how are they?' she asked rather guiltily, afraid that she had hurt them by her silence.

As indeed she had, it seemed.

'Not very happy I'm afraid, Lily. I'm the big bad wolf who's taken you away from them again, to live in a children's home,' he told her wryly. 'Where, of course, you won't be able to rest because of all the racket! The sooner you write to them yourself, the better it will be.'

'Oh, the poor dears – I'll write, I really *will* write and tell them that I'm being well looked after and feeling much better – and you know, I *love* hearing the children, because – oh, after what I've seen and heard . . . oh, Dad!' She turned away, and he reached for her hand.

'Now, now, Lily, my dear, it's going to take time. I do have some idea of what you're going through, because I had some pretty gruesome experiences in the last war, and to be honest you never really forget – but you do get over it, and that's a promise. When you're ready, I'm here to listen to anything that's on your mind – about St Mildred's, maybe, or young Dr Dennis,' he added, carefully watching her response. 'He seemed a very decent sort of fellow, I thought.'

'He is, Dad, and a good friend, but nothing more than that,' she said, remembering that she had once considered herself in love with Wardley – until Redfern had come along. And there was no need to mention *him*, now that it was all over.

'Not on *your* side, at any rate,' said Knowles with a little smile, patting her hand. 'But I think I recognised certain symptoms in *him*. You say he lives at Northampton?'

'Yes, quite close to my grandparents. His father's their GP, and I met him at a dinner party Grandmama gave. Oh, Dad, I must write to that poor old pair, though I can't think what to say – not just now. I don't seem able to concentrate on anything.'

'When you're ready, then,' he said gently; 'and later on perhaps you'll visit them, but for the time being you need to recover.' He paused and then added, 'Little Beryl Penney goes to the hospital to help out for a few hours on weekday mornings, while the children are at school, and perhaps when you're feeling a bit more rested, you might like to do the same, to keep your hand in. It's entirely up to you, my dear.'

Lily noted that he had not suggested helping Mabel with the children, and thought perhaps Mabel didn't want her help. Belhampton War Memorial Hospital, with its twelve beds, operating theatre and X-ray department, served Belhampton and the surrounding villages, and Lily felt a reluctance to face local people who knew her as Dr Knowles's runaway daughter; she did not think she could cope with well-meaning questions about St Mildred's. Suddenly overcome with weariness, she decided to forgo the wireless that evening, and go straight up to bed.

'All right, my dear,' said her father. 'I'll send Daisy up.'

'Oh, don't bother her. She'd much rather listen in with Mabel! I'll be all right.'

But Daisy was dispatched upstairs with the nightly glass of stout.

We were so thankful and relieved to hear that you had survived the dreadful bombing of St Mildred's, Lilian, but our rejoicings were abruptly cut short when we heard from the

237

Wardleys that you had been snatched from your hospital bed at Queen Adelaide's and taken to Belhampton. We have anxiously waited for a word from you, but have heard nothing, only a telegram and letter from your father. We beg you to write and tell us how you are, and how long we must wait before we see our grand-daughter again. We cannot believe that you are willing to stay at that woman's house, and if you are being held against your will, you must tell us, and we shall inform the police. Only you must write to us, dear Lilian, and tell us exactly what your circumstances are.

. . . and so you see, dear Grandpapa and Grandmama, I'm being very well looked after by my aunt, Mrs Daisy Baldock, and I beg you not to worry. It was such a terrible night when St Mildred's was bombed and completely destroyed with so many of my friends, including Miss Russell, that I have lost the confidence I had in myself, also my concentration. However, as soon as I feel better and able to travel, I will come to visit you, and perhaps you can then help me to decide what to do . . .

Lily groaned, and rested her head in her hands for a moment; then, picking up the Doctor's fountain pen again, she added, 'My father has shown me nothing but kindness, and I can see that he truly wants to mend the rift in our family, so that we may all be friends again.'

It sounded rather melodramatic, and she could just imagine her grandparents' cynicism on reading it, but it was the best she could do.

'Hello, Lily. Have you finished writing? How about a nice walk in the fresh air?'

Daisy had come up behind her, and half a dozen of the older children were waiting in the hall for her reply. It was Saturday afternoon, and Miss Styles and Beryl were entertaining the younger ones indoors before tea.

'Thought it'd be a good idea for Mabel to rest for an hour, while you and I take the older ones up to Parr's Wood,' said Daisy, smiling. 'Come on. You look as white as a witch – let's get some colour into your cheeks!'

It was the first time that Lily had come into direct contact with the children since her return, and she found them full of lively curiosity. Enlivened by the blustery March wind, the bigger ones scrambled on ahead through last year's bracken, up the winding path to the tree-crowned summit of Parr's Wood. Before them stretched the common to the south and a spread of fields and pastureland to the west, beyond which lay Wychell Forest. The wind had brought a glow to their faces, and Lily breathed in deeply. The first daffodils were in bloom, and all around them were the signs of the earth waking from winter's sleep.

'There'll soon be lots of little lambs frisking away in those fields,' said Aunt Daisy, looking like a shepherdess herself, thought Lily, surrounded by her flock.

'It's good, innit, Miss Lily?' piped up ten-year-old Pip, who had made the change from street urchin in Wandsworth to country boy – thanks to the benevolent discipline of Tim Baxter, Beryl had said, adding wistfully, 'I can't tell yer how much we all miss him, Miss Lily.'

Lily looked down at his bright face. 'You'd find London very different now, Pip.'

'Wot, 'cause o' the air raids, yer mean?'

'Yes. A lot of people sleep down in the underground railway stations, and in shelters and basements,' she told him, remembering the crypt of St Mildred's.

'Me an' me pals used to sleep under them railway arches, but it wa'n't 'alf cold in bad wevver,' he said, nodding vigorously. 'But then we fahnd a carter's yard wiv 'ay for 'is 'orses, an' that was nice an' snug! But I'd raver be 'ere at Pine'urst wiv Mum – she's a good 'un, she is! Are yer goin' to stay wiv us, Miss Lily?'

'Oh, Pip, I don't know – I really don't know,' she said, smiling at the undersized child, while the thought came to her yet again that Mabel Knowles did wonderful work at Pinehurst, and whatever wrong she had done in the past, there was no doubt that she earned and deserved the love of her Waifs and Strays, and the universal respect of Belhampton. Lily's conscience whispered that it was surely time for her to start pulling her weight, to offer her services as a helper at Pinehurst or join Beryl at the hospital each day – or go to see her grandparents. But at the mere thought of taking any kind of action, a paralysing reluctance seized her, and she was incapable of making decisions, or even plans. As her father said, she was still suffering from shock . . .

While she pondered these uneasy thoughts day after day, and came to no final conclusion, Aunt Alice called with an invitation for her to go to tea with the Westhouses at Cherry Trees. Geraldine had forty-eight hours' leave from the WAAF, and wanted to see her cousin, so of course Lily accepted.

She put on a jumper and skirt that she'd left behind two and a half years ago, and, having washed her hair and let it dry naturally into soft, loose waves, she borrowed Daisy's bicycle and set off to Belhampton Park, feeling a little apprehensive as to her reception. How much had Geoffrey told them about her London life? Had he said how quickly he'd been superseded by Wardley? Had he mentioned Redfern at all? At once a wave of sadness swept over her, remembering Sandy's last words, 'Thanks for the memory!' which just about summed up their ill-fated romance. It had given her such joy, such tremulous happiness while it lasted, but she shuddered at the recollection of the consequences, and the incident that had mercifully released her. That *child* would have been almost due by now: what would they have said at Pinehurst? Or at Cherry Trees? Or Northampton? She closed her mind to speculations that simply did not bear thinking about.

There was no need to worry about her welcome at Cherry Trees, for she was completely outshone by Geraldine, a pretty, dark-haired twenty-one-year-old, looking smart and efficient in her blue uniform, basking in her father's pride and envied by her sister, Amelia, now eighteen and longing to follow her, but restrained by their mother who insisted that her youngest was needed at home.

On enquiring about Geoffrey, Lily was shown a cheery letter from Alexandria where he'd spent some well-earned leave, but of course the fact that he was out there at all was a matter of constant anxiety to them. No mention was made of his former attachment to Lily, which was presumed to be in the past, and Geraldine openly asked her if she had any boyfriends. She herself appeared to have plenty to

241

choose from at Upper Heyford in Oxfordshire, where she was stationed as a radio telephone operator, doing vital work for Bomber Command. Lily felt a quick stab of envy for the girl's enthusiasm, but repressed it at once: why shouldn't Gerry employ her newly acquired skills to serve the RAF in this way, and enjoy doing so? She would find out soon enough about the sadness of young lives wasted, of good-looking, daring young men who failed to return from operations and even from training exercises.

Amelia was frankly envious of her sister. 'Honestly, Lily, I'll go raving mad if I have to spend another year stuck here at home!' she confided. 'All that Mother and Dad think about or talk about is Geoffrey, who's been abroad for *ages*, and now here's Gerry coming home and preening herself in her uniform in front of everybody. It's absolutely *deadly*!'

Lily made vaguely sympathetic noises, and remarked that Beryl Penney helped out at the hospital on weekdays.

'Ugh, I wouldn't care for that at all,' replied Amelia with a grimace. 'Actually I've applied to the NAAFI at Aldershot, though I haven't told the parents yet. At least I'll get to wear a uniform, and I can travel there and back each day on the train. And I'll meet all three services,' she added in anticipation of a burgeoning social life.

Lily wished her luck, but privately wondered how the girl would fare at working in the heat and steam of a large kitchen, and serving meals in a busy canteen. And yet it might be the right thing for her – after all, the war was bringing radical changes at all levels of society, as she herself knew well.

After tea Aunt Alice and her daughters took Lily into the parlour where a wood fire had been lit. Its modest heat was welcome after the chill of the dining room. A girl from the village carried the tea-things through to the kitchen, and Alice dispatched Amelia to keep an eye on her and the delicate bone-china tea-service.

'Of course, it's next to impossible to get reliable domestic help now,' Mrs Westhouse sighed. 'I envy Mabel her Miss Styles and Daisy, not to mention the Penney girl and that wonderful cook – and the gardener who does all those extra jobs!'

'Your sister Mabel has a dozen kids to look after, and damned difficult brats they are, don't forget,' Gerald Westhouse cut in sharply, puffing on his pipe. 'Needs all the help she can get. I hope you do *your* share to help her out, my girl,' he added, sternly fixing his one eye on Lily. 'Seeing that she's been good enough to take you back again after all that was said.'

Lily blushed to the roots of her hair, and could not meet her uncle's eyes. Reports must have got through from Pinehurst to Cherry Trees and further afield, no doubt – of her angry leave-taking two and a half years ago, overheard by Tim, Miss Styles, the cook and Heaven knew who else.

Aunt Alice saw her discomposure, and put in a word. 'Oh, Gerald, be fair. The Pinehurst children are models of good behaviour compared to these frightful evacuees swarming all over Belhampton and Beversley. Absolute *savages*! And there's nobody but women to keep them in order, with all the able-bodied men in the forces.'

'Except for those Italian prisoners of war lying around on the farms and eating our food,' muttered Uncle Gerald. 'I'd round up the lot and shove 'em into internment camps to sew mailbags or break stones or whatever it is prisoners are supposed to do. Gave themselves up in their hundreds in North Africa – no heart for fighting, just wanted an easy war.'

Lily could not help thinking that this was just as well for the Allies, but hardly liked to say so, and she similarly noted that there were no evacuees at Cherry Trees. She turned rather thankfully to Geraldine, who was delighted to talk about life at Upper Heyford, where it seemed that all the women were pursued by dashing RAF types, and there was never a dull moment.

Lily had plenty to occupy her mind as she cycled back to Pinehurst. The days were lengthening, and as her young body responded to a healthy country life, she knew she could no longer continue to lead the life of a pampered convalescent. It just wasn't right to go on accepting hospitality from her stepmother, who had never once reproached her for the way she had behaved; on the contrary, Mabel had tactfully withdrawn herself, and generously given up Daisy to be Lily's constant companion, with plenty of opportunity to talk in private with her father. Lily belatedly saw how much her arrival had changed the domestic arrangements: everything had been made to fit in with her requirements, however inconvenient to the rest of the household, and with never a word of complaint.

What did Mabel really think of her? Had she forgiven her, or was all this thoughtful tact for her husband, for Stephen's sake? Ought she to seek out Mabel for an honest talk – to thank her, perhaps, and to apologise. She should at least make some acknowledgement of how much had been done for her. And perhaps the time really had come for her to visit her grandparents, though judging by Grand-mama's indignant letters, there was no change of attitude there: Mabel Knowles was still *that woman*, with Dr Knowles still hopelessly under her thumb – and he had literally kidnapped Lilian. They were imploring her to return to them, but she was confused, unsure of where her heart lay. It was time to make up her mind, and also to make arrangements about completing her training. Her grandparents had suggested applying to Northampton General Hospital, and the longer she put it off, the harder it would become.

Then something happened that helped Lily to see her way ahead . . .

'Miss Styles has got a nasty cough, and the Doctor's afraid it could be bronchitis,' Daisy said one Monday morning towards the end of March. 'I'll have to take over her duties, Lily, and Mabel has two children home from school with colds – and it's washing day, so –'

'Oh, let me give you a hand, please!' cried Lily. 'Just let me be useful. I'll do anything!'

She cleared away the breakfast things, and saw the children off to school, the little ones in the care of the older girls. A woman came in from Belhampton on Mondays to help with the weekly wash, and when Cheale had stoked up the boiler to supply a good, continuous flow of hot water, Lily spent the morning assisting her to soak, boil, scrub, rinse, mangle and finally hang out a row of sheets, towels and pillowcases in a stiff breeze that was mercifully dry. The children's cloakrooms and lavatories had to be cleaned and the floor scrubbed, then the bedrooms swept and dusted before making up the beds with

245

fresh linen. After a midday lunch of cold meat and bubble-and-squeak made from Sunday's leftovers, some of the washing was sufficiently dry to take in and fold ready for ironing. Mabel looked after the two flushed and fretful children in their little back room, and Daisy took drinks and a poached egg to poor Miss Styles, who was feverish and coughing up quantities of thick phlegm into a mug containing disinfectant.

'Lily, could you cycle into Belhampton for some more Jeyes Fluid? And we could do with another couple of bottles of friar's balsam for inhalations,' said Daisy. 'I'd go myself, only it'll be Homecoming in just over half an hour!'

'Course I will, straight away,' replied Lily, who had thoroughly enjoyed her busy day. Off she pedalled on Daisy's bicycle, and having called at the hardware shop and chemist, she stopped at the baker's to buy from her own purse a couple of dozen crumpets to toast as a special treat for teatime and Homecoming, as it was called. This was a time set apart at Pinehurst, from when the children arrived home soon after four o' clock, until supper at six. Every child had a duty to be done, from helping Cook in the kitchen to assisting Cheale in the garden, including cleaning out the rabbit hutches. The younger ones did simple craft work with scraps of material and raffia, and during those two busy hours Mrs Knowles spoke to each and every one of her children individually, finding out anything that was troubling them, any secret longing, any ghosts from the past, and did her best to comfort and reassure. Homecoming would be well under way by the time she got back, Lily reckoned, and planned to start on the ironing before supper; but circumstances intervened.

When she reached the corner where the main road from Belhampton joined Beversley Lane, she saw two soldiers who had obviously walked from the station and now stood talking on the Pinehurst corner. Their uniforms were smart, and of a somewhat greener khaki than the ones she was used to seeing; their forage caps were worn jauntily on the sides of their heads. As she drew nearer to them, she saw that one was young, while the other seemed to be at least forty. The younger one smiled appreciatively in her direction as she dismounted.

'Let's ask her,' he said in the transatlantic accent Lily remembered from the Covent Garden ballroom. Of course – they were Canadians.

'Excuse us, ma'am – we've just come over from Aldershot. That place over there – it's called Pinehurst, ain't it?'

'Yes, it is,' she answered, wondering what on earth it could mean to them. Three of the older boys working in the garden under Cheale's supervision had stopped what they were doing, and were staring at Lily and the soldiers.

'And does there happen to be a – a Miss Mabel Court in charge there?' asked the older man. 'Or maybe she's married? I don't know what name she uses now, but I was told she runs a children's home hereabouts, and – and there don't seem to be any others.'

Lily realised that for all his friendly politeness, he was nervous. He spoke hesitantly, as if he hardly expected her to know, and she had the strange sensation of having stumbled upon a matter of some importance. But – a *Canadian*?

'That is the Pinehurst Home for Waifs and Strays,

247

and the matron is a Mrs Knowles,' she replied cautiously. 'Her maiden name was Court.'

The two men looked at each other. 'Hey, that *is* the lady, then, George!' exclaimed the younger one. 'C'mon, let's go straight up and knock at the door!'

'No, wait.' The older man looked at Lily. 'Excuse me, ma'am, but you wouldn't by any chance be Mabel's daughter, would you?' he asked in a low tone.

'No, I'm her stepdaughter,' she answered, while her mind worked quickly. Might this man be an embarrassment to Mabel, somebody she did not want the Doctor to know about? *Was he a former lover?* She felt that a lot might depend upon what she said and did next.

'May I ask your business with Mrs Knowles?' she asked in a briskly polite tone.

'Why, sure, but – it's kinda difficult to say, ma'am,' replied the older man. 'Mabel and me, now, we go back a long way.'

'Is she expecting you?' Lily noted that her father's car was not there, so he must be out.

'No, ma'am.'

'We aim to give her a surprise,' grinned the younger man.

'Excuse me a moment.' Lily had made up her mind to let Mabel decide whether she wanted to see this Canadian or not. 'I'll go and find out if Mrs Knowles is free. What name shall I say, please?'

The older man's face had paled, and his mouth was tense. He hesitated.

'Just say George, will ya?' said the other man. 'Canadian Army! You just tell her that!'

Lily propped the bicycle against the wall, nodded briefly and unsmilingly to Cheale and the three boys as if to tell them to get on with their work, let herself in with her key and went inside, closing the door behind her. She was met by sounds of activity and a buzz of happy children's voices: Beryl Penney came into the hallway and smiled brightly, back from her daily stint at the hospital.

''Allo, Miss Lily! Been shoppin', 'ave yer?'

'Do you know where Matron is, Beryl?' Lily asked quietly.

'She's upstairs wi' the two little poorly ones, but Miss Daisy's in the kitchen,' said Beryl, wanting to be helpful. 'Miss Daisy! Can yer come?' she called out before Lily could stop her.

'Oh, don't bother Daisy, it's Mabel I want to speak to –' she began, but Daisy appeared in the passage leading to the kitchen.

'What is it?' she asked. 'Did you get the shopping, Lily?'

'Daisy, there are a couple of soldiers asking for Mabel.'

'Soldiers? Asking for Mabel?' echoed Daisy, her dark eyes widening. 'Where?'

'They're outside. They're Canadians, over from Aldershot. One of them seems to know her name, and he says he –' Lily stopped, surprised by the sudden incredulous look on Daisy's face.

'Did he give a name?' she asked in a low voice.

'The other man said to say his name was George,' answered Lily, and Daisy put her hand to her throat, almost as if she were afraid. Beryl stared from one to the other in bewilderment, and Lily knew that a crisis of some kind was about to break on them. She would have to ask Mabel to come downstairs and deal with it.

At that moment they heard a door close upstairs, and Mabel appeared on the landing.

'They're much better, and I've left them both asleep,' she said with satisfaction, but as she began to descend, she sensed the tension in the atmosphere.

'Is anything the matter?' she asked quickly. 'What's happened, Daisy?'

Daisy dumbly shook her head, and Lily had to reply.

'There are two Canadian soldiers asking for you, Mabel. Do you know anybody called George?'

Mabel's face drained of all colour. She stood stock-still and stared at them for a moment. Then: 'Where is he?'

Lily nodded towards the front door, and Mabel gave a cry as she rushed to open it. She saw who was there, and they heard his shout as she fell into his arms.

'*Georgie!*' she cried, and burst into hysterical sobs, utterly unlike the Mabel they all knew.

'*Mabel!* Oh, Mabel, you ain't changed a bit . . .'

'Me little brother! I thought I'd never see yer again in this world – oh, Georgie, Georgie!'

And while Lily, Daisy, Beryl, the other soldier, Cheale and the three boys stared in astonishment, Mabel and the man called George embraced each other and wept.

'I'm sorry, Mabel, I never knew what happened to yer after the war,' he was saying. 'Davy an' me, we moved on to Vancouver, an' there was no word from London.'

'Never mind, Georgie, ye're here now, an' I'm lookin' at yer face again. Daisy! Come out an' meet the brother we thought was lost to us for ever!'

Lily stood aside, witnessing an outpouring of emotion in which she had no part to play. Children's curious faces were peering round the door of the living room, and a little girl started to wail in alarm at seeing their beloved mummy apparently crying her heart out, along with Auntie Daisy.

Realising this, and the effect it could have on the children, Lily's training came to the fore, and as if she were dealing with an emergency in the theatre at St Mildred's, she took charge.

'All right, Cheale, take the boys and get on with whatever you were doing. Beryl, you take the younger ones and I'll see to the older girls. Come along, all of you. Quickly now, everybody back to their jobs while Matron and Mrs Baldock are busy with their visitors. Come on, who's going to toast the crumpets for tea?'

Having got the children out of the way, Lily suggested to Daisy that she and her sister took their brother and his friend, whose name was Bill, into the Doctor's study. She then called through to the kitchen for a tray of tea to be taken to them, and as soon as the children were re-established at their various tasks, she checked on the two little invalids upstairs, and found them sleeping. Miss Styles had heard the commotion and said she was feeling much better, so could get up and help, but Lily told her to stay where she was until allowed up by the Doctor.

At six o'clock supper was served in the dining room, and Mabel had sufficiently recovered her composure to thank Lily for her help and to say that George and Bill would be joining them at the table. Daisy also emerged, ready to supervise the ladling of beef and vegetable soup into bowls, accompanied by crusty bread and the few remaining toasted crumpets.

'Would it be easier if Beryl and I sit with the younger ones at the smaller table, to make more space?' offered Lily, and this convenient arrange-ment was the scene that met the Doctor when he came in. He stared in utter bewilderment at the two khaki-clad figures at the big table, and Mabel rose at once to her feet, pale but smiling.

'Stephen, it's *George*! Me little brother who went to Canada – he's come back in the army!' she told him, her eyes filling with tears again, and Knowles went straight to his brother-in-law and grasped his hand.

'George Court! Welcome back to the old country!' he exclaimed, smiling a welcome to both soldiers, and beaming round at all the children. He kissed his wife and looked anxiously into her face, then glanced towards the smaller table where his daughter sat with Beryl and the younger ones. She gave him a wide smile and a surreptitious wink, which he returned, leaning towards her with a whispered, 'Good girl!' It was all the reward she could have wished for.

George and Bill had to return to their barracks by ten o'clock, but promised another visit as soon as they could arrange it. The incident made a big impact on Lily, and reminded her of how little she knew about Mabel's family, which of course was Daisy's too, and in which she had never previously shown any interest. At the end of that momentous day, when she and Daisy were in their room preparing for bed, she begged to be told more about their lost brother.

'Mabel doesn't like talking about the past,' con-fessed Mrs Baldock. 'She says that most of her Pinehurst children had a worse childhood than she did, and now that she's got a happy life here with her family of Waifs and Strays and the Doctor, she doesn't look back to brood on what happened in days gone by.'

'Does she mean the time when – when she and my father were together at the children's hospital, and he was married to my mother?' ventured Lily, who had never before spoken to Mabel's sister on this painful subject; she had been a young child when Daisy had left Pinehurst after the incident with the curate, and her place taken by Miss Styles.

Her aunt looked up in astonishment. 'What do you mean by that, Lily? Who's been talking to you?' she asked sharply. 'My sister was engaged to a captain in the Salvation Army at that time, Harry Drover, the best of men. He was her first sweetheart, and she stuck with him to the end, even when he was badly shell-shocked and lost an arm. Bless him, he never wanted to go to the war and kill his brothers, as he used to say. Oh, it was tragic! He was never the same again, and died in Mabel's arms not long before the Armistice.'

Daisy's face reflected her memories of a dearly loved friend, reduced to a stammering wreck by his horrendous experiences. Lily was puzzled, and persisted with her questioning.

'I'm sorry, Aunt Daisy, but I really want to know – was this at the time when Mabel was at the children's hospital?'

Daisy frowned. 'No. She'd left the East London by then, and gone on to the district in Kennington as a midwife.'

'But she did work with my father at the East London, didn't she? At the time I was born, I mean?' asked Lily, remembering what her grandmother had said.

Daisy, who was sitting at the dressing table, now

turned round and looked very hard at the young woman beside her.

'I don't know what you've been told, Lily, but don't let me hear you say anything but good about my sister,' she said severely. 'Let me tell you that Mabel left the East London hospital, just to get away from your father, and stop all the talk. It's quite true that *he* wasn't blameless, but my sister certainly was. *That* was why she had to give up the work she loved – because *he* wouldn't leave her alone, even though he was married and she was engaged.'

'Oh. Oh, I didn't know,' Lily gasped, and felt her colour rising. 'That wasn't what I heard.'

'Maybe it wasn't, but it's the truth, and whatever *you* heard was a lie.' Daisy too had flushed in her defence of her sister. 'It wasn't until two or three years later – 1920, to be exact – after your mother had died in the flu epidemic, that Stephen Knowles came searching for Mabel here at Pinehurst. I remember the day. You were a little thing in a pink dress, holding on to his hand, and Tim Baxter – he'd have been about eight or nine – he went to the door with Mabel, and there you both were on the doorstep. Mabel let you in, and six weeks later she and Stephen were married. But don't let anybody tell you that Mabel had eyes for anybody else but Harry Drover, right up to when he died. Your father would have betrayed your mother, but Mabel never betrayed Harry – never!'

Lily trembled, and put her hands to her face. 'I'm sorry, Aunt Daisy. It was my grandparents who told me –'

'The Rawlingses – oh, yes, they were prejudiced because of their daughter – only natural, I suppose.' Daisy shrugged. 'I'm sorry if I've upset you, Lily, but it obviously needed to be said. Your mother was a sad lady, I've heard, and your father had a terrible time in France during the war – just like Harry, just like all the rest of those poor men. He wasn't the only one, but he felt he needed somebody to talk to about it, somebody strong to lean on, like Mabel. But I won't listen to any lies about her. She had a very hard life from the start, the eldest of six – five after little Walter died before I was born – and she had to look after us all while we were growing up. Our father was a drinker, and our poor mother took her own life. Oh, I shouldn't talk about it, but just thinking about that time, it brings it all back.' Daisy gave a sob and bit her trembling lip as if to stop herself from saying any more. Lily gazed at her, horrified at what she had heard, but still wanting to learn the rest of the sisters' family history.

'Go on, Auntie Daisy, what happened? Please tell me.'

'Mabel doesn't like it talked about, and I've said quite enough.' Daisy's voice was muffled as she got into bed. 'Can I turn off the light?'

'Yes, do, but – can't you just tell me about your brother George? You were so glad to see him again today, weren't you?'

'Yes, we'd completely lost touch, and he found us through the Salvation Army. It was such a long, long time ago.' Daisy faltered, and then went on, 'George was only twelve when our good old family doctor helped Mabel to get him on to one of those child emigration schemes, a ship taking boys to Canada. Dear old Dr Knowles – he was Stephen's father, and the best friend our family ever had.'

'*Twelve years old!* To send him so far away from you all! *Why?*' asked Lily, sitting up in bed.

255

'Perhaps you'd better not ask too many questions, Lily. You've had an easy life here at Pinehurst, very different from Mabel's upbringing.' Daisy took two or three deep breaths, and then continued, the words tumbling out of her as if she could not stop.

'Well, if you must know, after our mother's death our father suffered a fatal accident at home while he was drunk, and George was . . . involved. He was in a terrible state over it, poor little chap, and the family broke up. Our brother Albert went into the navy and was lost at sea in 1918, and your Aunt Alice and I were adopted by our aunts, our mother's elder sisters who owned Pinehurst. Aunt Kate left the house to Mabel at the end of the war, and at the same time Mabel inherited a fair bit of money from our father's mother, our Grandmother Court. She was a very devious old woman, and there were lots of stories about her, but I think even she respected Mabel.'

Lily's head whirled as this complicated tale unfolded. She got out of bed, and went over to the window, oblivious to the cold. 'And so Mabel then opened Pinehurst as a home for children?'

'Yes, thanks to the double windfall of the house and the money. She runs it for the Waifs and Strays Society, though it's her own house, and Stephen Knowles has been content to live here with her, because those were her terms. Look, Lily, I'm sorry if I've spoken harshly about your father, but I've only told the truth. I'm sure that he's suffered too, and he's been a good husband to Mabel and a good local doctor. He's looking a lot older now, and I worry about Mabel, who's getting towards fifty and works harder than ever – plus all the anxiety over Tim. But it would break her heart to have to give it up.'

Lily stood at the window, pulling back the curtains

and looking up into the night sky. There was a distant hum in the air, which she knew was bombers going out on a raid over Germany.

'You've told me a lot that I didn't know, Daisy,' she said slowly. 'I've sometimes wondered why you and Aunt Alice speak so differently from Mabel.'

'Oh, yes, we were brought up to be little ladies, and Mabel stayed a Londoner,' replied Daisy with heavy irony. 'Alice is a fearful snob, and I've been a stupid fool. Mabel has made a much better life than either of us, maybe not in worldly terms, but she's laid up treasures in heaven.'

There was a long pause, and Lily said at last, 'I'm glad your brother George found you again.'

'Yes, it's like a miracle, something we'd given up hoping for, though I know Mabel never forgot him. He and his friend Davy Hoek met on the boat going out, and they've stayed together ever since. Neither of them has married, but when George said he'd join the army and come over to fight for the old country, Davy said the old country had never done anything for him, and so George came on his own. He'll be another one to worry about when he's sent overseas.'

'Yes.' Along with Geoffrey and Tim and Sandy and all the others, thought Lily, shaking her head. 'I wonder how long it'll go on for.'

'God only knows,' said Daisy. 'But George has come back to us, and that means a lot to Mabel. She's always blamed herself for sending him off to Canada in a hurry, but it was for his own good, and old Dr Knowles knew that too.'

Lily's mind was working on the information she had been given, and of course she came to wonder how a twelve-year-old boy had been 'involved' in the accidental death of his drunken father at home;

whatever happened must have been an ugly scene. And why had Mabel and the family doctor – her own grandfather whom she had never known – conspired together to get him out of the country? Even while she thought about it, she knew that there were some questions better not asked.

As if reading her thoughts, Daisy spoke up again in the darkness. 'Lily! Promise me you'll never, ever ask Mabel about George. I shouldn't have said what I did, because I don't know exactly what happened. I wasn't there. I've never asked Mabel about it, and neither must you.'

'I wouldn't dream of mentioning it to her,' replied Lily, getting back into bed.

But my father will know, she reflected, if his own father helped Mabel to keep the truth a secret. It's another burden that he's had to carry, like his memories of my mother. Daisy had said very definitely that he had not been blameless, and yet . . . who was she to judge him? What would he have said if he had known about Sandy Redfern and the predicament she had been in? Somehow she knew that he would have stood by his daughter.

The war was teaching Lily Knowles many things.

Chapter 12

'Lily, my dear, a word – if you can spare me a few minutes.'

'Why, of course, Dr Knowles, at your service!' Lily grinned, pushing a damp strand of hair back from her forehead. 'Can we talk here, or do you want me to come to your study?'

'I'd rather we weren't overheard. I won't keep you long.'

Lily untied her apron and threw it over the old round-backed basket chair they used when supervising the children's baths. She'd had to do the lot this evening, with Miss Styles still on the sick list, and Mabel confined to her room after fainting at the foot of the stairs, an alarming moment, which had frightened the Doctor, who then discovered that her blood pressure was low and her pulse irregular. For three days he had confined her to strict bed-rest, cared for by her sister, and though she was now clamouring to return to her usual working day, her husband was reluctant to agree.

'Daisy says she's much better for the rest,' Lily remarked, following him into the study.

'Yes, but I should have seen the signs earlier. She was so obviously exhausted and anaemic. Sit down, Lily. I've promised Mabel to pass on to you her gratitude for all your help at a difficult time – especially on that evening when George and Bill turned up. It was a happy occasion, of course, but a

259

big emotional strain, and I'm sure it's what brought on the fainting episode. You rose to the challenge, Lily, and I'm proud of you.' He patted her shoulder. 'With Miss Styles ill as well, I don't know how we'd have coped without you, and Mabel has truly appreciated it, my dear. Well done!'

Lily glowed with pleasure at this unreserved praise, proof that she was now accepted as the maturer woman she had become, rather than merely as the Doctor's difficult daughter.

'It's I who should be thanking Mabel for having me back,' she said quietly. 'And for everybody's kindness, especially Aunt Daisy. And Beryl's been very good too. I think she's ready to take on more responsibility now.'

'Ah, poor little Miss Penney, she just lives for the day when Tim next gets leave,' said Knowles, shaking his head, and Lily felt a queer little lurch of the heart, for in spite of her commendation of Beryl, she hardly saw her as a worthy partner for the young seaman who had so often shown his preference for herself. She smiled, unaware that her father's sharp eyes had noted the momentary flicker in her own.

'Anyway, I've had time to think about the future now, Dad, and although I'll be happy to go on helping out while Mabel and Miss Styles are recovering, the time has come for me to get back to nursing, and finish my training.'

'Ah.' He had been wondering how long it would take her to reach this decision, and he waited to hear where she planned to go.

'As you know, my grandparents wanted me to leave London and transfer to Northampton General,' she went on, glancing at his face for a reaction.

'And is that where you intend to apply?'

'Yes, Dad, it is. And as soon as things are back to normal here, I'll make that visit to my grandparents. It's about time.'

'I think you're quite right. They've been very good to you.'

'Yes, they have. But . . .' She hesitated, and then continued quickly, 'but there won't be any more criticism of you or Mabel, because I shall explain to them how well you've looked after me for this past month. And I'll also tell them about the wonderful work that Mabel does here for the children. I've never properly realised before what a haven Pinehurst is.'

'Ah, yes. I'm very glad to know that you've come to realise her worth, Lily. She's made it her vocation, and I've been privileged to share it with her – though I don't expect your grandparents to forgive me.' He turned down the corners of his mouth and added in a lower tone, 'There's no reason why they should. I can't forgive myself.'

Lily could think of no reply to this, and he turned to her with deep sadness in his eyes. 'That's the trouble with growing older, Lily, you find that some memories – the most uncomfortable ones – grow sharper rather than fainter. They don't just fade away, they stay with you to the end. But I mustn't burden you with my regrets, Lily; it's enough that you've come to understand what Mabel means to me. I wasn't her first love, you know. She'd have married another if he'd survived, and I know she's never forgotten him.'

Harry Drover, she thought, the Salvation Army officer. She nodded, and felt that she should say a little more. 'Dad, I've seen a lot and learned a lot in these last few weeks. I thought I'd never recover after seeing St Mildred's bombed and all my friends killed, but now I want to get on with my life again, thanks to you and Mabel and everybody here. Thank you for coming to fetch me – for taking me back. Oh, Dad, I'm sorry . . .'

Her voice tailed off, and he drew her close to him, letting his stick fall to the floor.

'It's all right, dear. I'm sorry, too. About your mother.'

It was the first time that he had voluntarily mentioned his first wife and implied that he felt regret for the unhappiness she had suffered. What could Lily answer? Nothing. She put her arms around his bony, pain-racked frame in a gesture that she hoped would convey her understanding of his human frailty. He had not been blameless, maybe, but he had suffered remorse over the years. And whatever had happened had been in a time of war.

Lily's grandparents met her at Northampton Castle Station, and she stepped down from the train, to be greeted with hugs and kisses. Both looked noticeably older.

'We've got a taxi-cab, Lilian, and the driver's here to carry your luggage,' said Grandmama. 'Oh, my darling, we've so longed to see you again!'

'So have I. I've been worried about you, and so sorry that . . .' She found it very difficult to explain why she had not come straight to them from Queen Adelaide's.

'Never mind, dear, you're here now, and we shall make sure that you have a *real* rest, to get your strength back and your peace of mind after all you've been through,' the old lady declared, linking her arm through Lily's, while Grandpapa led them to the waiting taxi. 'You're looking tired, and no wonder, after a month in a children's home! But now you'll be properly looked after, I shall make certain of it.'

Lily's room had been lovingly prepared, with the framed photograph of her mother holding her as a baby placed in a prominent position on the dressing table. There was also an official letter from Northampton General Hospital, which Grandmama said had arrived two days ago. Lily quickly opened it and read the contents before being called down to the dining room for lunch.

'I'm afraid the casserole isn't up to the standard we were used to, Lilian,' Grandmama apologised. 'Less beef and more home-grown parsnips! Your ration book will be a help, dear.'

But not for long, thought Lily, who had been asked to attend an interview with the matron of Northampton General Hospital the following week. She had written the previous week, giving her grandparents' address, and now wanted to get back to nursing as soon as possible. Besides, it wasn't fair to plant herself on the old couple for too long. Signs of age were showing in Grandpapa's stiff joints and Grandmama's increasing deafness. They were in no state to wait upon a young woman who had now to all intents and purposes recovered from her brush with death. And there was the matter of her position at Pinehurst. That same evening she felt she had to make this clear to the Rawlingses, as gently and as courteously as she could.

'My father has aged a lot in the past couple of years, and gets considerable pain from his war wound,' she began. 'He's very anxious to mend the rift between us, and we've had some helpful talks. I feel that I understand him better now.'

Mr and Mrs Rawlings sat in unsmiling silence as she contined, 'I've also had talks with Mrs Baldock, that's Mabel's youngest sister, Daisy, who's now back at Pinehurst as secretary and book-keeper since the boy – the man who did it has been called up into the navy. Daisy told me quite a lot about the Court family history, which is terribly tragic, and Mabel had a very hard childhood. And Daisy also assured me that Mabel had nothing to do with my father while my mother was alive. The – the fault was on his side.'

'Well, she would try to defend her sister, wouldn't she?' Mrs Rawlings' voice was cold. 'It was not what *we* heard, Lilian. There was a big scandal at the East London children's hospital over those two, and that woman had to leave on account of it.'

'That isn't true, Grandmama. Daisy told me that she left of her own accord, although she loved it there, because she had to get away from – from him, my father, who was causing all the gossip by his – er – pursuit of her. She was engaged at the time to a Salvation Army officer who was wounded at the Somme and died just before the end of the war. It was only after my mother's death, when he – my father – came looking for Mabel at Pinehurst, bringing me with him, that she agreed to marry him.'

'Very convenient, I'm sure, the deaths of our darling Dilly and the unfortunate Salvationist,' said the old lady icily. 'As if we hadn't sorrow enough for our daughter, but he must come and take you away from us as well. We – I shall never forgive him.'

Her voice shook, and Lily felt pity for her. 'In that case I shall say only one more thing, Grandmama,' she said quietly. 'He can't forgive himself, either. He told me before I left that he'll be haunted by the memory of my mother for the rest of his life.'

'And so he should be. I'm glad to hear it,' replied Mrs Rawlings, but her husband spoke a little less harshly.

'I'm glad too, Lilian, that your father has shown remorse for his past wrongdoing. That much does him credit. May I ask about Mrs Knowles's attitude towards you? Did she look after you well? And did you part on good terms?'

Lily considered for a moment, wanting to be absolutely fair. 'Mabel has never treated me any differently from the rest of her family – I mean her children, her Waifs and Strays,' she said. 'And she's never reproached me for the frankly horrible things I said when I left Pinehurst to go to St Mildred's. When Dad took me back there a month ago, she went to a lot of trouble to make me comfortable, and practically gave up the services of her sister, Daisy, to look after me round the clock at first. When I left yesterday, I thanked her for everything – and, you know, she's much respected in Belhampton for all she does for those children.'

'Well, we can't say fairer than that, Lilian,' replied Grandpapa with an approving nod, though his wife's mouth remained tightly shut.

Lily felt that she had said all that was necessary, and there need be no return to the subject. What she had said was true – that she and Mabel had parted on good terms with smiles and a light kiss – but in her heart Lily had the feeling that Mabel had not been sorry to see her go, and who could blame her for that?

The interview with Miss Nelson, the matron of Northampton General, went well. The lady expressed her sincere sympathy for the fate of St Mildred's, and accepted Miss Knowles's application to continue her training as a third-year probationer at the large voluntary hospital, a nineteenth-century building with a total of six hundred beds and covering many specialities. She suggested – which meant that she insisted – that Miss Knowles should put in at least eight months before sitting for the State Finals in the New Year. Lily agreed that this was reasonable, and it was settled that she should commence duties on the first Monday in May, moving into the nurses' home that weekend to collect her uniform. Before then she would have her chest X-rayed and be inoculated against diphtheria, typhoid fever and tuberculosis.

Her grandparents protested that it was far too early for her to return to work, but in spite of a certain apprehension, Lily looked forward to hospital life again, the familiar sights, sounds, smells and constant activity – a hive in which she would be just one small worker bee. News of two terrible air raids on London in mid-April sent shudders down her spine, and she felt all the more urgently called upon to give her unique contribution to the war effort.

Lily's first day on Victoria ward, female medical, came as a mental and physical shock. It was like being plunged into a whirlpool of new impressions, names to learn, routines to be followed, rules to be obeyed. Her fellow probationers all knew each other and looked askance at this girl who had not shared their experiences; everybody was busily engaged on what they had to do.

Victoria seemed enormous, with a large main ward of twenty beds, ten on each side, and a balcony with six more. On each side of the central block consisting of Sister's office, kitchen, treatment room and sluice, were corridors, each with two single rooms and a four-bedder. From seven o'clock in the morning until eight-thirty at night, with a two-hour break in either the morning or afternoon, or an evening off from six o'clock, the nurses tramped the length and breadth of the ward, giving out meals, feeding helpless patients, giving out bedpans and wash-bowls, making beds, doing the 'back rounds' to prevent pressure sores, changing water jugs and glasses, doing all the nursing procedures that Lily knew from St Mildred's, but with three times the number of patients – and no useful nursing orderlies to do the mundane domestic jobs.

Lily discovered very early on that it was the probationers who did the ward cleaning, from damp-dusting of bedsteads and lockers to sluicing mackintosh sheets, scrubbing bedpans and polishing the brass plaques on beds donated by such worthies as the Marquis of Northampton, the mayor and mayoress, and the various shoe manufacturers that gave the town its distinction. Even the wheels of the portable screens had to be scraped twice weekly, and the stains of bladder drainage bottles removed with a mixture of nitric acid and lead shot.

Lily felt awkward and uncertain in this environment where first-year 'pros' knew the routine better than she did, and Sister and Staff Nurse eyed her with suspicion, waiting to see how this newcomer coped. She felt herself to be on trial, and was not allowed near the medicine trolley or special treatments, intravenous infusions or catheterisations; even her recordings of temperatures and pulses were checked if abnormally high or low. Her head and feet ached, she dithered and stammered, and by the end of the first day was so utterly weary that she collapsed into bed as soon as she reached her room. When the alarm woke her the next morning at six fifteen for breakfast at six thirty and to go on duty again at seven, she honestly wondered if she could keep up the pace. Would she ever get used to it? Would she make it to the weekend? She remembered St Mildred's and her friends, dear Hetty Tarrant who was dead, and Beatrice and Cicely; Miss Russell, so stately and defiant against the enemy until struck down in her own beloved hospital – and she knew that she couldn't let them down. She had to go on, and somehow or other that first week was completed, and she began to know the patients and staff of Victoria.

Then came the Saturday, and the worst raid ever on London that night. The Sunday papers reported tremendous damage to the City, the very heart of London. Westminster Hall, the House of Commons, the British Museum and the capital's four largest railway stations were hit. The papers refrained from giving the exact numbers of killed and injured, but in this most ferocious of air raids, the numbers were obviously very high.

'D'you want to see my paper, Nurse?' asked old Mrs Whicker as Lily was tidying her bed halfway down the main ward. 'Those poor Londoners have had a battering again.'

Lily picked up the *Sunday Pictorial* and glanced at the headlines. There was a picture of Big Ben, scarred but still chiming the hours. She began to read, then put her hand to her mouth, as her breath seemed to be stifled in her throat.

'Oh, my God – my God,' she gasped, and the old lady looked alarmed, as did the women in the beds on either side of her.

'Are you from London yourself, Nurse?' asked one of them sympathetically.

'I – I worked in a hospital in the City,' Lily answered, whispering; her fingers trembled as she held the paper. 'It was b-bombed. All my – all my friends were killed.'

'Oh, Nurse, that's awful,' said Mrs Whicker. 'I'll tell you what, though, dear – they haven't got St Paul's Cathedral. Look, it says here, "bombed but still undaunted amidst the ruins" – oh, Nurse, don't cry, dear, don't cry!'

But Lily could not help herself. All the grief and sorrow of bereavement that had lain like a silent weight on her heart for two months now poured out in a great flood of tears, and she stood at Mrs Whicker's bedside, shaking from head to foot while the tears poured down her face, weeping for St Mildred's and the life she had known there, the friends she had made and lost – and for London, that great city, now facing total destruction.

The women looked at each other in helpless pity, and one on the opposite side of the ward got out of her bed to come to Lily's side.

'Come on now, duck, you're not in a fit state to be workin'. Can somebody ring the bell and fetch one o' the other nurses to come and take care of her?'

But third-year Nurse Hamilton was already striding down the ward.

'Good heavens, Nurse Knowles, what an exhibition in front of the patients! Come to the office at once, and try to get control of yourself!'

'Oh, don't be hard on her, Nurse. She's been bombed out of her hospital – it's a shame!' protested several patients as Lily was seized by the arm and marched out of the ward to Sister's office. The young staff nurse who was in charge that morning hardly knew how to deal with her.

'You'd better sit down, and have a cup of tea, Nurse Knowles,' she said. 'I can't send you off duty without asking Matron's permission. You were all right yesterday, weren't you? What brought this on?'

Lily made a tremendous effort to compose herself. 'There was – there was another terrible air raid on London last night, Staff Nurse, and it brought it all back to me,' she mumbled. 'My hospital was – my colleagues – they were all killed in a night.'

'She was reading one of the patient's Sunday newspapers,' put in Nurse Hamilton.

'Well, look here, Nurse Knowles, if you want me to ring Matron's office and ask if she will see you, I will, but otherwise you'll have to pull yourself together and carry on working. What do you want me to do?'

Lily knew that to leave the ward would count against her. She drew a deep breath, and wiped her eyes on the back of her hand. 'If I could sit down for a little while and have that cup of tea, Staff Nurse, I think I'll be all right.'

'Well, I hope you will. I'll go and put the kettle on, and you'd better go to the staff cloakroom and wash your face in cold water. I'm sorry about what happened, Nurse Knowles, but the war affects all of us. Some of the nurses have got brothers and boyfriends in the services, and we worry all the time about them, but we have to carry on. We've all got to be brave, haven't we?'

And so Lily stayed on the ward, carrying out her duties, and found her best comfort in the patients' kindly smiles, winks and thumbs-up signs.

'You're a brave girl, Nurse!' said Mrs Whicker, giving her hand a squeeze.

Lily knew that in her heart she did not feel at all brave, but put it down to her St Mildred's training that she could still face the world.

And a few days later she was rewarded. Visiting her grandparents on an afternoon off, she found a letter with a Devizes postmark waiting for her. The handwriting looked vaguely familiar, and her heart gave a leap: Beatrice Massey's Wiltshire home, Thorpe Place, was in that area, near to Wilsford Down. But Beatrice was . . . Lily tore open the letter.

Beatrice was alive! Rescued from the ruins of St Mildred's after many hours, her right leg had been so badly crushed that she had needed an above-knee amputation, and her back had also been injured. She was now home from hospital, confined to a wheelchair, and had thought, like Lily, that she was a sole survivor, until a letter had arrived from the Dowager Countess of Suffolk with the news of Lily's escape.

'Beatrice is *alive!*' shouted Lily. 'I must go and see her, I *must!*'

'But, my dear, it's a long way to travel when you only get one day off a week,' Grandmama pointed out.

'But I must see her and talk with her – it's like having somebody back from the dead!' Lily longed to see the friend who had shared her life at St Mildred's, with all their special memories. 'She says she wept for joy when she got the Countess's letter, and can't wait to see me! Oh, I wonder if Ned Carter has been to visit her!'

Letters were exchanged, and Lily wrote to Hanna Blumfeldt with the news. Hanna was still cycling around Clerkenwell with Nurse Terry, and would soon be sitting her midwifery exams. She and her father had also received letters from the Dowager Countess; there was to be a memorial service in St Paul's Cathedral on 25 June for all the staff of St Mildred's who had 'given their lives', as the Countess put it, on 8 March, and the few survivors were invited to attend. In addition to themselves there were two nurses who had been away from Bread Street that night, and a few domestic assistants who lived out. Professor and Frau Blumfeldt would be present at this ecumenical ceremony, with Dr Edlinger, and several consultants from St Bartholomew's and Moorfields. Beatrice said that she would be there with her parents and sisters, and Lily immediately put the date in the off-duty request book: it would be a day of sadness, yes, but also a day of reunion.

And there was another treat to look forward to: a letter from Aunt Daisy brought news of Tim, who would be coming home for a brief shore leave when the *Defiant* docked at Southampton for repairs and refuelling. Mabel and Beryl were preparing his room and excitedly counting the days, Daisy said. Lily knew that there would be no time for him to see her, and told herself not to be selfish for even wishing it.

And then, suddenly, his leave was cancelled. Just two weeks after that last terrible air raid on London, news came through that the battle cruiser HMS *Hood*, the largest ship in the navy, had been sunk in the Atlantic by the new German battleship the *Bismarck*, and only a small handful out of a crew of over fourteen hundred men had survived. Lily felt herself go cold at the thought of all the mourning parents, sisters, wives and sweethearts bereaved by this grievous loss, and knew that Mabel and Beryl would be feeling the same sick apprehension. And not without reason, for the Prime Minister now gave out an order to sink the *Bismarck* at all costs, and every British vessel in the vicinity was brought into the engagement. *Sink the Bismarck!* became the rallying cry against the pride of the German Navy, and reputedly unsinkable; within two days she was pursued, surrounded and repeatedly torpedoed and shelled until she broke and was submerged beneath the Atlantic with all hands.

When the news came through on the wireless, it was announced in the dining room at lunch-time. A great cheer went up: it was the first good news of the war for a very long time, and Lily cheered with the rest.

'Are any of us going to spare a thought for the families who've lost their sons and brothers and husbands from the *Bismarck*?' piped up a first-year sitting near Lily. Her fellow probationers turned to stare at her.

'Oh, trust Bailey to say a thing like that,' muttered one of them irritably 'She's one of these fanatic Roman Catholics – gets up at some ungodly hour on Sunday mornings to go to her church and pray for her co-religionists in Germany and Italy, I dare say.'

Nurse Bailey calmly went on eating her corned beef hash and cabbage. 'We're asked to pray for the Church and the world,' she said simply 'And that means everybody, especially those who're suffering because of this horrible war.'

'You'd better try saying that to Nurse Knowles,' said one of the others. 'She was bombed out of her London hospital, and lost all her friends.'

'Yes, and I've got a – a brother in the navy whose leave was cancelled because of the *Bismarck*,' added Lily. 'And if he's lost at sea, don't ask me to weep for the crew of the U-boat that kills him.' Her voice shook as she spoke, and Nurse Bailey, a fresh-faced girl of eighteen, replied quietly, 'I shall pray for him, Nurse Knowles.'

It was easy to dismiss the girl as a little prig, but her words disturbed Lily, and made her think of Mabel, who saw no difference between mothers sorrowing for their sons, whatever their nationality.

The latest news of Tim, now a leading seaman, was that his postponed leave had also been curtailed to a mere two nights at home, after which he and Billy Webb had been sent to join the crew of the aircraft carrier HMS *Ark Royal*.

'The time went by in a flash,' wrote Aunt Daisy, 'and we were all very upset at having to say goodbye again so soon.'

'*Lily!* How good to see you. I couldn't believe that you were back at work again – and here in Northampton! Oh, Lily, Lily!'

And before she had realised it, she was seized in Dennis Wardley's arms and kissed, while her grand-parents looked on in some surprise, but not displeased by this display of affection from the young doctor they had known from childhood. Lily had quickly fended off their questions about the brave fighter pilot she had mentioned, informing them that he had been posted away and had lost touch. But now here was Dennis, and there was no doubt about *his* regard for her.

'I've actually been sent home for a week's rest, Lily,' he said, settling beside her on the sofa in the Rawlingses' comfortable drawing room. 'And as soon as I heard you were here, I came straight over. It's just wonderful to see you, especially after that

274

ghastly business at Queen Adelaide's. Oh, I just wanted to grab you out of that bed and carry you off! And I *would* have done too; I'd have defied your father if you'd given me the slightest signal – but now you're back with your grandparents, and they must be overjoyed!' He smiled in their direction, and they nodded happily.

'It's a long story, Dennis, and I'm on good terms with my father again – and his wife, which I'm glad about,' Lily answered. 'He was perfectly happy about me coming back here to finish my training – but, Dennis, you look dreadful! Have you been ill?' she asked as she took a long look at him. 'You're so thin – and pale – and . . .' Her words tailed off in dismay as she noted his muddy complexion and red-rimmed, sunken eyes. 'What's happened to you?'

'Passed out in the middle of a ward.' He shrugged almost apologetically. 'The chaps in the services think it's an easy way out of the war, Lily, but when you're the only house officer on the horizon for days on end, it's no picnic. Remember how I used to say I hadn't time to get my hair cut? Well, just lately I've hardly taken my clothes off – it's been night and day. So when I literally fell down in the shafts, they sent me back home for a breather.'

'Then you ought to be catching up on sleep, Dennis!'

'That's the general idea, but as soon as Ma and Pa told me that you were here, I was on my way! When are you back on duty?'

'Four o'clock. I'm on an afternoon off.'

'Then I'll see you whenever you're off tomorrow, and the day after. We'll go for a drink – a walk beside the Nene. Oh, Lily!' He took her right hand in both of his. 'Remember that Sunday afternoon up at Ken

Wood, with London shimmering below us – and the music? I've never forgotten, have you?'

She smiled and nodded. 'I remember. It was just before the war began – another world.'

And I remember who else was there on that sunny afternoon when the orchestra played the 'Intermezzo' from the *Karelia* suite, she thought. Yes, that had been another world . . .

'Come on, I'll escort you back to the hospital,' he said. 'And we'll arrange an evening out together. Don't worry, Mrs Rawlings, I just need a little time with her all to myself!'

'It's quite all right, Dennis, dear. We know that she's in good hands with you,' said the old lady, catching her husband's eye.

But Lily knew that she would have to be careful not to raise the hopes of this good friend. The long, unsocial hours of a probationer's life would have to be made an excuse for limiting their meetings during his brief leave. The probationers were allowed one late pass per month, and when Lily obtained hers for his last night, she begged him to take her to the Northampton Repertory Theatre to see a performance of Shaw's *You Never Can Tell* rather than go for a drive in the country. They strolled back to the nurses' home, and he got a good night kiss, with which he had to be content.

'Good night, dearest Lily. I can wait, you know,' he told her, and kissed her again.

Halfway into June Lily was transferred to Gribble ward, male surgical and orthopaedic. The first-year probationer was young Nurse Bailey, a conscientious worker but with no knowledge of men, and an easy target for their good-natured but embarrassing jokes.

'I'm not lucky enough to have a brother, like you, Nurse Knowles,' she confided. 'I was an only child, and went to a convent boarding school.'

'Oh, how could your parents send you away like that?' Lily asked in surprised indignation.

'It was because my mother died, and my father couldn't be expected to look after me on his own,' replied the girl in a matter-of-fact tone. 'I had a very good education, and the nuns thought I'd got the makings of a nurse. I like it well enough, but I prefer looking after women!'

Lily found herself warming to the girl, and noticed that she was in fact very attractive to the younger men, such as the dark-eyed Italian prisoner of war who had been injured in an accident with a farm tractor. His name was Giancarlo Bottiglieri, which nobody could pronounce, so Sister gave the nurses permission to call him Mr Carlo. The other patients were suspicious of him, especially when discussing the apparent lull in the progress of the war. There had been no further serious air attacks for a month, and old Mr Pardoe in the end bed didn't like it.

'I bet that ol' bastard 'Itler's cookin' up somethin' new an' 'orrible for us,' he predicted.

'Mind what yer say in front of Signor So-So over there,' warned the man in the next bed.

'Go on, 'e can't make out a word we're sayin',' retorted Mr Pardoe.

'Don't be too sure. I wouldn't trust any o' them Eye-ties further'n I could spit – they're our *enemies*, if you ain't forgot, Granddad.'

Seeing them looking in his direction, the young man gave them a brilliant smile.

'*Va bene*,' he said, waving his good arm, the other being in plaster.

'An' the same to you with knobs on, mate,' growled Mr Pardoe's neighbour.

Lily hid a smile. 'Come on, Nurse Bailey, it's time to give out urine bottles. I'll wheel the trolley, and you pull the screens across the door.'

But at that moment the ward doors opened and Sister appeared to make an announcement. It seemed that the wireless had just broadcast the amazing news that Germany had turned upon Russia, her former ally, catching the Red Army totally unprepared, and German panzer divisions were smashing ahead in an invasion that must surely have Moscow in its sights. Mr Churchill had responded by promising the Russian leader, Marshal Stalin, what help Britain was able to give, but the general response was shock and disbelief.

'Well, if it means that he lays off us for a bit, so much the better,' said one of the men, voicing the general opinion, though nobody could decide whether this was good or bad news.

Mr Carlo smiled delightedly, though whether he understood or not was doubtful.

'Hitler must have tremendous military strength,' remarked Nurse Bailey. 'Either that or he's completely mad.'

Lily could not work up much interest, and in any case she was getting more and more excited as Wednesday, 25 June drew closer, until it was next week – and then it was tomorrow – and finally it was *today*! Oh, to see London again, even after the savagery of the bombing . . . and to see Beatrice and Hanna – it would be like coming home.

And there it was, as the train drew into Euston Station: it was still standing, the buses were still running, and the people were out enjoying the midsummer sunshine. It was not yet noon, for Lily had caught an early train, and now she decided to walk all the way, so as to take in as much as she could of the city she loved. When she saw the dome of St Paul's, her spirits lifted in thankfulness; here she would rest and wait until the service was due to begin.

Waiting at the top of the broad flight of steps, she wondered who would be the next to appear. She was about to go inside and sit down when she caught sight of an RAF officer coming up the steps towards her. Was it . . . Could he be . . . ? Her heart leaped, but it was Ned Carter who approached her, whipping off his peaked cap and smiling in recognition.

'It *is* Lily Knowles, isn't it? I heard from Beatrice that you'd escaped by a whisker, and I was so glad. How are you?' he asked, kissing her, and she saw that he was wearing the Distinguished Flying Medal. 'Beatrice is already here, you know, and sent me to look out for you. They came in by the north transept. Come on, there's a place reserved for you!'

She followed him up the nave to the seats below the dome, where Beatrice Massey sat in her wheelchair beside her parents and two sisters. Her body was rigidly encased in a spinal jacket beneath her dress, but she held out her arms to Lily.

'Lily, you're here! We're both here. Oh, who'd have believed we'd ever meet again?'

Lily bent over her friend to exchange a kiss – and received another kiss from the Dowager Countess whose soft, papery skin trembled against the faces of her surviving nurses. Lord Portland, Hetty's father, and his wife and family were there with other bereaved parents, so there was much mournful hand-shaking and whispered condolences. The seats gradually filled, and solemn music was playing as Nurse Blumfeldt burst in at the last moment, having been delayed by a maternity case, to take her place beside her parents and Dr Edlinger.

The service lasted an hour, the lessons were read by visiting consultants, and the eulogy was given by the Dean, on behalf of the Dowager Countess. The final hymn was 'For all the saints who from their labours rest', and after the final farewells the Masseys invited Lily, Hanna and Wing Commander Carter to tea with them at Claridges, where they were staying for two nights. Hanna made her apologies, whispering to Lily that she did not want Dr Edlinger to think that she was hanging around just to see *him*, but Lily gladly accepted, noting that she would have to leave in time for her train. It was a wonderful opportunity to talk with Beatrice, who looked better than expected, though she was rather tired by now.

'I've got to go back into hospital for more tests on my lumbar spine before I can be fitted with an artificial leg, Lily,' she said. 'That's if I can ever stand upright again, of course.'

'Beatrice dear, your consultant has every hope of you walking within the year,' said her mother with a significant nod towards Lily. Ned Carter was all attention, and seemed chattily at home with the whole family, so Lily decided to ask him the question on her mind.

'Er – do you ever see anything of Sandy Redfern these days, Ned?' she asked casually, and saw him hesitate. He glanced at Beatrice who gave a little nod.

'Not a lot, Lily. He's been off on ops all over Europe and North Africa, and besides, there's been a bit of a – a shenanigans over a – a lady,' he said, sounding oddly embarrassed for a man well experienced in the ways of the world. 'There's a divorce coming up, actually.'

'Divorce? D-do you mean he's married?' gasped Lily.

'No, no, *he's* not. It's the lady who's left her husband. Didn't you meet the Palmer-Bournes, Lily? She's something of a beauty.'

'In more ways than one, by the sound of it,' said one of the married sisters drily, but Beatrice saw the shock on Lily's face.

'I'm sorry, Lily, but I did hear something about it – and it'll be all over the papers soon,' she said in a low voice. 'Hetty said how badly he'd behaved towards you at that Covent Garden ballroom, but I never thought he'd go off the rails with the wife of a friend. He was – is – a very brave man, but – well, you never know what things people will do in a time of war, do you?'

Lily shook her head. It was another of those moments when she must hide what she truly felt. And she did, quite successfully.

'I'm surprised too, Beatrice, but we weren't in touch any more, so it doesn't really make any difference,' she managed, speaking lightly. 'Is there any more tea? Oh, thank you, I'd love another cup. And what about you, Beatrice? Shall I pour you one? Milk and sugar?'

Which made them both remember the Honourable Henrietta Tarrant, and the tea-dances at the Queen's Theatre in Shaftesbury Avenue.

Beatrice was right: before the week was out the more sensational newspapers seized on the romantic affair of the beautiful Daphne, a former débutante whose lavish wedding to Air Commodore Peter Palmer-

Bourne in the mid-1930s had now brought her into new prominence as a service wife, bravely supporting her husband on the home front and holding down an important job with the Ministry of Information. She was like a more glamorous version of Mrs Miniver in the much-acclaimed film of that name – until in a turn of events worthy of a Hollywood drama starring Bette Davis or Merle Oberon, this woman had renounced convention to follow the dictates of her heart. She had fallen in love with Battle of Britain hero Group Captain Alexander Redfern, holder of the Distinguished Flying Cross and double bar, and for love's sake she had left her Maida Vale home and husband, to live openly with him. They were to be seen everywhere together, holding hands, gazing into each other's eyes, oblivious to the clicking cameras; they were the golden lovers of the moment.

And the British public lapped it up. They rushed out to buy their popular newspapers, depleted in size but full of details of the delicious scandal, complete with photographs of Daphne and her group captain. It provided a real-life love story, a much-needed change from the dreary news of the war, the black-out, the shortages, the increasing pinch of rationing.

At Northampton General, the opinions on Gribble ward were divided between the nurses who pitied Redfern for falling under the spell of a woman who had neither principles nor virtue, and the patients who thought him a lucky devil: for who could condemn a war hero?

'I suppose she sees herself as a modern version of Lady Hamilton,' said a third-year, but Lily had to keep her thoughts to herself as she heard the comments all around her. What would they say if they knew that Alexander Redfern had once made love to *her*, Nurse Knowles? Now he was getting all the passionate lovemaking that he could desire, from an older and experienced woman who knew how to avoid the natural consequences of the act of love. Beatrice had hinted that he was not worth Lily's tears, but only Lily knew how sharply she still felt the pain of rejection, remembering those golden hours they had shared together.

'Nurse Knowles – Nurse Knowles, there's been a serious house fire in the town, and a whole family has been brought in with severe burns, so can you get up and come on duty early this morning?'

It was five o'clock, two hours before her normal time for going on duty, and the home sister, wearing a dressing gown, had brought Lily a cup of tea.

'What? Oh, yes, Sister, I'll come right away,' Lily replied, leaping out of bed.

'I believe you have some experience of air-raid casualties and burns?'

'Er – oh, yes, I saw some bad burns,' she mumbled in reply, pulling off her nightdress as the sister withdrew, closing the door.

She dressed in haste, swallowed the tea and made her way over to the main hospital block. It was already light at the start of a summer's day as she pushed open the doors of Gribble ward and was at once assailed by a horrible smell of burning: it was a *dirty* smell.

'Ah, there you are, Nurse Knowles. Matron suggested calling you over,' said the night sister, her uniform smeared with brownish stains. 'You're to attend the patient in the first single, a Mr Childs, an elderly man. He and his daughter, son-in-law and two grandchildren have been in a house fire, and he has severe injuries. He'll need constant specialling.' She paused to draw a breath and then added, 'It won't be easy, Nurse. You'll have to stay calm. There's a pile of clean barrier nursing gowns on that trolley. Put one on over your uniform, and theatre gloves. The doctors are with him now.'

Lily entered the cubicle and saw the figure lying on the stripped bed. It was blackened by charred fragments of pyjamas and burned flesh. The face was unrecognisable, and exposed skin surfaces were blistered and red-raw. The smell was like roasted meat with smoky, sooty overtones. For one moment Lily thought she was going to retch, but repressed it, took a breath and nodded to the doctors. 'Good morning, sir.'

'Oh, hello, Nurse. We've got a bit of a problem here,' said the consultant surgeon. 'This old boy managed to set fire to a highly inflammable armchair, and has got second- or third-degree burns over about seventy per cent of his body area. So we need to keep him warm, replace lost body fluid, and clean him up – which means virtually hosing him down with saline solution to get the bits off – and giving him morphine, intravenously if we can find a vein.' He pursed his lips and shook his head, indicating that there was little hope for Mr Childs.

The morphia was duly administered, and Lily assisted the registrar with the cleaning-up process, using warm, dripping-wet saline compresses and forceps to pick off fragments of clothing and detached skin. The registrar looked sick.

'His son-in-law's in the next cubicle with burns of chest and neck – he'll need a tracheotomy if his throat swells,' he muttered. 'The woman's over in female surgical, and the kids have gone to children's. I don't know how bad they are, but Granddad here will have to be covered all over in some sort of oil or jelly and slung up in a hammock, I should think. God!'

Lily spent all that day with Mr Childs, with just half an hour's break to have a midday meal and change her soiled clothing. Even her underwear was permeated by the sickly odour that filled the cubicle and wafted down the corridor. She watched the old man's condition deteriorate, until, just after six that evening, his heartbeat stopped. When she had wrapped him in a covering shroud, Lily was sent off duty to take a bath and rest.

Exhausted, she slept for part of the night, but then lay awake with troubling thoughts. It had been her first experience of actually nursing a patient with extensive burns, and it had left her feeling useless and inadequate. She almost dreaded going on duty the next day, assuming that she would be sent to 'special' the younger man. In fact she was sent straight to the end four-bedder where she and Staff Nurse shared the care of Mr Willows, the son-in-law, and his wife who had been brought over to be nursed alongside her husband, so as to pool resources in this particular emergency. Lily hoped that the couple would benefit by being nursed together.

It was exacting work, and constant vigilance was needed. A tracheotomy tube had been inserted into Mr Willows' throat to assist his breathing, and it needed to be kept clear. Intravenous fluids were running, sulphonamide therapy had been commenced, and the radiators turned up to keep the room temperature high. It was the changing of dressings that was by far the worst part: whatever ointment or medicated jelly was used, the dressings

285

adhered to the raw flesh, and large doses of morphia could scarcely deaden the agonising pain, until both nurses tearfully pleaded that some other treatment be tried.

'I've been in touch with the RAF hospital at Halton, and they say to lower them into baths of warm saline, to let the dressings float off,' the surgeon told them. 'They get a lot of airmen with extensive burns there, and they say that it's the best way. We'll have to get the plumbers to install a couple of baths in their room, connected up to the water supply, and work out how much salt we need per gallon, and then get hold of hoists to lift them in and out. Quite an undertaking.' He grimaced.

Lily never forgot how thankful they all were on Gribble ward when the saline bath treatment proved its worth and removed the fear from the patients' eyes. After immersion for an hour, light dressings were applied of gauze netting impregnated with paraffin and halibut liver oil, and these stayed on until the next immersion. The couple began to improve, and to ask about their children, who had burns of their legs and buttocks, which were responding to the same treament.

It transpired that old Mr Childs had caused the fire by lighting his pipe downstairs and igniting the armchair in which he sat. Being a hot July night, the flames had quickly spread to curtains and within minutes had roared up the wooden stairs, trapping the couple with their children.

'We should be thankful that it was the old man who died,' said Lily with a sigh.

'You mean his daughter and her husband would never have forgiven him?' asked the staff nurse on duty with her.

'I mean that he'd never have forgiven himself, poor old man,' replied Lily, for whom the tragedy of the Willows family had put her own disappointments into perspective.

And had also made her think about where her nursing skills might be employed in the future.

Chapter 13

'They thought at first I'd be paralysed from the waist down for life, but luckily the spinal cord was only bruised and not permanently damaged,' said Beatrice, shifting in her wheelchair and wincing. 'Oh, Lily, I'll never forget the day I first wiggled my toes! And when I was able to control my bladder, what a relief *that* was. It's been a bit of a stalemate since, though.'

'Your specialist says you will walk again, though it may take some time. You'll just have to be very patient with yourself,' said Lily gently. The lines around her friend's eyes and the tension of her jaw were evidence of her battle against pain and discouragement at her slow progress. Six months after the night of her ordeal she could only walk a few tottering steps with crutches and a newly fitted artificial limb, but the pain in her lower back and stump was so severe that she dreaded her daily practice.

'Yes, I know I must persevere, because – well, if I don't, I can't marry Ned – or anybody. Not in this condition.' She spoke calmly, but Lily knew that she meant every word.

'You will, Beattie dear, I know you will. He loves you, and what better reason is there for you to persevere?' Lily reached for her hand. 'We're survivors, you and I.'

There was a click as the casement door opened and

Mrs Massey came out on to the terrace with a tray of coffee, which she set down on the table beside the two young women.

'There's not a servant to be had for gold,' she shrugged. 'I'm lucky to have a woman from the village who comes in to do the heavy cleaning – otherwise I have to cope on my own.'

'Oh, thank you, Mrs Massey!' Lily exclaimed. 'I was just thinking how lovely and peaceful it is here. After night duty, it's paradise!'

They were seated on the sunlit terrace of Thorpe Place, and below them lay the garden. Half the lawn was given over to vegetables, and the central fountain no longer splashed over the three nymphs entwined on their stone plinth. Major Massey, a survivor of the Great War and now nearing seventy, was digging up potatoes ready for lifting, and beyond the garden wall was a green meadow where his dairy herd grazed. The piggeries were hidden by a small orchard with ripe apples, pears and plums ready for picking. It was a perfect rural scene.

'Coffee's ready, Farmer Jack!' Mrs Massey called, and the major straightened up and planted his fork in the ground. Within minutes he had joined them.

'How's my best girl today?' he enquired, anxiously regarding his daughter.

Beatrice smiled and said she was much better for having Lily with her.

'Lily's been saying how peaceful it is, but things aren't always what they seem,' smiled Mrs Massey. 'We had three evacuees and their mother staying with us at the beginning of the war, but they went back to London, and I'd like to say I was sorry, but I wasn't. I've said I can't take any children while

289

Beatrice is convalescing here – and they've sent us Italian prisoners of war to work on the farm instead of land girls!'

'Do they work well?' asked Lily. 'We sometimes get them in as patients, and they're really no trouble at all – quite helpful, in fact, once they're up and about.'

'A mixed bunch,' replied the major. 'You have to watch them the whole time, or they'll sit around and babble all day. Good with the evacuees from the village, though – it's amazing how the kids rush to join them as soon as school's out – and there's an end to work for the day.'

Not surprisingly, thought Lily; prisoners or evacuees, they're all away from their homes, and living among strangers.

Beatrice was telling her parents about the Willows family, and how the man and wife had been immersed in baths to remove their dressings.

'And even after all that, Mother, Lily said the poor husband's burns turned septic and he died of blood poisoning in the isolation ward at Northampton. Wasn't that dreadful?'

Lily closed her eyes at the memory of how they had all cried over Mr Willows' death, five days after his father-in-law, leaving Mrs Willows a widow with two young children to bring up. The fact that her husband would have been badly disfigured was no consolation.

'I thought these new M and B tablets were able to kill germs,' remarked the major. 'They cured Mr Churchill's pneumonia, didn't they?'

'Sulphonamides only prevent the spread of bacteria, they don't actually kill them,' explained Lily. 'Sepsis is what we fear most on all the wards. It's the big killer.' She sighed, and Mrs Massey abruptly changed the subject.

'How do you like night duty, Lily?' she asked, pouring coffee.

'It's not so bad if you can sleep in the daytime, and it's lovely to see the dawn rise if we're not too busy to notice it,' Lily answered. 'But the best thing about night duty is that we work for six nights and then have two off – and I've saved a night from last time, so now I've got three off in a row, which gives me time to come here. It just wouldn't have been possible on day duty.'

She did not add that coming to Wiltshire meant forgoing a visit to Pinehurst for her twenty-fourth birthday; she felt that Beatrice needed her more, and planned to visit Pinehurst on her next nights off.

Their talk turned to the progress of the war, and the cessation of bombing raids.

'Hitler's ranged all his available forces, including the Luftwaffe, in this assault on Russia,' said the major. 'Be thankful we're not in Leningrad. It must be hell on earth.'

Lily was silent, remembering the hell on earth of the Blitz. As at Northampton, she sometimes found it difficult to listen to observations on the war from people who had not personally endured night after night of aerial bombardment, the death and destruction.

Major Massey continued to talk about the situation abroad, particularly in the Western Desert of North Africa, where there had been a lot of fighting around Tobruk. 'The Eighth Army will find that General Rommel's Afrika Korps is a force to be reckoned with,' he said gloomily.

Lily knew that the British Commonwealth forces

had been restyled as the Eighth Army, the 'Desert Rats', and thought of Geoffrey Westhouse. Poor Geoffrey, was he a Desert Rat too? It seemed so long since they had walked and talked in London while the shadow of war loomed.

'It's high time America woke up and did something more than sending us a few food parcels and these damned films,' the major grumbled, adding cryptically, 'They may find that this time next year they'll have no choice. I don't trust those little yellow bastards out there in the South Pacific.'

'That's enough, Jack,' said his wife with a frown. 'Lily doesn't want to hear all this war talk when she's on a visit. Let's just be thankful for a respite from those horrible air raids, and hope that the Russians can defend themselves.'

'I doubt it,' he muttered darkly, and Beatrice looked worried, which made Lily quite cross with the major and his glum forecasts. Of course, he must be terribly worried about Beatrice, she reminded herself. *Oh Lord, please let her walk again, and find happiness with Ned – let them both be spared, please!* she prayed.

But at a time like this, nothing seemed certain, nothing could be relied upon. Lily tried to cling to her faith and to believe, with Mr Churchill, that victory would be won over the powers of evil, but there was bitter news that November.

The blow fell with casual unconcern while she was assisting in the theatre. It was the last operation on the list, and the surgeon relaxed a little as he put in the skin sutures to a hand wound.

'Sounds as if Hitler's panzer divisions have nearly reached Moscow,' he remarked to the anaesthetist.

'Ah, but he's coming up against another enemy,

the same one that did for Napoleon,' came the reply. 'The Russian winter will slow them up! Thirty degrees below freezing, and the worst is still to come. I think he'll find he's made a big mistake – and so will his troops, poor devils.'

'Let's hope you're right. We need some good news after this appalling loss of the *Ark Royal*,' went on the surgeon, taking a threaded needle from Lily's hand; she hesitated only for a second, and proceeded to thread another.

'Yeah, that's a big blow. Bloody Italian submarine, according to the wireless this morning. Just off the coast of Gibraltar, they said.'

'Not far from land, then. A fair chance of the crew being picked up, wouldn't you think?'

'Depends. According to what I heard, she started to list as soon as she was hit, and sunk while under tow – it'll be in the papers tomorrow.'

'Hm, after they've changed the facts round a bit.' The surgeon gave a final touch to the incision. 'All right, Nurse, we want a tulle gras dressing here. Sulphonamide powder? – good. Cotton bandage – thanks. Everything OK your end?' The anaesthetist nodded. 'Right, let's get the porter in. Don't know about you, but I'm ready for my lunch.'

Somehow or other Lily got the trolley cleared and put the instruments to rinse. In the changing room she took off her theatre gown and replaced her uniform dress and cap. Instead of going to the dining room she went up to her own room and kneeled down beside her bed.

Her absence was noted, however, and in a few minutes there was a gentle tap on her door.

'Are you all right, Nurse Knowles?' asked a familiar voice. 'Will you open the door, please?'

When there was no reply, Nurse Bailey turned the door handle and found it unlocked; she went in, to find Lily standing and staring at her with horror-stricken eyes.

'It's the *Ark Royal*,' she whispered. 'Oh, Nurse Bailey, it's the *Ark Royal*.'

'Is that the ship your brother's on? Oh, Nurse Knowles – it's been hit, hasn't it?'

'They were talking about it in theatre.'

'Don't give up hope – don't give up hope, Knowles,' urged the first-year, dropping the formality of the title while off duty. 'He may have survived. It wasn't as if they were out in the middle of the Atlantic.'

'Oh, I don't know. I'd give anything to know. And somehow I've got to go on working.'

'Yes, and it's the best thing for you, really, isn't it? Only you must eat as well! I shall come with you to the dining room and see that you do.'

'Thank you, Bailey, you're very kind, but – thank you, I suppose you're right.'

Other probationers looked askance at the 'hob-nobbing', as they called it, between a first- and a third-year, with six years' difference in their ages, but Lily took no notice of them. Bailey's early experiences had given her a maturity beyond her years, and Lily was thankful to unburden herself to a sympathetic ear. She confessed that Tim was not actually a brother, but that they had grown up together and were especially close.

'Do you mean that you're in love with him, Lily?' asked Bailey in her direct way. It was the first time that anybody had asked Lily this question, and the first time that she had actually considered it. She shook her head, remembering how she had felt for

Sandy Redfern, the joy and the overwhelming passion.

'No, I'm not in love with him – but I think he may be with me. And we *all* love him at Pinehurst. Oh, Nurse Bailey, pray that he's alive and not drowned. Oh God, let him be saved!'

The newpapers carried the details the next day. The aircraft carrier had been struck as she was heading for the shelter of Gibraltar, and had sunk very quickly. There were rumours of all her crew being lost, of all being saved, and varying reports of men being picked up out of the water by a destroyer.

The telegram from Dr Knowles arrived at Matron's office, and Lily was called from the operating theatre where she was currently working a late afternoon shift. She closed her mind to the possibilities as she made her way over to the administrative offices to find the deputy matron, Miss Scott, waiting for her with the telegram in her hand. And she was smiling.

'It's from your father, Nurse Knowles, and it's good news. I know, because he has spoken to me on the telephone. You may open it now if you wish, or take it to read in private.'

Lily tore it open and saw the words: TIM ARRIVED SOUTHAMPTON STOP TAKEN TO HASLAR FOR CHECK THEN HOME STOP DAD.

She stared stupidly at the row of capital letters, unable to make any sense of them.

'It is good news, isn't it, Nurse Knowles?' said Miss Scott gently. 'Would you like to read it out aloud?'

'"Tim arrived Southampton" – oh, yes, Miss Scott, *yes*! It's wonderful news – thank you!'

Letters followed, including one from Tim himself, and this time Lily was determined to make the journey to Belhampton to see him during his leave;

he would be home until mid-December, he said. When working in the general theatres, staff had alternate weekends free, so that the department was open for emergencies. Lily put in her special request for the Saturday and Sunday of 6 and 7 December, and waited with bated breath for the duty roster to go up.

And she had it! Plus an early shift on the Friday, enabling her to get off duty at half-past three, in time to catch the afternoon train to Euston. Crossing London might take anything from half an hour to an hour – and from Waterloo to Belhampton would take another hour and a quarter; she reckoned she would be at Pinehurst by nine o'clock.

In fact it was past ten when the train steamed into the little station after a long, cold, dark and uncomfortable journey, including an interminable wait at Waterloo, which seemed to be full of sailors returning from leave and ambulances waiting to receive wounded from Southampton, on the last lap of their journey from North Africa. At least London was now considered relatively safe for them, she noted thankfully.

Her train was the last to stop at Belhampton before the morning mail delivery, and the old porter and ticket collector was waiting to lock up and go home.

'The Doctor's been down an' says ye're to go up to Station Cottage, Miss Lily, an' tell Hyde ye're here, an' he'll take ye up in his ol' bone-shaker!'

Lily shivered as she walked out of the deserted station into the raw December night. She had not expected to be met at such a late hour, but she now realised how tired and chilled she was, after being up since five o'clock. Mr Hyde, the taxi-man, was waiting for her.

'C'mon, Miss Lily, ye're late – they'll be wonderin' where yer got to. Give us yer bag, an' in ye get. Let's hope she'll start on her own – she been playin' up lately.'

Two attempts at ignition failed, and Lily sighed with relief at the vibrating chug-chug-chug on the third.

'Have you seen Tim, Mr Hyde?' she asked as they rattled up the lane.

'Brought him up from the station like I'm doin' now, Miss Lily – poor lad was just about done in. Ye should ha' seen Mrs Knowles's face when he got off the train! "Tim, me own dear boy," she said, "thank God ye're home!" Always been like a son to her, has Tim. Well, here we are – no lights on, but I bet yer dad an' Tim'll be waitin' up for ye. No, no, Miss Lily, the Doctor's already paid – here's yer bag an' there's the door openin'. Must ha' heard us comin'. G'night!'

The door was open, and Lily almost stumbled over the step in the darkness – but she was at once caught up in a man's arms and held against his chest. Against his heart.

'Lily – oh, Lily, ye're home at last, me own darlin' Lily.'

A lamp burned dimly in the hall where the long-case clock kept time, ticking away the hours. Over Tim's shoulder she saw her father's tired smile, and there was Mabel and Daisy and Miss Styles and Beryl, all waiting to greet her, to ask about her journey, what time she had left Northampton – and to say her supper was in the oven, and did she want a hot drink?

And to apologise for not meeting her at the station. 'I'm so sorry, Lily,' said her father, 'I went down a couple of times, and then Mabel wouldn't let me out

297

again – and *I* wouldn't let Tim out, although he was begging to go – he's a bit chesty after all he's been through, so in the end I asked Hyde to wait for you. I hope you didn't feel let down, my dear.'

'Of course I didn't, Dad. I'm just so happy to be home,' she said, hugging him.

'Christmas has come early this year!' smiled Daisy. 'How long have you got?'

'Got to go back Sunday night, but never mind, there's all day tomorrow, and I'm going to make the most of every minute. We'll forget all about the war, just for two days!'

Only Beryl Penney's pale, anxious little face was not smiling as she watched Tim Baxter kissing the girl he called his 'darlin' Lily'.

That Saturday was a day to remember. After the midday meal Tim wanted to take Lily and the older children for a walk along the footpath that skirted the top of the common and up to Parr's Wood. Mabel shook her head.

'Yer can take the five big ones, Tim, but not Joe. He's just gettin' over a cold. And Daisy and Beryl can go along with yer, otherwise they'll be runnin' all over the place. Me and Miss Styles'll stay home with the little ones.'

As always, Mabel's word was law, and Beryl noticeably brightened as she put on her hat, coat, scarf and gloves, and saw that the five delighted children were similarly wrapped up against the winter weather. Daisy smiled and gave everybody their orders.

'Right, Beryl, you and Tim go on ahead with the three boys, and Lily and I will bring up the rear with the girls. Be careful how you go, the footpath's bound

298

to be muddy. Now, Lily, I want you to tell me all about those enormous wards at Northampton General – and that dreadful case of the family who were burned in the house fire.'

Lily was quite happy to walk and talk with Daisy, who was now more like a sister than an aunt, and Tim had to hide his disappointment as they trudged the first couple of miles, but when they began the ascent to Parr's Wood, he waited for the others to catch up, and said they must climb in single file, with himself at the back. As they proceeded, Lily begged Daisy to bring her up to date with the local news.

'Did I tell you that Bever House has been taken over as a convalescent home for the military since you were last here?' asked Daisy. 'Poor chaps with mental problems, so I've heard, so it's a nice country retreat for them.'

'Ah, yes, that lovely old manor house overlooking Beversley,' said Lily, nodding. 'Wasn't it built in the eighteenth century for the de Bever family?'

'Yes, but it was a sad story. The young bride died in childbirth, and the husband, Lord de Bever, was the last of the line. The house passed to a nephew, but there were tales of gambling and debts, and at the turn of the century it was a girls' school. Well, now it's got a new lease of life. Oh, this is hard going, isn't it? The ground's slippery after the rain – whoops! Watch where you're going, Dickie!'

At the summit they were rewarded for their effort, for the sun came out from behind a cloud bank and poured rays of winter sunlight over fields and farmland; further to the west they could see the beginning of Wychell Forest, dark and dense. To the south lay the ancient village of Beversley, separated from Belhampton by the five-mile stretch of common.

299

'Isn't it a sight to behold, Lily?' Tim whispered to her. 'I reckon there's somethin' special about the beauty of a winter afternoon, don't you? Look at how the kids are starin'!'

'Yes – oh, yes, it's like a promise of hope – of victory at the end,' she replied, remembering that other winter climb, two years ago at Box Hill. Oh, why did *he* have to keep coming back to mind? She felt Tim's gloved hand in hers.

'This is what I've dreamed about at sea, Lily – you an' me with the children, lookin' after 'em like we are now.' His voice was low and urgent, as if he wanted to say what was in his heart before they were interrupted. 'Yer dad's not too well, Lily, and Mum isn't as strong as she was. One day, after the war's over, Pinehurst'll need another matron an' – husband, if my prayers are answered, I know who –'

'Now, now, you two gossips, it's getting chilly,' said Daisy briskly. 'Soon it'll be dark, and we don't want to be stranded likes babes-in-the-wood, do we? Off you go, Leading Seaman Baxter, and take Beryl and the boys with you. Lily and I will follow with the girls. Come on, everybody, we've got muffins for tea!'

Tim looked blank for a moment, but Lily was thankful; she felt shaken by what had been so nearly said. Now she knew that there was no mistake: Tim loved her and wanted to marry her. She blamed herself for being so blind, and knew that she must give him no encouragement. And yet – should she send him back to sea with no hope at all? She loved him so much as a brother, and dreaded hurting his faithful heart. Could she confide in Daisy? Some inward sense told her that she would not find much sympathy in either Mabel or her younger sister. They

300

would probably both look more favourably on little Beryl Penney, who so obviously adored him.

That evening Lily deliberately engaged Miss Styles in conversation over the toasted muffins, and listened to the deliciously creepy ghost story on the wireless that the older children were allowed to stay up to hear, seated around the fire in the Quiet Room. Her father looked tired, she thought, but was enjoying the cosy winter evening; Mabel looked from him to Tim and back again, rejoicing in having them both near to her. Beryl smiled shyly at Tim, and they exchanged a couple of remarks about the play, but it was obvious that his eyes were only for Lily.

On Sunday morning they all trooped off to church, where the vicar gave thanks for the preservation of Tim Baxter's life from the wreck of the *Ark Royal*, and after dinner Tim asked Lily to put on her coat and walk in the garden with him. Now there was no getting out of it: the moment had arrived.

'Lily dear, you know what I'm going to say.'

'Yes, Tim, I think I do, and the only answer I can give you is that we must wait until the war's over. It's not a good time to make commitments of any kind,' she said in some agitation, avoiding his eyes.

'But, Lily, if we could just reach an understandin' between ourselves, it'd mean so much to me, dear.'

Poor Geoffrey Westhouse's words were being repeated in her ears, and she had to give the same reply that she had given him.

'I honestly don't think it would be right for me to make such a – a promise, Tim. You know that I love you as a brother – more than anybody else in the world, I think, except for my father. But it's not in the way that you're talking – asking – oh, Tim, don't ask me!'

'Then I must ask yer somethin' else, Lily, an' I want yer to give me a truthful answer,' he said solemnly, obviously making an effort. 'Is there somebody else? Some doctor, maybe, like that one who lives in Northampton?'

'No, Tim, Dr Wardley's a good friend, but I'm not in love with him either,' she told him, and then feeling that she had to be absolutely truthful, she added, 'There *was* someone, an officer in the RAF, but he was – wasn't . . .' She faltered, and he reached for her hand.

'Dearest Lily, did he get killed? You can tell me, you know.'

It would have been so easy to say yes, but Tim Baxter deserved the truth. 'No, he was – he's in love with somebody else.'

'Ah, I see. Thank yer for tellin' me, dear. So there's hope for me yet, then?'

'Please, Tim, I can't say anything now. We must wait until after the war.'

'That could be a long way off, Lily.'

'Yes. A lot could happen. A lot could change,' she said resignedly. 'But not now, Tim. Not now.' She tucked his arm under hers. 'It's cold out here – come on, let's go indoors.'

And if the family had been expecting an announcement, they did not get one. Tim might be disappointed, but Mabel caught Daisy's eye and winked.

And then it was time to go to the station for the train back to Waterloo, then on to Euston and Northampton. Lily said goodbye to Mabel at the house, and only her father and Tim came to see her off. Knowles looked the other way when Tim kissed her lovingly and lingeringly, and then she was away.

'Thank you, thank you for a lovely weekend away from the war!' she called out as the train drew out; but by the time she reached Northampton again, the latest news had broken, six hours later than in America, where it was still afternoon: without any declaration of war there had been a terrible surprise attack by Japanese aircraft on the US Navy, the Pacific fleet at anchor in its home base at Pearl Harbor. In two hours some twenty ships and many aircraft had been damaged or destroyed, and between two and three thousand American servicemen were dead. The Japanese had now gained control of the Pacific, clearing the way for a seaborne invasion of Malaya and the Philippines. Hong Kong and the British naval base at Singapore were virtually undefended.

'It's an absolute disaster,' said Grandpapa when Lily next visited, and his gloom seemed all too justified when only three days later came the terrible news of the sinking of the British battleship HMS *Prince of Wales* and the battle cruiser *Repulse*, which, having sailed out to defend Singapore, were attacked by Japanese bombers. Again Lily felt her blood run cold at the thought of the lost crews, either drowned or taken prisoner by the new enemy. Suppose it were Tim – how would she feel at having refused to offer him even a glimmer of hope?

And then she thought of Major Massey, and wondered what *he* was now thinking: could he find a reason for rejoicing at this latest horror? Would he note with satisfaction that the 'little yellow bastards' had done the Allies an enormous favour by catapulting the United States of America into the war?

*

That dark Christmas was not accompanied by much festivity, though not all the disasters were suffered by the Allies; the tide was beginning to turn in Russia, where the German invaders were suffering a series of defeats at the hands of newly mobilised Russian armies. 'General Winter' was indeed on the march, and there was enormous sympathy for the new allies.

As was traditional, a Christmas ball was held at Northampton General, in the nurses' home. Nurses who had suitable partners were permitted to invite them, and invitations were also sent to officers stationed at the barracks in the middle of the town, and to the RAF base at Sywell, some six miles out. There was a great deal of chatter and speculation among the probationers, staff nurses and younger sisters; Nurse Bailey admitted that she would like to attend, though she had never been to a dance in her life and had no evening dress.

'Will you go, Nurse Knowles?' she asked.

'No, somebody has to stay on duty, and I'm happy to be Cinderella. You don't have to wear a long dress, Bailey. Your Sunday best will do! Go and enjoy yourself. It will be an experience for you,' advised Lily, thinking about the two-toned green dress she had lost in the bombing, and of course that lovely Molyneux gown lent to her by dear Hetty – when she had worn it to dance and dine with Sandy, and he'd kissed her in the taxi . . . She sighed, preparing to set the trolley for the first squint correction on the ophthalmic theatre list. She told herself that she was contented with her memories, and felt no inclination to go to the hospital ball at a grim time like the present. A letter had arrived from Tim, who was back on convoy duty in the Atlantic, reunited with the repaired and refurbished HMS *Defiant*, and also with young Billy Webb, who had got married to his sweetheart, Sally, during his leave in London. Lily trembled at the thought of the underwater enemies on their trail, the dreaded German U-boats.

But she reckoned without her grandparents, especially Grandmama's determination to bring her and young Dr Wardley together. She couldn't remember telling them about the date of the ball, but somehow they found it out and informed their GP and his wife, with the consequence that Lily received a note from their son.

'Is there any chance of an invitation to your Christmas hop, Lily? I can arrange to be free on the 19th if you haven't got a more agreeable partner, and need I say I'd be over like a shot!'

What could she say? How could she refuse? Especially when Grandpapa slipped her a ten-pound note to buy a dress at Adnetts, the big, imposing drapery opposite All Saints' Church – and Grandmama produced six clothing coupons from their own books. The clothes rationing system, introduced in June, had been hardly noticed by Lily, who wore uniform most of the time, and she had replenished her lost wardrobe in Belhampton before coupons were issued.

She accepted the money, but said she had enough coupons without taking theirs and, accompanied by Grandmama, she bought a pretty calf-length dress in a soft dove-grey satin. It left her shoulders bare, but had a separate little matching 'coatee', which could be put on and tied with a ribbon just above the bust. It suited her fair hair and skin, and showed off her figure to perfection – in fact Nurse Bailey was so impressed that she decided to attend too, even though partnerless. The dark-patterned print dress she wore for church accentuated her youth, and Lily thought how sweet and unaffected she was, whilst quite unaware of her own appeal.

And so Cinderella went to the ball after all . . .

'By Jove, Lily, you look ravishing!' exclaimed Dennis when he met her in the entrance hall of the nurses' home.

She blushed, as pleased with the compliment as any girl would have been. Heads turned in their direction, and some fellow probationers were frankly surprised at this transformation of the serious third-year who had few friends and spent most of her off-duty with her grandparents. Lily acknowledged their glances with a radiant smile, introducing her partner as Dr Dennis Wardley from Bart's, which sent their eyebrows up even higher, and clearly impressed Matron, who asked him about his plans for the next year or two.

'A good question, actually, Lily,' he said, taking her arm and leading her to the bar. 'I was going to ask you the same. You've done your eight-month stint here, haven't you?'

'Yes, at the end of the month. I sit for Finals in February, though I won't get the hospital certificate and badge – or the St Mildred's one either,' she said sadly. 'Never mind – and yes, I have got some ideas about what to do next.'

'Go on,' he prompted.

'I seem to have reasonably good theatre skills, Dennis, and I've heard about this place at Park Prewett where some chap's doing all sorts of things with skin grafts for burns.'

'Yes, it's called plastic surgery, and there's another

306

pioneer at East Grinstead. But, Lily, this is amazing, because I'd like to take it up too, as my war service. So guess what I'm planning, after all I've said to the contrary. I'm going to join the RAF as an MO, and take a course at Halton, where they've got a big burns unit – and it's expanding all the time.'

'Oh, Dennis, that's marvellous! Haven't we come a long way since that Christmas two years ago, when you came to the dance at St Mildred's, but we ended up in theatre with poor Mrs Young and her dreadful eye injury – remember?'

'How could I ever forget that night, Lily? Perhaps that's where it all began, even though I nearly passed out at the sight of that eye! But look, why don't you do the same, and join up? Become a – what do they call themselves? – a Princess Mary's Royal Air Force Nursing Sister! That would be the best way to get the widest experience – and think of the prestige!'

'Hang the prestige, I just want to do something worthwhile,' Lily retorted. 'But I'd have to think about it. Come on, they're playing "Follow the Yellow Brick Road" – listen!'

'How do you dance to that?'

'You link arms and skip, like this!'

It turned out to be an unexpectedly pleasant evening, and Lily was amused to see Nurse Bailey being taught to waltz by a young lieutenant; they both seemed to be taking it very seriously, but not without enjoyment.

After supper, while the orchestra was taking a break, Lily and Dennis retired to a quiet nook near the foot of the stairs, where a home sister discreetly sat on guard to deter visitors from attempting to climb them.

'Er – I suppose you've seen all this rather pathetic

stuff in the papers about the, er, great lovers of our time,' he said casually, and Lily stiffened.

'Why, is there any news? Are they married yet?' she replied in an equally off-hand tone.

'No, for the simple reason that the fascinating Daphne isn't divorced yet. Maybe Palmer-Bourne's hanging on and hoping that she'll go back to him – I don't know. I'd keep my options open if I were her. Redfern's not twenty-four yet, and she must be thirty-five if she's a day. What's the betting that he'll dump her when this show's over?'

Lily knew that Dennis was only trying to reassure her by belittling the couple, making it clear that he was entirely on her side but, even so, his words irked her; she had no inclination to gossip about Redfern's mistress.

'It's no concern of mine, Dennis, and quite honestly I haven't the slightest interest in their goings-on,' she said with a shrug.

'I'm delighted to hear that, Lily. Wise girl! There's the orchestra getting ready to start again – d'you think they'll play "The White Cliffs of Dover"?'

'No, they'll save that till last. This one's a quickstep – "Bless 'em All!" Shall we dance?'

Everybody seemed to enjoy themselves, and when Matron announced the last waltz, which was indeed 'The White Cliffs of Dover' in three-four time, Dennis drew Lily close in his arms and she let her head fall against his shoulder. She saw Nurse Bailey happily drifting past them with the young officer, her face aglow. What was it about service uniforms that stirred young women's hearts? She was glad that Dennis was going to join up and care for injured comrades in arms. He would be non-combative, but respected – not like the motley group of mainly arty types, poets, painters and musicians who worked as porters and mortuary attendants at Northampton General, rather than take part in the war. 'Conscientious objectors' had a much easier time in this war than the last one, so Lily had been told by her father and men like Major Massey, but they were still looked upon as cowards, especially by women who had husbands, sons and brothers on active service. As a doctor in RAF uniform, a commissioned officer, Dennis Wardley would command respect and yet not have to confront the enemy face to face.

Not like Tim Baxter, facing death at sea; or Geoffrey Westhouse, facing death in the desert; or Ned Carter, facing death in the air.

And Sandy Redfern too – though *he* had a warm, loving mistress to comfort him and satisfy his needs.

Chapter 14

RAFH Rauceby, Near Sleaford, Lincs
Sunday, 8 March 1942

Beatrice, dear!

What a *lovely* letter from you, so full of encouraging news! I can just picture you getting about on your 'tin leg', which of course is bound to be painful at first, and you must try to be more patient with yourself. Remember Douglas Bader, and how he persevered with his two tin legs. I'll bet *he* got impatient sometimes and thought his progress was slow. Think of what you've *achieved* in the past year – do you realise that it's exactly a year today since it all happened? Do you still get nightmares, Beatrice? I do, and my father says you never really get over it, but life goes on and we go on too, don't we?

Lily put down her pen, and looked out at the steadily pouring rain; should she start again, leaving out the last two sentences? It was important that Beatrice looked forward, not back. After a moment's consideration, she decided to leave it as written.

Anyway, enough of that, *she wrote*. I'm sorry I haven't answered your letter before, but honestly, life has been a whirlwind this year. You know I stayed on at Northampton until I sat my Finals, and as soon as I heard I'd passed I applied to the Air Ministry, and was called to an interview with a *very* grand dame at Adastra House – that's in Kingsway, the Aldwych end, not far from where Geoffrey worked as a solicitor's clerk. There was a bit of palaver about St Mildred's, because you know all the records were lost, but the General Nursing Council confirmed my date of commencement there, and the dear old Countess sent a very kind letter, plus the fact that my references from Northampton can't have been too bad. Anyway, the upshot was that I'm on trial for six months to show what I can do, and my dear Beattie, you ought to see where I've landed! Right out in the wilds of darkest Lincolnshire, an *awful* hole that was known as Rauceby Mental Hospital up to 1940, but now it's RAFH Rauceby, with a burns unit, orthopaedics, general surgery and medicine, even a maternity ward for servicemen's wives – a total of 400 beds. But to me it's creepy, as if the shadows of the past linger on. There's a forbidding main block, all long, bare corridors leading to padded cells, and several outbuildings, one across a garden for officers only. Even in the burns unit there's this insistence on rank, quite unbelievable, and the PM Sisters are all commissioned 'flying officers', which seems daft to me, seeing that most of them have never even been up in an aeroplane, and the doctors are addressed by their rank, like Wing Commander Goodhart, who's a senior surgeon.

Rauceby is at the back of beyond, about four miles from Sleaford, a quiet little market town, definitely not known for its night life. This whole place is overgrown with laurels, dark green and dripping with rain at present. Honestly, Beattie, what a *depressing* place to lock up the mentally deranged, though I suppose that was the idea – to keep them out of sight and out of mind. Goodness knows what happened to them when the RAF took it over, though a few poor souls have stayed on as domestic staff, like the old man who brings up the clean laundry and grins and nods at us. 'Pretty dear!' he says, Pretty dear!' Some of the nurses say he frightens them, heaven knows what they think he might do! I'm sure there's no harm in him, he's just simple, poor old thing.

So what do I do here? I'm somewhere below the Princess Mary Royal Air Force Nursing Sisters – what a mouthful! – with their smart uniform and veils, and above the VADs with their red crosses on their aprons, the ones who do most of the basic ward work, like our nursing orderlies at St Mildred's. I share a room with two of them, which made my heart sink at first, but it isn't so bad. They're nice girls from quite good backgrounds – well, they wouldn't have volunteered for this sort of work otherwise, would they? And we're all so tired by the end of a day on the wards that we fall asleep as soon as we collapse into our beds. There's a story going round about a VAD who was at everybody's beck and call, always being told off and chivvied – until she turned out to be the Marchioness of Carisbrooke! So I shall have to watch my step, won't I? At present I'm on orthopaedics, and the cases are fairly long term. Most of the men are quite young, and have every sort of fracture, from skull to pelvis. Two have spinal injuries and have to lie flat in complete plaster casts, while others are up and hobbling around on Thomas's splints and crutches. They have to wear 'hospital blue' trousers, with white shirts and red ties. Their main problem is sheer boredom, although there are books and playing cards for them, also a gramophone. One of my room-mates, Joan Mastin, has a mother who comes in and teaches them *needlework* – yes, really! It's rather comical to see men with hands like shovels doing embroidery and patchwork, and of course they tease each other over it. Mrs Mastin gets them the materials and teaches them the basic stitches, and at least it keeps them occupied. It's like you with your knitting and crocheting – oh, and how kind of you to make that shawl for Grandmama. I was wondering if you could make one for . . .

Lily was about to write 'Mabel', but stopped and wondered if she should put 'Daisy' instead. Through the window she saw an ambulance making its way along the gravel track between the laurels, heading for the burns unit, so probably bringing another victim or victims from a damaged aircraft; the sight always made her think of the airmen she knew.

She screwed on the top of her fountain pen, and put aside the letter to finish later. It was almost time to report back on duty.

'Nurse Knowles, you're to go over to the burns unit for this evening,' said the PM Sister in charge of orthopaedics. 'They want somebody to "special" an admission who's come in with burns to face and hands.'

'Very well, Sister.' Lily wrapped her cloak round

her again and walked briskly over to the separate building, her heart beating a little faster; this was the reason she had come to Rauceby, to learn more about the treatment of burns and patients with skin grafts. What was she about to see?

Aircraftman Richard Parsley was not yet nineteen, a wireless operator and air gunner, the only survivor of a stricken Hampden bomber limping back to RAF Cranwell in Lincolnshire. In midair the fuel tank had caught fire, and Dick Parsley had sustained burns to his face and hands before bailing out over the Wash, where he had been picked up and taken to a civilian hospital at Boston. Here he had been treated for shock and given intravenous plasma to replace body fluid; he had also received the accepted treatment for burns – tannic acid sprayed on to the skin as a coagulant, to form a temporary 'skin' and prevent further loss of fluid. He had then been flown by air ambulance to Rauceby.

'Bugger,' said Wing Commander Goodhart. 'The stupid sods have sprayed him with that bloody Tannaflax, and you can see what it's done, can't you? The acid has drawn the skin together, and he's lost most of his eyelids. His nose will probably be all right, but it's essential to have eyelids that blink, or the cornea gets ulcerated and the sight goes. Get both those hands into Bunyan-Stannard irrigation envelopes, and keep his eyes covered with saline compresses. Continue the intravenous dextrose-saline, give morphia – a half to three-quarters of a grain two-hourly, and I'll get in touch with RAFH Halton to see what they advise about the eyes.'

He marched off, and the sister took Lily aside. 'Right, Nurse Knowles, this is a classic case of "airman's burn",' she said. 'You will stay with him and carry out all observations – his temperature, pulse, respiration, colour and response to stimuli. If he speaks, note what he says, and try to get him to take a little barley water through a straw.'

And talk to him, thought Lily. Nothing of the boy's face was visible; a little hole in the saline compresses gave access to his mouth. His body apart from his face and hands had been protected by his clothing, and had minor cuts and bruises, but was otherwise unharmed. Blue hospital pyjama trousers had been put on him, and his chest was bare beneath the bedclothes. And he was her special patient to care for, minute by minute.

She devoted herself to him, recording all observations, keeping his compresses moist, giving him tiny sips of barley water through a straw, placing a urinal bottle between his legs and measuring the output. And all the time she talked to him in a low, gentle voice, reassuring him that he was in a special RAF hospital where he was getting the best of care, asking if he was in much pain, did he want a little drink, did he want to pass water – and then telling him that his parents had arrived to see him.

The sister introduced Mr and Mrs Parsley to the unrecognisable figure that was their son, and Lily's heart ached for them, unable as they were to kiss him or even hold him by either of his hands, encased in silk-coated envelopes of saline solution. So far he had scarcely spoken since his arrival at Rauceby, other than giving faint moans or grunts, but when he heard his mother whisper, 'It's us, Dick – it's yer mum an' dad,' he made a sound that showed that he understood, and nodded slowly.

Somehow or other the couple managed to keep their emotions under control for the five minutes that they were allowed to stay. Lily reckoned them to be only in their late forties, and noted that they spoke to Dick of his younger brother and two sisters.

'Ye're a very brave boy, an' we're proud o' yer, son,' his father managed to say, while Mrs Parsley told him that he was in a good place and would be all right. They touched his knees and feet, and then they had to leave, just as Wing Commander Goodhart returned and informed the sister and junior doctor that A/C Parsley's eyelids were to be operated on the next morning.

'They're sending an ophthalmic bod up to do a graft from his armpits, so he'll need the usual skin preparation. Damned intricate job, though this chap McIndoe at East Grinstead has done quite a few, apparently. I'll be assisting – hell of a responsibility.'

In the event the operation was actually performed jointly by the visiting specialist, who did the right eyelid graft, and Goodhart, who did the left, under supervision. An experienced theatre sister officiated with the instruments, and Lily was theatre 'runner' at her own request, backed up by a VAD. She was able to observe that a postage-stamp-sized piece of skin was taken from an area just below the armpit, where the skin was soft and free from hair, using a special razor or dermatome, to slice the exact thickness required; this was cut to shape with McIndoe scissors, and sewn into place as a replacement eyelid: it was then covered with tulle gras, a dressing made from sterile netting impregnated with Vaseline and a sulphonamide preparation.

The young aircraftman made a good recovery, and when Goodhart removed the dressings after five days, the skin graft had taken satisfactorily, though the disfigurement of his newly stitched lashless eyelids and surrounding raw skin was a dreadful sight for his parents to see; a lot more healing would need to take place before his face was anything like presentable, and Goodhart mentioned the possibility of a further operation at some future time.

'A cosmetic job might improve the look of his eyes, but the first priority was to save his sight, and we've done that,' he said with a satisfaction that was shared by them all.

After six weeks at Rauceby, Dick was transferred to a RAF convalescent unit at the spa resort of Matlock in Derbyshire for rehabilitation to be commenced. He was the first patient that Lily nursed with 'airman's burn' of face and hands, but as spring passed into summer that year she saw a steady stream of such cases pass through Rauceby, some complicated by broken bones and internal injuries. She felt that her experience of air-raid casualties at St Mildred's and her introduction to delicate eye surgery in that little ophthalmic theatre, followed by the Willows family's tragedy at Northampton, had all been a preparation for the vital work she was doing now. She earned the approbation of the surgeons and PM sisters, who could rely on her cool head and steady hands, and even more rewarding was the trust of the patients and their relatives, their confidence and gratitude. It wasn't always easy, and the despair of healthy young men who had lost limbs, sight and former good looks could be very difficult to deal with. More and more of them needed neuropsychiatric care, and units sprang up in various parts of the country, to which they were sent for rest and assessment, both officers and aircrews. Lily noted that one of them was sent to Beversley in Hampshire, and realised that it must be Bever House, the eighteenth-century manor that Daisy had mentioned as being taken over by the military.

One morning a distinguished visitor arrived to tour the burns unit, and Lily was told that this was Mr Archibald McIndoe, consultant surgeon to the RAF and pioneer in plastic surgery. He turned out to be a cheery, tubby man of middle height, about forty, with a knack of putting men at their ease. Sitting on a patient's bed, strictly against all the rules, he said things like, 'I think I could do something with that eye –' or ear, or nose or hand – 'how would you like to come to the Queen Victoria Hospital at East Grinstead, and let me try out an idea I've got?' His informal manner won over staff and patients, and Lily wondered if she would ever see the hospital at East Grinstead, where men from all the services, some from overseas, found their way to his Ward 3, already a byword for his innovative treatment of badly scarred burns victims.

The PM sisters often spoke eagerly of postings abroad; new RAF hospitals were opening as the need arose, from the Gold Coast to Egypt, and a large draft of nursing sisters was required to staff them. It was looked upon by many young women as an opportunity to see the world and have a wonderful social life of parties and picnics, but Lily had no desire to leave England; she wrote to her father saying that she was doing the type of work she most enjoyed, and intended to continue improving her skills on the home front.

'We're all very glad to hear of your decision, Lily,' he wrote back. 'Mabel worries enough about Tim and others of her boys in the services, without adding you to the list. Her brother George is still kicking up his heels on training courses like tank practice, and getting rather fed up, but it will be one more to worry about if he gets sent abroad.'

Daisy's letters said much the same, and added a piece of news: Geraldine Westhouse had been transferred to RAF Waddington, one of the larger bomber stations, where her skill as a radio telephone and wireless operator would mean she'd be responsible for giving instructions to pilots on bombing operations, both on taking off and returning to base.

'That's in Lincolnshire, not so far from you, Lily,' wrote Daisy. 'Will you two be able to meet on a day off?'

Lily had only two days off per calendar month and usually spent her free time exploring the countryside on the battered bicycle she had bought for ten shillings in Sleaford; Waddington was about twelve miles north on the Lincoln Road, but there was an erratic bus service, so she wrote to her cousin, suggesting that she might come up to Waddington on her next day off. For a week there was no reply, and then a brief note arrived to say that Geraldine was far too busy at present, and a certain squadron leader demanded all the time she was able to spend with him between ops – 'which I'm sure you'll agree is far more important, Lily.'

Ah, yes, thought Lily, remembering those blissful snatched meetings with Sandy, and wrote back to say that she quite understood, and maybe there would be an opportunity later.

It came sooner than she expected, and in much less agreeable circumstances. The following week one of the PM Sisters asked if Nurse Knowles might accompany her to assist with a FFI – free from infection – inspection of WAAF personnel stationed at Waddington.

'Their numbers are growing all the time, and it'll take me practically the whole day on my own,' she explained to the matron, and Nurse Knowles was accordingly sent along with her in a staff car.

'These inspections are not too popular among the girls, but they're a necessity, Nurse Knowles, as you will discover,' she said. 'The girls come from very mixed backgrounds, and sometimes they need advising on personal hygiene. FFI inspections cover general health, skin conditions, head-lice – yes, we usually find a few cases of those, and they get reported to the MO. Not only that,' she added, pulling a face, 'we do sometimes find problems that have to be sent to the Special Treatment Centre at Evesham. You know what I'm talking about, don't you, Knowles?'

'Er – d'you mean VD?' asked Lily warily.

'Yes, I'm afraid so, mostly gonorrhoea. And the occasional pregnancy. A lot of these girls have come into the service with no knowledge at all. They're plunged into a situation among a lot of young men, and before they know where they are . . .' She shrugged meaningfully.

Lily shifted uncomfortably in her seat, realising too late that she had been brought on an unpopular exercise, as much to share the sister's embarrassment as to assist her.

The inspection took place at the station sick quarters, in a bare, clinical room with a chair on which the WAAFs sat for the head inspections, and a narrow couch for more intimate examinations. Inevitably there was a smell of female bodies, especially from those who were menstruating, and Lily found a few septic spots, blackheads and decaying teeth; she did not find any nits, but some of the girls had hair that would have benefited from more frequent shampooing. She recognised a case of scabies, which she referred to the sister.

When Geraldine came in for her turn, Lily avoided her eyes and concentrated hard on the girl she was inspecting, so that her cousin was seen by the PM Sister, who had just reduced one WAAF to tears by asking when her next period was due; it was in fact three months overdue, and she confessed to morning sickness and a feeling of fulness in her breasts.

Sister wrote all her findings in an official report, and singled out a group of young WAAFs for an informal talk on personal hygiene, recommending that if a daily bath was not possible, a daily shower was a necessity.

The two of them were about to take their leave of the base when they saw a contingent of four smartly dressed WAAFs marching purposefully towards them, obviously with no goodwill. To her dismay Lily saw that her cousin was the spokeswoman, and her eyes were blazing.

'Just a minute, you two, we want a word!' she demanded. 'We intend to protest against the outrageous way you treat responsible servicewomen who are doing an important job. In future we shall refuse to submit to any further so-called inspections – especially by such a person as *you*, Nurse Knowles. You're not even a PM Sister!'

'Look, I'm most terribly sorry,' Lily began. 'I didn't know –'

'How *dare* you!' stormed Geraldine, getting into her stride. 'You of all people, coming here and subjecting respectable girls to this sort of thing, as if we were no better than the unfortunate kids *you* were brought up with! Well, we'll see what my father has to say about this – and what he'll have to say to *your* father!'

'Oh, Geraldine, *please* don't make it a family matter,' pleaded Lily, her face as beetroot-red as her cousin's. 'I honestly didn't know that the – the FFI – what it entailed. I'll write and apologise to – to –'

'Come on, Nurse Knowles, there's no point in standing around arguing,' said the PM sister, somewhat disconcerted by the encounter, but not intimidated. 'We were sent to carry out a routine inspection, and we can't help it if some people object to it. Kindly let us get to our car, will you?' She shoved her way past the four angry WAAFs, and Lily had no choice but to hurry along beside her, almost on the verge of tears.

'You didn't tell me you had a *relative* at Waddington,' the sister said crossly as they drove out of the base.

'And you didn't tell *me* that it was such an infamous inspection,' Lily snapped back. 'The Westhouses will never speak to me again after this.'

'It's something that has to be done, and there's no sense in making a big issue of it,' said the sister. 'At least I'll know not to ask *you* again.'

Lily did not reply. The damage was done.

As always, work was the great consolation, the means by which ruffled feathers were put into perspective against the sufferings of the wounded. The young patients at RAFH Rauceby were a constant reminder of the war, which otherwise seemed to have retreated from everyday life on the home front, and gone to other parts of the world. Singapore had fallen to the Japanese, and the United States Air Force had bombed Tokyo. The Russians were putting up a tremendous defence against the German invasion, and the industrial city of Stalingrad was bracing inself for an all-out onslaught. In North Africa General Rommel was driving the Eighth Army back in a series of defeats towards somewhere called El Alamein, while the RAF had embarked on a fearful bombardment of German cities, destroying arms factories, shipbuilding yards and with them a great number of civilians; under Air Marshal Sir Arthur Harris the Germans were getting more than a taste of what the British had endured in the Blitz of 1940–41.

And London – ah, her London! – had not been destroyed. Lily received a first-hand account of its emergence from the bombing in a rare letter from Hanna Blumfeldt.

'I did not expect to live to see the end of the Blitzkrieg, but thought I would be killed like my friends,' she wrote, almost as if she'd been disappointed at surviving. 'Now I work as a midwife at Queen Adelaide's Hospital, and I see London like a big wounded animal raising up her head and licking away the blood. Wild flowers grow in the bomb craters and birds sing. Children play in the open spaces where houses stood, and the postman and the milkman go on their way as before. I deliver babies of the war, and trust that they will see the end of it.'

Lily stopped reading and hugged the letter to her heart. She could picture it so well: the great city reviving as it always had done, through war, plague and fire, all kinds of changes as the River Thames flowed on, century after century. And here was an alien German Jewess describing its latest renaissance – and why not? Hanna had reason enough to be grateful, to adopt London as her home, and to serve its citizens now in the way that she had chosen. Lily read on.

'But all is not good. Our city is now flooded with American soldiers, all big and strong and healthy, but I am ashamed of the cheap girls who smile and hang round them for whatever they can get. It is a very shameful picture of the British woman, which not all of us deserve.'

Lily sighed, and thought about the pregnant WAAF – and the outrage of Geraldine and her friends; there would always be the good who had to suffer for the behaviour of the bad, and this was borne out by a letter she received from her father, whose handwriting, she noticed, had become rather shaky lately.

Yes, it was unfortunate about your FFI inspection occurring when it did, and upsetting Geraldine, *he wrote*. I know only too well that these checks have to be made, and the majority of girls must naturally find them humiliating. There have been a few rumblings coming from the direction of Cherry Trees, but it doesn't bother me, and Mabel is far too taken up with worrying over Tim, because British shipping losses have been so heavy. Alice is probably worrying about Geoffrey, as things don't look at all good out in the desert, and we don't seem to have anybody to match Rommel. What a pity he's on the wrong side.

Going back to the little rumpus over the FFI, I see that the government has taken note of reports of 'loose morals' in the women's services, and have appointed a committee (who'll be on it, I wonder?) to look into the matter. It'll probably turn out to be a case of the few giving a bad name to the many, but it won't do anything for recruitment of the better sort.

Your six months' trial at Rauceby is getting near to its conclusion, so we soon expect to hear that you are a fully-fledged Princess Mary's Royal Air Force Nursing Sister! How's Dennis Wardley getting on in the RAF? Do you hear much from him these days?

And the answer to that was yes, she did. He was at the RAF General Hospital at Ely in Cambridgeshire, on a course in maxillofacial surgery, which dealt with jaw and teeth injuries, often complicated by facial burns. And he was wanting to see her.

'As a doctor I get a special petrol allowance, and can get up to Sleaford in no time,' he wrote. 'All you have to do is tell me when you're off, and I'll find a way to synchronise watches! And, Lily, as soon as you're in the PMRAFNS, do you think we could get a posting together? Or is that too much to ask for?'

Dear old Dennis, he never gave up. And there was surely no harm in meeting just for a day. An idea occurred to her, and she wrote back to suggest it to him.

'Yes, I'd like to spend a day with you, and catch up on all the news. Could you arrange to be off on Saturday, 22 August? If it's so easy for you to get here, would it be possible then to go to Northampton, so that you could see your parents and I could visit G and G? They would so appreciate it, Dennis, and so would I.'

'Done!' came back the reply. 'I've put a red ring round the 22nd on the calendar, not that I'm likely to forget it. It will be such heaven to see you again, Lily.'

And so, in their own way, said Grandmama and Grandpapa.

But it was not to be. Lily's life was changed in a moment, by a telegram from Aunt Daisy on the eighteenth, to say that Dr Knowles had collapsed while on his rounds, and asking her to come home at once.

Chapter 15

'Look 'ere, Mrs Baldock, I've put up with more'n my share o' sauce from these young blighters, but I ain't takin' *that* sort o' caper from nobody!'

Cheale was holding a wriggling eight-year-old boy by the ear, his broad and usually good-humoured face red with indignation. 'Peein' out of a tree on me, 'e was, pardon me sayin' so.'

''E ain't supposed to wallop me, Miss Baldock!' whined the culprit, vainly trying to free himself from the gardener's grip.

'Shut up, or I'll box yer ears for ye again, ye dirty little beast. Just 'cause the doctor's bin taken bad, ye think ye can play up. If I 'ad my way, ye'd get a good hidin'.'

'Leave him to me, Cheale,' said Daisy hastily. 'Come indoors at once, Stan, and you won't be allowed out again until you've apologised to Mr Cheale. In you go – quick! Oh, my goodness, here's Lily, home already, and nobody to meet you at the station. Hello, Lily dear – you must remember what it's like here when school's out – sheer pandemonium!'

Lily put down her canvas holdall to return Daisy's kiss. 'I came as soon as I got your telegram. How is he? Is he –'

'He's in the hospital, Lily. Dr Jarman's calling a specialist over from Basingstoke to see him.'

'Is it his heart?'

'I don't really know. He just seems absolutely worn out. Of course he's been overworking for years, and since the war it's been harder still, night after night on call and –'

'And never any peace and quiet,' muttered Lily, 'I'll go up to see him straight away. Can I borrow your bike?'

'Of course, but won't you stop for a cup of tea first? Mabel's visiting him at present, and we're all at sixes and sevens here.'

'No, thanks, I want to see him for myself.' And Lily marched off to the shed to get out the bicycle. Within two minutes she was pedalling towards Belhampton War Memorial Hospital, leaving Daisy staring after her and wondering what to do with that little monster Stan Ditchfield. She had never before seen Cheale so put out, and was secretly inclined to agree with him about a good hiding, but Mabel forbade any form of corporal punishment.

Mabel was sitting beside her husband's bed, and a nurse had just taken his temperature. The August sun was slanting through the open sash windows on to the pale green walls, and the parish church clock struck six as Lily walked into the ward.

'Oh, look, Stephen, here's Lily come to see yer,' Mabel said, smiling, and his tired eyes lit up at the sight of his daughter.

'What, all the way from Lincoln, Lily?' he said weakly. 'There was no need to bother you, my dear, I just had a bit of a blackout, that's all.'

Lily quickly hid her dismay, and forced a smile at the shrunken figure lying so flat in the bed, with little humps where his bony hips, knees and feet showed beneath the green counterpane. The skin of his face wrinkled like paper when he smiled, just like an old man's. She leaned over to kiss him, and took hold of his hand.

'So, Dad – how are you feeling now?'

'Much better. More rested.' He looked unutterably weary.

'Ye'll be all right once we get yer home, Stephen love, and yer can sleep right round the clock if yer want to,' Mabel said fondly, adding, 'Nice to see yer, Lily. Dr Jarman says yer dad's goin' to have to retire, not before time, I reckon. This could be a blessin' in disguise.'

'Shan't know what to do with myself all day.'

'Yes, yer will. Ye'll enjoy yerself potterin' around, not havin' to go out at night any more. That's right, i'n't it, Lily?'

Lily could think of no reply, so shocked as she was by the change in her father. Couldn't Mabel see that he was a dying man, or was she deliberately deceiving herself and him?

He closed his eyes and give a tiny sigh; his hand lay limply in Lily's, as if he had not even the strength to return the pressure of her fingers.

'You're tired, Dad – I expect you'd like to go to sleep,' she said softly. 'I'll say good night now, and come to see you again tomorrow.' She kissed his cheek. 'Good night, Dad. Bless you . . .' She longed to tell him that she loved him, but merely repeated the 'Good night'. She kissed his hand and laid it down on the sheet. Nodding to Mabel, she got up and turned from the bed.

'Right oh, Lily, I'll be comin' in a minute,' said Mabel as Lily walked away. It seemed only tactful to leave the couple alone for a few more minutes, but after waiting outside for a while, Lily realised how tired she was after her long journey, and began to cycle slowly back to Pinehurst. No doubt Mabel would prefer to walk the mile on her own anyway, she thought.

'Ah, Lily, I've got you a nice salad for your supper, and opened a tin of sardines for a treat,' said Daisy. 'Sorry about the upset when you arrived! Come and sit down with me and talk – Miss Styles and Beryl can cope. How did you find your father?'

'Thank you for sending for me, Daisy. He's not long for this world, is he?'

'You don't know that, Lily dear. He might rally and be spared for a few years of retirement.'

'When shall we know what this specialist says?'

'Tomorrow, I think. Look, Lily, you're tired out. Why don't you go up to bed and I'll bring your supper on a tray?'

'I'd better stay and see Mabel. It must be a very hard time for her – and all of you.'

'It certainly isn't easy, especially during school holidays – and no Tim!'

When Mabel arrived, Daisy got up to make a fresh pot of tea, but Mabel was at once waylaid by Miss Styles, at her wits' end with two defiant children, Stan and Cissie Ditchfield, who were refusing to obey her, and encouraging rebellion in the others.

'I'll deal with them, Mabel,' said Daisy. 'You go and get your supper and talk to Lily.'

But Mabel took Stan aside and listened to his tale of woe and mistreatment by Cheale, gently asking him about his own misdemeanours; she then had a long talk with ten-year-old Cissie, explaining to her that because the Doctor was ill they all had to be extra good. She ended with a hug and a promise from the girl to be more helpful in future and to say sorry for being rude to Miss Styles.

By which time Lily had eaten her supper and taken Daisy's advice about retiring to bed. Something told her that tomorrow was going to be another very long day.

The morning brought news of an Allied landing at the port of Dieppe, and a large number of troops with heavy equipment were said to be engaged in fierce fighting. The news broadcast was not very clear about numbers, or what the purpose of this manoeuvre was – whether it was the start of an invasion or a single raid on an enemy-occupied position. There was not time at Pinehurst to give much attention to the broadcasts, but the cook listened to her own wireless in the kitchen while she worked, and told Daisy that a lot of Canadian soldiers were involved.

'I s'pose that means yer brother George, Mrs Baldock. D'ye think he's with 'em?'

Daisy had no idea, but decided to say nothing to Mabel, who had enough to worry about at present. The children were starting on their morning tasks with varying degrees of unwillingness, and Lily donned an apron to assist with the general routine work, which was much more demanding during school holidays.

'What would I give to see Tim stroll in and take over these boys!' sighed Daisy. 'He'd get them out kite-flying or exploring on the common with a picnic. He was *so* good with them.'

'Well, *I* could take them out for a picnic,' volunteered Lily. 'Beryl could help me, and then you could get on with your office work. Miss Styles could stay here with the little ones, and Mabel could visit Dad – just as long as I can see him this evening.'

'Are you sure?' Daisy sounded dubious. 'They're much harder to look after these days – but it would be a great help.'

The picnic was duly decided upon. Lily consulted with the cook about packing sandwiches and biscuits, and said she would leave at two o'clock with eight of the children, five boys and three girls, leaving only the four youngest ones with Miss Styles.

At one o'clock the news broadcast revealed that some two thousand Canadians had been in the Dieppe raid, and that many were killed or wounded, and large numbers taken prisoner. The women at Pinehurst gradually began to realise that this had been a failed mission, an assault that had gone tragically wrong. Mabel was appalled.

'To think that our dear little brother Georgie came back to us after all those years, only to be lost again, Daisy!' she lamented. 'What a wicked waste! I wish he'd stayed in Canada like his friend Davy. Fancy sendin' a man of his age into such danger!'

The uneasy atmosphere affected the children, and Lily was glad she had arranged the picnic, though just before they set out, Dr Jarman arrived to tell Mabel the specialist's opinion on her husband. Daisy and Lily joined her in the Quiet Room to hear the verdict.

'At sixty, the Doctor's got the body of a man about fifteen years older,' said Jarman, a GP in his fifties who now had to look for another partner. 'Years of coping with the pain of that war wound have taken their toll, and arthritis has set into the right hip. His heart is enlarged, he gets breathless on exertion, and in fact he's just worn himself out.'

'I can see that for meself, Dr Jarman,' replied Mabel rather coldly. 'And I'm surprised *you* never noticed before. Now I want to get him home to his own bed. I've done up his study on the ground floor as a bedroom where he can be nice and quiet.'

Jarman looked doubtful. 'He certainly needs to be able to rest, with access to the garden while we've got this fine weather.' He paused significantly. 'I feel that Pinehurst is hardly an ideal environment for him, Mrs Knowles, as I'm sure you must appreciate. It's time to give some thought to the future, you know.'

'What? But my children have never been more in need of a home like Pinehurst!' cried Mabel, clasping her hands together. 'Stephen's never minded living here all these years. He's used to the children. They're our family; it's our life!'

'Ssh, Mabel, don't upset yourself, we'll just have to wait and see how things go,' said Daisy quickly. 'You've got me and Miss Styles and Beryl and Cheale – and now Lily's come home to help us as well. We'll manage together, you'll see!'

And now Lily's come home to help us as well.

Lily excused herself and withdrew. It was time to set out for the picnic.

'Yer can feel the fresh air doin' yer good up here, can't yer, Miss Lily?' cried Beryl, her round face glowing. 'I'm ever so glad yer thought of a picnic!'

It was true. By the time the little party reached the broad open space of the common, they were all in better moods, striding out or running ahead under the blue arch of the sky. Beryl chatted away happily, keeping an eye on the girls.

'Ye're good with the boys, aren't yer, Miss Lily? They upset poor Miss Styles with the horrible words

333

they use – ever so rude, they are sometimes. Miss Daisy – Mrs Baldock – tells them off, but they won't take any notice of *me*. In fact Mother's the only one they take any real notice of – apart from Mr Tim. Things just aren't the same without him here.'

Her eyes brightened as she uttered Tim's name. It was common knowledge that she received an occasional letter or postcard from him, and kept them wrapped in a silk handkerchief under her pillow.

'I find that it's best just not to take any notice of bad language, Beryl,' Lily said. 'If you show that it upsets you, they'll try it on all the more. Now then, boys! Who can play leap-frog? How many leaps can you do in a row? Careful, you'll get your foot stuck in a rabbit hole, Jack! Now, girls, who's got a skipping-rope handy? Nobody? Well, then, it's a good job I brought a couple in my bag! And what else have I got here, boys? Yes, a football! And plenty of space to kick it around in, no windows to break, no fences to send it over. Ready? Here it comes!'

For the next hour the children gave rein to their natural energy and earned their refreshments at four o'clock. Afterwards Lily got the girls to gather wild flowers and make up a bunch of the prettiest ones for Mother, as they called Mrs Knowles. Bell heather, stonecrop and yarrow with its daisy heads, willow herb and wild clematis – 'Does anybody know the other name for it?'

'I do, Miss Lily, I do! Dirty ol' man's beard!' shouted Cissie Ditchfield, to muted giggles.

'Girls are much easier than boys, aren't they, Miss Lily? I don't have any real trouble with them at all,' said innocent little Beryl, but Lily had noticed how the Ditchfield girl made faces at Miss Penney behind her back, to the furtive amusement of the others.

Young Cissie was devious, pretending friendship to coax out secrets and then making them a subject of public ridicule and scorn, while passing on the blame to somebody else. Lily found her difficult to like, and knew that the girl sensed this.

'Come on, it's time we were gathering our bits and pieces together. Don't throw away any litter, will you? Give me that bottle, Stan, or it'll get broken. I saw that, Cissie – give Nellie back her sun-hat at once. No arguments, please. Are we all ready, Miss Penney?'

A scornful, squeaky voice repeated, 'Are we all ready, Miss Penney?' – followed by a stifled burst of laughter, like somebody blowing a raspberry. Lily stared hard at Cissie Ditchfield.

'That wasn't me, Miss Lily, it was Jack farting – ooh, I'm sorry!' Cissie clapped her hand to her mouth, and Lily quelled her with a withering look that had its effect; not another word was spoken as they marched home two by two, with Beryl at the front and Lily at the rear, inwardly trying to come to terms with her resentment towards a ten-year-old underprivileged child.

Back at Pinehurst, they were greeted with joy. They'd had a telephone call from George! Miss Styles had answered, and when George asked, 'Is that you, Mabel?' she had replied, '*George!*' Thinking she was his sister, he had gone on to explain that he was still at Aldershot, having not been sent to Dieppe because of his age. At first he had been furious, but as the news reports had filtered back, he realised that he had been lucky to escape. His young friend Bill had been lost, along with many other boys he had come to know well.

'Oh, *George!*' Miss Styles had cried out again,

whereupon Mabel, just back from the hospital, had heard her and rushing into the study, snatched the receiver from her hand and made her brother begin explaining all over again. Daisy was also called to speak with him, and the evening passed in rejoicing that he was still alive, well and free – though their thankfulness was overshadowed by the loss of Bill and so many of his compatriots.

When Lily cycled to the hospital that evening she was able to spend time alone with her father, as Mabel had visited in the afternoon. After telling him the good news about George, their talk was mainly about her experiences at Rauceby and, weak though he was, he was eager to listen.

'You will go back there, won't you, Lily? You *will* become a PM Nursing Sister?'

'I'll go back to the kind of work I was doing there, Dad, when things have settled down a bit at home,' she replied with a smile. 'But I'm not quite sure that I want to be a PM after all.'

'Why on earth not? You've got this far.'

'It would be too much of a commitment, Dad. I mean, they might want to send me abroad or somewhere, and there's plenty of nursing to be done at home. Like at East Grinstead, for example, where this Mr McIndoe is doing all sorts of new plastic surgery operations. And there's another place at Park Prewett, not so far from here. There's plenty of time to decide.'

What she did *not* say was that she had no intention of leaving Belhampton while he was in his present condition. And even if he made a reasonable recovery – or if he died – would she then be free to live her own life? In the short time since her arrival she had thought she sensed a downturn in the atmosphere of Pinehurst; it was less happy, the children were more difficult and demanding. Mabel was now forty-eight, looking older and tireder, and Dr Jarman had hinted that Pinehurst could not go on for ever under her rule. One day a new matron would have to be appointed, and Lily remembered what Tim had told her about his secret dream of their lives after the war. Was that what *she* wanted out of life? At present she was missing her work with injured airmen, but for the time being she had to stay here, to be on hand for her father. And for Pinehurst, her childhood home.

When she got back she went straight to her room and wrote a letter to the Air Ministry, withdrawing her application to the PMRAFNS, and another to the matron at RAFH Rauceby, informing her that she would not be returning there because of family commitments.

'Why, Lily, you've been scribbling all the evening since you got back from the hospital,' said Daisy, coming in with a cup of tea. 'The children say they had a wonderful picnic, and Beryl's singing your praises to the skies – and we're all overjoyed that George is safe! But you look worried, Lily. What have you been writing? Is it a letter to that nice Dr Wardley?'

'No, Daisy, I've been writing to – to say I'll be staying here for a bit, until – until –'

'Oh, Lily! Lily *dear*, don't cry,' said Daisy, holding out her arms. 'You know, I feel pretty sure that the Doctor's going to get over this, at least to be well enough to come home and lead a quiet life for a year or two. Try not to be too upset about him, dear. You've been through so much worse than this, haven't you? But you're right, we do need you here.'

337

Lily wiped her eyes, blew her nose, drank the tea and made an effort to put on a brave face. For how could she explain to her kind Aunt Daisy that not all her tears were for her father? Some of them were for herself.

Lily wrote next to Dennis Wardley, telling him of her changed circumstances, and he at once wrote back to say he would collect her belongings from Rauceby and deliver them to her grandparents' home.

'Of course I'm very sorry to hear about your father's enforced retirement, but I don't see why this should interrupt your own career,' he wrote. 'At a time like this, when more and more burns victims are in need of expertise like yours, it's important that your skills should not be wasted. Dr Knowles must surely agree?'

Lily groaned inwardly, unable to explain that Pinehurst and its Waifs and Strays were equally in need of her while her father remained ill. The years of estrangement seemed to make it more necessary for her to show loyalty to Pinehurst by taking the place of Tim Baxter to the best of her ability and soothing her father's anxieties for his wife. She could see that Mabel was torn between her duties to her husband and the children she regarded as her family, and so for the time being – for the foreseeable future, in fact – Lily was obliged to stay.

She and Daisy heaved a huge sigh of relief when September called the children back to school. A series of misty mornings heralded an abundant harvest of fruit and vegetables, the precious local home-grown produce that was annually donated to Pinehurst. It had to be carefully preserved in a time of scarcity: runner beans had to be salted down, apples wrapped in newspaper and spread out on the floor of the loft; pears and plums were bottled in sealed jars, blackberries made into jam and jelly, eggs immersed in a covered bucket of water glass solution kept at the back of the larder.

On Dr Jarman's insistence, backed up by the specialist, Dr Knowles remained in hospital until school had recommenced, and then he was brought home and installed in the newly furbished study, which now became a bedroom for him and Mabel, while Matron's office had been converted into a small sitting room. The Knowleses' former bedroom on the third floor was now Mrs Baldock's office, in which she did all the administrative work of the Home – the record-keeping on each child, the accounting, staff wages and planning the catering. A telephone extension was installed for her, and she said that the inconvenience of having to climb two flights of stairs was more than compensated for by the quietness, as the third floor was out of bounds to the children. Her bedroom was next to her office, while Lily shared Tim's room with Beryl, so as to be on hand for the children in the night. Miss Styles, in charge of linen and laundry, had her own room and the title of deputy matron, though Daisy was really Mabel's second in command. The days were full, but at least the Doctor was home again, a familiar sight sitting in his basket chair against the south wall in the mellow afternoon sunshine, exchanging pleasantries with Cheale.

'He's lookin' much better, i'n't he?' said Mabel. 'We'll feed him up an' get him back on his feet in no time!'

But Lily saw how her father's head drooped as he fell into a doze, his thin, veined hands lying on the blanket covering his knees.

'All right, Dad? Had a nice little sleep?'

His faded blue eyes seemed to look beyond her at something or someone else in the distance. 'Thank you, dear,' he said softly. 'Thank you for coming back to me.'

'I'm glad to be here, Dad.'

When Mabel appeared with three cups of tea on a tray, Lily caught an unguarded expression in her eyes: she knew then that Mabel was not deceived, but just wanted to do all she could to make her husband's last days a time of tranquillity, even in a home for Waifs and Strays.

'Ssh, the Doctor's asleep,' the children would say to each other, arriving home from school.

'Just pipe dahn, Joe, will yer?' ordered Cissie. 'Shut *up*, Dick, d'yer hear?' And in fact the presence of the invalid made Pinehurst more like a real home, Lily thought, one with Granddad sitting in a corner, unable to join in the life of the household, but still a part of the family.

The wireless and daily newspaper brought them the news of the war, the tremendous resistance by the Russian industrial town of Stalingrad against the German onslaught, with hand-to-hand fighting in its streets. In North Africa the British line at El Alamein was said to be holding against General Rommel's hitherto unstoppable advance. The children's games at Pinehurst took on a warlike aspect, with invisible rifles noisily bang-bang-banging as boys crawled on their bellies under bushes or across the linoleum, while the air resounded with the 'Yeee-ooo-ow! Yeee-oo-ow!' of dive-bombing aircraft. Miss Styles thought it all very wrong, and said it ought to be stopped, but Lily agreed with Daisy that such games worked off the children's frustrated aggression.

Mabel only asked them to quieten down if they were disturbing the Doctor: the closing of doors was usually all that was needed.

They did not see much of the Westhouses, though one Sunday afternoon Lily was invited with her father and Mabel to tea at Cherry Trees. Uncle Gerald came for them in his car, and told Lily that he was very pleased to see her helping out at Pinehurst, the inference being that it was not before time. Aunt Alice received them graciously, and avoided any reference to the unfortunate incident of the FFI inspection at Waddington, where Geraldine had been promoted and was preparing to take an important examination that would qualify her to become a radar mechanic. The Westhouses saw little of Amelia these days; Alice said that she had progressed from the NAAFI to the ATS and was learning to drive.

'Of course we're very proud that all three of our grown-up children are playing such an important part in the war effort,' said Alice, though the frown lines in her forehead and the encroachment of grey hairs were evidence of her constant anxiety for Geoffrey.

'It's been so long since we last saw him,' she sighed. 'And we don't hear much because of censorship, but we feel that he must be right in the thick of this awful desert war.'

Nobody enquired about Lily's experiences at Northampton or Rauceby, but she did not mind; poor Aunt Alice must be so desperately worried for her son, she thought.

Gerald drove them home before it was dark, so that the Doctor could get to bed, tired after the exertion of the visit. 'Take care of him and Mabel,

341

Lily,' muttered her uncle as they got out of the car. 'You couldn't be doing a better job.'

Lily was less sure, especially as regards her management of the children. The very next day brought trouble at Pinehurst, and it was all her fault – well, hers and Cissie Ditchfield's. Except that Cissie was only a child, and Lily had just had her twenty-fifth birthday.

A letter had arrived from Tim Baxter, enclosing a separate one for herself. Mabel opened the letter at the breakfast table, and the enclosure fell out on the floor. In an instant Beryl Penney was on her knees, picking it up and pressing it to her heart. Mabel smiled.

'Ah, yer got one o' yer own, have yer, Beryl?' she teased. 'We won't ask to see it!'

But alas, when poor Beryl looked at the name on the letter, it was not hers but Lily's. Her eyes filled with tears as she handed it over, and an awkward silence fell on them all.

And it didn't end there. Cissie Ditchfield had noted this little scene, and made it an occasion to take revenge on Miss Penney, who had given her a telling-off for swearing – 'as if *bleedin'* was a really bad word. Blimey, I could tell Miss bleedin' Penney a few worse ones'n that!' she said to Nellie Cook, who thought she was a very rude girl, but didn't dare to say so.

'Are you all ready for school, girls?' Beryl Penney stood at the door of the girls' cloakroom. 'All got yer coats buttoned up? Sandwiches in satchels? All right, then, off yer go!'

But Cissie suddenly dropped to her knees, and scrabbled about on the floor. 'I've lost me letter, me letter from me sailor sweet'eart!' she said, pretending to cry. 'Quick, I must find it to put under me piller

342

tonight, 'fore that Miss Lily gets 'old of it!'

Miss Penney reddened. 'Get up at once, Cissie – at once, d'yer hear? What sort of an example is that to give the little ones?'

Emboldened by the sniggers of some of the girls, and Miss Penney's discomfiture, Cissie continued to crawl around on the floor.

'Boo-hoo, I can't find me letter! Miss Lily's taken it orf me!'

'What's going on here?' Lily's voice cut in. She had just seen the boys off to school, and heard the disturbance in the girls' cloakroom. 'What on earth are you doing, Cissie?'

Cissie remained on all fours and looked up at Lily slyly, wondering how far she dared go.

'I'm lookin' for Miss Penney's letter,' she simpered, and Lily's face froze, remembering the scene at breakfast.

'Get up at once – this minute! *Up* with you!'

The girls held their breath as Cissie hesitated. Miss Penney was in tears, and Lily felt her temper rising. She made a sudden grab at Cissie, seized her by the shoulder and hauled her up bodily to her feet – and slapped her face. There was a gasp. Cissie stared open-mouthed for a moment, and then gave a howl like an enraged animal.

'*Bitch*!' she spat out. 'Bleedin' Nazi! I ain't stayin' 'ere to put up wiv it, I bleedin' well ain't!'

And still yelling, she flew out of the house, leaving Lily trembling with rage and frustration. She had made a serious mistake in striking a child, something forbidden at Pinehurst.

'Very well, the rest of you can leave for school,' she said, her heart thudding as the girls trooped out, silent and scared-looking.

343

'Don't worry, Beryl, it wasn't your fault.' She willed herself to stay calm. 'Go and get a cup of tea. I shall go straight to Mrs Knowles and tell her what happened.'

And she did, confessing that she had slapped Cissie's face in the heat of the moment.

'I'm very sorry, Mabel, and I'll apologise to her if she apologises to Miss Penney,' she said evenly. Mrs Knowles, as expected, viewed the matter gravely.

'I know that girl's difficult, but she's had a terrible childhood, and yer know I don't allow any form o' corporal punishment here. I'll see yer both together when she comes home from school.'

But a telephone call from the school informed Mrs Knowles that Cicely and Stanley Ditchfield had not arrived that morning with the others. At once the home was thrown into chaos.

'I've never had a child run away from Pinehurst before, not in twenty-three years!' Mabel exclaimed in shocked accusation. '*Now* I shall have to tell the police. Oh, where are those two poor children?' She went on to remind Lily that the Ditchfield brother and sister had been sent to the country with the first wave of evacuees, but had been so unhappy that they'd returned to the East End of London, where their home had been destroyed in the Blitz, and they were the only survivors of their family. Taken up by the Waifs and Strays Society, they had been sent to Pinehurst because of the matron's excellent reputation.

And now *this* had happened, and all because of Lily's ill temper and lack of understanding.

The agony of suspense was soon ended. The children were discovered begging outside the Wheatsheaf Inn in the centre of Belhampton, to raise

344

money for their train fares back to London, they said. Lily felt faint with relief, and even Mabel's wrath was somewhat abated, especially when the children were returned, and a very penitent Stan begged to be taken back.

'It was all *'er* doin'. I never wanted to go,' he pleaded, almost in tears. 'I don't blame Miss Lily for cloutin' Ciss. She's daft in the 'ead!'

Lily was ready for an exchange of apologies with Cissie, but Mrs Knowles decided that everybody concerned had learned their lesson, and wanted no more emotional scenes. It was to be forgotten but not repeated, she said.

And when the Doctor squeezed his daughter's hand and told her to put the whole thing behind her, she resolved to forgive as she had been forgiven in the past. She treated an astonished Cissie Ditchfield as if nothing had happened; nothing that mattered, anyway.

The end came swiftly and peacefully, without a struggle. When October came in with chill winds that sent the leaves whirling and rattled the window-frames, the Doctor took to his bed for the last time. Mabel called on Lily to assist her with his nursing care, and the next seven days and nights blended together in a firelit vigil of watching and waiting: one or other of them was always at hand for him during the day, and at night Mabel slept beside him while Lily rested on a couch in the adjoining former office.

By common consent Mrs Baldock took over the day-to-day running of the home, with Miss Styles as housekeeper. Miss Penney assisted both of them as necessary, and showed a new authority in her deal-ings with the children. Mrs Knowles still presided over the Homecoming hour, when she spoke to each child individually, and Lily saw and understood that this was as necessary to her as to the children. They crowded round her, touching her dress and holding on to her as if to make sure that their mother was still there for them, though so much of her time was taken up in looking after the Doctor. He was very tired, she told them, so they would have to go on being very, very good.

The summons came in a dark, early hour before dawn on a Sunday morning. Lily rose as soon as she heard Mabel's whisper at the door, and hurried into the bedroom. By candlelight she looked down at her father's face, calm and untroubled in the repose of death. With tear-filled eyes she bent down and kissed his forehead. 'Dad,' she whispered. 'Oh, Dad.'

'I suddenly woke up and knew straight away that he'd gone, just like when my Harry went, all them years ago,' Mabel said quietly, holding his lifeless hand.

'I – I'll go up and fetch Daisy, shall I?' faltered Lily.

'No, leave her till it's light. No point in disturbin' everybody – and I don't want the children bothered, not before I'm ready to tell them in me own way. Yer could make us both a cup o' tea, Lily, and we'll lay him out together, you an' me, but not for another hour. I want to spend some time with him, nice and quiet. I'll ring up Dr Jarman later, when he's up.'

Lily boiled the kettle on the gas-ring in the kitchen, and made the tea, which she took through to her stepmother.

'Thanks, Lily. An' thanks for comin' back. It meant a lot to yer father, and he wanted yer to go back to yer nursin'. I don't s'pose either of us know what to say, so let's both kneel down by his bed and say the

Lord's Prayer, 'cause that just about says it all.'

For the next hour the two women sat in silence, each with her own thoughts of Stephen Knowles. Lily gave thanks for his life and for the healing of the rift that had separated them. She felt that she now understood the choice he had made when he married Mabel, knowing that he would have to live in her house and share her with the twelve Waifs and Strays that were her family. He had knowingly given up the comforts of a normal home life because of his need for her, and had never once complained.

Lily could not guess at Mabel's thoughts, but she had mentioned her first love, Harry Drover, and so was probably pondering on both the men who had loved her. When she rose at last to draw back the curtains on the cold, clear light of an autumn morning, Lily was aware of a sense of duty done, as if a debt had been paid and a burden lifted: Stephen Knowles was at rest, his personal regrets and conflicts over.

And Lily was free again.

Chapter 16

'You won't leave us yet, will you, Lily?' Daisy asked anxiously. 'We need to get back into a routine, and Mabel's looking so tired. You will stay until after Christmas?'

The funeral was over, and they had returned to the house. There had been an enormous turn-out at the parish church and at the graveside, to honour a well-respected family doctor. The vicar had given him a glowing eulogy, saying that many thousands had benefited from Dr Knowles's ministrations over the twenty years he had served Belhampton, to numerous murmurs of agreement and much wiping of eyes.

'Worked hisself into the ground, poor devil,' muttered a voice in the crowd, and Lily noted that this too was met by nods and sighs.

A buffet, luxurious by wartime standards, was prepared and set out in the church hall by the ladies of the parish, and all the mourners were invited to partake of it after the burial. Mrs Knowles had shaken hands with them all, but had not lingered, though she told Daisy and Lily to stay and mingle with those who had come to pay their respects. She said she needed to get back to her children and reassure them that the life of Pinehurst would go on, even without the Doctor who had gone to rest in heaven.

'An' now we've got a special treat – toasted

crumpets for tea, with Miss Styles's plum jam on 'em, 'cause ye've all been so very, very good!'

She held out her arms as if to enfold them all in one enormous hug, just as Daisy and Lily came in at the front door.

'It's always been her way, to lose her own sorrows in the lives of her children,' murmured Daisy, and then asked, 'You won't leave us yet, will you, Lily?'

'Well, I had intended to get back to nursing as soon as possible,' Lily admitted. 'I'd thought of applying to the burns unit at Park Prewett.'

'Oh, not yet!' pleaded Daisy. 'Look, leave it till after Christmas, and then why don't you apply to Bever House? You'd be only five miles away if we needed you. It's been expanded quite a bit, with two new wards built on at the back – well, not exactly built on – they're separate huts with a lot more beds. It's a proper hospital now.'

Lily remembered that a couple of patients from Rauceby had been sent to RAFH Beversley, as Bever House was now known, and she thought of cycling across the common one afternoon to take an unofficial look at it. The trouble was that her bicycle had a puncture, and she was hopeless at replacing tyres.

Before she could make a move, a wave of colds and coughs swept through Pinehurst, and two of the children became bronchitic. Sore throats and high temperatures took their toll, and Lily's dilemma was solved for the time being when Mabel actually asked her to stay on and assist at this difficult time. The only cheering ray of light was the news from North Africa, where the battle of El Alamein was raging. General Montgomery had broken through Rommel's front line, and by early November the Germans were in full retreat. Whenever any member of the

Pinehurst staff could slip into the Quiet Room or the kitchen to hear the latest news on the wireless, there were smiles and muted cheers, and though it sounded as if the casualty lists were heavy, it was undoubtedly the turn of the tide in the desert war.

As 5 November approached, the older boys demanded to have a celebration bonfire, more for El Alamein than Guy Fawkes' night. Cheale had plenty of leaves and garden prunings to dispose of, and had intended to burn them anyway, though because of the blackout the bonfire would have to be in the daytime. In the end it was decided to have it on Saturday, 7 November, in the afternoon, and as most of the children had now recovered, this was to be a real treat, with roasting chestnuts, and gingerbread men still warm from the kitchen.

'Make sure they're all well wrapped up, and don't let them go too close to the fire,' warned Mrs Knowles, though she kept a watchful eye on the proceedings from the back door.

Lily found it quite exhilarating. Cheale lit the bonfire on what had been the potato patch and, the day being fine and clear, the dry twigs crackled and pungent blue smoke rose up very satisfactorily, to the children's delight.

'Look over there, Lily,' said Beryl Penney, nodding towards the hedge that separated the garden from the farmer's field beyond. 'They look as if they'd love to join in, don't they?'

Lily vaguely recognised the two young men gazing wistfully at the bonfire and the small circle of children surrounding it. One of them called out, 'Hollo! Is good fire, yes?'

'Nicky!' shouted Stan Ditchfield, and young Pip's face lit up.

'Johnny!' he cried, waving to them. 'Yeah, it's good, innit?'

The onlookers were Italian prisoners of war who had been working on farms around Belhampton all through the summer. They were about twenty years old, and Beryl was right, they did look rather lost.

'I don't suppose there's so much for them to do now,' Lily remarked. 'Repairs and repainting of sheds and things – a bit of hedging? What else do farmers do in the winter?'

'Miss Lily, can Nicky an' Johnny come an' see the bonfire close up?' asked Pip.

Mabel was standing on the back door step, and in response to Lily's questioning look, she gave a nod and a smile, at which the two men eagerly climbed over the gate. They were greeted by a roar from the children, and Cheale handed one a rake and the other a pitchfork.

That was how Niccolo and Gianni first set foot in Pinehurst, and by the time the farmer had agreed to share their labour, and the Waifs and Strays Headquarters had given official permission for them to assist the staff of Pinehurst under careful supervision, they had already become a part of the family, or so it seemed to Lily.

Their practical skills were variable: they were neither better nor worse at stoking the boiler, mending fuses, cleaning windows, repainting walls and woodwork than any other young men of their age, but they proved to be experts with bicycles and could mend a puncture in minutes, for which both Daisy and Lily were grateful. But their good humour and popularity with the children was something that could not be measured. Saturday afternoons were given over to football matches on the common, when

Nicky and Johnny opposed each other, supported by teams of two, three or more players, often augmented by other boys from Belhampton. When Mabel mentioned that Tim had flown kites, the two boys from the Abruzzi set about learning how to make and fly kites that would stay up in the air when handled by a Pinehurst child. They showed their photographs of their parents, brothers and sisters, sweethearts and pets; they sang their favourite songs, and were happy to be taught to read English by Cissie Ditchfield and Nellie Cook, using Miss Styles's copy of *Woman's Own* as a primer.

'I've torn out the problem page,' explained the lady, who disapproved of the shameless frankness of some of the letters sent in by readers, and Lily smiled to herself as she heard Gianni stumbling his way through an advertisement for Pond's Vanishing Cream, a product recommended by various ladies in society.

'"The b-beauty se-secret of the l-love-ly D-Dap-Dapnee Pal-Palmer – Bo-Bournee wh-whose f-flawless com-plex-shun ees a seem-seembol of Eng-English wo-woman-hood,"' he stammered, much to the mirth of the girls. '"Sh-she says she al-always uses P-Pond's Van-Vanish-ing C-Cream to t-take c-care of her deli-delicate" – what ees that, her delicate?'

Cissie and Nellie shrieked with laughter, and Beryl Penney nodded.

'It's true, Lily, the chemist in the square has sold out o' Pond's Vanishing Cream. I've got some, it's really nice. Yer can have some if yer like – it's on our dressing table.'

'No, thanks, Beryl, I'll stick to Wright's Coal Tar Soap. It smells better,' said Lily drily. 'But well done, Gianni!'

'Worth their weight in gold, them two,' declared Mabel. 'No doubt about it, boys need a man, it stands to reason.' And both she and Beryl sighed for Tim Baxter, far away and facing the dangers of the deep.

A laughing, crying Alice Westhouse came flying down from Cherry Trees with the news that Geoffrey was in a military hospital in Cairo after being wounded at El Alamein. She did not know the extent of his injuries, only that he was alive and out of the fighting! She was hugged and kissed by her sisters and Lily at this welcome news, and they all speculated on whether Geoffrey would be brought home in time for Christmas.

'We've sent a telegram to Geraldine at Waddington,' said Alice happily. 'I know she'll do her best to get a forty-eight hour pass as soon as her brother gets home!'

As if in special honour of Geoffrey and all the men who had fought at El Alamein, the sound of church bells rang out all over England on Sunday, 15 November. They had been silent for over two years, following a decision to ring them only in the event of an invasion. Now that threat had passed, and El Alamein was a historic victory to be celebrated nationwide. Lily stood entranced by the sound, thinking of the bells of St Paul's Cathedral ringing out over London at this moment, leading a chorus from the few remaining City churches.

'Are yer cryin', Miss Lily?' asked Nellie Cook.

'No, dear, I'm just so happy to hear the bells again.'

What should she do now? Was it time to get back to nursing? She had cycled across the common to Beversley on her newly repaired bicycle, and looked at Bever House on a gloomy November afternoon. Its

353

swimming pool was empty and silent, and the two hutted wards at the back of the house seemed oddly devoid of any sign of life. A little shiver ran down Lily's spine as she wondered what suffering might lie within their wooden walls. Were they for the growing number of 'neuropsychiatric' cases, men whose nerves had given way under intolerable stresses? Was RAFH Beversley to be her next destination, and if so, was it time to send in an application? Of course she would need to discuss it with Mabel before making a move, and also write to Grandmama and Grandpapa to ask their opinion, though she knew that they would want her to move nearer to them – and to 'that nice Dr Wardley'.

She sighed, for the old couple troubled her conscience when she stopped to think about them. After her father's death they had assumed that she would leave Pinehurst straight away, and it was very difficult to explain to them why she hadn't.

Before the end of November something happened that helped Lily make up her mind.

It was after dark, and the children's tea had just finished when there was a loud ringing of the doorbell, the sort of ring that heralds urgent news. Mabel went white, and leaped to her feet.

'Tim,' she whispered, and dashed to open the door. For a moment she hardly recognised the figure on the doorstep, who was neither Tim nor a messenger with ill news of him, but a young woman in a distraught state.

'Auntie Mabel,' she sobbed. 'Can I come in? I've got nowhere else to go.'

'*Geraldine!* 'Course yer can come in, dear, come to yer auntie!' cried Mabel, opening her arms to enfold the young woman in a bear hug. Lily and Daisy, still seated at the table, exchanged significant looks. 'Geraldine' could only be Geraldine Westhouse, the proud WAAF who was her parents' pride, the apple of her father's eye. Mabel called out from the hall.

'Just carry on without me for a bit, will yer, Daisy? I'll be in me office – an' can somebody make us a pot o' tea?'

'What on earth can be the matter?' muttered Daisy. 'And why has she come here and not to her own home?'

Lily turned down the corners of her mouth. 'We'll hear all about it in due time. I'll make the tea and take it in to them.'

In her own mind Lily could make a fair guess at her cousin's predicament; it was likely to be the same one that had befallen many other girls in the women's services. She could picture all too clearly Geraldine's whirlwind romance with the squadron leader who might not return from his latest bombing raid over enemy territory: the moments of passion, his persuasive whispers, the loving and giving – and then the consequence, the growing suspicion deepening into certainty: pregnancy. Lily had been spared, but it looked as if Geraldine was now 'in trouble', like any other unmarried pregnant girl, disgraced and discharged from the WAAF – or the ATS or the WRNS – 'on compassionate grounds'. Poor Geraldine.

When Lily took the tray of tea into Matron's office, her suspicions were confirmed. Mabel was rocking the tearful girl in her arms, and comforting her with common sense.

'Now, now, dear, it's not the end o' the world, an' yer mother an' dad'll come round to it, just see if they don't. Look, here's Lily with a nice cup o' tea.'

'Lily! Oh, what will she think?' wailed Geraldine, hiding her face in her hands.

'Now then, Lily's seen enough o' life not to be surprised at anythin', just like meself – i'n't that right, Lily?' said Mabel, giving Lily a wink.

'That's right,' smiled Lily, pouring out two cups of tea. 'We're cousins and friends, aren't we, Geraldine?'

'They'll all have to know sooner or later, so we might as well tell them now,' said Mabel kindly. 'Geraldine's going to have a baby, Lily, an' her young man's been killed – that's the real tragedy. Her parents are a bit cut up at present, so she's come to us till Alice an' Gerald've got themselves sorted out. When did yer say it was due, dear – March?'

'The doctor I saw at Waddington thought it would be March or April,' mumbled Geraldine despondently. 'But Aunt Mabel, I can't go home to Cherry Trees. My parents are in the most fearful rage, shouting and saying terrible things – oh, it was dreadful, dreadful!'

Geraldine could not see the expression on Mabel's face, but Lily was almost shocked by it, so grim did she appear.

'Shoutin' at *you*, were they?' she asked, frowning.

'No – well, Mother was very cross at first, and said she couldn't believe it, such a disgrace to the family and how was she going to face her neighbours in the Park – but then Father started shouting at *her*, and said all she cared about was Geoffrey, and she told him he *didn't* care about Geoffrey and all he'd been through in Africa – and then – and then – he lost his temper completely and said it was true, he *didn't* care about Geoffrey, because he wasn't his son! Oh, Mabel, that's what he said – "He's not my son, he's

356

your bastard." It was the worst thing I've ever heard in my life, they spoke as if they hated each other!' And Geraldine collapsed into fresh sobs of misery.

'I'm sorry to ask yer this, Geraldine, dear, but what did yer mother say to that?' enquired Mabel gently.

'Oh, she screamed and hit her head with her fists like a madwoman – and he slapped her face and said, "It serves you right," or something like that. He started to speak to me, but I couldn't stand another minute of it. I just turned round and ran out of the house and came here. Oh, Auntie, what shall I do?'

Mabel held her close, but her face was full of anger. 'Wait till I see them two. I'll knock their blinkin' heads together,' she muttered. 'Carryin' on like that in front o' their own poor girl.'

'You won't send me back to them, will you, Auntie?'

'What? No, no, dear, ye'll stay here with yer Aunt Mabel. We could do with an extra pair o' hands, as it happens. We'll find yer a room in Pinehurst, never fret – i'n't that right, Lily?'

'Yes, the children will love having Geraldine here,' answered Lily, suddenly smiling broadly, because in that moment she saw her own way ahead. 'She can share with Beryl, and I'll move out. Yes, Mabel, it's just the right time, especially now that we've got Nicky and Johnny. I was waiting for the right moment to apply to RAFH Beversley, and this is it!'

'Bless yer, Lily – ye've proved yerself to be Stephen's daughter, an' I can't say better'n that,' said Mabel with real satisfaction. 'Now, come on, Geraldine, let's get yer sorted out. Better go an' wash yer face first, an' when ye're ready we'll introduce the children to another auntie!'

*

Gerald Westhouse walked down from Cherry Trees later that evening; having the sight of only one eye, he avoided driving in the pitch-darkness of the blackout.

'Good evening, Mabel,' he said with his usual deference towards the sister-in-law he had always admired. 'Thank you for your phone call. It's very good of you to be so concerned for Geraldine, and I'm deeply grateful. I've come to take her home.'

'Well, she's not comin', not today, anyway,' was Mabel's sharp reply. 'That girl's in a terrible state, no thanks to you an' Alice, an' she's restin'.'

'Look, Mabel, I'm very sorry about what happened this afternoon –' he began, but she cut him short.

'Not as sorry as ye'd've been if she'd gone an' drowned herself or jumped in front of a train. It's happened before with girls in that sort o' fix.'

He looked appalled. 'Oh, my dear Mabel, don't say such a thing! If I could just have a word with Geraldine – tell her I'm sorry – that we're both sorry –'

'I've already said she's restin', and I'm not havin' her disturbed. She's had enough upset for one day. I'll tell her ye've called, and what ye've said, and it'll be up to her to say when she's ready to see yer. Meanwhile I've offered her work at Pinehurst. That's all I've got to say, Gerald, and – well, I'm sorry if this has brought up old memories, but Alice hasn't been a bad wife to yer – though neither of yer should've said what yer did this afternoon. Right, I'll wish yer good evenin', then.'

Gerald Westhouse knew very well that he could legally demand to see his daughter and take her away, but he was shamed by his sister-in-law's reproaches, and saw that it would be best to withdraw until the situation had calmed down.

'Very well, Mabel. As I've said, I'm most grateful for what you're doing for my daughter, and I'll be in touch again with you tomorrow. Please tell her that I called and said –'

'I've already told yer I will.'

'All right, then. Good night, Mabel. Thank you.' They shook hands, and he left.

Before breakfast the next day, a red-eyed Alice Westhouse arrived and asked to speak to her sister in private. Mrs Knowles took her into the office, and they sat down.

'I've had a terrible night, Mabel. I haven't slept at all. I've been half out of my mind,' said Mrs Westhouse, beginning to cry.

Mabel did not move from the desk where she sat as if interviewing a member of staff. 'Yer seem very concerned for yerself, Alice. I hope yer can manage a bit o' pity for yer daughter.'

'Oh, Mabel, don't start lecturing me. Don't take that hard attitude when I'm so worried about my poor son,' wept Alice.

'Yer mean the son yer wanted to get rid of?' Mabel's tone was indeed hard. 'All them years ago, in this very room when it was our Aunt Kate Chalcott's office, and Pinehurst was a convalescent home for men wounded in that other horrible war – must've been 1916, and yer told me yer was carryin' Guy Savage's child – remember, Alice?'

'Oh, Mabel, how could you be so cruel? That's all past history, a quarter of a century ago! Why must you rake it all up now?'

'Because I think yer need remindin'. Gerald was

here last night, as I suppose yer know. He wanted to take her home with him.'

'Yes, and you told him she was staying here, which was very good of you, Mabel, and I want to accept your offer, because I'm sure it's the best plan for the time being. We'll pay you, of course, for having her here –'

'Excuse me, Alice, but I don't want yer money. Geraldine can have her bed and board in return for light duties, and yer can give her pocket money if yer like. At least the poor girl won't be pointed at here.'

'It's most kind of you, Mabel,' sniffed Alice, wiping her eyes. 'You've always been so good.'

'D'yer want to see yer daughter?' asked Mabel. 'Show her a bit o' sympathy for the loss o' the young man?'

'Yes – yes, of course I'd like to speak to Geraldine,' said Alice hastily. 'I want to do whatever's best for her.'

And to her mother's relief Geraldine Westhouse chose to stay at Pinehurst.

Lily's interview with the well-built, rather formidable matron of RAFH Beversley went very well. Miss Bertha McGawley was a Princess Mary's Royal Air Force Nursing Sister, but the resident medical officer was an army man, Colonel Lloyd-Worth, RAMC, a veteran of the last war. There were two other PM Sisters and half a dozen VADs.

'So although we are primarily a Royal Air Force hospital, Miss Knowles, we take cases from all three services, because of our specialities,' Matron explained as she showed Lily around the two post-operative wards, each with six beds. 'We do some plastic surgery, mostly second or third operations to improve the appearance of existing skin grafts. A specialist comes over from Park Prewitt once or twice a week.'

Lily immediately thought of Dick Parsley and the hasty operation that had saved his sight but left him very disfigured.

'Our highly experienced theatre sister will be leaving us in the New Year for service at the RAF General hospital at Calcutta, so your theatre skills will be invaluable, Miss Knowles. We're most impressed by your references from RAFH Rauceby.'

Lily glowed. This was exactly the sort of work she was longing to return to. Matron then led her upstairs to half a dozen single and double rooms, very comfortably furnished with a library and billiard room, piano and gramophone.

'These are for the use of "neuropsychiatric" cases, for want of a better word, Miss Knowles — men needing rest and recuperation from horrific experiences that we can scarcely imagine. The main problem is keeping them occupied, especially at this time of year. The swimming pool and tennis courts haven't the same attraction as in the better weather. There's a psychiatrist who visits and gets them to write down their dreams and such like, but,' she sighed and shrugged, 'it isn't easy to know how best to help them.'

Lily thought of Mrs Mastin teaching needlework in the orthopaedic ward at Rauceby: it was something that might be tried at a future time.

'And then there are the hutments, Hut One and Hut Two, each with twelve beds,' said the matron, glancing at Lily a little cautiously. 'A speciality we don't – er – broadcast outside the hospital. Have you any experience with treatment of venereal diseases, Miss Knowles?'

Lily hesitated. She remembered the brigadier at St Mildred's, in the last stages of tertiary syphilis, his mind gone, his body prematurely aged.

'Er – no, not really, Matron,' she replied.

'You wouldn't have a lot to do with them, though you might have to relieve the sister in charge on occasion. We have two well-experienced male medical orderlies who carry out most of the treatments, under the direction of Colonel Lloyd-Worth. The Huts are completely separate from Bever House, with their own dining room and facilities.' She glanced at her wristwatch. 'They'll be resting this afternoon after their treatments, but I'll just take you over to peep inside.'

The patients were all in bed, and most appeared to be sleeping in the silence of the winter afternoon: the treatments must be exhausting, Lily thought.

'Bever House is beautiful, isn't it?' smiled the matron as they returned to the eighteenth-century manor house. 'We think that Jane Austen may well have visited here – she didn't live too far away.'

'It must seem like a haven after all that these men have been through,' Lily remarked.

The matron did not reply directly, but showed Lily where the resident nursing staff slept on the third floor, and said that as a trained nurse, she would have a room to herself.

'Well, Miss Knowles, that leaves only one question: how soon can you commence duties?'

Grandmama's letter left Lily in no doubt of her keen disappointment, not to say disapproval.

Your grandfather and I find it hard to understand why you have chosen to stay in the vicinity of Belhampton instead of returning to Rauceby where you were doing so well, Lilian. If you could have seen the look on poor young Dr Wardley's face when he called here with your belongings, it would surely have touched your heart. With the death of your father, we hoped that you would be able to put that part of your life behind you for good, but apparently not . . .

Lily wrote back saying that she was very sorry, and asked them to try to understand how difficult life had been at Pinehurst in recent weeks.

'But now that the staff situation has improved, I'm able to accept a post as staff nurse at the RAF Hospital at Beversley,' she told them. 'It will give me plenty of scope for using the skills I've acquired at Northampton and Rauceby.'

She sighed, knowing that they would still feel hurt and annoyed by her prolonged stay at Belhampton.

And then, on the very day before she was due to leave for Bever House, Tim Baxter walked in at the back door, causing Cook to exclaim and drop her wooden spoon.

'Where's Mum?' he asked. 'And Lily, is she still here? I've only got a few hours – where are they?'

He soon found out. Like bees to a honey-pot they came from whatever they were doing: Mabel, Daisy, Beryl and Miss Styles, all excited at this unexpected appearance of the man everybody loved. Geraldine hung back shyly in the background while Mabel hugged her precious boy, and after tenderly returning her embrace, he looked around for the other one he had come to see.

'Lily – darlin' Lily! I've been hopin' an' prayin' I'd see yer!'

'And here I am, Tim.' She smiled and let him enfold her in front of them all, but as soon as she felt his lips pressing upon hers with all the yearning of one who has waited a long, weary time, she drew back from his arms.

'Tim, dear – we're *all* glad to see you, so say hello to everybody,' she said breathlessly, her heart pounding.

'Yes, dear, o' course – bless yer.' He reluctantly released her and turned to hug Mabel again.

'Dearest Mum, I'm so sorry I wasn't here when the Doctor . . . but yer had Lily. That must've been a big comfort to yer.'

He proceeded to kiss Daisy, Miss Styles and the cook, but Beryl Penney burst into tears and ran upstairs, unable to bear his obvious preference for Lily. Mabel did not miss this little drama, though she looked lovingly upon the young man she had always regarded as her own special son.

'Come an' sit down to dinner, Tim,' she said. 'Cook must've had a premonition, 'cause we've got yer favourite rabbit stew an' Hampshire puddin'!'

'Sounds good, Mum – oh, it's wonderful to see yer!' But he kept hold of Lily's hand, and she and Mabel sat on each side of him at the table while Daisy served the delicious stew and soft, suety pudding, followed by rhubarb and custard. He explained that he had only a few brief hours before he was due to join the *Defiant* again at ten o'clock that night – and after the meal was finished, the reason for his whirl-wind visit was made clear.

'Come for a walk with me, Lily.'

How could she refuse? Under the gaze of Mabel and the rest of the staff, she put on her coat, hat and gloves, and accompanied him a little way down Beversley Lane, until they were out of sight of the house.

'I had to see yer, Lily, an' by what yer say, I've caught yer just in time before ye're off again. It must be fate that brought me into Portsmouth this mornin', Lily. Yer won't send me back to sea this time without a promise for the future?' he asked her anxiously. 'I know yer won't, dear. This war won't go on for ever, but if we can make each other a promise for when it's over, we'll have somethin' to work for an' live for – an' don't yer feel the same, dearest Lily?'

He put his arms around her as they stood in the deserted lane on that dull winter afternoon. She heard his urgent whispers, the loving words uttered in his native Cockney, now overlaid by a softer Hampshire burr. Her heart swelled with affection for this true and honest man who had never once given her a moment of unhappiness – not like Sandy Redfern, who had said he loved her and then left her humiliated. Now Tim was holding her close to him, trembling as he waited for her answer.

She could not send him back to sea without the assurance he craved, and so she nodded and whispered consent to an unofficial engagement. He gave a great sigh of relief.

'Oh, Lily, me darlin', darlin' Lily, I love yer so much!' And before she knew it he had taken the glove off her right hand and slipped a silver ring over her third finger. A single lustrous pearl gleamed on it, a rare gem, and she caught her breath.

'Oh, *Tim*!'

'I had it done for yer specially, Lily – an' I'll be that happy, thinkin' about yer wearin' it for me. Kiss me, darlin' – ah, me own dear girl.'

It was done. She had given her word, and they turned back to the house where she soon discovered that unofficial or not, the news was immediately proclaimed to all and sundry, including the children when they arrived home from school. Their shouts of glee at the sight of Tim turned to groans when he said he had to return to his ship, and there was no more time for him to spend alone with Lily. What a dear, good man he was, she thought, so kind and courteous towards Geraldine, whose situation she quietly explained to him – and the friendliness he showed to the two Italian boys, thanking them for all the help they were giving.

'Even when you think it was an Italian U-boat that sunk the *Ark Royal*,' whispered Miss Styles in awe, though Lily suspected that the thought had hardly occurred to him – or to them.

There were more kisses and hugs all round, and though Mabel's expression was difficult to fathom, she declared that Tim's happiness meant more to her than anything else in the world.

'A lot could happen between now and the end o' the war,' she muttered to Daisy. 'If my boy's life's spared, he can marry whoever he pleases – but poor little Beryl's breakin' her heart.'

They all went to see him off at the station, and Lily was clasped in his arms for one last time, one last kiss – 'God bless yer, Lily!' – and he was gone.

Had it all actually happened? Yes, it had, for there was the gleaming pearl on her finger. And perhaps it was just as well that she was leaving Pinehurst the next day, for Mabel's manner was somewhat distant, and Daisy was doing her best to comfort poor, broken-hearted Beryl.

What else could she have done, Lily asked herself. There was nobody she loved more than Tim Baxter – not any longer. Of course she felt badly about Beryl Penney, and she knew that Tim did too, but she had never been able to see the girl as a wife for Tim or a future Matron of Pinehurst.

She gave a long, resigned sigh. Everything was so much more complicated in time of war.

Chapter 17

'Remember that it's early days as yet, Platt,' said Mr Day, the surgical registrar from Park Prewitt who had performed the operation five days earlier, and had come over to remove the bandages from the flight lieutenant's face. 'Hm, yes – what d'you think, Matron? The edges are healing well – little bit of inflammation below the right nostril – yes, it was well worth doing. We'll leave it exposed now, let the air get to it. Good!'

Staff Nurse Knowles hastily composed her own face, to hide her dismay at the sight of poor F/L Platt's. She had left her ward to come and see the removal of his dressings, having assisted in theatre at the operation, and knowing how desperately the man hoped for a good result. As had just been said, it was early days, but the swelling and discoloration was not a pretty sight.

'Is there a mirror handy?' asked Platt, and the surgeon and Matron both shook their heads.

'We don't think mirrors are a good idea in the early post-operative phase, old chap. Wait until it's had a chance to settle. Now, Matron, did I hear you mention coffee?'

Matron's silver tray with coffee-pot and Scotch whisky was traditional at Bever House, and Platt got a generous dose from the bottle, twice the amount poured for the surgeon. Lily had to return to her ward, while Matron and Day sat down to talk with

Platt. Lily knew he had a young wife and a four-month-old baby daughter, and of his anxiety about the effect his disfigurement might have on his marriage and career prospects. It would be up to the young woman to give him back his faith in himself, for the child would not notice anything amiss. Would Mrs Platt be equal to it? Would she accept his ruined looks, or would she turn away in revulsion? Lily had seen both reactions, and the tragic consequences of rejection.

The Blue Room, once an elegant eighteenth-century drawing room on the first floor of Bever House, was now a six-bedded ward, and the portraits of former owners gazed down on the occupants in their 'hospital blues' and red ties, lounging on their beds or loping on crutches.

'Can we have a window open, Nurse? It's pretty rank in here.'

'All right, but it's a bit breezy outside. You know they say March comes in like a lion and goes out like a lamb!' Lily laughed, and threw up the sash of one of the long windows. A cool current of air stirred the curtains, and she breathed in the tang of the awakening earth. The days were getting longer, and the first daffodils were already out. It was spring again, two years on from the night when St Mildred's had been destroyed. In some ways Bever House reminded Lily of her training days, a small hospital with forty-four beds in all, and a matron, affectionately known as Big Bertha, closely involved with patients and staff.

'Phew, that's better, Nurse – the sweet smell of fresh air! We can do with a bit of it in this place. Pooh, what a whiff!'

Lily frowned at the speaker and shook her head,

369

nodding towards the pallid, listless man whose rotting plaster was not due to be changed until the end of the week, and meanwhile added to the stale odour of men's bodies and secretions, the universal smell of sickness.

'Why can't they change his plaster now, Nurse?' muttered one of the men. 'It can't be doing him any good in that state.'

Lily shook her head. 'No, it's been found that it's better to leave plasters on and let healing take place beneath them, rather than disturb the wound.'

'Phew! I reckon they'll find it crawling with maggots by the time they finally take it off.'

Lily gave a little shrug. 'That's not necessarily a bad thing,' she said in a low voice, at which he grimaced and shuddered.

The Blue Room housed post-ops with wounds and fractures, and the Green Room, a former library, was for burns and plastic surgery cases such as F/L Platt, often following primary surgery at one of the larger centres for this speciality. Lily did duty on both wards and took the weekly theatre sessions with Mr Day. Otherwise the wards were largely staffed by VADs who assisted with such basic necessities as feeding, dressing, using the lavatory and ablutions. It was Matron McGawley's policy to encourage the men to help each other, not only to keep them usefully occupied, but to increase their sense of comradeship and stimulate new ideas for making such tasks easier.

The daily newspaper and the wireless set in the ward kept them all up to date with the progress of the war. El Alamein had proved to be a very costly victory, with thirteen and a half thousand British and Commonwealth troops killed, and enough wounded to fill every military hospital in Egypt. While in the Far East the Japanese had overrun Malaya, Singapore and the Philippines, the news from Russia was better, for in January the siege of Stalingrad had ended in abject defeat for the Germans. And although London was sporadically under attack by enemy bombers, the RAF was smashing the heart of Germany's war production in heavy raids on the Ruhr towns of Essen and Düsseldorf, and on Berlin, which of course also killed civilians and destroyed their homes.

'Serve 'em bloody well right, after the pounding they gave London and the rest,' was the general reaction from the Blue and Green Rooms, but the effect on some bomber crews was devastating. Michael Smart, a rear gunner who had returned from fourteen raids over Germany, now occupied a room on the second floor of Bever House with 'neuro-psychiatric' cases, or NPs, shut away in bleak isolation for hour after hour, refusing to speak and hiding his face from all comers – doctors, nurses, relatives and the visiting RAF padre. He had been transferred to RAFH Beversley in the hope that the peace of the countryside would have a beneficial effect, but so far there was no improvement, and Colonel Lloyd-Worth was hinting darkly at electric-shock treatment and force-feeding, though Matron had tried her best to gain the man's trust and get him to talk about his breakdown: the conflict between grief for his friends who had not returned from raids, and guilt for the suffering caused to innocent German families.

'It's the fact that he's a hero that's the problem,' muttered the colonel. 'If he was just a shirker, I wouldn't waste my time on him, but by his gallant service to his country he's earned the right to our consideration. Damned if I know what to do with the fellow, though.'

Three months at RAFH Beversley had taught Lily Knowles many things, one of which was that far from being a haven, it was filled with fear and pain and anxiety at every level – and nowhere more so than in Rose Cottage and Ivy Cottage, as Huts 1 and 2 were called by their inmates, just as they referred to the MO as Colonel Chinstrap, after the character in *ITMA*, a small gesture of defiance against a despot who ruled them with a rod of iron.

Lily knew that the colonel was not a bad man. On the contrary, he had an exemplary record as an army doctor in the First War and, now in his late sixties, he might have retired honourably and taken up a senior position in the Home Guard; but he chose instead to be medical superintendent of a RAF hospital, treating its various casualties of war with stern conscientiousness. In appearance he reminded Lily of Field Marshal Montgomery, the hero of El Alamein, firm of purpose and correct in manner, with his cane tucked under his arm. He never mentioned his private life, but Matron said he was a widower. He could be kind and patient towards men with obvious physical injuries, and he tried to be fair to the loonies, as he referred to the neuropsychiatrics, though he'd been heard to say that they'd have received short shrift in *his* war, and should count their blessings and look around at men worse off than themselves. But as for the men in the Huts, they had only themselves to thank, and he warned them that lack of perseverance with treatment would result in every dire consequence, from blindness and arthritis to paralysis, insanity and early death. And worse even than that . . .

'If any of you men marry within five years of commencing treatment for syphilis, without assurance that the Wassermann test is negative, you will show no love for your wife and no care for the children who will inherit this terrible disease. And if you marry while still harbouring the organism of gonorrhoea, your children will be blinded at birth. See here . . .'

And he showed them on his slide projector a photograph taken at a Sunshine Home for Blind Babies, a pathetic row of young children toddling one behind the other, each holding the one in front as they made their slow progress.

'Such a hideous consequence is a disgrace to any civilised community,' thundered the colonel. 'Do you know that twenty per cent of world blindness is due to gonorrhoea?'

And drastic indeed were the treatments meted out to the men infected with syphilis or gonorrhoea or both, in primary and secondary stages. Injections of compounds containing arsenic, mercury and bismuth were given intravenously by himself or the brisk, efficient sister in charge of the Huts. Intramuscular injections were given by one of two medical orderlies, Mr Weldon, a conscientious objector whom Lily quite liked, and Ernie Price, who leered and joked with the men in a way she found objectionable.

'Them who was out in the desert can say yer was bitten by a camel!' he guffawed. 'Full o' syphilis, them brutes are s'posed to be!' – though this traditional fiction was only repeated when the colonel was out of the way.

The side-effects of these draconian remedies often seemed worse than the symptoms of the diseases: jaundice, stomach upsets, nausea and diarrhoea prostrated the victims, and some developed skin rashes that were difficult to differentiate from the syphilitic; patients had to treat both by dabbing with hydrogen peroxide and dusting with zinc oxide powder. There was a total ban on alcohol in the Huts, and a strong laxative was given every day. It was generally agreed that the colonel intended to kill or cure: there were no half-measures.

The other regular treatment for gonorrhoea was by irrigation with a solution of potassium permanganate, and this was carried out by the orderlies using rubber gloves and bladder syringes filled with the purple fluid. It gave relief from the irritation and temporarily dried up the discharge, and the men were taught how to administer it themselves.

As with the NPs, so with the outcasts in the Huts: Matron McGawley visited Rose Cottage and Ivy Cottage every day, and chatted informally with individual patients, finding out their special fears, which were usually about the reaction of their relatives, few of whom visited, because few knew that their sons or brothers – or husbands or sweethearts – were in hospital, and for what reason. Staff were told not to talk about this speciality outside, and the Huts were generally believed to be for nervous disorders, as Lily had at first assumed.

'I know they call me Big Bertha behind my back, Nurse Knowles, but at least I know they trust me,' said Matron in her easy way. 'We have some very sad cases in the Huts, as in Bever House. Take that poor boy Andrew Sharpe. I was pleased to see you talking with him.'

Lily nodded. This was a nineteen-year-old boy, the son of a Methodist minister in Newport.

'It would kill my mother if she knew I was in here,

Nurse Knowles,' he said, hardly able to meet Lily's eyes. 'I let myself be tempted just that once – only the once, Nurse, when I was out with some chaps and we'd had a bit to drink. If I'd known half of what I know now . . . But I just feel like one of the lepers in the Bible, unclean. I can't pray any more, or – or anything.' His eyes filled with tears, and Lily saw the depth of his shame and desolation.

'Have you spoken to the padre at all, Andrew?'

'Yes, he's been very decent – says he sees a lot of it, and that I'm lucky to be getting the best treatment, and that I should pray for the woman who – who . . .' He left the sentence unfinished. 'He says I should keep myself occupied, and I've tried writing – but it's hardly a subject for poetry, is it?'

'What sort of poetry do you like?' asked Lily.

'My mother's sent me this book, *The Unutterable Beauty*, by a padre who was in the last war, Studdert-Kennedy. The men loved him, and called him Woodbine Willie.'

'Oh, I think I've heard of him,' said Lily. 'Do you like his poems?'

'I did, until I came across this one,' he said miserably, and handed her the book, open at a poem entitled 'Idols'. She began to read the eleven four-line verses, and gasped in dismay.

> Still Venus stands with swelling breasts
> And sidelong glancing eyes,
> And lures lust-drunken devotees,
> To trust her when she lies.

Here was no gentle Christian padre-poet: this was an angry man, condemning the wartime spread of venereal disease. Lily read a few verses on:

375

> She smiles and counts her victims up
> Young wife and little child,
> The festering filth of bodies
> By lures of lust defiled.

'Oh, this is awful,' muttered Lily. 'I think Woodbine Willie got a bit carried away with himself!'

'No, read it right through, Nurse – the bit about the blind babies – here, look.'

Silently she read a verse that the colonel might have written.

> Blind babies crying for the light,
> Strong men with open sores,
> The never-ceasing sacrifice
> Streams through her temple doors.

'Oh, I can't read any more of this, it's horrible!' said Lily, distressed on his behalf. He took the book back and nodded.

'Yes, Nurse, you're right, it's horrible. And it's true. I've made myself one of those devotees, and now I've got to pay the price by being an outcast.'

And he turned away from her, leaving her unable to offer a word of comfort. And wishing that Woodbine Willie had not felt the need to be quite so graphic.

Cycling along the chalky track across the ancient common, a five-mile stretch of heathland beneath an arching sky, Lily breathed in the clear air and reflected that she was travelling from one place of refuge to another. She enjoyed the work at RAFH Beversley, and Matron had been urging her to apply for a PMRAFN Sister's post, for which she was now eligible.

'There are no staff nurses in the PMs, Nurse Knowles, and it's more than time that you were made up to sister's rank,' she had said. 'Mr Day asked me why you weren't!'

A sister's rank, uniform and pay would indeed be acceptable, but something held Lily back; to sign on would mean that she could be transferred to anywhere at home or abroad, and she was very reluctant to make such a commitment when she might suddenly be needed at Pinehurst; but she found it very difficult to explain this to Matron.

She slowed as she approached the bracken-covered summit of Parr's Wood, and the steep downward incline to Pinehurst Corner, where the chalk track joined the Beversley Road. And there was the house standing firm and solid, its bricks and mortar a shelter in all weathers, a place where unloved children discovered a home in every sense of the word, through Mabel Knowles's devotion and care. As Tim Baxter had. And would it be theirs one day, his and hers? It seemed too far away in the future to be imaginable.

Daisy greeted her warmly, Beryl a little less so. 'Miss Styles has gone into Belhampton, and Mabel's resting before the Homecoming hour – but Geoffrey will be over soon, and you must tell us all about Big Bertha and Colonel Chinstrap!'

They sat down with a cup of tea, and Lily enquired about Geraldine.

'Alice keeps thinking that she's starting in labour because she gets a lot of backache and is an enormous size – but Mabel says it's just something called "fixing pains".'

'Is she having it at home?'

'Yes. They've booked a midwife to deliver her at

Cherry Trees. Goodness knows what will happen about the baby, though. If she keeps it, she'll be dependent on her parents for years to come.'

'Poor Geraldine. By the way, I was surprised to hear that Geoffrey's helping out with the boys.'

'Oh, yes, he's very good with them – thrills us all with his stories about the Desert Rats!'

Geoffrey Westhouse had arrived home in mid-January, thinner and looking much older, his fair skin lined and leathery from exposure to the desert heat. He had been pulled out of a blazing tank, and suffered superficial but widespread burns to his back and buttocks; and he had also fallen head over heels in love with the Queen Alexandra's nursing sister who had cared for him and dressed his raw flesh daily. It seemed that Sister Dinah Hall returned his feelings, and had promised to keep in touch and visit him when she next had leave. Lily had been touched by his attitude towards his sister Geraldine, for the first thing he did on arriving home was to insist that she came home too.

'You mean you shunted her off to Aunt Mabel, of all people, who's already got twelve children to look after?' he said to his parents incredulously, brushing aside his mother's protests that it had been Geraldine's choice and that she helped Mabel with the children. So to Gerald's delight and approval, the disgraced daughter was reinstated, and a new and easier relationship began between Geoffrey and the man he had always called Father.

The Pinehurst children's Homecoming was made all the more exciting by Miss Lily's visit on her half-day, and Cissie Ditchfield and Nellie Cook entertained her with a song-and-dance act they had been practising, in imitation of the Andrews sisters.

'Mum'll play for us on the pianner – won't yer, Mum?' And Mabel duly obliged.

They sang with gusto, exhorting Lily not to sit under the apple tree with anyone but them, their feet tapping on the lino and their hands flapping in time to the music. Lily clapped and begged for a repeat performance, and they would have willingly given a third, but were interrupted by the arrival of Geoffrey, who accepted a cup of tea, and sat down to chat with Lily.

'It's very good of you to spend time at Pinehurst with the boys, Geoffrey,' she said.

'Well, it was damned good of Mabel to take in Geraldine the way she did, and now that the Eye-ties are needed on the farms for ploughing and sowing and what-not, and I've got time on my hands – well, it's the least I can do.' He smiled. 'Dinah got me doing all sorts of jobs for the other fellows in that Cairo hospital ward – she's the most wonderful girl in the world, you know! There were some pretty bad cases, yet somehow a marvellous atmosphere among them all. I was sorry to leave them, actually, especially Dinah – and I enjoy helping with the lads here, though I could never be as good as Tim. You know, Lily, I was surprised to hear that you and he were engaged. I've always thought of you two as brother and sister.'

There was a slightly awkward pause, and Lily noticed Mabel looking in their direction. Times had changed since her father and Mabel had disapproved of her flirtation with Geoffrey Westhouse, and she suspected that Mabel would look upon him much more favourably now; but he was in love with his Dinah, and Lily had consented to an engagement to Tim – and far from being unofficial, everybody seemed to know.

She smiled and shrugged. 'Yes, and I suppose I did, too – until we grew up and –' she hesitated, unable to think of the right words, and ended rather lamely with – 'and of course the war has changed everything.'

'I'll say it has! I don't mind telling you, Lily, I was at a pretty low ebb when I was sent to North Africa, but if I hadn't been at El Alamein, I wouldn't have met Dinah!'

Mrs Platt burst into tears when she saw her husband, but was comforted by her parents and by Matron, who told her that his future and hers, and that of their little girl, was entirely dependent upon the way she conducted herself now, as the wife of a hero. To everybody's relief she dried her tears and assured her husband that she loved him as much – or even more – in his present state than when she had first set eyes on him at a RAF dance. Then he had been a charming, teasing boy in his smart uniform; now he was her husband and the father of her child. She kissed his scarred face, and said they would face the future together.

'It was like seeing a renewal of marriage vows,' said Matron, surreptitiously wiping her eyes.

Two other events occurred at that time, which were less happy. The man with the stinking plaster had it changed, and the wound appeared to be healing slowly; but within a week he was dead from septicaemia, the killer that no amount of careful nursing, nourishment and strict cleanliness could overcome.

And the rear gunner Michael Smart threw himself out of a second-floor window in the middle of an April night. The amazing thing was that a patient in the Green Room heard a noise, got out of bed and looked out of the window at the very moment that Smart fell and landed in a thick buddleia bush, just sprouting its new spring foliage. It broke his fall, and he sustained a fractured left tibia and fibula and an assortment of scratches. The alarm was raised, the night sister and a couple of VADs got him on to a stretcher and into the house. The colonel was called, and said he would have to be put in the Blue Room as a surgical case, so Smart was no longer able to hide himself away with his misery, but had to conform to the fairly relaxed routine of the ward, and 'muck in', as the colonel expressed it, with the other fractures and the amputees. Having a broken leg, he was now a bona fide patient and, immobilised in a plaster on traction, he had leisure to look around at his fellow sufferers and through the high window to see the bright April sky. At the end of a week, he asked the man in the next bed to scribble a note to his parents and ask them to visit. He was also able to talk at some length with the visiting padre.

'It's the effect of being with other fellows worse off than himself!' declared the colonel, but Matron said that the time of solitude and seclusion had also been necessary – and even perhaps the failed suicide attempt.

Geraldine was delivered of a baby son, and as soon as his grandfather saw him, his future was assured: young Robert Westhouse would grow up at Cherry Trees, adored by his mother, grandparents, Aunt Amelia and Uncle Geoffrey – and Aunt Lily, who visited him and saw the sadness in his mother's eyes.

'I shan't ever marry, Lily,' she said. 'Nobody will want me, anyway, and I'll always have my memories of Robert's father – but oh, if only he was here to see his son!'

'Geraldine, dear, try to be thankful that you're able to keep your baby,' said Lily gently. 'Lots of girls have to give them up, and never see them again.'

'That's what Mabel said when she came to visit us,' sighed Geraldine. 'She said that she had a very dear friend who was in the same situation during the last war, and had to give up her little son, and it completely broke her heart.'

And Geraldine held her baby boy close, kissing the top of his downy head.

'I'm afraid I'll have to ask you to go on night duty for a week or two while our night sister is away, Nurse Knowles,' said Matron at the beginning of May. 'It will mean that you'll be acting as night sister in sole charge of the whole hospital. I'll be available if you need any help, of course, though on the whole it's fairly quiet, and you'll have two VADs on with you.'

Matron was clearly mystified by her excellent staff nurse's refusal to take up a more senior post, but Lily stood firm on this point. She agreed to cover the night shifts and to be on call for emergency theatre cases at any time.

It was a different world. She had been on night duty before, but not at a small rural unit such as this; St Mildred's had been in the heart of the City of London, and Northampton General and Rauceby RAFH were large hospitals with hundreds of beds. The work here was not particularly heavy, and after tucking-down between nine and ten o'clock at night, and the morning awakening from six onwards, her main responsibility was to do two-hourly rounds, check dressings of wounds and inspect plasters, and note if patients were in pain and discomfort, in which case pain-relieving injections or tablets were given, and hot milk drinks offered.

The atmosphere was strangely unreal at night. She heard the songs of nightingales in the ancient beech wood above Bever House, and the occasional mournful call of an owl or the yelp of a fox contrasted with the groans and mutterings of troubled sleepers. The fresh fragrance of lilac drifted in through the open windows, sweetening the odour of septic wounds and discharges. Passing between the two rows of beds in the Huts, she was aware of the unquiet slumbers of the inmates, watched over by a VAD clicking her knitting needles or writing her brief report on each: *Slept well, no change*.

But the night brought its own opportunities, and sometimes in the small, dark hours she would find one of the NPs awake and willing to talk. She then sat down with a cup of tea and listened to accounts of experiences hitherto repressed: she had learned not to discourage tears, for these could be a healing stream. When NPs turned away from her, bound by their demons, she would smile and pass on, hoping that they would emerge from their personal hells in the course of time. The chances were good, as they were for the most part healthy, normal young men who had broken down under intolerable pressures – and inevitably Sandy Redfern came to her mind: how was he bearing up? Was Daphne Palmer-Bourne keeping him from falling into such sloughs of despair as she saw here?

'It's a bit of all right, isn't it, Nurse?' said a voice at her side early one morning, and she turned round to see a flight sergeant in his hospital blues and dressing gown, standing beside her at the open window, smoking a cigarette. The sun was rising, and soon the Hampshire patchwork of fields and farmland would shimmer in all its May beauty of foliage and blossom.

'My leg's healed up a treat, and I'll be out by the end of the week,' he went on. 'And I'll never forget this place, Nurse. It's done me a world of good. You wouldn't think there was a war on, would you, looking out over that green countryside? Paradise!'

She smiled, but inwardly found it quite impossible to forget the war at RAFH Beversley, where damaged bodies and shattered minds were a constant reminder of it – and within an hour the latest war news was on everybody's lips.

They heard it first in the Green Room, where a VAD had switched on the wireless as she went in with the tea-trolley: a minute later she ran through to the Blue Room and told them to tune in as well to the news broadcast on the BBC Home Service. Silence fell as they heard that a specially trained squadron of the RAF had carried out a daring operation over the Ruhr. Two great dams that supplied energy to Germany's heavy industry had been hit by a specially designed bomb, and substantially damaged, resulting in a gigantic flood over an enormous area: factories, farms, coalmines and ironworks were swallowed up in a seething lake of water that the raiders could see below them.

'The Prime Minister describes this operation as being of strategic importance in the progress of the war in Europe,' said the newsreader, and at RAFH Beversley their rejoicings reflected those of the whole nation.

Matron McGawley came on duty early, to be joined by Colonel Lloyd-Worth, who twirled his cane

like a mace, throwing it up in the air and catching it
neatly.

'We must drink a toast to those courageous boys of
the Royal Air Force, and observe a minute's silence
for those of them who did not return,' said Matron,
and to everybody's amazement she produced a
whole cask of beer, which was brought into the Blue
Room by the two medical orderlies, lifted on to the
table and duly breached.

'I've heard that Mr McIndoe keeps a barrel on tap
in his ward at the Queen Victoria Hospital at East
Grinstead,' she said, 'and I've been saving this for a
special occasion. Do we all agree that this is a good
time for a special celebration?'

There were no objections, and the cask remained
on the table all day for the men to refill their glasses.
The NPs were not left out, and even the Huts got a
half-glass per man, although Andrew Sharpe refused
it, having vowed never to touch alcohol again as long
as he lived.

'Here, have a whisky before you go to bed, Nurse
Knowles,' said Matron genially. 'It'll help you to
sleep after all the excitement!'

Lily duly downed a small Scotch, and fell asleep
quite quickly, though she was seized by fearfully vivid
dreams about water – towering walls of it sweeping
along streets, washing away houses, shops, churches
and schools, submerging men, women, children and
animals on its heaving waves. And then it was rushing
down the Beversley valley, flooding the village and its
surrounding farms – now it was pouring into Bever
House. She tried to cry out, but she was choking – she
was drowning with her patients!

'Nurse Knowles – Nurse Knowles, wake up. Wake
up, my dear.'

'What? Who is it?' Lily opened her eyes and saw Bertha McGawley bending over her.

'My dear, you must wake up. There's been a telephone call from Mrs Knowles.'

'What?' Lily was shaking from the terror of her nightmare. 'What's happened?'

'It's Leading Seaman Baxter, Lily. He's in Haslar – ssh, it's all right, Lily, he's safe at Haslar. Mrs Knowles is going to visit him, and if you get up now, she'll take you with her.'

Within the hour Lily was on her way to Portsmouth with her stepmother.

Haslar Naval Hospital at Portsmouth had a long history of service to the Navy, and Tim Baxter had encountered it briefly after his rescue from the *Ark Royal*. Now he lay in a ward full of injured men from various backgrounds, and behind a screen the boy in the next bed lay dying.

'I can't speak any German, can you?' one nurse asked another, and Tim realised that this patient was German, picked up out of the oily wreckage of his scuttled U-boat, and ending his young life in a British hospital.

Tim's right shoulder was intensely painful, and his arm was strapped to his body, to immobilise the shoulder joint. His head was also roughly bandaged, and he ached in every part. He wondered what had happened to young Billy Webb who had been longing to see his wife Sally: had he survived the sinking of HMS *Defiant*, as Tim clearly had? He closed his eyes, thankful at least to be in a bed and not adrift on the open sea . . .

'Tim – Tim, dear – it's Mum.'

Was that really the sound of Mum's voice, or was

it a dream? He hardly dared to open his eyes in case
he was only imagining that she was there.

'Hello, Tim,' whispered another voice, the unmistakable sweet voice of the girl he loved – his own
darling Lily! Now he opened his eyes, and there they
both were, standing one on each side of him, their
faces anxious and pitying – but real!

'We heard ye'd been torpedoed again, Tim, but
praise God, ye've been saved a second time. When
yer get out o' here, we'll have yer home an' get yer
right!' Mabel's hand shook as she held his, her tears
falling while she smiled and soothed.

'Are you in much pain, Tim dear?' asked Lily
gently, having looked at the chart at the foot of his
bed. Somebody had scribbled 'Compound fracture
right scapula/shoulder joint/multiple contusions/
scalp wound. For X-ray, morphine 4-hourly prn.'

'A bit, but nothin' I can't put up with – now that
ye're both here – darlin' Lily.'

Tears welled up in his eyes, and Mabel lightly
smoothed a hand across his forehead. 'Don't upset
yerself, dear. We'll soon have yer home, and then
we'll look after yer, don't worry.'

Lily stood rather helplessly by the bed, and gave a
little nod, as if to agree with Mabel.

But she didn't agree, that was the trouble. Tim was
a badly injured man who would need careful
specialised nursing for some time to come. He would
need assessment of his fractures and a plan of
treatment, and might still be left with a permanently
stiff shoulder and limited movement of his right arm.
He could not be properly nursed at Pinehurst, that
much was evident to Lily, whatever Mabel said.

So Lily smiled and said nothing, but her mind was
busy. She knew how valuable she was at RAFH

Beversley, and Matron had begged her not to stay away for longer than was absolutely necessary. All right, then: when Tim was well enough to be moved, he would be transferred from Haslar to Bever House, where she could look after him every day, and stay at her post. That would be her condition, and Matron would have to accept it, or lose her.

Beryl Penney had a horror of drunkenness. The menacing spectacle of a man reeling mindlessly out of control filled her with fear and revulsion. As a young child she had run away from a drunken father's violence, and was found hiding in a tool-shed, a cowering four-year-old taken in by the Waifs and Strays Society and sent to Pinehurst. She had remained a nervous child with a propensity for forming devoted attachments to anyone who showed her kindness, and as she grew up she had adored both Tim Baxter and Lily Knowles. Now twenty-three, she had been broken-hearted by their engagement, and what she saw as Lily's treachery. The news of Tim's second escape from shipwreck and the prospect of having him home again threw her into confusion.

When she heard the loud, insistent knocking at the door on the following Sunday afternoon, she answered it in some trepidation. Mother was away visiting Tim at Haslar, and Mr Westhouse had taken the children out to play on the common. Mrs Baldock was dealing with a new girl who threw tantrums, and Miss Styles had fallen asleep over her knitting.

Beryl opened the door and at once drew back in horror at the sight of a very drunken sailor swaying on the step, hardly able to stand upright.

'Oh, I think ye've come to the wrong house,' she

said, and was about to shut the door, but he managed to focus his eyes on her, and she saw the utter misery in their depths.

'Tim,' he mumbled. 'I wanna shee Tim – good mate o' mine – mush shee Tim.'

'Oh,' said Beryl uncertainly. If this young man was a sailor and knew Tim, he must have a reason for coming to look for him – but what a horrid state he was in!

He lurched forward, nearly falling through the doorway, and Beryl called out in alarm. 'Daisy! Can yer come? Quick!'

All at once he collapsed, banging his head on the door-step as he fell. A thin trickle of blood began to ooze from his forehead. Beryl called out again to Daisy, but it was Miss Styles who came hurrying into the hall.

'What's the matter? Oh! Oh, my goodness, whoever's that? What's he doing? Is he ill?'

'I don't know who he is, but he's drunk an' he knows Tim an' he's in some bad trouble an' his head's bleedin',' gabbled Beryl. 'What can we do with him?'

'We must telephone the police,' said Miss Styles. 'This is a respectable household!'

'But if he's a friend o' Tim's –' Beryl began, remembering Tim's stories about his mates on board, and Miss Styles must have been thinking along the same lines, because she suddenly came out with the name, 'Billy Webb.' And repeated it like a question: 'Billy Webb?'

The man groaned. 'Tha'sh me, missus – Billy Webb. Poor ol' Billy, ish luck's at the bottom o' the shea.'

Beryl realised that a decision had to be made and

action taken. 'In that case, Miss Styles, we'll have to take him in, for Tim's sake. He must've been rescued from the *Defiant*, but somethin's gone wrong, an' he's come here. Come on, help me get him indoors.'

'Good heavens, Beryl, what on earth will Matron say?'

'Nothin' as bad as what she'd say if we turned a friend o' Tim's away from the door. All right, Billy Webb, Tim ain't here but we'll clean yer up an' give yer a cup o' strong coffee.'

When Daisy Baldock arrived on the scene she was truly astonished – not so much by the strange young sailor who appeared to be dead-drunk, as by the way little Beryl Penney had taken charge of him. Together they held his head under the cold tap in the kitchen, made up a cup of milkless Camp coffee and stood over him while he drank it, and then helped him up the stairs to Tim's bedroom where they left him to sleep it off.

When Mrs Knowles returned from Haslar, she exonerated Beryl at once. 'Yer did right, ye're a good girl. An' Billy'll tell us all about it in his own good time,' she said, adding that Tim would be so happy and relieved to know that his young friend was alive and well.

Even if he was as drunk as a lord and his luck was at the bottom of the sea, thought Beryl, though she glowed at Mabel's praise.

The three weeks that Tim Baxter spent at Haslar were extremely difficult for Lily Knowles. She could not visit him more than once a week, for she needed to retain her bargaining power at RAFH Beversley, which meant putting in full-time duties, not spending time at Portsmouth. And she found that

Matron McGawley could also make conditions.

'Colonel Lloyd-Worth has been in touch with Haslar and with the Air Ministry, Sister Knowles, and a transfer has been agreed to, provided that Haslar is satisfied with his condition, and that the bed is not needed for an airman of any rank. Is that quite clear?'

Lily stared. *Sister* Knowles?

'Yes, that's the other matter to be settled,' Matron went on. 'Our sisters are leaving to go abroad – to Africa and India – and I need your skills here as a PM Sister. You may well have to deputise for me at some stage, and a staff nurse can't do that. So that's my ultimatum, Sister Knowles, and I look forward to Leading Seaman Baxter's arrival here.'

She smiled, and Lily had no choice but to agree. And yet as soon as she put on her sister's grey-blue uniform dress with matching shoulder-cape and the triangular veil, equal in rank to a flying officer, subject to King's Regulations, she thought of her father, and how proud he would be; so she wore it with pride, smiling at the patients' congratulations.

'Well done, Sister! You deserve it!' they chorused, to a round of applause.

Able Seaman Webb wanted to accompany Mrs Knowles on her visits to Tim at Haslar, but she said it was too early. Billy needed to recover, not only from the shipwreck but the double shock he had received on his return to London: first, that his wife had been flagrantly unfaithful, and second, that his mother and grandmother had both been killed in a bizarre accident at an underground station. He could not speak of it without shaking, and Mrs Knowles feared that he and Tim were both at too low an ebb to benefit from meeting as yet. She wished that she had more time to spend with him, but meanwhile she told him he was very welcome to stay at Pinehurst as long as the navy allowed him leave.

So he turned to gentle Beryl, who had taken him in without question or condemnation.

'Yeah, I was lucky,' he told her as they sat on the garden bench. 'I got picked up straight away by this destroyer – we was packed together like sardines, but none of 'em was Tim. Soon as we got into port I looked everywhere for him, but nobody had seen him, an' I thought he might've drowned. Anyway, I took meself off to London to see Sally, an' that was when . . .'

He stopped speaking, and Beryl touched his hand. 'All right, Billy. Tim told us that yer was married on yer last leave.'

'Yeah. My gal Sal, I called her. Kissed her photo every time I got into me bunk – kept it in me wallet. Oh, Christ, Beryl, I worshipped that gal. The thought of her kept me goin'.'

'I know, Billy, I know.' Beryl's face was full of pity. 'I been in love too. So – you got home?'

'Yeah, we'd got a little flat not far off Fleet Street where I worked. I found her – she wasn't expectin' me, though, an' there were these GIs – an' not only GIs, there was all sorts, they was round there every night, so this neighbour tol' me. And me poor ol' mum, she'd had a bust-up with Sally, an' they'd called each other a few names – it was the talk o' the street, this woman said. An' yer should've seen Sally. She didn't look like the gal I knew – standin' there defiant, like, with this guy grinnin' . . . He said he didn't know she was married, an' when I went for him, he soon scarpered. But I still can't believe it o' my Sally, turnin' out like that.'

Beryl continued to sit quietly beside him, her little fingers upon his hand. 'An' then yer went to see if yer mum was –'

'Me mum was dead, Beryl, an' I never knew – I hadn't been told. It happened weeks before. She and Gran were at Bethnall Green – she used to go there sometimes to see her sister – an' there was a sudden daylight raid an' a lot o' people ran to the tube station for shelter. They said a woman was carryin' a baby, an' her foot slipped on the stairs an' she fell – it was like a pack o' dominoes, they said, people fallin' on top o' one another, pilin' up at the bottom, suffocatin' – nearly two hundred of 'em. Oh my Gawd! My Gawd! Me poor mum an' Gran, never done any harm, in fact they worshipped me mum in Lambeth. Nurse Webb, she was, went all through the Blitz, got knocked orf her bike, but kep' goin' like a trooper – an' now she's gone, an' dear ol' Gran. They loved – they loved me, Beryl – an' now there's nothin' left. I wish I'd drowned with me mates, I tell yer, I wish I had!' And poor Billy gave way to tears.

Instinctively Beryl put an arm on his shoulder. 'Ssh, ssh, Billy, don't say that. I can see why yer came here to find Tim. I'm so sorry, Billy, dear – so sorry.'

'I ought to be ashamed o' meself, carryin' on like this to a sweet little country gal like you,' he mumbled wretchedly, hanging his head.

'Oh, Billy, I ain't no country gal! I'm a Londoner, same as you!'

'Go on! Are yer really?'

'Yeah, I was brought up here, same as Tim, sent by the Waifs an' Strays when I was little, 'cause . . . but yer don't want to hear that, Billy.'

'Yes, I do. Course I want to hear about yer, Beryl.
Did yer lose yer parents?'

'No, but –'

And for the first time in many years, Beryl Penney
recounted her history, and was surprised at how
those early years came back to her, details she
thought she had forgotten, and which caused her to
tremble at the memory. But then she felt two strong
arms around her and Billy Webb's words in her ear,
both tender and regretful.

'Yer poor little dear – an' here's me feelin' sorry for
meself. I'm sorry, Beryl, I really am – but thanks for
tellin' me, 'cause it makes us sort of in the same boat,
don't it?'

'I s'pose it does, Billy – an' I'm glad yer came here
– really glad.'

'This is terrible, Sister Knowles. Another death from
sepsis – and he was doing so well, it's such a
tragedy. Oh, just think of the shock to his poor
parents!'

Matron McGawley was very upset, for the death
had been completely unexpected. A young aircraftman had had a bullet removed from his abdomen,
and at first the wound seemed to be healing; but
suddenly it had begun to ooze foul-smelling pus. His
general condition rapidly deteriorated, and although
a surgeon came over from Basingstoke, it was
obvious that nothing would halt the infection. Within
two days he was dead from septicaemia.

'I feel the shame of it for our hospital,' said Matron,
shaking her head in distress. 'It's as if our standards
of hygiene are not all they should be, though, heaven
knows, we do the very best we can.'

'It's something that happens from time to time,

394

Matron,' said the colonel with a fatalistic air. 'There are some virulent organisms that just spread through the system and can't be stopped.'

Lily shuddered, thinking of Tim Baxter . . .

Chapter 18

An influx of new patients at Haslar hastened Tim's transfer to RAFH Beversley on a sunny day in June. Even Mrs Knowles had to agree that he was still in need of hospital care when he was brought up from Portsmouth by ambulance and installed in the Green Room. Lily was taken aback by his wan appearance, having not seen him for over a week; he had lost weight and had a cough that made him wince with pain. The spica bandage of the right shoulder restricted movement of his chest, and with his arm immobilised in a sling he found it difficult to get a comfortable position in bed.

'We'll have to get you up and exercising your legs, young man,' declared the colonel. 'Get your circulation going!' But Tim seemed drained of energy, and lay on his bed with his eyes closed, reminding Lily of a pale marble effigy in Winchester Cathedral.

Mrs Knowles was early on the scene, though she had to travel by a slow local bus that ran a circular route from Belhampton to the surrounding villages. She bustled around his bed, plumping up the extra pillows she had brought from Pinehurst, offering him fresh salad vegetables and eggs, and seldom arrived without home-baked titbits from the kitchen.

'My Tim won't be goin' back to sea again,' she was heard to say. 'He's done his bit for his country, good an' proper!' Lily could see that he had a long way to go towards recovery of his former strength, yet his eyes brightened at the sight of her, and his good humour and gratefulness for everything that was done made him a favourite of staff and patients alike.

Just as he was everybody's favourite at Pinehurst, thought Lily with a pang, and Matron did not miss the pain in her eyes, nor the heightened tension when Baxter's mother visited.

'Strong competition there, Sister Knowles,' she remarked. 'You'll have to put your engagement on hold for a while, and let him be a boy again, with his mother. When he's better he'll need you more, but for the time being . . .' She smiled, but Lily was suddenly choked by tears. She mutely nodded her gratitude for the older woman's understanding, and applied herself to her work in all areas of the hospital.

RAFH Beversley was a self-contained little world, a law unto itself, ruled with a deceptively light hand by Bertha McGawley. Lily Knowles had her own important part to play in it, and knew herself to be valued, so hid her unease under bright smiles and reassuring looks, enjoying the happy relaxation of visits from Daisy, who in spite of being once again largely responsible for the day-to-day running of the Home, still found time to cycle the five miles across the common to see Tim. She always seemed able to make him chuckle at stories about the children, their little scrawled cards and gifts made of raffia, string, buttons and coloured paper.

Billy Webb also visited him before being recalled to convoy duty. Something about this lad seemed oddly familiar to Sister Knowles, and when the story of Sal's betrayal was told again, Lily remembered the belligerent young Cockney printer of Fleet Street and his girl. It was a memory best forgotten, she thought, especially as he told Tim that Beryl had promised to write to him regularly, and the Westhouse firm of solicitors had undertaken to start divorce proceedings on his behalf, on grounds of his wife's adultery.

'There's going to be a record number of these cases,' predicted Gerald Westhouse when he visited with his daughter Geraldine and baby Robert, now two months old and smiling up at the nurses who clustered round to coo over him.

And there was another flying visit that took Lily by surprise and gave rise to a certain awkwardness. Beatrice Massey appeared at the front entrance with Wing Commander Carter, who was driving her to London for the funeral of the Countess of Suffolk. Lily was able to invite them to take coffee at a garden table, where she complimented Beatrice on how well she was walking, using a single stick – 'though I manage without it indoors'. The young couple were now officially engaged, and Beatrice's glowing looks testified to her happiness. Ned was a flying instructor, and tested out new equipment.

'And what about *you*, Lily?' asked Beatrice, smiling. 'Is there any news of that nice young doctor from Bart's?'

Lily shook her head, and proceeded to tell her friends that she was engaged to a sailor. An explanation was needed about Tim's lifelong relationship to her, their shared childhood at Pinehurst – something that Lily had never truly confided to her friends at St Mildred's, for though they knew she had been brought up in a children's home, they had understood that her Rawlings grandparents were her only family connection after her father's remarriage.

Beatrice was a little puzzled. 'Was he – is he the young sailor who came to see you at St Mildred's

House that time, Lily? I remember Hetty teasing you
and saying you were a dark horse, but we didn't
really think it was serious. After all, you were seeing
the Bart's man and –'

'And Sandy Redfern, yes – and we know what
happened to *him*,' said Lily, striving to sound casual.
'Well, Beatrice, I'm engaged to a much better man,
one who genuinely loves me. At present he's quite
poorly in hospital with a badly fractured scapula
after being torpedoed for the second time, but he's
getting better.'

'Oh, Lily, how dreadful! At least he was spared,
thank heaven. Which hospital is he in?'

This was a difficult one, and Lily was strongly
tempted to say that her fiancé was at Haslar. Her
conscience prevailed.

'Beatrice, dear, Tim's *here*, at RAFH Beversley, by
special arrangement. But his mother will be coming
to visit soon, and he's not at all well, so if you don't
mind . . .'

'Of course I understand, Lily, don't worry,' replied
her friend quickly. 'One day in the future – some
happy day when this horrible war's over – we shall
meet him, I'm sure. Ned thinks that the war's
probably about halfway through now – don't you,
Ned, darling?'

'What? Oh, yes, it's the Far East that's the worst
problem now. Hitler's lost the war in Europe, thanks
to the pounding he's getting from the RAF, worse
than we ever had,' said Ned.

After a pause Lily asked, 'Is Group Captain
Redfern still with Bomber Command?'

'I'll say! Leads the most extraordinary life, constantly flying out there, bombing 'em to hell, and
coming back every time. Terrific record.'

Another pause. 'And – Mrs Palmer-Bourne?'

'Shares it all with him, short of actually accompanying him on the raids – and there's even been a rumour about *that*. They seem to revel in the danger, and she travels to be wherever he is. It's one of the great romances of the RAF, I suppose.' He glanced at her, and then at Beatrice. 'Well, there you go, other people's lives, always more exciting!'

'You don't think about him any more, do you, Lily?' Beatrice asked in a low voice.

'No – oh, no, not at all,' Lily answered, in spite of having enquired about Redfern. For now she was engaged to Tim – dear, loving, faithful Tim.

'We'd better be on our way, darling,' said Ned, standing up, and they both kissed her and sent their very best wishes to Tim.

'We'll see him next time,' said Beatrice as Ned helped her into the passenger seat.

'We'll dance at your wedding!' laughed Ned, turning the car towards the London Road.

London. Another world to Lily now, another time. She waved until they had turned the corner, and hurried back to her patients.

It was Mabel Knowles who first remarked that Tim was feverish and restless. For some days he had been running a mild temperature, and the pain in the right side of his chest was worse. Colonel Lloyd-Worth listened with his stethoscope, and repeated his recommendation that Baxter should exercise more.

'The trouble is, he doesn't move about enough, and his lungs aren't filling,' the old doctor grumbled. 'He needs to get out of that bed and into the fresh air on a beautiful day like this!'

But when Lily and a VAD got Tim out of bed and

walked him to the door, he collapsed on the threshold, and had to be carried back to bed. He had hypostatic pneumonia, and Mabel was frantic, while the colonel hid his alarm under a series of orders.

'Better get him out of the ward and up to a room on the second floor; it'll be quieter. We can't give morphia – it'll depress his respiration. Get a cylinder of oxygen to the bedside, and let him have a few puffs at that.'

Matron reproached herself, saying she should have seen it coming. 'It's always a possibility with fractures, and I suggest we get that shoulder bandage off, and let him breathe more freely – the scapula should be knitting together by now. We'll keep him sitting up on pillows, apply kaolin poultices to his chest, and top him up with fluids every hour.'

The two medical orderlies Weldon and Price got Tim on to a stretcher, and carried him upstairs to a single room formerly occupied by a neuropsychiatric patient.

Mrs Knowles fussed over him on her daily visits, and Lily hid her own fear under outward composure, going about her duties, sharing the nursing care of Tim and spending off-duty time at his side, reapplying his poultices, adjusting his oxygen mask and persuading him to take drinks. Miss McGawley noted her pallor and the dark circles under her eyes, and worried that she might break down, which would be a calamity; but Lily had discovered new reserves of strength during the past two years, and had no intention of dissolving in tears while on duty.

Matron put down the telephone on her desk, and turned to the medical superintendent with a resigned air.

'As if we hadn't enough to put up with, we've got an officer from the RAMC coming to see us for our sins, Colonel. He's bringing samples of some new drug they're trying out on the armed forces. It's called penny-something, and comes from a mould.'

'A what?'

'A mould – as in food that's gone mouldy, I presume. I've to get all the trained staff together to hear him tell us how we must use it. It's very expensive, and has to be kept in a refrigerator, he says. Ours is in the kitchen, and I don't like the idea of putting a mould in with the food!'

Lily gasped as soon as she saw the grave-faced man standing beside the colonel in the annexe between the two wards, ready to give his talk and demonstration.

'Good morning. I am Lieutenant Edlinger of the Royal Army Medical Corps,' he began, and there was a stir among the listeners: he was a *German*!

'I am visiting certain service hospital units in the area with samples of a very important drug that will revolutionise the treatment of infection,' he said in what was obviously a prepared speech. 'It was first discovered by Professor Fleming at St Mary's Hospital in 1928, and is derived from a fungus called penicillium. I have been part of a team working on the isolation of the active ingredient. It is already being used with excellent results on front line troops in the Mediterranean arena of war, and at home here in trials at ophthalmic units and for burns.'

Lily nodded, for Dennis Wardley had mentioned something about a new experimental treatment in a letter from Halton, in which he described it as 'precious as gold dust'.

'It is most important that you understand the

nature and the use of this unstable substance, which has to be kept refrigerated,' the speaker went on. 'It is in the form of this powder, as you see, which must be mixed with distilled water in its phial, and then drawn up into a syringe, where it becomes a thick, dense liquid for intramuscular injection, usually into the buttock. Because of its consistency, it is a painful injection, and should be given deeply into the muscle.'

The nurses looked askance at the yellowish powder, while the lieutenant went on to list the organisms that it was able to kill without injuring healthy human tissue: the staphylococcus, streptococcus, gonococcus, pneumococcus, meningococcus, spirochaeta pallida and the diphtheria bacillus. The colonel looked unconvinced, and at the end of the talk he did not detain the lieutenant for further discussion, though Matron invited him into her office for coffee, and said that if any members of staff had a question to ask him, they might do so.

Lily took this opportunity to reintroduce herself, and addressing the visitor as Dr Edlinger, she politely asked after the Blumfeldts, which caused Matron's eyebrows to rise.

'The professor and his wife are well, Sister Knowles,' replied the doctor with a little bow.

'And Hanna?' Lily ventured.

'I believe the daughter is a midwife at Queen Adelaide's.' He did not smile, even though he had recognised and remembered her.

'I'm interested that you two have already met,' smiled Miss McGawley, clearly intrigued.

'Yes, we met while I was at St Mildred's, Matron, through another student nurse who was a great friend of mine,' replied Lily, resenting the lieutenant's dismissive attitude. She looked at him directly as she added, 'I didn't know that you had joined the British Army, Johannes.'

'Er, yes. When I had finished my work at St Mary's Hospital, I knew that I must fight for the country that has – has become my own. The obvious choice was the Medical Corps, and I hope to go abroad with the Allied forces.' He stood up. 'I must thank you, Matron, for your kindness, but I have another journey to make. Good morning.'

He quickly took his leave, reminding Matron to keep a record of all injections of penicillin given, and a report on the progress of the patients selected for treatment.

'What a strange man!' commented Matron. 'Do tell me more about him, Sister Knowles!'

Lily recounted as much of the doctor's history as she knew from Hanna Blumfeldt. And I can understand why poor Hanna was so disappointed in him, she thought to herself.

There was no time like the present for starting the trials of the new drug, and Colonel Lloyd-Worth and the Matron decided on two patients: L/S Baxter, and a Flight/Sergeant Talbot, who had lost his left foot, and had an inflamed abscess of the stump. Following the guidelines left by the lieutenant, both were prescribed a dose of 300,000 international units four-hourly.

'But what about the Huts?' asked Lily. 'Dr Edlinger said that it was effective against the –'

'The colonel says he's not wasting such an expensive drug on them,' Matron replied with a little shrug. 'Come on, Sister Knowles, let's check these doses together, and you can give Talbot his first one, and I'll give Tim's.'

They checked the amounts and drew up the mixed solution into their syringes, using large intramuscular needles because of the density of the fluid, which had an oddly musty smell.

'All right, Talbot – here's your first injection of penicillin,' said Lily, screening off the bed. 'I'll give it into your bottom – on the right side. Now, then . . .'

Talbot gasped and groaned as the injection was forced through the needle. 'Good God, Sister, it's worse than the pain in the stump! Will there be many more?'

Lily simply had not the heart to say that it was only the first of four-hourly injections round the clock for five days, and could only hope that he would get used to it.

Mrs Knowles was visiting Tim, and Matron asked her to wait outside the room while the injection was needed. His agonised yell of pain brought her back in, just as he gave a jump that caused the needle to be withdrawn too soon.

'I won't have him experimented on, an' that's final!' Mabel exclaimed, and a brief, angry exchange took place between the two women.

'Do you realise that this new drug is literally worth its weight in gold, and you've made me waste half of it, Mrs Knowles?'

'I don't give a fig how much it costs! All I know is that my boy's suffered enough, an' I won't have him tortured any more!'

'Very well. You have denied your son the privilege of being among the very first patients to receive a new drug, and that's your responsibility,' said Bertha McGawley, disappearing before anything else could be said, though Lily overheard her talking to a VAD in her office.

'Ignorant woman! If it wasn't for poor Sister Knowles I'd have her escorted off the premises!'

'But, Matron, it's horrible stuff,' protested Lily, who had come to report that F/S Talbot had begged not to be given any more injections of the new drug. 'He says it's worse than the pain in the stump, and he – oh, it's too *cruel* – and we don't really know how effective it is, do we?'

'What the hell's going on here?' demanded the colonel, striding in at that moment with his cane under his arm and a frown on his face. He glanced at Lily. 'What's the matter with her? She's usually such a sensible girl – and I've never seen you hysterical before, Matron!'

'I'm *not* hysterical, I'm just thoroughly annoyed, Colonel. We're not having much success with Lieutenant Edlinger's revolutionary penicillin!'

And both she and Sister Knowles told him in some detail of their unfortunate experiences.

'Hm! Damned namby-pamby attitudes these days. If they'd gone through the Somme in 1916, they'd have had something to whine about – if they'd survived,' blustered the old colonel, somewhat at a loss. He sniffed, rubbed the side of his nose, tweaked at his moustache and finally pointed his cane in the direction of the Huts.

'All right, then, we'll try it out on those buggers over there – a five-day course for Hut One only, and then compare with Hut Two. The medical orderlies can give it under my supervision, only you'd better check the doses with me, Matron.' He sighed heavily. 'I don't know – women!'

And within an hour the first round of penicillin injections had been given to the inmates of Rose Cottage – men whose buttocks and thighs were already bruised black and blue from injections of arsenic and mercury compounds.

Lily never forgot that week. Like doctors and nurses in service hospitals around the world, the staff of RAFH Beversley watched as miracles happened before their eyes: the yellow powder with the musty smell was to change the treatment of septic wounds and infections for ever. In Rose Cottage the men's symptoms had noticeably diminished after twenty-four hours, and two days later they were incredulously comparing the effect of penicillin with each other. At the end of the course they were cured of gonorrhoea, and depending on the stage of syphilis, that too retreated before the powerful drug. The news permeated Bever House like wildfire, and not only did the inmates of Ivy Cottage demand penicillin, but L/S Baxter and F/S Talbot decided to persevere, with good effect; Tim recovered from pneumonia and Talbot's stump healed cleanly.

'It's truly a miracle,' said Bertha McGawley.

'It works, just as that Jerry MO said it would,' marvelled Lloyd-Worth.

'It's saved him, Lily – it's cured my Tim,' confessed Mabel, and went to apologise personally to Matron, and to thank her. 'I'll never forget what yer done for him here.'

Lily rejoiced at Tim's recovery, and gave thanks for it, but a special little corner of her heart was reserved for Andrew Sharpe, whose life had been transformed by the cure of two hateful diseases. He was ready to be discharged and to rejoin his squadron.

'I've been cleansed, Sister Knowles,' he told her with shining eyes. 'I'm like the leper who was made whole again by the touch of the Lord's hand. I'm a new man – and the rest of my life is going to be devoted to His service.'

'Why, what are your plans, Andrew?' asked Lily, smiling.

'If I survive the war, I'll follow my father into the Methodist Church – and I know I'll be a better minister for this experience, Sister. I'll be able to understand my fellow men – and women – much more than if I hadn't had this affliction. Oh, Sister Knowles, it's just as the Psalm says – how wonderful are the works of the Lord, and His ways past finding out!'

'I'm sure He's got great work for you to do,' said Lily, who wished Andrew well with all her heart, silently remembering her own deliverance from a disgrace that would have ruined her career. 'But let me just say one thing. Don't tell your parents. Don't upset them. God knows about it, so there's no need for anybody else to know.' She hesitated. To say 'good luck' sounded inappropriate. 'Goodbye, Andrew.'

He took her hand and said, 'God bless all of you here – every single one of you.'

It was one more thing she would not be able to tell Grandmama and Grandpapa when she next wrote; neither had she told them about her engagement to Tim Baxter . . .

On the day of Tim's discharge Matron and the colonel shook his hand. Michael Smart, now walking on crutches, was especially grateful for the talks they had shared, the impression made on him by a man who had never had money, status or rank, but whose good nature had made him as popular in a hospital ward as he had been on board ship and in a children's home.

Tim clung to Lily before stepping into Mr Hyde's taxi with Mabel. 'I'll miss yer so much.'

'I'll come over to see you whenever I can, Tim, dear.'

'At least his mother's happy,' remarked Matron when they'd waved goodbye, but Lily felt dejected, knowing that her visits to Pinehurst would necessarily be brief. A PM Sister in wartime did not get holidays, only forty-eight-hour leave passes, and she would have to make the most of precious free afternoons and evenings. And heaven only knew when she would be able to visit her grandparents: her conscience troubled her when she thought about the old couple whose letters reproached her regularly. Recalling their kindness and generosity throughout her nursing career, she would also sometimes remember the Redferns, and she wondered how the old lady was reacting to her grandson's daredevil existence, the constant dread of bad news – the worst news . . . but it was no longer her concern.

The announcement of the landings in Sicily by British, American and Canadian forces brought more personal anxieties to Pinehurst and Cherry Trees, for both Mabel's brother George Court and her nephew Geoffrey Westhouse were involved in this first step towards the liberation of Europe. Hopes began to rise of an earlier end to the war, but for Tim Baxter active service was over. After attending a medical examination he was given six months' sick leave on full pay, and then to be discharged from the navy on health grounds. As Lily had feared, his right shoulder and arm had been permanently damaged, but being left-handed, he was able to take over the administrative work from

Daisy, and free her for the running of the home and care of the children.

Which was just as well, for Mabel, now in her fiftieth year, was showing signs of strain on her heart, and Dr Jarman warned her that she could not continue working at her present pace. Chronic fatigue, an irregular pulse and sudden fainting attacks alarmed her family and caused Daisy to put her foot down and insist that Mabel handed over the reins of Pinehurst to herself and Miss Styles, at least for the time being.

'With Tim home again to do the books, and Miss Styles and Beryl to help me, we'll manage perfectly well,' Daisy insisted, and even on her brief visits Lily saw how the balance of power was subtly changing at Pinehurst. Mabel presided over the Homecoming hour as she had always done, and the children gathered around her with their stories of the day, but Daisy and Tim between them gradually took over the day-to-day management, exercising the benign discipline that had always been a hallmark of Pinehurst.

Lily's twenty-sixth birthday fell on a Friday, and she had promised to cycle over to Pinehurst for tea. It was a mild September day, and on arrival she went straight in through the open door, stopping short on the threshold of the living room. Mabel had fallen asleep in her armchair, a letter from George on her lap; she had been reading it aloud to Tim and Daisy, who sat together on the old sofa, newly re-covered in a tough, child-resistant cretonne. Daisy gave Tim a smile, nodding affectionately towards Mabel, and as he turned his head he caught sight of the figure in the doorway.

'Lily – oh, Lily, ye're here! How long've yer been

standin' there? Happy birthday, darlin'!'

He got up to embrace her, and Daisy rose to put the kettle on.

'We're savin' yer presents till the children come home, Lily,' he said, ''cause they do love to see 'em bein' opened! How long can yer stay this time?'

Mabel woke up with a start, and Lily sat down beside Tim in Daisy's vacated place. When the children came running in from school, the Homecoming was largely taken up with opening her presents to exclamations of delight. There was a leather purse from Mabel, an umbrella from Daisy, and a brush, comb and mirror set from Tim – 'much too extravagant!' she told him. Miss Styles had knitted a matching hat and scarf, and a friendlier Beryl produced a jar of Pond's Vanishing Cream. Some of the children had made cards for her, and Daisy made sure that none of them was left out of the proceedings.

How well Daisy has taken over, thought Lily, and how tactful she is towards her sister – 'Now Mabel dear, don't *fuss*! We've got it all in hand, and there's no need for you to worry. Just sit down and talk with the children, that's what they want the most!'

This really meant 'don't interfere', Lily realised, but was so nicely expressed that no hurt or offence could possibly be taken. And there was no rivalry between the sisters regarding the children, for Mabel was always Mother or Mum, and Daisy was Auntie.

She's much better with them than I ever was, thought Lily; she'd never hit a child – not that Cissie Ditchfield harboured any grudge. On the contrary, she was full of questions about nursing the wounded, and confided that she too wanted to be a nurse when she grew up.

The time slipped by, and Lily noticed that the sky was darkening. She stood up.

'I'm afraid I shall have to be off now,' she said, to a chorus of disappointment from the children. The presents and cards were put into her leather shopping bag and deposited in the bicycle basket. They all crowded to the door to see her off.

'I'll walk with yer as far as the ridge o' Parr's Wood, Lily,' said Tim.

She rightly guessed what he was going to say, and had her answer ready.

'*No*, Tim, we decided not until after the end of the war, didn't we? I'm in the RAF now, and I've got a job to do, just as you have at Pinehurst. I'm sorry to disappoint you, Tim dear, but we can't be married until it's over.'

'But now that I'm back at Pinehurst, Lily, we could run it together, just as I've always dreamed we would,' he pleaded.

'*No*, Tim, I'm not ready for that. I've got my nursing to do, as I just said, and I can't leave it.'

'But we don't know how long the war's goin' to last, do we?'

'A year or two, who knows? Everybody says the tide's turning. Please, Tim, don't try to make me change my mind, because I'm not going to.'

'All right, darlin', I don't want to fall out with yer. It's just that it's such a hell of a long wait. Kiss me, Lily – forgive me, dear, I just need yer so much!'

They kissed, and she mounted the bicycle to pedal away as fast as she could in the fading light, as if pursued by her own troubled thoughts; and then, free-wheeling down the long, slow incline until the roof of Bever House appeared below the beech wood, it seemed that the confusion in her mind suddenly cleared, and the undeniable truth stared her in the face.

The first person she saw on entering was Matron. 'Ah, you're back, Sister. Did you have a nice time? How's Tim? Would you like a mug of cocoa?'

'Matron, I – oh, Matron, I've made the most terrible mistake!' she heard herself saying.

'My dear, whatever's the matter? What's happened?'

'I can't marry him, I can't, I can't!' she cried wildly, clasping her hands together. 'I *can't*! I'm not worthy of him – oh, my God, what shall I do?'

'Ssh, calm yourself, Sister, somebody will hear. Quiet! You don't want me to have to slap you, do you? Come into my office – now!'

Having made Lily sit in a chair opposite her, Bertha McGawley took hold of both her hands.

'Now then, Sister, let's have a bit of common sense. I've been wondering how long it would be before you realised that dear Tim Baxter is not for you.'

Lily stared at her. 'Is that what you really thought? I've never been worthy of him, never!'

'Don't be silly. It's not a case of being worthy or otherwise. You're not right for him, nor he for you. You made a decision on the spur of the moment, and it was the wrong one. No harm has been done. You only have to break it off and give him back his ring.'

'Only? *Only*, Matron? And break his heart when he's been through so much? How can I? His mother would never forgive –'

'Never mind about his mother. It's your life, Lily. And *his*, because there'd be no happiness for either of you. Look here, I suggest that you stay away from Pinehurst for a while, get him used to being without you, and when the opportunity arises . . . Have you a

413

mutual friend who could pave the way for you at all – a member of staff at the home, perhaps?'

'Not really. There's Mrs Baldock – Daisy, she's Mrs Knowles's youngest sister, a very good friend and wonderful with the children – but I don't know. She'd be so hurt and upset on his behalf. Oh, they'd all turn against me, I know they would!' And she sobbed bitterly.

'I wonder,' said Bertha McGawley thoughtfully. 'I think I know one lady who would probably be quite pleased.'

'Do you mean his mother?'

'Yes. And she only wants what's best for her son. Anyway, my dear, we're going to be very busy here, with all the reorganisation over the Huts. Now that there's no longer the need for long-term care for new VD cases, Hut One is to be given over to patients from reconstructive units between operations, men who need hospital care and dressings before going back for further surgery, and they'll be *your* special province. Hut Two is to be converted into a workshop to get the men occupied – anything from weaving to woodcarving, I gather, and there'll be instructors who go from place to place, but Weldon and Price will have to earn their keep as supervisors, and getting selected cases out of the hospital and down into Beversley village – which will mean straight into the White Hart, if I know Ernie Price.'

'So we shall have surgery and rehabilitation, then?'

'Yes. The idea is that the two will overlap when the post-ops progress from ward to workshop.'

'And into the pub,' added Lily, managing a watery smile.

'Exactly, Sister, and we've got to make it work. There won't be much time for a private life, and my suggestion is that you write a letter to poor Tim, breaking off the engagement as gently as you can, and say that life is hectic here at present, and Matron has forbidden you to cycle over to Pinehurst now the days are getting shorter, and it isn't safe. Yes, I think a letter would be best, to save you both embarrassment. Only do it soon.'

'Thank you, Matron.' Lily wiped her eyes, and Miss McGawley remembered that it was her birthday.

'Look, can I offer you a small Scotch? I often find it's a help at difficult times, as long as it's used sensibly, and never while on duty. Cheers! And many happier returns of the day!'

Gratefully Lily acknowledged the reasonableness of everything that this wiser, older woman had said, and yet Tim's devotion continued to haunt her, and the days passed by without the fatal letter being written. For how could there ever be a right time to break his faithful heart?

Work went ahead on the conversion of the Huts, but before it was completed the new surgical cases began to arrive, and Sister Knowles found herself trying to nurse quite seriously ill men in a dust-laden atmosphere of hammering and sawing. Matron begged for more trained staff, and in October a Sister Selleck arrived. She had previously nursed in Malaya as a civilian, and had succumbed to malaria. She had the dried-out complexion of an Englishwoman exposed to tropical conditions, and her skin was yellowed by mepacrine, but she quickly proved herself to be adaptable and well experienced in both theatre and ward work. When Lily casually remarked over coffee that malaria must be very unpleasant, Jane Selleck replied grimly that unpleasant or not, it had saved her life; she had got away just before the fall of Singapore.

'God only knows what's happened to my colleagues, but at the mercy of the Japs, I doubt if any of them will have survived. I haven't heard a word, and I suspect the worst.'

With the extra help and the completion of the new ward and workshop, life became a little less stressful, and two weeks later Matron produced a surprise for Sister Knowles: a forty-eight-hour leave pass.

'You need a complete change of scene and a rest, Sister. I'm sorry I can't offer you longer, but you can take the Friday afternoon off and stay away until Sunday night. Haven't you got a friend who lives on some grand estate in Wiltshire?' suggested Miss McGawley, who was in fact quite worried by her sister's weary, run-down appearance.

But Lily knew exactly what she would do with her weekend of freedom. At the earliest opportunity she hurried down to the Beversley Post Office and sent a telegram to Northampton.

The old couple were patiently waiting at the station when she eventually arrived at ten o'clock that Friday night. There was not a word of reproach in their welcome.

'Look, James, there she is – Lilian, *dear*!'

'Grandmama – Grandpapa – I'm sorry – I'm so sorry!' she repeated, hugging them in turn as they each took an arm as if she were an invalid, and led her out to the waiting taxi-cab.

'Tomorrow you can tell us all about your life as a Royal Air Force Nursing Sister, Lilian, but tonight you're going straight to bed with a hot milk drink!'

How good they were to her, she thought as she closed her eyes in the familiar pretty room with her mother's framed photograph on the dressing table. Thank heaven that there was now no need to tell them of her engagement to Tim Baxter . . .

Saturday began with breakfast in bed, followed by a leisurely morning of talking with Grandpapa in his study, and with Grandmama, who was preparing lunch in the kitchen, assisted by her daily help.

'I'm doing a chicken casserole, and all the vegetables are from the garden!' said the old lady happily. 'And I want you to put on the green velvet dress you'll find in the wardrobe, Lilian, and your pearls. James, make sure that the sherry's decanted, and get a bottle of claret up from the cellar! We've got a little surprise for you, Lilian!'

When she realised that Dr and Mrs Wardley would be joining them, she felt a little awkward, remembering how keen her grandparents had been on making a match with their son, but when Dennis himself appeared, Flight Lieutenant Wardley, surgical registrar from RAFGH Halton, she could not hide her astonishment. He kissed her in front of them all.

'Lily, this is wonderful! Thanks to your good grandparents, who tipped me off!'

'So I see,' she said, quite overwhelmed by the memories that flooded back at the sight of him. She took a glass of sherry from her grandfather and drew a few deep breaths.

'I want to hear all about RAFH Beversley, Lily.'

'And I want to hear about RAFGH Halton, Dennis. We've had one or two post-ops from you, and it sounds a splendid place. Mr McIndoe visits you quite often, doesn't he?'

'Oh, yes, he's a terrific character, right at the forefront of reconstructive surgery. And now that we've got penicillin, there's so much more we can do.'

They chatted easily together, and the two older couples exchanged nods and glances. When Grandmama announced that luncheon was served, they sat down to eat in style.

Over the meal the conversation continued to be dominated by hospital experiences, and Lily was asked about the impact of penicillin at Beversley; she managed to reply without reference to the Huts and their function at that time, in order to spare her grandparents.

'No doubt about it, it'll change the whole face of medicine,' Dennis declared. 'Wait until it's in general use, and we'll see the end of septicaemia. And the difference it's made to the treatment of burns – well, it's nothing short of a revolution. We've got these intravenous drips, creams and ophthalmic drops. Even with the most horrific facial burns we can use –'

'Oh, Dennis, I don't think we need to go into quite such detail while we're eating this excellent lunch!' protested Mrs Wardley, giving her husband a nudge with her foot. 'Change the subject!' she whispered under her breath. He cleared his throat.

'I think Dennis's excitement is quite understandable,' he said with a smile. 'Remember that he's seeing these cases at first-hand. They're men he has come to know personally, just as Lilian gets to know her patients as individuals – and as I do, of course, in my own sphere as a GP. Tell Lilian about that tragic case of the ace fighter pilot who went on to Bomber Command – the one who's lost –'

'Shut up, Pa,' Dennis muttered, and a sudden

silence fell on the small company. Lily stiffened, and put down her knife and fork.

'Really, Dennis!' said his mother in surprise, while his father looked bewildered.

'Er – have I said something out of turn, then?'

'More casserole, anyone?' asked Mrs Rawlings in an effort to disperse the tension. 'There are some runner beans left, and potatoes – do help yourselves.'

Lily spoke quietly. 'Go on, Dennis. Tell us about him.'

'Actually, Lily, I think Mother's right. This isn't the time or the place for gory details. We'd much rather hear about your eccentric old colonel!'

'Tell us about this pilot, Dennis,' she repeated. 'Please, I want to know.'

'I'm sorry, Lily, I didn't intend to mention it,' he replied, looking daggers at his father.

Lily's voice was a strained whisper. 'Are you talking about Group Captain Redfern?'

'Lilian dear, you've gone as white as a sheet!' cried Mrs Rawlings. 'Do you want to leave the table and go and lie down for a while?'

'Oh, my God, is he somebody you know, my dear?' asked Dr Wardley. 'I'm terribly sorry.'

Lily gulped a mouthful of water, and drew on the reserves of strength she had built up over the past five years: her training at St Mildred's, and all that had happened since.

'Are you saying that Sandy Redfern's at Halton?' she asked, facing Dennis squarely.

'Yes, he is, but –'

'How long?'

'About three weeks. Look, I never intended –'

'I want to see him, and I've only got forty-eight hours' leave. Will you take me to him today?'

'Oh, Lilian, not *today*!' Mrs Rawlings' protest was an old woman's wail.

'Will you take me to see him, Dennis, please? This afternoon?'

'It would do no good, Lily. He won't want to see you. Even McIndoe can't talk sense to him.'

'If you won't take me to Halton, I shall have to get a train. Will you all excuse me?'

'Lilian! For Heaven's sake get a hold on yourself!' her grandmother implored.

But she had risen from her chair, and would not be dissuaded.

'I shall have to get a train. I must go to Aylesbury,' she said. 'Is there a taxi service to take me to the station?'

Dennis rose and took hold of her arm, none too gently. 'Look here, I'll take you to Halton if you're absolutely determined to go,' he told her. 'But you can find your own way back again. My petrol allowance doesn't run to every female whim and fancy. Come on, then, let's go!'

And the luncheon so lovingly prepared and beautifully served was abandoned while Lily threw on her hat and coat over the green velvet dress, ignoring all remonstrances. She hurried out with Dennis and got into his car, leaving her grandparents to apologise to the Wardleys as well as they could.

'I'm really very grateful to you, Dennis.'

'Don't bother. I've no patience with you, Lily,' he answered angrily. 'This man cares nothing at all for you, as he's proved in the past – yet as soon as you hear his name you forget duty and dignity. You've behaved abominably to your grandparents and to my mother and father – and this is the last time you'll make use of me.'

'Dennis, I'm sorry. I'm honestly sorry, but I must see him, and this is all the time I've got.'

Wardley remained silent, fixing his eyes on the empty road ahead: the road that ran south into Buckinghamshire, to Aylesbury and the RAF General Hospital at Halton, where lay the man Lily was demanding to see.

When they were within about ten miles of their destination, Wardley appeared to relent a little.

'I'd better give you some idea of what to expect, Lily, though I can't guarantee what sort of a vile mood he'll be in.'

'Will he be blind?' she asked quickly, for this had been the thought uppermost in her mind.

'He's lost the left eye and ear and half the scalp. The right eye's had a lid transplant, with a fair chance of saving the sight. Both hands are burned, so he won't be able to see you or touch you. I suggest you touch his right shoulder to make contact. I'm sorry, Lily.'

For she had gasped and whispered, 'Oh, my God – Sandy.' But she quickly composed herself, and asked, 'Was this on a bombing raid?'

'Yes, over Stuttgart. He'd unloaded his high explosives and was on the way back when he was caught by anti-aircraft fire. Managed to limp home and crash-land in a field where the fuel tank blew up before he could crawl free. He was the only survivor – got taken to a civilian hospital and sent on to us.'

She took a deep breath and exhaled slowly. 'Do you think he'll survive, Dennis?'

'We've had cases just as bad that are doing quite well, but it's his attitude that's against him. He just wants to overdose on morphia, and refuses to go to East Grinstead on McIndoe's invitation. His poor old grandfather comes to see him, but all he gets is blasphemy, like the rest of us. I've never known a more recalcitrant patient.'

'And – Mrs Palmer-Bourne?'

'I'd rather not repeat what he called her. And whatever *you* do, don't cry.'

'Don't worry, I won't. Thank you, Dennis. Maybe I'll be able to get through to him, maybe not. At least you've given me the chance.'

He shrugged and said nothing more, though as he led her up the flight of stairs to the ward, he put an arm around her shoulders.

Chapter 19

Group Captain Alexander Redfern, DFM, DFC and double bar, is twenty-five years old and longs only for death – or failing that, the next injection of morphia – blessed morphine sulphate that takes away the worst pain he has ever known, and carries him up into that azure heaven above the clouds where he flies free as a bird. Below him the earth spreads out like a carpet – open country with farms and woodland, towns astride their rivers, linked by main roads and railways, bounded by the coastline and the sparkling Channel. He looks down on his country with pride, knowing himself to be a match for any marauding Messerschmitt, for this is the Spitfire summer of 1940, and he is one of the Few; and he knows too that on his return the sweetest of girls is waiting for him, that dear little nurse, his lovely Lily . . .

But after the dream comes the nightmare, the horror that he must re-live again and again. The sky darkens to pitch-blackness, and he is flying a Lancaster bomber with throbbing engines and a cargo of death. There is the familiar rush of adrenaline as the bombs rain down on Stuttgart and the explosions begin, a massive firework display lighting up the sky: and there are searchlights too, picking him up in their crossed beams while anti-aircraft fire crackles all around him. He smiles, for he has become a legend in the squadron. He leads a charmed life, and the flak always misses his crate by inches. Mission accomplished, he's heading for home and the woman who waits impatiently to fold him in her arms, to wrap her legs around him, recklessly matching his desire with her own. Daphne! Daphne the insatiable, who can never get enough of him – oh, Daphne, woman in a thousand, I'm coming home to you!

But something's wrong this time. There is a terrific bang and a jolt. The Lancaster has been hit, and he briefly dives and rises again. Now memory grows dark. He has got to limp back across the Channel if he can, and try to land on open ground. Lower and lower into the impenetrable dark, a crash and an enormous flash, a fireball and the sound of men's voices screaming in fear. Blackness. Pain. And the waking up to days and nights blurred by a pain that leaves no room for anything else. He's still breathing and his heart's still beating, but he's blind and he's lost half his head, or so it seems. The left side has been scraped off, leaving only a blazing agony in its place. Day – night – day – night – how long? A week? A month? He has had an operation on his right eye, but the only thing he cares about is the pain-relieving injection.

Voices, men's and women's, come to him through the mists – and he hears a nurse speaking in a low voice: 'Visitor for you, Alex.' There are footsteps and he picks up a familiar fragrance of perfume. Daphne! Has Daphne come to see him?

There is a gasp, a retching sound, and the nurse says 'Careful!' – because Daphne is vomiting where she stands. He hears the obscene splatter on the floor beside his bed. More gaggings and heavings, and the nurse mutters under her breath as she leads Daphne away, still heaving helplessly. He hears their departing footsteps, followed by the sound of somebody with a bucket and mop, coming to clear up the mess. So much for women's love . . . bitches on heat, more like it.

More voices come to him, kind and well-meaning, but he can't be bothered with them. A man is saying things like 'help' and 'co-operate', empty words with no meaning. Some poor sod's making a hideous noise like an animal caught in a trap – and he realises that it's himself, a sign that the pain is returning. Come on, Nurse, where are you? Got my injection ready? Hurry up, you silly cow, come on, come *on*!

Two pairs of footsteps again, and a man's voice saying, 'I've got a visitor for you, Redfern.'

'Is that Wardley?' he asks as somebody comes close to his bed. 'The only visitor I want is the nurse with the hypodermic.'

'Hello, Sandy.' He hears a new voice, calm and cool as a mountain spring. It sends a tremor through him.

'What? Who is it? Which one are you?' he demands. 'Have you got my injection?'

'No, Sandy, I don't work here, I've just come to see you. I'm Lily Knowles – remember me?'

'Lily? You can't be true – Lily? I can't see you or touch you . . .'

'I'll put my hand on your right shoulder – there.' He feels a gentle touch, as soothing as the voice. He is confused. '*Lily*? They said you were dead, but then I heard you'd escaped and left London. Is it really you – *here*?'

The fingers move on his shoulder. 'Yes, Sandy – and so happy to see you again.'

'Happy? Good God! Happy to see a man with half a head! Didn't they warn you?'

'Of course I was told what had happened, and of course I'm sorry to see you in a burns unit, but don't forget that I'm a nurse, and I've seen many cases of airman's burn, like yours.'

'Have you? But you looked after old ladies at that little hospital where Grannie was – you were arranging the flowers—'

'Ah, but I'm a nursing sister in the RAF now – and I have an uncle who had the same sort of injury as you in the last war. He wears a patch over his eye and practises as a solicitor. He's a good one too.' Her voice sounds so calm and matter-of-fact.

'Lily, I can't believe you're real. How did you know about me?'

'Flight Lieutenant Wardley told me – the surgical registrar here.'

'Wardley? Is he a friend of yours?'

'Yes, Dennis was a medical student at Bart's when I was at St Mildred's.'

'Dennis? Is that his name? Ah, don't tell me he was that tight-lipped bod with you at Ken Wood that Sunday afternoon we listened to Sibelius! I never realised. So good old Dennis stayed the course, and got you in the end, then.'

'I only wish that were true, Redfern.' Wardley's voice is coolly neutral. 'Look, Lily, I'll leave you here for half an hour, OK? I've squared it with Sister, and I'll telephone my parents to say that we're returning to Northampton this evening.'

'Thank you, Dennis, it's very good of you. I'll see you at about five, then.'

Wardley's footsteps depart, and for the next half-hour she talks quietly with him in that steady, low-pitched voice.

'How are your grandparents?' she asks.

'Grannie's dead. Her heart gave out – it was all the worrying over me.'

'I'm so sorry. And Grampy?'

'He comes over on the train to see me, not that it gives either of us much pleasure. James and Mary came once, but I couldn't be bothered with them, so they did as I suggested, and shoved off again.'

'And are you going to tell me to shove off too?'

'No. In any case, I don't believe you're really here. You must be a dream. Ha! I treated you badly, Lily, I was a selfish oaf – and now you've come to get your own back, fair enough.'

'How do you mean?'

'You've come here to pity me, like everybody else.'

She hesitates as if to consider her reply. 'Of course it's a pity to see you like this,' she says, and just for a moment her voice seems to shake, but she continues firmly, 'The sort of pity to beware of is self-pity, and I won't encourage you to indulge in that!'

'What will you encourage me to indulge in, then?'

'Well, if you've got any sense you'll stop resisting Mr McIndoe, and let him help you. Go to the Queen Victoria Hospital at East Grinstead, and let him see what he can do.'

'Oh, Christ, Lily, I can't be bothered. However he patches me up, I'll always be a freak, a bogey-man with half his face missing. I'll take the morphia and fly away, the sooner the better.'

'I see. So you don't want me to come and visit you again?'

'Y-yes, I do – that's if you're real, and willing to. How far have you come?'

'I'm stationed at RAFH Beversley in deepest Hampshire, quite a journey, and I only get one forty-eight-hour pass in a month – but it would be easier for me to get to East Grinstead.'

She's actually bargaining with him, so she must be real! If only he could see her face . . .

A nurse comes to take his temperature and pulse: she puts a thermometer in his mouth and places two fingers lightly on his temple. While she counts the pulse-beats Dennis Wardley returns to take Lily away. The half-hour has passed, the pain has come back, and his mouth stretches in a grimace.

'Time for your injection, Group Captain,' says the nurse, reading the thermometer.

'And time for me to say good-bye,' adds Lily, patting his shoulder before removing her hand. 'If you like I'll come to see you at East Grinstead when I get my next leave.'

She stands up and leans over him. He feels her forefinger touching his neck, stroking up towards his chin, trailing over it until she reaches his mouth, the only part of his face not covered by bandages. His lips close over her fingertip in a kiss.

'Lily, thou fairest one of flowers all – remember St Paul's?' he asks, and she puts her mouth close to his right ear, so that only he can hear her whispered reply.

'How could I ever forget? And I'll see you there again, Sandy.'

She straightens up and says aloud, 'Dennis will let me know when you're transferred to East Grinstead, but for now it has to be goodbye.'

He hears the departing footsteps. She has gone – but she has promised to return.

*

Once outside the ward, Lily Knowles's iron self-control gave way completely, and Wardley had to steer her into a small waiting room where she leaned against him and sobbed her heart out in mourning for Sandy Redfern's youthful good looks, his daring high spirits, his manly strength, all so tragically ruined. And his eyes, oh, those blue eyes!

'I'm sorry, Dennis, I'm sorry, I'm sorry . . .'

'So am I, but you've performed a miracle this afternoon, Lily. I've never heard him respond so well. Here, use this.' He produced a large white handkerchief, and she wiped her eyes and nose. 'I'll see if I can beg a cup of tea for you from one of the wards.'

'No, Dennis, let's be going. It's a long way to drive in the dark. You've been so good to me today, and I'm grateful, really and truly I am. Heaven knows what your parents will think, and my poor grandparents – but I'll never be able to repay you.'

'And just think, if I hadn't told Pa about Redfern in the first place, you wouldn't have known, and we wouldn't have come!'

'Which makes me believe that it was meant to be,' she answered.

He took her arm as they walked out of the building and towards his car. 'Redfern's going to need a different kind of courage now. McIndoe will have to do several operations on that face, and he can only succeed if Redfern really wants him to. If anybody can pull him back from the brink, you can – but he'll have to co-operate.'

'I've promised to visit him at East Grinstead,' she said as he opened the passenger door.

'Yes, he's got something to live for. Ha! Some contrast between you and that other woman!'

429

'Do you mean Mrs Palmer-Bourne? Did she come to see him?'

'She came, yes, and threw up all over the place. She couldn't stomach it. I saw her leaving the hospital, looking like a haggard old woman. I've never had a lot of time for her, as you know, but I actually pitied her then.'

'Poor Daphne,' murmured Lily, staring ahead into the darkness.

'Yeah.' And poor old Dennis too, Wardley thought to himself, for he understood now that he had no chance with Lily Knowles as long as Redfern survived, however disfigured he might be.

'It was too bad of you, Lilian!' Mrs Rawlings made no attempt to hide her indignation at the humiliation she and her husband had suffered. 'How could I possibly excuse you to the Wardleys?'

'I'm terribly sorry, Grandmama.'

'I'm afraid that *sorry* isn't good enough, Lilian. You stay away from us for months at a time, yet you're off to Belhampton as soon as that Knowles woman beckons. After your father died, we thought that would be the end of it, but for reasons best known to yourself you stayed on at that place instead of returning to Rauceby.'

'I know I must have seemed ungrateful, but—'

'But this has been inexcusable. James and I had been so looking forward to seeing you again at long last, and poor Dr Wardley went to a lot of trouble to get this Saturday off. And what do you do? You force him to rush you off at a moment's notice to visit this airman, without any apology or explanation. It was so embarrassing for us! And let me tell you that his parents are deeply offended. I'm very disappointed in you, Lilian.'

'Oh, Grandmama, if you could only see his injuries –'

'*Whose* injuries? Who *is* this mysterious pilot you had to rush off to see?'

'He's the RAF officer I told you about, the one who was brought up by his grandparents. Don't you remember, I went to dinner with them in St John's Wood, and you wrote back to say that you'd like to meet him?'

'Yes, I do remember. But later you said that he'd drifted away, and you'd lost touch.'

'Yes, he found somebody else, but – but that's all over now, Grandmama, and when I heard that he was in RAF Halton with terrible burns, I just *had* to see him again, can't you understand that? And as soon as I saw him I knew that I must do what I can to help him recover, though he'll always be badly scarred. Oh, Grandmama, please try to understand!'

But Mrs Rawlings was not yet ready to forgive her wayward granddaughter. 'Oh, you silly girl, throwing your life away when you could have Dr Wardley, such an excellent young man in every way, and so devoted to you. You've treated him shamefully, and I've no patience with you. You must have inherited a wilful streak from your father, because Dilly would never have caused all this trouble!'

Lily saw that it was useless to argue, and was silent and subdued for the rest of her visit. She accompanied her grandparents to church on Sunday morning, and after lunch took her leave of them and set out on the long and tedious journey, first to Euston, then by underground to Waterloo for the train to Belhampton, and Hyde's taxi to Beversley.

'Ah, the wanderer's return,' grinned Jane Selleck.

'You've got some explaining to do, madam! Your fiancé has been round to see you, and Matron had to tell him you were away on weekend leave, visiting your grandparents – and the band played "Believe it if you like!"'

'Oh hell,' muttered Lily – and found Miss McGawley equally unsympathetic.

'I have to say I think you've treated Tim Baxter most unfairly, Sister Knowles. You should have broken off the engagement before now. The poor fellow came here to ask why you hadn't been home – to Pinehurst – for the last fortnight, and I had to say you'd gone to Northampton. He looked absolutely stricken, and I suggest you get in touch with him as soon as possible and tell him the truth. You owe him that much, surely!'

Lily apologised as well as she could, and promised that she would write to Tim Baxter at the earliest opportunity. But how could she break the unwelcome news? Should she perhaps write to Mabel at the same time?

Yes, that would be best, and on Monday afternoon, when she had a couple of hours off duty, she sat down to write the two letters. Should she tell Tim about Sandy Redfern, and how he had come back into her life? Yes, she must be truthful, and so she spent an hour writing and rewriting the fatal letter, begging his forgiveness and saying that she was not the right woman to be his wife, nor could she ever aspire to being Matron of Pinehurst.

When it was finally written, signed and sealed, she put it aside and took another sheet of paper to write to Mabel – but before she had dipped her pen in the ink, one of the VADs came to summon her to Matron's office. 'There's somebody to see you, Sister.'

Tim! He must have come over again, she thought, bracing herself for the encounter; but the visitor was not Tim but Mabel, standing by Matron's desk like an avenging angel. Even Miss McGawley had been taken aback by her forthright demand to see Sister Knowles.

'I'll leave you two here in the office,' said the matron as she retreated, closing the door behind her, but not moving out of earshot.

Mabel came straight to the point. 'Right, Lily, where had yer gone when Tim came lookin' for yer yesterday?'

Lily swallowed. 'I was visiting my grandparents at Northampton,' she replied, 'and I was also taken to seen an injured pilot at RAFH Halton – an officer I knew when I was at St Mildred's.'

'Oh, yes? And is this injured officer important in yer life? More so than Tim Baxter?'

'Perhaps. I'm not sure, Mabel – he might be if he survives. He's very badly injured, and I – I shall have to give him what help and encouragement I can.'

'And what about my Tim? Doesn't *he* come in for any o' this help an' encouragement?'

'Oh, Mabel, I should never have got engaged to Tim, and I'm so terribly sorry!' Lily burst out. 'I just hadn't the heart to refuse – and then I hadn't the heart to break it off. I've written him this letter   ' She held out the envelope with shaking hands. 'Will you please give it to him?'

Mabel Knowles made a clucking sound with her tongue against her teeth. 'An' does this letter make it quite clear about breakin' it off?'

'Yes, Mabel, it does.' Lily hung her head, avoiding Mabel's eyes as fresh tears gathered in her own. 'If you'll take it and give it to him, I'll be most grateful.

I know what you must think of me, but it can't be any worse than what I think of myself. I'm a coward, and not worthy of him.'

If Lily had looked up then, she would have seen a softening of Mrs Knowles's stern gaze.

'I'll see that he gets it, don't worry. It'll break the poor boy's heart, but it could be worse – at least ye've found out in time. All I ask is that yer keep well away from Pinehurst for a while, certainly for the rest o' this year.' She stepped closer to Lily, patting her on the shoulder. 'I'll break it to him as well as I can. War's a terrible thing, an' people do things they wouldn't've done in better times. I wish yer well with yer airman. Goodbye, Lily.'

'That's a good job done, Sister Knowles,' said Matron with an approving nod after Mabel's departure, but Lily felt utterly wretched as she washed her face, drank a cup of tea and reported back on duty in Hut 1, the surgical ward. Her work had always been her best consolation, but her heart went on aching for both the men who so clearly needed her love.

There were two letters for Lily at coffee-time on the following Wednesday morning. She recognised Daisy's handwriting, and opened it first, hoping to find at least a degree of understanding. The letter was blotted and had obviously been written in haste – and anger. Lily gasped with dismay at the reproaches in every line:

Dear Lily,

I wish you could see the trouble you have caused here. Tim is distraught by your cruel letter. It is the collapse of all his dreams at a time when he is not yet recovered from all he has

434

been through. Not only that, but Mabel has suffered a heart attack over it and is in Belhampton War Memorial Hospital on complete bed rest, and mind that you keep away from her. Miss Styles and Beryl and I are doing our best to care for the children, but we are shocked and appalled by the heartless way you have treated our dear friend and brother as Tim has always been. Keep away from Pinehurst because you are not welcome here.

D. Baldock.

It was a bitter blow to read such words from somebody Lily had known and loved all her life as a kind and indulgent aunt, and later as a sister. Oh, what harm she had done to these dear people, especially to Tim and Mabel! And there was nothing she could do to make amends.

As soon as she was able, she put through a call to Belhampton Hospital to enquire about Mrs Knowles.

'Are you a relative?' asked a brisk female voice.

'Yes, I'm her stepdaughter, Miss Knowles.'

'Can't you contact her sister at Pinehurst Home for Waifs and Strays?'

'Well, actually it's rather difficult. You see, I'm a sister at the RAF Hospital at Beversley. Oh, please tell me – is she dangerously ill?' Lily's voice trembled as she begged for information. She heard a muttered exchange at the other end of the line, and a different voice came back to say merely, 'Mrs Knowles has had a good night, and is comfortable. Good morning.'

At least this meant that Mabel was not in immediate danger. Lily must somehow hide her misery and carry out her duties. She put the other letter in her pocket to read later.

'You all right, Sister Knowles?' asked Jane Selleck at lunch-time. 'You look a bit white around the gills.'

'I'm all right – well, no, I'm not, really,' faltered Lily. 'Problems with relatives; it's all a bit complicated.' She tried to speak lightly, but failed completely.

'Anything to do with your weekend leave?'

'Well, no, not directly, although – the trouble is that I've had to break off an engagement, and it's upset everybody.'

'That's a shame, but as long as *you* know you've done the right thing, that's all that matters. These things blow over in time. Er – I suppose there's somebody else. Want to talk about it?'

Lily could not reply for the choking sensation in her throat, but forced herself to eat some lunch and excused herself, murmuring, 'Mr Day's coming over to do two ops this afternoon, and I'd better go and get things ready.'

By the time she eventually got off duty and fled to the privacy of her room, she allowed herself to give way to tears. Daisy's rejection had hurt her more than she had realised at first, and it almost seemed as if time had rolled backwards, and she was once again the rebellious twenty-one-year-old, defying her father and Mabel, being rude to Tim and leaving Pinehurst under a cloud. She had gone to her grandparents and found sympathy there, but now they too were disappointed in her, and so were the Wardleys; even Dennis's patience was wearing thin.

And then through her tears she remembered her father, and how he had looked when he'd visited her at St Mildred's House. She saw again his bowed back and his sorrowful eyes.

I only hope that you are never in the same situation as

we were, Lily – but if you ever are, perhaps you might understand – and forgive.

'Oh, Dad, I do, I do!' she said aloud. 'I'm sorry now for all the cruel things I said. Forgive me, oh God, forgive me!'

It was some comfort to know that she had made her peace with him before he died, but she was utterly miserable at being alienated from Mabel and the home in which she had grown up. She longed to go to Mabel and beg forgiveness – but that was impossible now that she had been forbidden access to her and to Pinehurst.

Only Sandy Redfern, badly injured and hovering between life and death, had shown the slightest need of her: and he was so far away. Any messages between them would have to be relayed by Dennis Wardley, and she had no idea when she would be able to see him again.

Then she remembered the other letter, and took it out of her pocket. The writing was in an old-fashioned hand, rather spidery and unknown to her. She tore open the envelope, and found two closely written pages.

'My dear Miss Knowles,' it began, and Lily glanced at the address at the top of the page: Elmgrove, Hamilton Terrace, St John's Wood – the home of the Redferns! She eagerly read on.

When I visited my grandson this afternoon at the RAF Hospital at Halton, I could not believe the change in him. All his former cynical harshness had gone, and the poor boy actually asked my pardon for his earlier behaviour. This of course was freely given, especially in view of his completely changed demeanour. To my joy I

437

found that he has regained *hope*, and told me that he is soon to be transferred to a specialist hospital in Sussex for skin grafting, which he had hitherto refused. At first I could not believe the evidence of my own ears, but I soon discovered that the reason for it was your visit to him on Saturday afternoon. How can I thank you, my dear Lily, for this miraculous change? And I beg you to visit Alex again whenever you can. I shall be happy to pay your travelling expenses.

As you will know, Alex is at present unable to read or write, but I have gladly agreed to act as a go-between, to carry messages for you. You can write to him at my address, and I will read your letters to him with all discretion and confidentiality. He can then dictate his replies to me, which I will then send on to you. It will be a happy task for me, I assure you, dear Lily, and I enclose a few stamped, addressed envelopes for your use.

I now live alone since my poor wife's death, with the daily charwoman's assistance. How times have changed since those happier days when Alex brought you to our home! We were very sad about the bombing of St Mildred's, but greatly relieved to hear many months later that you had not been killed on that terrible night. Life has been a nightmare since Alex became a bomber pilot, and we could not condone his way of life. My wife's heart succumbed to the constant anxiety, as she had always feared that he would meet his death in the same way as his father, a flyer in the last war.

Just to know that you have renewed your

friendship with Alex in these tragically altered circumstances is the best news I have had for years, and I shall be forever in your debt.

I am, dear Miss Knowles – let me call you Lily –

Your obedient servant,
Alexander W. Redfern

Once again Lily's tears flowed, but this time they sprang from the fullness of her thankful heart. Here at any rate was one who did not accuse or reproach her, who did not warn her to stay away. On the contrary, this man begged her to visit his grandson. How eagerly would she take up his offer to act as go-between! She got out her writing-pad, pen and ink straight away, and before retiring to bed she had written to both father and son. Her letter to Sandy was encouraging and affectionate without being intimate, and had no stronger endearments than 'dearest Sandy' – but she knew that her mention of St Paul's Cathedral would remind him of their first kiss, and the line 'London, thou art the flower of cities all' would be changed into his own special version of it in praise of her.

Before getting into bed, Lily kneeled down beside it in the way she had been taught as a child at Pinehurst. There was much cause for sorrow: Sandy's dreadful injuries, the loss of an eye and the possible loss of the remaining one; his grandmother's death, leaving his grandfather a sad and lonely old man; she herself had been rejected by Mabel and Daisy because she had broken Tim Baxter's faithful heart; she was out of favour with her grandparents and she had disappointed Dennis Wardley; even Matron McGawley had chided her for her poor judgement. Yet in spite of everything her first prayer was one of thanks for Redfern's reappearance in her life, for his grandfather's letter, and the prospect of visiting him again at East Grinstead. She prayed earnestly that she would be able to fulfil old Mr Redfern's hopes and give Sandy the sort of help he needed. A burden was lifted from her heart, and in the days that followed it showed in the brightness of her eyes and the new spring in her step.

'You look pleased with yourself this morning, Sister Knowles!' said the men in Hut 1. 'Have you had good news?'

'Er, yes, you could call it good news – after a lot of bad news,' she answered, smiling.

'Heard from your young man, Sister?' asked one of them with a wink, and Lily nodded a little self-consciously.

'Which one?' muttered a VAD nurse who had looked after Tim Baxter and grown to like him, as everybody did.

'Ssh, keep your voice down,' said the nurse who was making beds with her.

'Why should I? I don't wonder that Tim's mother has been on the warpath – coming round here at the weekend when *she* had tootled off to see some RAF type. She's a right little goer, is our Sister Knowles.'

Lily heard every word of this exchange, and caught the look of unapologetic defiance directed at her. What *was* it about hospital grapevines everywhere, she wondered, always humming with the latest news, ahead of all official announcements.

'Right, gentlemen, it's time for the medicine round,' she said brightly. 'And there's a whole basketful of clean laundry to be checked and put away, Nurses – all right?'

And she smiled, because deep down in her heart was something very much like happiness – and no amount of antipathy could diminish it.

'IS YOUR JOURNEY REALLY NECESSARY?' asked the poster at the railway station, but Lily had no doubt about her own; it was just a week before Christmas, and at long last she had got another forty-eight-hour pass. Getting to East Grinstead involved a cross-country journey on suburban lines and unreliable buses, and she decided it would be best to go up to London and come down into Sussex on the Southern Railway line.

The original Queen Victoria Hospital had started as a local cottage hospital, but it had greatly expanded, and with two hundred and thirty beds had become nationally famous as a centre for reconstructive surgery under the leadership of Archibald McIndoe, whose innovative and unconventional approach to injured airmen with burns of the face and hands had become a byword. He looked upon these intelligent, often very handsome young men as fellow human beings rather than as patients, and aimed at giving them back their self-confidence as well as rebuilding their faces. As Lily approached the hospital she saw a signpost indicating a large hut to the left of the original building: this was Ward 3, where she would find Sandy Redfern.

It was like no other ward that Lily had ever seen. A grand piano was being played, and some of the patients were strolling around in sports flannels, shirts and pullovers; there was no sign of the regulation 'hospital blues' with the red tie. One man was tapping away at a typewriter, while others were playing cards or chatting. She at once recognised a faint, unpleasantly sweetish odour as the smell of burned human tissue, but this was overlaid by a stronger and distinctly pub-like aroma, emanating from a large barrel of beer at the end of the ward, which she discovered was on tap to anybody at all times. A coke stove stood in the middle of the ward, and a couple of men sat beside it, reading newspapers and warming their feet.

And there, halfway down on the left, sitting on his bed and anxiously looking out for her with his one eye was Sandy Redfern. He was wearing a dressing gown, and stood up as soon as he saw her. She put on a smile as she walked towards him, instinctively holding out her arms. He drew back slightly, as if fearing that she would be repelled by the sight of him, the ugliness of the lashless eye, now uncovered and functioning with the newly grafted lids. His head was still bandaged, as was his left hand, but the right was exposed and, although raw-looking, was healing and growing new skin.

'Sandy – oh, Sandy, you look so much better,' she told him breathlessly, resting her hands on his shoulders, and looking into the uncovered half of his face. 'So much better,' she repeated softly, and kissed his right cheek. She lifted her trembling hands up and clasped them behind his neck, closing her eyes as their lips met in wordless affirmation that she loved him still, a love unaffected by external appearances.

A round of delighted applause from the other occupants of Ward 3 brought her back to their surroundings.

'Nice one, Sandy, let's have another one!'

'So *that's* why he was squirting posh aftershave all over the place!'

Such was the irreverent atmosphere of Ward 3,

and she drew back, smiling and blushing in self-conscious acknowledgement of their cheeky comments, but not really embarrassed.

He spoke for the first time. 'Not much privacy here, Lily, I'm afraid. They don't mean any harm. In fact, I suppose it's an ideal place to be – you can always find somebody worse off than yourself here. See that chap at the end of the row, the one in the wheelchair. Face and hands burned, and *no legs* – they had to amputate them both. And yet he propelled himself down the ward to speak to me on the day I came in, and said, "What happened to you then, mate?"'

'Ah, and I'll bet that was the moment you started to recover,' she replied, lightly holding his right arm.

'No, *that* was when I heard your voice on that Saturday afternoon at Halton. That was my turning-point, and I'll always be grateful. But first let's get out of this noisy hole. Sister has said I can take you over to a little annexe where we can talk without being overheard.'

She followed him through a door along a covered passage that led to another hut. 'This is for physio-therapy, and we can talk in here,' he said, showing her into a rather comfortless storeroom where they sat on two wooden chairs.

'Oh, Sandy, I'm so happy to see you again!' she said, still holding his right arm. 'I've booked in at a hotel for tonight, so I can stay all day and come back tomorrow morning. Do you realise it's been seven weeks since we first met again?'

He cleared his throat. 'I knew you'd come as soon as you could, because you'd promised, Lily – and every time Grampy read your latest letter, it was just as if you were talking to me.'

'I felt exactly the same when I got your letters, Sandy, written by dear old Mr Redfern. They seemed to bring me closer to both of you. I've really come to love your grandfather, and thanks to him it's just as if we've been meeting regularly – don't you think so?'

'Ah, yes, Lily, I know exactly what you mean – and I wish I could take you out for a drink or a meal, but we're not allowed out while we've still got bandages on. You'd never believe how informal it is here. Some of the chaps go out to the pictures or the pub, and a few come back a bit the worse for wear, but the nurses are fantastic. They're specially trained to care for normal, healthy men who are injured but not ill – there's a difference.'

Lily nodded. 'I know. And is it true that all McIndoe's nurses are pretty?' she asked, smiling.

'Yes, but as far as I'm concerned, *all* nurses are pretty, and none more so than you, Lily.'

'Oh, Sandy, dearest Sandy, what joy to hear that!' she said, her eyes sparkling. 'But tell me what's been happening to you here. How long have you to stay?'

He explained that since his transfer to Ward 3 he had had two further operations, one a skin graft to his scalp, using skin from his thigh, and another on his left hand, from which the ends of his fingers had been amputated.

'I'm to have another op on my head, and then I'll be due for a break at Sainthill Manor, that's a convalescent unit near to East Grinstead,' he told her. 'They've got workshops there.'

'But I *told* you that you'll come to RAFH Beversley between ops, Sandy!' she cried. '*We've* got a workshop and instructors, and – I – we – oh, it would be so wonderful to have you there, and see you every day! Oh, Sandy, you *must* ask to be sent to Beversley!'

But to her surprise he shook his head doubtfully. 'Lily, dear, you mustn't sacrifice too much of yourself on my account. Perhaps it would be best if –'

'*Sacrifice?*' she broke in. 'What do you mean? It would be nothing but happiness to have you near to me and to use the skills I've learned for *your* benefit – can't you *see* that?'

'Ah, but what about Wardley?'

'Wardley? *What* about him?'

'Well, he's obviously loved you for a long time, Lily, since before we ever met. He can offer you much more than I can now, and he has the first claim on you – a first-rate doctor in the same special field as yourself, a fit man who's proved his worth and stayed faithful to you.'

'Oh, Sandy! Dear old Dennis is a fine man, an excellent surgeon, everything you say, but I've never been in love with him, not in the way that I –' She only just checked herself from saying, 'the way that I love you.'

'But surely he deserves a chance, Lily. He's far more deserving of you.'

Lily now began to see that she might have shown her feelings too openly, both by her words and the letters she had written via his grandfather. Yet surely at a time like this, with Sandy badly and perhaps permanently injured, there was no virtue in hiding her love? She longed only to comfort this man and give him a reason for living.

After a short pause, she said, 'Truthfully, Sandy, I've never been in love with Dennis, though he's been a good friend, and I hope he'll find the right girl one day. To be honest, I actually became engaged earlier

445

this year to another man, a sailor, somebody I grew up with in the children's home run by my step-mother. You know, I gave you a wrong impression, Sandy, when I said I'd been brought up by my mother's parents. In fact, there's a lot you don't know about me, and it will all have to be told – but there will be time for that.'

'You say you were *engaged* to this sailor, Lily? When did you break it off? Was it after you visited me at Halton?'

'Yes, but I'd made up my mind to break it off before I heard from Dennis that you were in RAFH Halton, Sandy,' she said, realising that she sounded unconvincing. 'Tim and I weren't suited to each other. I didn't love him in the way he loved me – but he'd gone through so much. He'd been torpedoed twice and was very ill and I pitied him. I mean I –'

Sandy drew in his breath sharply. 'Ah. Beware of pity. That's what you said to *me*, didn't you, Lily?'

'No, I said beware of *self*-pity, Sandy – that's a different matter. I just wasn't right for Tim, but it's been a very painful business, and has upset a lot of people. I regret getting engaged, but not breaking it off. And now that I've met you again, I – I just want to do what I can for you.'

A note of pleading had crept into her voice, and as he slowly shook his bandaged head, she began to be aware of unforeseen difficulties looming between them. He did not share her eager joy: there was a weariness, a deep disillusionment in his voice and manner. She considered her next words carefully.

'Sandy – I've been so happy, knowing that we've met again – your grandfather's happy too. There's no other man for me, no one but you.'

'But I treated you despicably, Lily, and humiliated

you with that – that other woman. I was a swine. And now I've got to find my own way back. I'd despise myself completely if I took advantage of your forgiveness now – and I've already made up my mind not to come to Beversley for convalescence between ops. If I've learned anything from my behaviour with that other woman, it's that I'm utterly unworthy of you.'

Lily suppressed her desire to protest, to beg him not to turn away from her love. Whatever I do, I mustn't cry, she thought.

'Don't be too hard on Mrs Palmer-Bourne,' she said. 'Dennis told me how she reacted, and I've seen it happen before. Don't forget that I'm a nurse and well experienced in these sorts of injuries. Dennis said he actually felt sorry for her, and so do I, but that's nothing to do with us.' In spite of herself her voice shook. 'Look, Sandy, I've come a long way to see you, and I intend to enjoy our time together. Let's go back to Ward Three now, it's a bit chilly here. Only before we do, kiss me again.'

He did so, but with a kind of despair. 'Oh, Lily, you lovely girl, you're much too good for me.'

She stayed with him for the rest of the day, and left at ten o'clock that night to go to her hotel room. She came to him again the following morning until midday, and then had to return to Beversley, insisting that she would come again and continue to write via his grandfather.

No matter what he said or thought, she was quietly determined to make him change his mind by one means or another. She had got him back, and did not intend to lose him again.

Chapter 20

Bertha McGawley had a headache. A post-Christmas torpor hung over RAF Beversley, and some patients were resentful that the workshop was still closed on the 27th because it was officially Boxing Day, the 26th having fallen on a Sunday. Sister Selleck had a cold, and Matron had told her to go to her room and stay there, rather than risk spreading it through the wards, and that meant that there were only two trained staff on day duty, herself and Sister Knowles, assisted by three VADs. And now Knowles wanted to see her about a personal matter.

'All right, Sister, sit down. We haven't much time, with so few staff on duty.' She pushed a cup of coffee across the desk. 'What's it about? I hope you're not thinking of leaving us.'

'No, Matron, I hope to stay here for the duration of the war, however long that will be. I have a request to make concerning a patient at the Queen Victoria Hospital at –'

'At East Grinstead,' Matron broke in. 'Yes, word gets around, Sister. I believe this is another case of airman's burn of the face and hands?'

'Yes, in a very distinguished officer, Matron. He fought in the Battle of Britain, and has since flown on more than twenty operations over enemy territory. His bomber was hit towards the end of September, and he managed to make it back across the Channel and crash-landed in flames. He was at RAFH Halton for two months, and was transferred to East Grinstead early this month. He's lost his left eye and ear, both hands are burned and he's had three operations – and he'll need more. I met him while I was at St Mildred's, just before the war, and his name's Redfern, Group Captain Alexander Redfern.'

Lily had been speaking quickly and nervously, and now paused to get her breath.

'I see. So he's one of Archibald McIndoe's "guinea pigs", then,' Miss McGawley remarked.

'Yes, Matron, you could say that.'

'And I suppose you want him to come here between operations.'

'Yes, Matron. I'd like that very much.'

'Well, it's nothing to do with me, Sister. It's up to Mr McIndoe where he sends his patients for convalescence and rehabilitation. Your group captain had better speak to him about it.'

'But, Matron, you see, that's the trouble. Sandy – I mean Group Captain Redfern – is going through a period of depression and, er – self-accusation, similar to what we've seen here in our NPs, and he says he might as well go to Sainthill Manor – that's a convalescent unit near to East Grinstead. But he'd be so much better off coming here, Matron! He doesn't really care for the constant noise and camaraderie of Ward Three – that's Mr McIndoe's ward, a quite amazing place, always something going on and everybody seems to do as they like . . .'

'Yes, I've heard it's been compared to an ongoing party in a pub,' said the Matron drily. 'McIndoe's a law unto himself, apparently, but a great surgeon. But I don't see how this officer can be forced to come to Beversley if he doesn't want to, however much *you* want him here, Sister Knowles.'

449

'But if Mr McIndoe himself recommended it, Matron – if he told Sandy that he wanted him to go to a quiet place out in the country where he'd have good nursing care and rehabilitation in our Hut Two,' pleaded Lily, her greenish-gold eyes earnestly searching the older woman's face, 'it would mean so much!'

'So much to whom, Sister – him or you? I'm sorry, but I just don't see that any request on my part would count with McIndoe. And I have a sensation of *déjà vu* on this matter, remembering how you bargained with me over bringing Leading Seaman Baxter here, your fiancé at the time, and only six months ago. Then we had all the trauma of your break with him, and the rift with Pinehurst. How are things there now? Did you hear from them at Christmas?'

Lily's face fell. 'I sent cards to them individually, Matron, and I had a card from them all, signed by Mab— by my stepmother, and one from Tim and three from children.'

'Hm. Poor Tim. And now you've found – what's his name, Sandy?'

'I've found him *again*, Matron. We'd lost touch, but now he needs me, and I know I can help him to recover, mentally as well as physically. And – and I told Tim and my stepmother about him, when I broke off the engagement.'

'I see. Well, I'm sorry, Sister, but I really don't see what I can do, especially if this officer says he doesn't *want* to come here.' She glanced at the clock. 'Good heavens, look at the time! We must get back to our patients. Good morning, Sister.'

Lily politely replied, 'Good morning, Matron, and thank you,' as she was dismissed, and that evening she wrote an impassioned letter to old Mr Redfern, begging him to use what influence he had, if any, in persuading his grandson to request Beversley as a place of convalescence. She no longer needed to enclose her correspondence to Sandy, who could now read for himself her friendly, hopeful letters with their amusing anecdotes and avoidance of sentimentality.

The situation between herself and Pinehurst continued to bother her. The only source of news was Geraldine Westhouse, who worked there on a daily basis, leaving eight-month-old Robert in the care of Mrs Westhouse. Geraldine wrote that Mabel's condition was stable, but that she was now only nominally the Matron of the home: the administration and supervision was carried out by Mrs Baldock and Mr Tim, assisted by Miss Styles and Miss Penney.

'Aunt Mabel is still very much "Mother" to the children, and they go straight to her with their stories and problems,' she reported. 'It's impossible to imagine the place without her. I owe her so much for her kindness to me when I was in trouble, and I'm very sorry that you no longer visit, Lily, but the news that you have a friend in the RAF has upset Mrs Baldock very much. I never hear Aunt Mabel or Tim speak a word against you, but I'm afraid Aunt Daisy is adamant.'

Lily was sometimes tempted to go and visit Mabel uninvited, because she felt sure that she would be kindly received as Stephen's daughter; but if it caused a scene with Daisy, and led to Mabel having another heart seizure, she would never forgive herself. She had been ordered to stay away, and that's what she had to do. It served her right, she thought sadly.

Geraldine's letters also brought intermittent news of the two serving soldiers in the family – her brother, Geoffrey, and Mabel's brother George, both engaged in the Italian campaign. The news on the wireless had announced that tens of thousands of British, American and Canadian troops had stormed ashore at Anzio, thirty miles south of Rome, to be greeted with joy by civilians but fierce resistance from Germans; it was impossible to guess the truth about what conditions were like, as very few letters found their way home.

The New Year of 1944 dawned on a war-weary population that could hardly believe that hostilities might be over before its close. The war was going well for the Allies in Europe, Russia and North Africa, though there were stories of terrible suffering, but the Japanese still seemed to be keeping the upper hand in the Far East. And there were whispered rumours of US troops being stationed at various points along the southern counties, engaged on training exercises for some highly secret manoeuvres. This news gave rise to much speculation, and Colonel Lloyd-Worth thought that it could mean only an invasion of Europe.

Mr Day had just completed a further operation on A/C Don Smith's left eye, assisted by Sister Knowles with VAD Nurse Griffiths as runner. A previous attempt to graft on a lower eyelid had been unsuccessful, and Day had thought carefully before trying again.

'Well, that's that, and we can only wait and hope,' he said, pulling off his theatre cap and mask. 'Thanks once again, Sister, and I know you'll keep a very close watch on that dressing. It's having a good surgical sister that gives me the courage to do things like this. McIndoe takes risks, and isn't always successful, but he tries again, and the more you do, the better you get at doing it.'

'Yes, sir,' said Lily automatically, rinsing her hands in a bowl of warm water. 'Get Price to help you lift Don on to the trolley, will you, Nurse Griffiths?'

'I'll help you,' said Day with a smile at the nurse who was known to have started a romantic friendship with the young aircraftman. 'Here we go – whoops! – tuck in his blanket, good girl.

'Er – talking of McIndoe, Sister Knowles,' he continued casually, 'I believe there's an RAF officer at East Grinstead who's a bit unclubbable – doesn't take to the jollifications there.'

Lily's mouth dropped open, and she raised her eyes from her instruments to the surgeon's face. He looked slightly amused.

'I beg your pardon, sir?'

'Mm, yes, I've had a word with the great McIndoe on the phone – blew my own trumpet a bit as a burns and eye man, mentioned that I'd got a very good theatre staff, said perhaps this chap might do better at Beverley – just a suggestion, you understand – and he seemed quite happy about it and said he'd send the chap here for post-op next month.'

Lily could scarcely believe her ears. 'Oh, Mr Day – I can't tell you how much . . . Matron must have said something.'

'Yes, Sister, you owe a lot to Big Bertha. In fact we all do. Salt of the earth.'

'Thank you, thank you so much, Mr Day. I'm so grateful!'

'All right, Sister, no need for histrionics. And this chap had better co-operate. He sounds a bit of a nutcase – sorry, neuropsychiatric – and may need very careful handling. But of course you're used to those too. Anyway, keep an eye on Smith, won't you?'

The patient was wheeled back to Hut 1 by Nurse Griffiths and Ernie Price; she gazed down fondly on his flushed, expressionless face, half obscured by the eye bandage.

Sister Knowles was ready and waiting for the new admission, who had been flown by helicopter from East Grinstead and brought by taxi from the little landing strip on the edge of the common. It was one of those clear February days with a promise of spring in the air, and her heart was full of hope as she stepped forward to greet the group captain. This time there were no bandages to be seen, but he wore an airforce-blue scarf around his head, a black patch over his left eye and a glove on his left hand.

'Welcome to Beversley!' she said with a smile, and he raised his right hand in a half-salute.

'This is your doing, yours and Grampy's,' he said flatly. 'Did I feel a fool when McIndoe said he'd heard from the old chap. I'd half a mind to refuse point-blank.'

'Thank goodness for Grampy's sake you didn't,' she replied, though this was news to her; McIndoe had been got at on two fronts, then, and Sandy's next words proved that he knew.

'And when that eye surgeon of yours put his oar in, I hadn't much chance of getting out of it, but it's only on the understanding that I can transfer to Marchwood Park down by Southampton Docks,' he said as he walked through the imposing entrance to Bever House and into the reception area, ignoring her proffered arm. The taxi driver followed with his suitcase.

'Oi'll take this up to y'r ward for 'ee,' the man said, but Lily told him to set it down as the group captain was going to a single room upstairs. The patient raised his eyebrows.

'Am I? That's something, anyway.'

'So far, so good, then,' murmured Lily, hiding her apprehension under the cool, professional smile that matched her uniform. 'Will you come this way, please?'

His room was the one in which Tim Baxter had recovered from pneumonia, and Redfern was clearly pleased by its comfort and privacy.

'You can come down to the wards at any time and have your meals with the other men, or trays can be sent up to you here,' she said. 'The bathroom and WC are just across the corridor. When you're ready, you can view the rehabilitation unit and workshop, and you'll be assessed and advised about the type of occupation to take up.'

'Thanks, Sister Lily.' He allowed himself a brief smile. 'I'd rather take meals here. Any tea going?'

'I'll have some sent up, though you can boil a kettle on the gas-ring at the end of the corridor, and there's milk and sugar on the shelf. Lunch will be at half-past twelve.' She put her hand on his shoulder as he sat on the bed. 'And welcome to Bever House, Sandy. I'm sure you'll be glad you came here, as many other men have been. It's quiet, it's peaceful, and Mr Day –'

'And good old Mr Day tricked me into coming,' he finished. 'Must remember to thank him.'

It was on the tip of Lily's tongue to say that he could go to Marchwood Park any time he liked, and she wouldn't try to stop him; but she remembered that she was a Princess Mary's Royal Air Force Nursing Sister, and he was a courageous man damaged in body and mind in the service of his country. So she simply smiled and replied, 'Just as you say, Group Captain. Please excuse me now, as I'm needed in the theatre this afternoon.'

Nurse Griffiths sniffed when she heard that Sister Knowles's officer had got a room to himself, while A/C Smith was in Hut 1 with its chatter, wireless and constant comings and goings.

'You can't get away from class distinction, not even in a place like this,' she muttered just loud enough to be heard. 'I see that her ladyship's officer is getting the full VIP treatment.'

'Did you say something, Nurse Griffiths?' asked Matron, suddenly appearing behind her. 'Group Captain Redfern was ordered to go into a single room by Colonel Lloyd-Worth, if you want to take it up with him.'

The VAD blushed and mumbled some sort of an apology. Miss McGawley nodded and passed on, but that afternoon she paid a visit to the group captain's room and initiated a long talk about his injuries, his background, his feelings about his stay at Halton and at East Grinstead, and any hopes he had about the future. She looked at his head, the area of bald, shiny skin over the left side, the external auditory passage that was all that remained of the ear, and the empty hole beneath the eye-patch; she nodded approvingly at the healed lids of the other eye. She looked at the short, nailless fingers amputated at the first phalangeal joint on the left hand and the newly healed scars on the right one.

'Good movement,' she commented. 'I'd get you doing some tapestry with those fingers.'

'Oh, very suitable, that's what I was hoping to do,' he replied. 'Christ!'

'Mm, yes, you've come a long way, but you've still got a fair way to go, Sandy – or would you rather be called Alex?' Her voice was motherly and matter-of-fact. 'McIndoe's done a splendid job so far – how long is it – four or five months? Another year, and you'll be that much more advanced – and the war might actually be over! Have you thought about civvy street at all?'

He could not help admiring her audacity, her chatty, natural attitude to what he saw as a gross and hideous disfigurement. He paused, considering his reply. If she could be aggressively frank, so could he.

'I've learned to respect the RAF sisters,' he began, and she bowed her head slightly in acknowledgement. 'But I know when I'm being softened up, Matron, so don't bother to patronise me. I know very well that it was Lily Knowles who schemed to get me here, using a surgeon and my grandfather to influence McIndoe. I've no objection to spending time here before going back for more surgery, but it's only fair to tell you that I have no feelings of a sexual nature towards Lily Knowles, and you'd better tell her so, to avoid misunderstanding.'

'Oh, thank God for that. I was afraid you were planning to marry her, and I couldn't spare the best surgical sister I've ever had. What a relief! Thanks so much for telling me.'

He was a little surprised by this reaction, but merely shrugged. 'Glad to hear it.'

'And while we're on the subject of sexual attraction – or its opposite – may I ask you something else?' she asked pleasantly. 'Is it only Sister Knowles who has this off-putting effect on your libido, or does it extend

457

to all nubile females? If so, it's very typical, and quite understandable. You're at a low ebb, Alex, and it's bound to affect your sexual drive. Don't place too much importance on it – it'll certainly come back as you regain your strength.'

He glanced at her and hesitated. 'It seems pretty obvious to me that with the sort of ghastly mess I've got for a face, there's not likely to be much – er . . .'

'Don't be too sure. And don't underrate your hero status. Ask Ernie Price to tell you his rude joke, though I'm sure you'll have heard it before.' She laughed. 'Actually Mr McIndoe is very much aware of the need for acceptance of burn scars, not only by the world in general but by the patients themselves. Anyway, I'll leave you to think things over and get used to your new surroundings – and I'll try to warn Sister Knowles not to throw herself at you! Do try to visit the rehab unit tomorrow in Hut Two.' She stood up. 'Well, I've enjoyed our useful little chat, but I'd better be getting along now. And, Sandy, I do hope that you'll enjoy your stay at Bever House.'

She left him pondering on their 'useful little chat'.

'Stone the crows,' murmured Group Captain Redfern.

Old Mr Redfern lost no time in travelling down to visit his grandson, and Lily arranged for him to put up for two nights at the White Hart. She greeted him with real affection, warning him that Alex was not easy to deal with.

'In fact you could say that he's uphill work, Grampy. If you could persuade him down to the private bar of the White Hart this evening, I'll join you later, as soon as I get off duty.'

She took Mr Redfern up to Sandy's room, where he

greeted his grandson warmly, grasping his right arm and putting a hand on his shoulder.

'I can't get over the change in you, my boy,' he beamed. 'Standing – walking – and you've put on a bit of weight. It's a miracle!'

Sandy's shadowed face expressed some bewilderment at the old man's enthusiasm, but Lily understood only too well that Mr Redfern was thinking of the unrecognisable, pain-racked figure in the bed at RAFH Halton, with head and hands swathed in bandages and a mouth full of cruel obscenities. By contrast, the morose man now before him was a cause for rejoicing.

Sandy flatly refused to face a company of strangers at the White Hart, so the grandfather and grandson took their tea and supper together in his room; Lily begged for an extra portion to be sent up on the tray. She also offered to show Mr Redfern the facilities of the workshop in Hut 2, and he eagerly accepted, though Sandy refused, saying he had no interest in knitting or embroidery.

'Here we are, Grampy, and you'll see that the workshop covers many skills at different levels of ability,' she said, switching on the lights, for the day's activity finished at five thirty. 'Woodwork's popular, whether it's practical, like making foot-stools and putting up shelves, or ornamental, like carving figurines – look at this Madonna and Child! Or the model Spitfire over there. We do painting and sketching, picture-framing, typewriting and using the telephone with one hand. As for the weaving and tapestry that Sandy's so scornful about, it's wonderful exercise for the hands. I've seen men with only stumps for fingers, persevering to thread needles with coloured wool, even when they hurt and bled.

Sandy has lost the phalanges of his fingers on the left hand, but he still has the thumb, and he's going to have to learn to do all the things that a normal hand can do.'

'And he will, Lily, he will,' said Mr Redfern, nodding vigorously. 'And it's all thanks to you, my dear. I look upon you as a daughter, you know, and I can wish nothing more for Alex than such a fine young woman as yourself. My wife and I were deeply grieved when he drifted away from you, and we couldn't condone his open flaunting of that married woman, the wife of a brother officer. We felt the shame and disgrace of it. Oh, how I wish that my wife could know that he's found you again!' And to Lily's embarrassment he took hold of her hand and held it to his lips.

'Thank you, Grampy. As I said, it's not going to be easy, and we must both be patient and help Sandy to help himself. That's the aim and object of rehabilitation.'

'He didn't like the atmosphere of McIndoe's ward, Lily – the frank way of talking, you know, the jokes and leg-pulling. Yet he used to be so *outgoing*, and loved parties, drinking, dancing – and of course that mad infatuation – so distressing, and we felt helpless . . . Oh, Lily, dear, how good of you to forgive him!'

'But, Grampy, think of the danger he was in, risking his life night after night,' said Lily softly. 'He needed the partying and the company of – well, a woman like Mrs Palmer-Bourne.'

'Oh, don't mention her. She wasn't fit to lace up your shoes!'

'But I *will* mention her, Grampy,' said Lily steadily. 'She was available to give him what I was no longer willing to give. Because of the obvious risk to myself.'

'I understand you, my dear – but I still don't see how he could possibly prefer her to you.'

'It's not for us to judge others, Grampy,' she said, thinking of her father. 'Let's just be thankful that we've got him here at Beversley, and I intend to see that he gets the maximum benefit from it – but it will take time. He needs to find his own way back, and mustn't be rushed or he'll dig himself in and refuse to budge!'

Grampy must have taken her at her word, Lily decided, because the next day Sandy allowed himself to be persuaded to go for a walk with his grandfather, up through the beech wood and on to the common. Their progress was slow, and Grampy's legs ached by the time they got back to Beversley village, while Sandy was more tired than he cared to admit; but both agreed they felt better for the exercise and fresh air, and that evening Sandy accompanied his grandfather to the private bar of the old inn, to drink a couple of bitters with him.

They chose a dark corner, and Sandy sat with his back to the room. At first they were the only patrons, but within a quarter of an hour a couple of khaki-clad officers came in, followed by a man and a woman who had eyes only for each other. Having downed their bitters, Grampy ordered two more, asking what food was on offer. The landlord produced a freshly baked game pie, and served them generous wedges with mashed potatoes, which they ate with a good appetite and without talking to anybody other than each other.

Then Ernie Price came in with a flight sergeant on crutches. They sat themselves at a table in the middle of the room, and looked around to see who else was in.

461

'Hey, look who's here. It's the elusive group captain!' said Ernie cheerfully, and nodded to Mr Redfern. 'Visiting yer son, eh?'

'Grandson,' corrected Grampy. 'And you are . . .?'

'Price, Ernie Price, medical orderly from up the road, and this is Ron, on his first visit to the local hostelry. So what are we all havin', then? My round!'

Four bitters were brought to the table, and Ernie got up to move their chairs, so that all four were seated at the central table. Two bitters downed in quick succession had relaxed Sandy Redfern, and although he had not spoken previously to either Price or Ron, he was made aware of their complete indifference to his appearance.

Ernie got out a pack of cards. 'Who's for a round o' rummy?'

'Er – I'd have to be reminded how to play it,' said Mr Redfern, glancing at his grandson. 'Are you familiar with it, Alex?'

'Is it anything like whist?'

'No, that's an old women's game. C'mon, we'll have a dummy run, and ye'll soon get the idea.' Ernie shuffled and cut the cards, and dealt out seven each, face down. He put the rest of the pack on the table, and turned up the top one.

'Oho, the queen of hearts, that's a good start. Your lead, Granddad, and I'll show yer what to do. The object o' the game is to make up a run or a flush, and yer throw out any card yer don't want, like this, see?'

When Lily Knowles put her head round the door of the private bar soon after nine o'clock, she found three convivial players exchanging mock insults and poor Grampy struggling to keep his eyes open.

'So this is where you are!' she said sternly, though

her eyes twinkled. 'I had no idea you were a cardsharper, Sandy Redfern!'

'Yeah, he's a right demon. We got to watch him all the time,' grinned Ernie.

'And poor Mr Redfern's tired out – it really is too bad of you!' she scolded. 'Come on, Grampy, let's leave them to it, and get you up to your room. I can take your place, though I haven't the slightest idea how to play.'

When she had seen Grampy thankfully to bed, she sat down in his chair to be instructed in the rules of rummy while keeping her eyes on Sandy. His face was flushed, and the drink had loosened his tongue: he kept up a continual argument with the other two men.

'Hey, it's my go, not yours! You shouldn't have thrown out that ten of clubs!'

'Ah, but you can't see what I've got here, mate!'

'And you can't see mine – I got a hand like a foot!'

'Why, you misbegotten son of a . . .!'

As accusations and counter-accusations flew back and forth, mixed with loud laughter, the evening quickly passed, until, to Lily's horror, the landlord announced, 'Last orders, gentlemen, please.'

'Oh, my goodness, we've completely forgotten the time!' Lily cried.

'Oh calamity!' Ernie Price rolled up his eyes in dismay, though he'd been well aware of the hour. 'Tell yer what, Lily, take the group captain home an' creep in through that door by Hut Two. I unlocked it before we came out, but be as quiet as yer can. Me and Ron'll follow yer up.'

'Just a minute, Ernie,' said Redfern. 'The matron told me to ask you to tell your rude joke.'

'Which one?'

'I don't know. She only mentioned one.'

'What were yer talkin' about?'

'Oh, er – depression and – er – not much interest in – er . . .'

'Why be down an' out when yer could be up an' in? Was that the one?'

'Watch it, mate, there's a lady present,' said Ron.

'Yes, and *this* lady's leaving *now*,' said Lily, firmly taking hold of Redfern's right arm. 'Good night, all!'

Walking along the old High Street arm in arm with the man she loved, Lily savoured the moment. She felt grateful to both Grampy and Ernie Price, who in their different ways had given Sandy a day of healthy exercise and social contact. She mentioned this to him.

'God, I'm tired, Lily,' was all the reply he gave her.

'Shows you've had a good day,' she said briskly. 'You won't need any rocking tonight!'

They reached Bever House and followed Price's advice, going round to the back of the house and approaching Hut 2. Sure enough, the door that led to the covered walkway connecting the Huts with the main building was unlocked. They entered and silently made their way towards the house; just before the covered way reached the back door, it broadened out into an L-shaped annexe where theatre trolleys and empty gas cylinders were stored. It was from here that they picked up a strange, rhythmic banging sound, and looked at each other.

'Something's going on there,' whispered Lily. 'It could be an intruder of some kind. I'll go and have a look.'

'I wouldn't if I were you, Lily,' he whispered back. 'Let's just get into the house.'

But Lily's curiosity was aroused, and she crept towards the annexe and the odd noise. Redfern followed her, fearing that she might be in for a shock if his suspicions were correct.

And they were. Lily stood stock-still at the sight that met her horrified gaze: a man and a woman in the act of copulation on a theatre trolley that banged on the wall in time with the man's thrusting movements. He lay on top of her, fully clothed, and her nurse's uniform was pulled up to reveal her knees on either side of him.

'Don! Oh, Don! Ah – ah – ah!' she was gasping in time to his pleasurable grunts.

Lily was pulled back sharply by Redfern's right arm.

'Don't let them see you,' he whispered.

'Nurse Griffiths! On duty – in uniform!' she said incredulously. 'I shall have to tell Matron.'

'No, don't – don't get her into trouble, Lily. Neither of them saw you, did they?'

'No. He was looking down at her, and she had her eyes shut tight. Sandy, this can't be allowed. I'll have to speak to her tomorrow, and say I'm reporting her to Matron. So *flagrant*!'

'Please, Lily, don't make a big fuss about it. She's doing him a world of good – I mean, she's showing him that she doesn't mind his face.'

She turned and stared at him. 'I don't mind *your* face, Sandy, but that doesn't mean I'd jump up on to a theatre trolley and – when somebody might come along at any moment . . .' She stopped speaking, overcome by embarrassment.

'Wouldn't you, Lily? Wouldn't you really?'

To her further vexation she saw that he was laughing at her.

'Sandy Redfern, you've had too much to drink! What a thing to say!'

She turned on her heel and marched off through the back door, and he followed her along the old kitchen corridor to the reception area. There she stood and faced him, he faced her, and they both collapsed into stifled giggles. So great was Lily's joy at seeing him laugh that she decided then and there not to report Nurse Griffiths; she would simply tell the girl that she had been seen, and warn her that if it ever happened again she would be in serious trouble – in more ways than one, Lily would tell her severely.

And then she realised that she was actually grateful to the shameless couple, just as she was to Grampy and Ernie. Thanks to all of them, Sandy Redfern had taken a big step forward on his road to recovery.

Chapter 21

'Cheer up, Lily,' said Sister Selleck. 'Haven't you noticed the date? March the twenty-first, the traditional first day of spring – and isn't is heavenly to see the almond blossom out? And all the daffodils? It's what I missed most when I was in Malaya – the beauty of an English spring!'

Lily knew that her colleague was trying to raise her spirits following Group Captain Redfern's return to East Grinstead for further operations on his head and left hand. She nodded and forced a smile.

'I know, Jane, I know. It's just that poor Sandy's going to need a lot more surgery, more than he realises, I think, and I miss him so much.'

'I miss *my* friends, and one doctor in particular,' went on Jane Selleck quietly. 'There's been no word from any of them since Singapore fell to the Japs over a year ago. I try to hope that some may have survived, but – well, I daren't think about what might have happened to them.'

'Now you've made me feel terrible for moaning over Sandy. I'm sorry, Jane.'

'Don't be, old thing. Just think about the terrific progress he made while he was here. Let's face it, he's got some pretty horrific facial injuries, and it was no wonder that he was a bit of a – I mean, you've done a great job with him, Lily, getting him started at the workshop – and wasn't it good to see him going down to the White Hart with the others, after being so unsociable at first?'

'Yes,' smiled Lily. 'I even got him to come to Great St Giles's with me on Sunday!'

'So you did, and we all remarked on it. It's a medieval church, isn't it?'

'Yes, it dates back to the fourteenth century. You get a sense of history there, thinking of all the generations that've come and gone over the centuries.'

'Did the vicar speak to Sandy at all?'

'Just a handshake on the way out, the same as for everybody – yet in a way he *did* speak to Sandy, through his sermon. He based it on a text from the Book of Job, and I noted it down.'

'Can you remember it?'

'Yes, I looked it up. "He knoweth the way that I take, and when He hath tried me, I shall come forth as gold."'

'Oh, that's wonderful, Lily, so appropriate! What did Sandy think?'

'He didn't actually comment on it, though I know he took it in. I just touched his arm when the vicar repeated it for emphasis.' She paused for a moment, and then went on, 'There are some things that aren't easy to talk about. It was like when I wanted to take him to visit my Aunt and Uncle Westhouse in Belhampton Park. Uncle Gerald lost an eye when he was shot down in the last war, and wears a patch. He was in the air force, the Royal Flying Corps it was called.'

'So they'd have a lot in common, then.'

'So *I* thought, but Sandy wouldn't go – said he didn't want to meet more strangers, didn't want a lot of fuss; he'd feel self-conscious, et cetera, et cetera – so I gave up.'

468

'Perhaps he didn't want to be paraded in front of them as your new fiancé,' suggested Jane Selleck bluntly. 'Or he might have been afraid of meeting your uncle with the eye-patch, in case he saw a reflection of himself in twenty or thirty years' time.'

'I don't know, but I didn't argue with him. I just long for him to come back to us. I reckon he should be ready by the end of April. It'll be so beautiful here by then!'

'I'll keep my fingers crossed,' smiled Jane, 'but I wouldn't bank on it if I were you. And when he *does* come back, may I suggest that you don't appear to be too eager?'

Her doubts turned out to be justified, for Redfern's road to recovery was beset by setbacks and disappointments. An area of skin grafted from his right thigh to the left side of his head failed to establish a good blood supply and sloughed off. Mr McIndoe wanted to make a second attempt, and meanwhile he had grafted skin from the inner aspect of the thigh to the palm of the left hand. It was taking longer than expected, and Redfern had become depressed; his letters were brief and scrappy, and by mid April ceased altogether. Grampy wrote sadly that Alex had 'lost heart', and begged Lily to visit if possible, but Matron said she could not be spared for a long weekend; only when Sister Selleck volunteered to be on day and night call for forty-eight hours was Lily able to set out on the long journey by train, going via London.

As soon as she saw Redfern lying on his bed in Ward 3, Lily knew at once that he had lost the ground he had gained at Beversley.

'You shouldn't have come,' he said as she sat down beside him.

'Thank you for your warm welcome, Group Captain,' she replied, determined to remain calm and to sound light-hearted. 'And in spite of it I'm happy to see you again! I know your op wasn't a success, but Mr McIndoe will have another go. It's all happened before, you know.'

'If I consent to it,' he said. 'I'm sorry, Lily, but you could never understand what it's like in the small hours of the night when you can't sleep, your graft hasn't taken, and your thigh's bloody sore from where the skin was sliced off. You just feel too fed up to go on. You just want out.'

'It's true that I haven't had that experience, Sandy, but the other men in this ward have all suffered something similar, some not so bad, some much worse, so you can't say you're the only one,' she said in a low voice. 'You've got lots of reasons for pressing on. Let McIndoe try again.' She looked at his bandaged left hand. 'He operated on that, didn't he? How's it doing?'

'Dressings off today, so you can see for yourself,' he answered briefly, and when the sister came along to remove the dressings in a bowl of warm saline solution, Lily was allowed to watch. With bated breath she saw the hand revealed, puffy and purplish-red in colour, with four nailless stumps that ended at the proximal phalangeal joint; the thumb was normal.

'Very nice,' said the sister. 'The swelling and discoloration will go in time, and you'll be surprised at what you can teach those short fingers to do. Well done!'

'So that's good news, Sandy,' Lily said with conviction. 'And you're going to have that graft to the head done again, and this time it will take, you'll see! I'll be thinking of you and praying for you, like all the rest of us at RAFH Beversley, and you'll "come forth as gold" – remember that?'

He sighed heavily and lay back on his pillows, closing his one eye. 'You're much too good to me, Lily. If you've got any sense you'll go back to your sailor and make him happy.'

There was a long silence while Lily debated with herself and her surging emotions: how should she best reply? She finally spoke quietly, close to his ear.

'But apparently I haven't got any sense because I've chosen *you*, Sandy, that's the trouble. Now, what about me reading the newspaper to you? There's a terrific battle going on in Italy, around somewhere called Monte Cassino – and there are lots of whispers about a big invasion of Europe to take place soon, but nobody knows when or where the Allies will land. They're saying that the war could be over by the end of the year.'

'Doesn't affect me whether it's over or not – I'm out of it.'

'I have a cousin and an uncle out in Italy, so it'll certainly affect them, like hundreds of thousands of others – and just think of our prisoners of war, longing for the day!'

'Yes, of course – I always was a selfish swine.'

'Selfish or not, you've shown tremendous courage – and you persuaded me not to report Nurse Griffiths, for which she is truly grateful! Come on, Alexander Redfern, you must look forward and find your way to a new life in the future. And this time I'll be there to help you.'

And it's going to be uphill work, she added silently to herself.

*

The burgeoning Hampshire countryside was at its loveliest when the group captain returned to RAF Beversley in mid-May. This time he did not come as a stranger, but was eagerly welcomed by both patients and staff. The colonel shook his hand, and Matron actually gave him a kiss on his right cheek, and so did Sister Selleck. Nurse Griffiths smiled shyly: Don Smith had been discharged, but she now wore his engagement ring.

And Lily? She had decided to be discreetly cool towards this man who had the power to set her pulse racing and turn her knees to water. She now had to show him to his bed in Hut 1, where he would be with other post-operative patients, Matron having decided that it would be better for him to have company, and besides, the single rooms were all occupied. He grimaced briefly at hearing this, but made no objection.

'I've been in touch with my relatives in Belhampton Park,' Lily told him, 'and Aunt Alice has invited us to dinner at Cherry Trees; Uncle Gerald will pick us up in his car, and we have only to name the day.' She watched his face closely as she spoke, and seeing a completely blank look, she went on quickly, 'I've got a half-day on Thursday, and I shall accept. I'll give my aunt and uncle your apologies, and say that you'd be bored stiff and would rather stay here and sulk – that's right, isn't it?'

'Now then, Lily, there's no need to make me out to be an ill-mannered bore –'

'You said it, I didn't. Suit yourself,' said Lily airily, hoping against hope to call his bluff and make him change his mind.

She need not have worried. A second stay in Ward 3 and a successful skin graft had influenced

Redfern's outlook on life, and Lily's words about looking forward to the future had had an effect, even though he might not admit it. He therefore shrugged and remarked that he supposed it was only polite to accept the invitation, and that he'd better make the effort.

'Thank heaven it worked!' Lily confided to Jane Selleck in relief.

Gerald Westhouse arrived punctually on an afternoon of clear skies and snowy May blossom. He shook Sandy's hand cordially, and remarked lightly on their similar injuries. On arrival at Cherry Trees, Lily at once saw that little Robert, not Redfern, would be the centre of attention.

'He's into everything; I daren't take my eyes off him,' said his fond grandmother. 'Geraldine will join us later when she finishes work at Pinehurst, and Amelia's away with the ATS on some *very* hush-hush business.' She chatted away happily, making a point of not looking at Redfern.

'Have you heard from Geoffrey lately?' asked Lily.

'Oh dear me, yes, it's frightful out there. Geoffrey says that the tanks and infantry are wiping out the last of the German resistance, but the condition of the ordinary Italian people is heart-rending, especially the children – he gives away half his rations by the sound of things.'

Lily saw to her satisfaction that Sandy had made friends with Robert. The child took no notice of his bandaged head, being used to his grandfather's eyepatch, and was chuckling away happily at the farmyard noises Sandy was making for Robert's wooden animals – 'moo' and 'baa' and 'cock-a-doodle-doo!'.

Alice took advantage of this diversion to tell Lily

that Gerald had gone out again to fetch another visitor. 'And who else do you think is coming to dinner, Lily?'

'Not Mabel?' said Lily, her eyes widening. 'Oh, Aunt Alice, am I going to see Mabel again?'

'Yes!' smiled Alice. 'We know that she wants to see you, and it's Daisy who's keeping you away, so – he's bring Geraldine back from Pinehurst, and Mabel's coming too!'

Lily's heart was in a flutter. She had so long wanted to heal the rift with her stepmother, but she wished that their reunion could have taken place in private, rather than in front of their Westhouse relations – not to mention Redfern, the man who had replaced Mabel's beloved Tim in her life. She glanced towards Sandy, and saw that he was down on his knees with Robert and the toys. How on earth was she going to introduce him?

They heard the car arrive, and within minutes Mabel was in the room, her eyes seeking Lily. She held out her arms. 'Lily, me dear! Thank God to see yer again!'

'Oh, Mabel, I've missed you – so many times I've wondered how you were . . .'

The two women held each other in a long embrace. 'It's been too long, Lily.'

'Oh, yes, it has, it has – but there's somebody here that I – I want you to meet,' faltered Lily. 'This is my friend Sandy – er – he's staying in RAF Beversley at present, between operations.'

Sandy had got up from the floor when Geraldine claimed her son's attention, and he now held out his right hand to the pale, thin-faced lady.

'Good afternoon,' he said, looking to Lily for more information.

'Sandy, this is Mabel – Mrs Knowles, my stepmother – my late father's wife.'

Mabel was staring at the man who stood before her. 'I'm sorry, I didn't know – I didn't realise ye'd been injured so – so badly,' she said almost apologetically. 'Yer poor face – an' yer hand.'

'Yes, I was, er, singed a bit when I crash-landed. Lily's been a tremendous help to me.'

His tone was matter-of-fact, but Mrs Knowles continued to stare at him in a rather disconcerting way. 'Did Lily say yer name's Sandy?'

'Yes, short for Alexander. Call me Sandy or Alex!'

'Alex?' she repeated. 'I knew an airman called Alex in the last war. He was engaged to one o' me dearest friends, but he got shot down an' killed, leavin' her expectin', poor ol' Maudie.'

'Er, Mabel, we won't talk about that now,' said Alice, glancing significantly at her daughter, whose circumstances were embarrassingly similar. 'Are we all ready for a cup of tea?'

But Mabel went on speaking as if she had not heard. A painful memory had been awakened, and she had to follow it through.

'Maudie nearly lost her life havin' that baby, an' so did poor ol' Dr Knowles, me father-in-law. I know, 'cause I was there – I was the midwife. It was in Maudie's little lodgin'-house, an' there was only the landlady and me friend Norah to help when he put the forceps on an' pulled the baby out – then he passed out himself, an' we had to lay him on the bed along o' Maudie –'

'Mabel, that's enough!' hissed Alice. 'There are men present, and we don't talk about those sort of things in mixed company.'

475

'No – let her go on,' said Redfern. 'What happened to the baby, Mrs Knowles?'

'Ah, that was the worst of it. His blinkin' parents stole the baby off her. She had childbed fever an' was put in the infirmary, and along came the Redferns an' took him! *She* was an ol' bitch if ever there was one – treated Maudie like dirt, and turned her away from the door o' that posh villa up in St John's Wood. Nearly broke her heart, it did – it was wicked. Wicked!'

A silence had fallen on the company. Mabel stared again at Sandy, who had gone very pale.

'Yer face is scarred, poor boy, but there's somethin' about yer . . . What's yer family name?'

His answer was scarcely above a whisper. 'My name's Redfern, and my father was an airman in the last war. He was killed before I was born, and I was always told that my mother – that she had given me up willingly. Mrs Knowles, I think I was that baby . . .' His voice tailed off, and Lily came to his side; she put an arm on his shoulder.

'That was a lie! A wicked lie!' cried Mabel, as Alice made her sit down. 'She loved yer! She worshipped yer! Yer was all she had left of Alex Redfern!'

'Tell me what happened to her, Mrs Knowles,' he said urgently. 'Where can I find her?'

'Oh, yer poor dear boy, yer can't. She died back in 1928 or 9, only thirty-six she was – but she made a name for herself, oh yes! She an' her young brother went down to Twickenham, an' she got a job in films. Oh, there was nobody to touch Maud Ling, oh, my!'

'*Maud Ling?*' whispered Sandy. 'Do you mean the film actress – that beautiful woman?'

'The very same. That was her, that was yer mother!' said Mabel triumphantly. 'We lost touch

476

after I'd opened Pinehurst, but Daisy an' me used to go an' see all her films. They were silent films, o' course – I heard Maudie couldn't do the talkin' pictures 'cause of her London accent. She was a real Cockney, was Maudie, bless her heart. Terrible childhood she had, both parents drank, an' she used to beg in the streets and got sent to the Waifs an' Strays in Dulwich.'

By now Sandy Redfern was crouching down beside Mabel's chair, listening intently to every word. Lily kept her hand on his shoulder.

'And she – she died about fifteen years ago, you said?' he asked.

'Yes, it was TB. Caught up with her in the end. An' she never saw her son again.' Mabel paused, and then had a sudden thought. 'Oh, my Gawd, I called Mrs Redfern a – sorry if she was yer grandmother, but it nearly killed Maudie, losin' her baby like that.'

'It's all right, Mrs Knowles,' he said. 'Grannie died last year. Grampy's still around, and he's been very good to me since – since what happened. You've given me back something I'd lost, and I'm grateful.' He leaned over her chair and kissed her. 'Thank you!'

By now there was silence in the room, as everybody present became aware of what had been revealed. It was as if a reconciliation had taken place. Mabel kissed Lily again, and then Sandy; she put her arms around them both, as if giving them her blessing.

'Mabel dear, you do know that I wouldn't have been the right wife for Tim, don't you?' Lily now asked. 'Nor yet the right matron for Pinehurst? You knew that all along, didn't you?'

'Yes, dear, an' ye've made the right choice, though it was hard on my Tim at first. But I'll tell yer somethin',' she added with a smile, 'I think he *has* found the right one now, just under his nose, one who'll be a good matron as well, much as I'll be sorry to hand over.'

Lily stared. 'But I thought Beryl Penney and Billy Webb were . . . Has she changed her mind?'

'Ha! No, not little Beryl, she an' Billy were made for each other. No, I mean me sister Daisy. I've known for ages that she likes him, and now that he's not got – er – any other ties, why not?'

'*Daisy?* But she's so much older!' said Lily in surprise.

'Is she? She'll be forty this year, and he's thirty-three. Seven years isn't such a big gap, an' Tim needs a mother as much as he needs a wife. It couldn't be better. Mind yer, this is between ourselves for the time bein', Lily. We must give them time to come round to it.'

The dinner that followed was a celebration of a kind, and Lily glowed in the warmth of Sandy's loving looks and Mabel's newly discovered closeness, both to herself and the man she loved. Thanks to her he had discovered his mother and knew that she had not abandoned him, but had loved him with all her heart.

And if Gerald Westhouse recalled reading something about Group Captain Redfern's torrid and much-publicised affair with some society woman, he wisely decided to forget it.

It was a perfect evening. Gerald Westhouse had dropped Mabel off at Pinehurst and then took Lily and Sandy as far as the southern edge of the common, near to the beech wood.

'Save your petrol ration, Uncle Gerald, and put us

478

down here,' said Lily. 'We'll walk down through the wood.'

'Just as you please. Nice evening for a stroll.' Did Westhouse give them an amused look as they got out of his car? 'Good night, Alex – come and see us again. You too, Lily.'

They waved as he drove away, and then turned to each other and linked arms.

'It's been a most extraordinary visit, hasn't it?' said Lily as they walked along the track beneath the bracken-covered bank on the edge of the wood. 'You never expected such a revelation when you reluctantly agreed to meet my Westhouse relations – though I'm only related by my father's marriage to Mabel. Aunts Alice and Daisy are her sisters.'

'I feel as if I'm in a dream, and will have to wake up at some point,' Sandy mused. 'In a way I feel that I've found my mother, even though she died so long ago. It makes such a difference to know that she really loved me, Lily – it means far more than the fact of her being Maud Ling the actress, though God knows that's incredible enough. Do you remember going to the cinema in Leicester Square to see her in an old film about the early days of flying?'

Lily nodded. *'On Wings of Love,'* she replied. 'And you said she was as beautiful as Vivien Leigh! And do you remember the silence when you praised Maud Ling to your grandparents? Your grandmother changed the subject quite abruptly, I thought.'

'Yes, you're right, I do remember,' he said. 'They knew who Maud Ling was, of course. How strange that they never told me.'

'I think your grandmother was afraid of losing you,' said Lily, looking thoughtful. 'Think what she

479

must have felt every time Maud Ling's name was mentioned – and it may have preyed on her mind, the way she'd kept you away from your mother. But she's not here any more, and it isn't for us to judge her.' Lily tried to be charitable about a woman she had instinctively disliked from their first meeting. 'You must tell Grampy that you know,' she added quickly. 'Somehow I think he'll be pleased, don't you?'

'Yes, I'll tell him. Oh, bless you, dearest Lily, if it hadn't been for you, I would never have met Mabel, and never known about my mother. I owe it all to you!'

She stopped walking, which meant that he had to stop also. 'I've benefited too, Sandy. I've found Mabel again, and I can see why my father needed her so much – for her understanding, her sheer goodness of heart. Even at a time like this, there's so much that's good in the world!'

They had reached a point where the bank curved down to the level of the track, and a path turned off into the ancient wood. Lily turned and put her arms up around his neck. They were free to exchange a kiss, unwatched by the occupants of Ward 3 or the staff at Beversley, and he could not help but respond to her.

'Lily – thou fairest one of flowers all . . .'

'Sandy – Alex – don't let's waste this lovely evening,' she urged softly, taking his hand and leading him into the cool dimness of the wood. 'Show me I've really, truly got you back again.'

She began to unbutton her summer frock, and he drew a long, shuddering sigh. He could not refuse: he had not the will to deny her, and yet – did he still have the strength? Would his blood run hot again as it had in the past, before he had been so changed? His hands trembled as with hope and fear he took off his uniform; their clothes seemed to melt away as they sank down together on the forest floor.

'I love you, Sandy,' she murmured. 'I've always loved you, ever since that day in St Paul's.'

It was so natural, so inevitable, and he was surprised at how quickly he was stirred by her kisses, her warm flesh, her breathless whispers. He was astonished at his own arousal and the ease with which he entered her. A gasp, a cry, a mix of tears and laughter as they were swept along together towards a shared climax – and within minutes they were satisfied and lay replete in each other's arms. There were words of love, of gratitude, of utter contentment.

But very soon for Redfern there was a moment of doubt, of questioning.

'Dearest Lily, ought I to have done that? Will you be sorry, as you were after that other time at Waltham Abbey?' he asked her.

'No, no, no, it wasn't you who made this happen, it was me – and I've got no regrets at all,' she reassured him. 'And you've made me happier than ever before.'

He held her closely in his arms, thankful beyond words for knowing that he was still the same whole man, as fit and able as he had been before his terrible accident – and yet there was a change in him: he was now more appreciative of a woman's love. His desire was to please her rather than himself, and in achieving that desire, he was richly rewarded.

The light was fading, and the air was cool upon their skin. It was time to put on their clothes and go home to Bever House. So great was Lily's happiness that she hoped she would not meet anybody on their return – for surely both staff and patients would take one look at their faces and know what had passed between them!

As the days passed, and May gave way to June, it was indeed obvious to Matron, Sister Selleck and the nursing staff that Lily was a woman in love, though Redfern's emotions were less easy to fathom. Everybody agreed that he was much nicer, willing to join in the talk in the ward, and the growing speculation about an Allied invasion of Europe; but there was also an inevitable sadness at the loss of his former good looks. To Lily in the happy blindness of love he was as handsome as when they first met – but to the rest of the world he was a pathetic sight, and he knew himself to be so; and whereas she looked confidently ahead to the end of the war and a shared life together, he could see no further than a series of operations, shuttling backwards and forwards between East Grinstead and Beversley. And what would he look like at the end of McIndoe's reconstructive surgery? What kind of work would he be fit for? How could he ask any woman to share such a limited existence?

While smiles and glances passed between them in public, they no longer had the privacy of his single room. He made friends with the other men in Hut 1, and joined them in the workshop and in their explorations of the village and visits to the White Hart. After a few days Lily realised that he was avoiding occasions of being alone with her, and she thought she knew the reason: he did not want to make a serious commitment until his operations were completed and he could start making plans for the future. In this she was correct, but what she did not guess was his decision never to marry – and therefore that he should not take advantage of her again, as he saw it. He told himself that he had no right to use her as he had used Daphne for his own gratification, willing though that woman had been; and sooner or later he would have to tell Lily this, though he shrank from the scene that would ensue, the hurt it would cause her.

And so he put it off from day to day, until the sudden momentous news of the invasion of France put all private concerns into the background. The landings on the Normandy beaches became the only subject of conversation, and the end of the war in Europe now appeared much nearer. Would it be over by Christmas? They all listened to the wireless, which gave limited news on that memorable 6 June, named D-Day, and on the days and weeks that followed. Exciting as it was, there was a sense among the patients at Beversley RAFH of being only spectators now, out of the battle and watching as others forged ahead. RAF and USAF bombers pounded German defences along the coast, while airborne troops landed behind enemy lines. Inevitably the Allies suffered heavy casualties, and the families of men involved lived in constant anxiety. Lily was frankly relieved that Sandy was now out of the arena.

Less than two weeks after D-Day another terrifying weapon of war appeared over southern England, the pilotless planes named by Hitler as V1s and by the Londoners as doodlebugs, robotic machines resembling aircraft, with orange flares streaming behind them: when their engines cut out they fell randomly to earth and exploded, wreaking death and destruction on the civilian population. Was this to be another Blitz? It seemed like it, and once again children were evacuated from the capital as the hideous machines streamed in over an area of Kent and Sussex that became known as 'bomb alley', with East Grinstead right in their path.

It was time for Redfern to return to the Queen Victoria Hospital for further surgery, and Lily was determined to arrange a time for them to be alone together. On the day before his departure she persuaded Jane Selleck to invite Raymond, an officer in Hut 1 whom she quite liked, to join her in an evening stroll to the White Hart, while Lily invited Redfern to make up a foursome. They strolled out together, enjoying the warm evening air, chatting about the progress of the Second Front, and went into the private bar of the old inn where Redfern's appearance was known and accepted by the landlord and locals, though inevitably there were some whispers like 'Don't look now, but . . .'. He had almost learned to take these in his stride, but Lily saw how his whole body stiffened in embarrassed resentment.

The four of them left shortly before closing time, and walked at a leisurely pace up the High Street; the sky was clear, with a glowing sunset over Wychell Forest to the west, and when they reached Bever House Jane caught Lily's eye and suggested they sat in the garden for a while. As planned, Lily gave Sandy's arm a tug.

'Let's leave Jane and Ray together,' she whispered. 'That's what they'd like us to do! We'll walk up a little further to have a last goodbye before you leave tomorrow. Oh, *do*, Sandy, *do*!'

He knew what would happen if he gave in to her, and his better judgement dictated that he should gently refuse; but three half-pints of ale had weakened his resolution, and Lily's greeny-gold eyes gleamed in the fading light, pleading with him. He could not refuse, but took her outstretched hand and let her lead him into the rustling dark of the beech wood, as ready, as eager as herself to make love again.

'Lily, you enchantress, you witch of the wild wood, you've cast a spell on me,' he whispered, folding her in his arms.

'You're leaving me again tomorrow, and who knows what may happen, my love, before we meet again?' she answered. 'We've only got tonight for certain – only tonight!'

'Tonight,' he repeated as they lay down together at the foot of an ancient tree. 'Tonight, Lily, fairest of flowers all.'

Tomorrow there would be time enough to repent . . .

The advance of British, American and Canadian forces into Europe progressed, and on the Italian front the Allies had reached Rome. At home the terror of the doodlebugs continued, and they were occasionally seen over Belhampton. People gazed up at the mindless machine, praying that the buzz of its engine would not cut out while it was directly overhead, and feeling guilty relief when it passed on to cause havoc elsewhere.

A heavy influx of patients injured in the aftermath of D-Day kept the staff at RAFH Beversley busy, and all leave was cancelled; Lily could scarcely find time to visit Belhampton, let alone travel to East Grinstead, but on one occasion when she cycled over the common to Pinehurst, she was warmly welcomed by

Mabel, Miss Styles, Beryl and Geraldine; Daisy and Tim had gone to Belhampton where Daisy had a dental appointment, and as Tim needed new bicycle tyres, he had gone with her. Lily suspected that Daisy wanted to avoid a confrontation between Tim and the girl he had loved for so long and so unreservedly, but she accepted the explanation at face value.

'How's Alex gettin' on, Lily?' enquired Mabel. 'Has he had his next operation? Can he write to yer?'

Lily confessed that most of her information about Alex, as she was learning to call him, came from his grandfather, who sent her detailed accounts of him after each visit, while Alex was only able to scribble brief notes, and after his operation had asked another patient to write on his behalf.

'He hopes to be discharged again some time around the beginning of August,' she reported.

'Good! An' yer must make sure to bring him to see us. I could tell him a lot about his poor mother. Wasn't it a shame, the way she was kept away from her own son?'

'I know he'd love to hear anything that you could tell him, Mabel.'

And who knows, there may be something else to tell him, she thought to herself with a secret little thrill. It was now six weeks since her last menstrual period, and she daily looked out for other signs such as a tingling and swelling of her breasts, a queasy stomach on waking: was she imagining it, or was it really true? Was her body again preparing to nourish a child – *his* child? Was this to be the affirmation of their love, the proof that she now belonged to Alex Redfern, his future wife and helpmate? Oh, let it be so, she prayed, for the circumstances were very different from what had happened three years ago.

She could not yet be sure, and hugged her secret to herself. By the time he returned to Beversley she might be able to whisper it in his ear, and their future would be assured – for what greater incentive could there be for him to face the world as a fit man, healthy and whole, the possessor of a wife and child?

The summer days passed, and by August Lily was certain of her pregnancy. She had told no one, wanting Alex to be the first to know; but when he did not return she began to be anxious about him, and then came a worrying letter from his grandfather.

My dear Lily, *he wrote*

I am hoping that you will be able to obtain permission to visit Alex, who was in a very low state when I saw him yesterday. You have always had such a good effect on him, and I now beg you to use your influence again. Mr McIndoe says he will not be able to remodel that left ear without lengthy surgery, and Alex has been depressed by talk of a glass eye and a half-wig that would be held in place by a removable fixative. The thought of depending upon such necessities for the rest of his life has understandably upset the poor boy, and nothing that I could say was of any help. In fact he got angry with me and spoke as harshly as in those dark days at Halton. He actually told me not to visit again.

I am therefore begging you, my dear Lily, to visit him if you possibly can. Only you can restore the hope that he now seems to have lost.

The letter was signed, 'From your humble and grateful friend, Alexander W. Redfern.'

Lily went straight to the matron and showed her the letter, for it was more eloquent than any words of her own; Miss McGawley was naturally sympathetic.

'You know the staff situation here, Sister Knowles, and the burden that will fall on the rest of us when you are absent. I can let you go to East Grinstead on Saturday, but you must return on Sunday as soon as you can. Is that quite clear?'

Lily thanked her, and wrote to tell Mr Redfern that she would visit Alex in two days' time. She promised to do all that she could to lift his spirits, and smiled secretly to herself when she thought of the news she had for him: what better news could there be to restore his hopes for the future?

On Saturday she set off early on the London train to Waterloo, took the underground railway to Victoria, and travelled down to East Grinstead, arriving at the Queen Victoria Hospital well before noon. She went straight to Ward 3 – and received news that almost caused her to faint on the spot.

'Why didn't you telephone before coming all this way, Miss Knowles?' asked the ward sister. 'You could have saved yourself the journey. Group Captain Redfern was transferred to our rehabilitation centre at Marchwood Park on Thursday.'

'B-but he was due to come to RAFH Beversley again,' stammered Lily, thinking there was some mistake. 'He's to have all his convalescence with us.'

'Was he? All I know is that he specifically asked to be sent to Marchwood Park – that's near Southampton, you know,' said the sister, noting Lily's obvious shock. 'Would you like to sit down for a while, Miss Knowles? Can I get you a cup of tea?'

'No, thank you, Sister, I must go. I'd better be off to

Southampton,' said poor Lily, hardly knowing what
to say or think.

'Your best plan would be to go up to London
Victoria, and travel down to Southampton from
Waterloo,' said the sister kindly. 'You could be there
this afternoon if the trains are on time.'

Lily nodded and made her way out of the hospital
and towards the railway station where she got a
London train to Victoria and went to find a taxi. Her
thoughts were whirling around in her head, sapping
her confidence and sowing doubts abut Redfern.

*He doesn't want to see me again. He's deliberately gone
to Marchwood instead of Beversley. He must be regretting
what happened between us. He's left me for a second time*,
said the voices in her head. And another voice asked,
*Has Daphne Palmer-Bourne come back to him? Has she
taken him away from me again?*

No answer came, and Lily stepped into the taxi,
trying to think clearly.

'Where d'yer want to go, miss?'

'Er – I think I want to go to . . .'

'Pardon, what did yer say, miss?'

'Yes, er – Elmgrove, please.'

'Where's that, miss?'

'Oh, I'm sorry, that's Hamilton Terrace – St John's
Wood,' she said vaguely. 'Yes, that's it, St John's
Wood.'

'Are yer sure, Miss? Hamilton Terrace, St John's
Wood?'

'Yes, that's the place,' she said, because she knew
she had to see Alex's grandfather and tell him the
news – *all* the news. She hoped he would accompany
her to Southampton, for she now felt very much
alone. Yes, she needed to see Grampy.

*

489

'Lily, my dear! Come in, come in!' Old Mr Redfern held out his arms and kissed her cheek.

'Have you seen him? How did you find him? Is he any more hopeful? He'll have been glad to see *you*, I don't doubt!'

'Oh, Grampy!' was all she could say, and burst into tears.

'My God, Lily, what's happened? Tell me at once!' he said in alarm.

'He's at Marchwood Park, Grampy. He didn't want to see me – he's gone to Marchwood Park!' she sobbed as he led her into the living room and sat her down in a comfortable chair.

'Lily, my dear girl – try to tell me exactly what's happened. Have you seen Alex?'

It took her several minutes to compose herself sufficiently to tell the story of her fruitless journey to the Queen Victoria Hospital and her conviction that Alex had wanted to get away from her. Saying these words, she sobbed afresh, and he poured her a small brandy.

'Drink this, my dear. It will help to calm you,' he said, but she instinctively shook her head.

'Oh, no, Grampy, I mustn't drink alcohol.'

'But, my dear Lily, it's only a little drop. I'll add some soda water to it. It'll do you good.'

'No, I mustn't, because . . . oh, Grampy!'

He looked into her face, and she stared back at him. He gave a gasp of realisation.

'Lily, my child,' he said solemnly, 'are you . . .?'

'Yes, I'm expecting a baby, Grampy – *his* baby. It will be born next spring.'

Her voice was low, for she had not intended to reveal this to anybody before telling Alex, but now that the words were spoken, it seemed inevitable that

Mr Redfern should know, just as everybody would know soon – Matron and the staff at Bever House, Mabel and the staff at Pinehurst – and Alex Redfern himself.

But she was not prepared for Mr Redfern's reaction. He stood up straight, looking very stern.

'What? By God, he'll marry you or he's no grandson of mine! I'll see that he does his duty by you, or the doors of this house will be closed to him!'

'But I haven't told him, Grampy. I was going to tell him today, but – he doesn't *know*!'

'Then he damned soon *will* know! He knew what he was doing! You're a good woman who's always been faithful and loyal – which is more than I can say for *him*! I'll see that he marries you, Lily, and takes care of you, and so will I. Come on, my dear, we're going to Southampton!'

And by four o'clock they were on a train out of Waterloo; Lily leaned her head back against the worn red plush and closed her eyes. She found Grampy's presence comforting, and his concern for her reassuring; even if it was true that Alex no longer loved her, she knew that she would be cared for. She had no wish to coerce Alex into a shot-gun wedding, and also she was well aware that she had pursued him – tempted him, even – and so had nobody but herself to blame for her present situation. And yet . . . and yet . . . she still rejoiced that she was carrying his child, for she had loved him above all her other admirers. And always would.

The repetitive rattling of the train lulled her into a doze, and Grampy had to wake her when they arrived at Southampton. He helped her down from the train and sat her on a platform seat while he went to find a taxi-cab.

491

On that first Friday at Marchwood Park, Group Captain Redfern soon discovered that there would be no special favours as there had been at RAFH Beversley. The convalescents went straight to the workshops each morning and got down to serious training.

'No basket-weaving or rug-making here, old son,' said the man next to him. 'We produce items for aircraft navigation to the very highest standard, and they'll soon get your left hand doing just as well as your right.'

In the workshop in Hut 2 Redfern had learned to thread needles with wool for tapestry work, and his stumps had acquired a certain amount of dexterity that had impressed the instructor. On Saturday the workshop closed at noon, which annoyed him: his only aim in life now was to become proficient with his hands and able to live an independent life without being a burden to anybody, and especially to Lily.

Having nothing else to occupy him that Saturday afternoon, he went off on his own for a stroll in the grounds, which overlooked Southampton Docks. Below him the Channel lay blue and sparkling in the August sunshine, in contrast to his sombre reflections.

Lily had given him back the will to choose life rather than death; she had led him to discover the truth about his mother, in place of the lies he had been told about her; and he had lain in Lily's arms and known the deep satisfaction of pleasuring her, feeling his manhood restored to full vigour by her passion.

And now he had turned his back on her, or so it

would seem to her and the world in general; only he knew that it was not a rejection on his part, but a sacrifice. He had to make her despise him, when in fact he was giving her up to save her from a lifetime tied to a man with half a face, a false eye, false hair and ugly, unnaturally shiny skin made from patches cut from his thigh – a monstrosity that had made Daphne Palmer-Bourne vomit at the very sight of him.

He got out a packet of cigarettes, put one between his lips with his stumpy left hand, and struck a match, shielding the flame with his right hand.

Lily, oh, Lily, my love, I'm doing this for your own good if only you could know it.

Tears came to his eyes, his fingers shook and the flame went out. He was about to light another when a man's voice called to him across the lawn.

'Redfern! I say, Redfern, you're wanted at Reception.'

'Why?' he asked irritably, not turning round.

'There's an old cove breathing fire and demanding your presence forthwith!'

Guffaws of laughter greeted this, and another voice shouted, 'And he's got a young woman with him!'

'Oy, oy! Looks as if you could be in lumber, mate!' More laughter.

'Yeah – either take to the hills or get yourself over to Reception at the double, old son!'

Redfern's heart raced, and he could feel the blood pounding in his head. Because of course it could only be his grandfather – and Lily? – who had come to seek him out. And yes, there they were, coming across the grass towards him, Grampy looking flushed and angry, while *her* eyes were full of reproach. What could he say? Tell them to go away? Was he strong enough to turn his back on love?

They stood beside him, and his grandfather came straight to the point. 'You may have been a hero in the air force, Alex, but that doesn't give you leave to ruin a girl and then desert her!'

'Grampy, it's for her own sake –'

'Oh, don't talk rubbish! I've seen with my own eyes what this girl has done for you. She's pulled you back from the very jaws of death, and this is how you treat her – I'm ashamed of you, Alex!'

'Grampy, please, I –'

'Shut up!' shouted the old man with uncharacteristic vehemence. 'Your father was killed and left your mother with a child – and, God forgive us, we took that child away from her – but you've been spared, Alex, thanks to Lily, and you'll marry her and take care of *her* child, or you're no grandson of mine!'

Silence. The words hung in the air around them. A slight southerly breeze blew in from the sea. Redfern stared at his grandfather in blank unbelief, and then turned his eye on Lily. She gave an almost imperceptible nod, whereupon Redfern's face came alive.

'*Lily!* Lily, my love, why didn't you tell me?'

'I wanted to be certain, and then I went to East Grinstead and you weren't there. Oh, Sandy, I'm sorry, it was all my fault –'

She got no further, for he stepped forward and threw his arms around her, holding her close to him, kissing her and trying to shake his grandfather's hand at the same time.

'Oh, Lily, forgive me, please forgive me. I only wanted to save you from a life tied to – oh, Lily, is it really true? Am I going to be a father? Lily, will you marry me? Will you have me?'

'Will I, Alex? Will I? Oh, yes, yes, yes, I will!'

They clung to each other for a moment, and then turned to Grampy to include him in their joyful reunion, a three-part embrace.

They had not noticed a gathering circle of eager spectators, men of all ranks convalescing after or between reconstructive operations. These now began to clap and cheer.

'It's as good as going to the pictures, this is!'

'No, it's better – 'cause it's real!'

And they were right. It was certainly real.

Chapter 22

On the whole it was agreed that the September wedding at Great St Giles's had been a happy occasion, even though it was generally known that the bride had had to get married. She wore her Princess Mary's Royal Air Force Nursing Sister's uniform instead of the traditional white gown, and carried a bouquet of freshly picked garden flowers. There were sniffs and nose-blowings in the church when she and her tragically scarred bridegroom, also in uniform, made their marriage vows in firm, clear voices, and then, as a married couple, progressed very slowly down the aisle, exchanging smiles with relatives, friends and well-wishers. All the children from Pinehurst were there, with Mrs Knowles, Miss Styles and Miss Penney; Mr Baxter and Mrs Baldock sat smiling happily together, for their own wedding was soon to follow. A rather pale and peaky Canadian soldier, Sergeant Court, was sitting with his sister Mrs Knowles, having been sent back from Italy after a near-fatal attack of enteritis.

Mr Alexander Redfern, senior, beamed on all present, and did his best to make the bride's grand-parents feel at ease, though Mr and Mrs Rawlings were clearly disappointed; they had hoped for so long that their granddaughter would eventually marry Dr Dennis Wardley, and they had been further dismayed by the group captain's appearance. Meeting his grandfather, however, had been an agreeable surprise, and they were pleased to find that he was staying at the same Belhampton hotel as themselves, where Wing Commander Ned Carter and his wife Beatrice were also staying with their baby girl; Ned was Alex's best man, and the Rawlingses were impressed by their friendliness and courtesy.

The meeting they hoped to avoid if they could was with Lily's stepmother, whom they had never met. They had always pictured her as a bold seductress who had enticed their daughter's husband into an illicit affair, and were taken aback when she turned out to be a tired-looking but perfectly respectable widow of fifty, obviously loved by the children in her care. She stepped forward with her hand out-stretched to introduce herself in a friendly, unpretentious London accent, and said she was pleased to meet them at last; so having at first almost refused to attend the wedding, they were now more or less reconciled to it.

Gerald and Alice Westhouse were there with daughters Geraldine and Amelia, and little grandson Robert. Their son, Geoffrey, was still in Italy on 'mopping-up' operations after the retreating Germans.

Miss McGawley and Colonel Lloyd-Worth sat with Sister Selleck and other staff from RAFH Beversley, plus a fair sprinkling of ambulant patients. A dark-eyed, dark-haired woman with an unsmiling expression sat next to Mrs Carter, and when the bride saw her she broke away from her new husband's arm to kiss her friend Hanna Blumfeldt and thank her for coming.

The reception was held at Bever House, and Matron McGawley thanked heaven for a fine day, which meant that the guests could wander outside in the garden and grounds. A wartime buffet of sandwiches, home-made cakes and scones was laid out on the work-benches in Hut 2, the rest of the equipment having been pushed against the end wall. The colonel was in charge of the bar, and watched as Weldon and Price carefully dispensed measured amounts of beer and wine into glasses, with fruit juice for the children, who seemed to be swarming all over the place: this was better than any Sunday School treat!

When the bride bent down to accept a posy and a kiss from little Robert Westhouse, she turned round to find herself face to face with Tim Baxter.

'I'm so glad to see you here, Tim,' she said. 'Please accept my warmest congratulations!' And with the privilege of a bride, she gave him a kiss on the cheek.

'Same to yerself, Lily,' he said a little awkwardly, and immediately Daisy was at his side.

'Yes, I'm sure we all wish you happiness, Lily, you and – er – the captain,' she added, and she too was kissed by the bride.

'I'll never forget how kind you always were to me, Daisy, and I'm so happy for you and Tim. He couldn't have made a better choice.'

'Well, thank you, Lily. We wish the same for you and your captain.'

And so the last shreds of hostility vanished like a vapour in the sunlight.

Lily complimented Beatrice on how well she was walking. 'Nobody would guess you had a tin leg, Mrs Carter!' she teased, and then went in search of her other old friend from St Mildred's.

'Hanna, dear, how are you? Are you still at Queen

Adelaide's? And how are your parents? And Dr Edlinger?'

'My parents are well enough, and the doctor is with the liberators of Europe,' Hanna replied in her deep, grave tones. 'There are terrible rumours, and we must all be prepared to be shocked as never before.'

'Oh, Hanna! Surely it's good to know that Johannes is taking part in the liberation of Europe? And of his – his own country?' smiled Lily, trying to lighten Hanna's habitual pessimism.

'Germany is no longer his country, or mine,' Hanna answered sharply. 'And there is little *good* that he will find there.'

A shiver ran down Lily's spine, even though it was her wedding day and the sun was shining. She was to remember her friend's words at a later date.

The happy couple had arranged to spend their short honeymoon – the rest of that weekend – in London at Elmgrove, their future home where they would live with Mr Redfern senior; but for the time being, Sister Redfern was to continue working at RAFH Beversley while her husband continued to shuttle between the Queen Victoria Hospital at East Grinstead and either Beversley, or Marchwood Park, which had more advanced workshops. On their wedding night they heard the explosion at Chiswick of the first V2, a long-range rocket launched from bases in Germany and Holland, adding to the havoc of the V1s or doodlebugs. How many more 'secret weapons' might Hitler have up his sleeve? While the Allied advance continued through Western Europe, and the Russians liberated in the East, capturing town after town from the enemy, Londoners battened down their hatches once again in preparation for a second Blitz.

On the Sunday morning after their wedding, Lily begged to be taken to the morning service at St Paul's, and Alex willingly agreed. They were both deeply affected by the majesty of the great cathedral, a symbol of London's survival, and kneeled down together; Lily gave thanks for Alex's recovery and their reunion, and asked the Lord's blessing upon their child; her husband's loud and emphatic 'Amen!' caused heads to turn to look at them. It was not now possible to climb up to the galleries, for there had been some bomb damage, though the structure of the building itself was still sound; but in a quiet corner of the north transept they remembered their earlier visit to St Paul's and their first kiss, now celebrated with another.

Alex had at first wanted his wife to stop working after their wedding, but faced with the new terror of the V2 rockets, he was thankful that she was to stay in Hampshire. When he advised Grampy to leave London and live in a Belhampton hotel for the duration of the war, the old man refused point-blank, saying that he had come through the Blitz, and wasn't going to leave his home now, though he agreed that Lily should stay away from the danger of V1s and V2s.

Life resumed its busy daily pattern at RAFH Beversley, and the failure of the British and American attempt to take Arnhem during the last week in September was a bleak reminder that the war in Europe was not yet over; it resulted in enormous loss of life. Lily was getting much tireder, and spent much of her off-duty time resting, though she attended the quiet October wedding of Tim and Daisy at their parish church. There was a flurry of surprise when Daisy was described as a 'spinster of this parish', and her title given as Miss Court, not Mrs Baldock; it seemed that she had assumed the 'Mrs' on her return to Belhampton, as it sounded more respectable, though there was some speculation about her relationship to Mr Baldock, if in fact he had ever existed. In the church Lily joined Mabel, who sat watching her beloved Tim getting married to her own sister; she smiled when she saw Lily, for they both knew that the newly married lady would soon become matron of Pinehurst, and that it would be in safe hands.

By mid-November Lily's pregnancy was beginning to show, and she could feel the baby's movements. Alex had been reassessed by Mr McIndoe, and further surgery was discussed. Alex said that enough surgical reconstruction of his face, scalp and hand had been done, and he now wanted to start earning his living again. He had been offered a desk job in the RAF Administration and Special Duties Branch, which meant he would be involved with personal problems of officers and other ranks. It was thought that his own experiences would be put to good use when dealing with other servicemen.

'But he finds it very difficult,' Lily confided in Miss McGawley and Jane Selleck. 'He's not used to office hours, and when he doesn't see eye to eye with his seniors he lets them know in no uncertain terms! Consequently there's often a bit of an atmosphere.' She sighed. 'It's not easy to advise him, but I don't think he's cut out for a desk job. He says, "You can't fly a desk," and I know he dreams of getting back to flying – but how can he, with only one eye?'

When she was out of earshot, Sister Selleck told Matron that Sister Redfern was going to find marriage to the group captain an uphill road.

'I think she knows that, Sister,' replied Miss McGawley. 'She knew that before she married him. The answer is that she loves him, and that's what's most important in these cases. He's very lucky to have her. Not all of McIndoe's guinea-pigs have the backing of a woman like Sister Knowles – I mean Redfern. She'll have to stop working soon, though I don't know how we shall manage without her.'

Lily worked her last shift on 30 November, and was given an affectionate send-off by staff and patients, which made her feel both grateful and tearful. She packed her belongings and travelled up to London to join her husband at their home in St John's Wood. The number of V1s and V2s was diminishing, and proved to be Hitler's last strike against England, the death-throes of an evil regime, now facing final defeat.

She was warmed by her father-in-law's hearty welcome and, in spite of wartime shortages, he made sure that she had every comfort he could provide. As an expectant mother she was entitled to extra rations, and after the long hours of work at Beversley, she found housekeeping for her husband and father-in-law easy by comparison. Alex continued with his desk job until Christmas, but in the New Year he had decided to let McIndoe perform another operation on his scalp, after which he would apply for work in a small manufactory south of London where precision tools were made to a very high standard of accuracy.

'I think that will suit him better, Grampy,' Lily said. 'He doesn't really get on very well with other men who can't help looking at his face. And he doesn't want any special privileges.'

'Poor boy,' sighed the old man. 'I'm afraid a lot of Alex's problems spring from the fact that he was robbed of a mother's love. If only I could have my time again, I would never allow that poor girl to be denied the right to care for her baby. We thought it was for the best, you see – she had nothing, and we could give him everything that money could buy. But we denied him something much more important.' He sighed deeply. 'Maud was our housemaid, a pretty, saucy little thing – and I caught her in what is usually called a compromising situation with our younger son, Alex. My wife dismissed her at once, but he kept in touch with her. He was shot down before the baby was born. It was tragic, so tragic. And I've regretted it ever since. I should have been firmer, but my wife could never take to the girl.'

Lily hardly knew what to say, for she had sometimes wondered if this early deprivation had contributed to Alex's fickle temper and sudden changes of mood.

'But *you* will be able to help him, my dear,' went on Grampy with conviction. 'He needs you more than anything else in the world, just as his father needed Maud Ling, the only person who truly understood *him* – I can see that so much more clearly now. You helped him when he was at his lowest ebb – not like that other woman who only wanted to possess him and parade him in defiance of convention. Oh, how my wife grieved over her influence! And then when he was most in need of encouragement to survive, she vanished like the shallow-hearted creature she

503

was. And then you came, and I'll be forever in your debt, Lily. You saved him.'

He took her hand in both of his, and Lily said softly, 'I think the baby will be a great help to him, Grampy. When he can hold it in his arms and know that he's a father, I'm sure it will do wonders for his self-confidence.' She spoke from the heart, for she was feeling progressively more tired as the weeks went by, and longed for the day of the baby's arrival. A district midwife was booked for the confinement, a Mrs Tressell, who popped in sometimes to feel Lily's abdomen and listen to the baby's heart with a little metal stethoscope like an ear-trumpet. She told Lily that everything was normal, and how fortunate she was compared to some poor women with large families and low incomes. Lily was therefore reluctant to complain of her tiredness and headaches.

Christmas passed quietly at Elm Grove, and January brought news of more triumphant liberations of Europe. The war would surely be over soon, although Alex remarked gravely that it would take another two or three years to beat the Japanese. Then news filtered through of a terrible discovery the Russians had made as they advanced through Poland: they had come across a concentration camp at a place called Auschwitz, where Jews from all over Europe had been herded and slaughtered. The gas-chambers and crematoria were there to be seen, along with mounds of corpses, and some five thousand survivors, dying from starvation.

As soon as Lily read this in the newspapers and heard it on the wireless, she thought of Hanna and her relatives left behind in Germany. In spite of headaches and swollen ankles she hurried to Lisson Grove and Queen Adelaide's Hospital, which was within walking distance. On arrival she asked to see Sister Blumfeldt, and was told to wait in the office of the Labour Ward until the sister was free. After a quarter of an hour Hanna appeared, her usually serious expression darkened still further by what she had heard. Lily stood up and held out her arms.

'I heard the broadcast about that dreadful c- concentration camp, Hanna,' she faltered, 'and I – I can't think of anything to say, but I just wanted you to know that I . . .'

Words failed her, for what words could express sympathy for such horror? If Hanna's grandparents and other relatives had been sent to that place, there was no hope for them. She could only hold her friend's hand as they stood in silence.

It was Hanna who spoke first. 'I do not know, but I think it unlikely that my mother's people were sent to that – to Auschwitz,' she said. 'Mother said they were being taken to a place called Bergen-Belsen in Germany.'

'Then perhaps we can still hope?' ventured Lily.

'After more than five years? I doubt it,' replied Hanna. 'Thank you for coming, Lily. You have always understood why I am as I am.'

She let go of Lily's hand and looked at her critically. 'How are *you* keeping?'

'Oh, very well, never mind about me,' Lily said quickly.

'When is the baby due?'

'I've been given March the twentieth as the approximate date, but honestly, Hanna, don't –'

'About seven and a half months. When did your ankles swell up like this?'

'I really don't know, but all expectant mothers are the same, aren't they? It's the pressure!'

'Who is your midwife?'

'Mrs Tressell – she's very good.'

'I will have a word with her. Does she take your blood pressure?'

'No, my GP does that when he sees me.'

'How often?'

'Er – I really can't remember – it was before Christmas.'

'I will take it now, before you go. Wait here.'

Lily was embarrassed, and hoped that Hanna would not antagonise Mrs Tressell. When she reappeared with the stethoscope and cuff, they both watched the mercury fall in little jumps corresponding to the heartbeat.

'It is much too high, Lily. Have you any headache or flashes in front of your eyes?'

'Sometimes I do, but –'

'I will ask the consultant to see you. Come with me, please.'

Lily followed her into a room with an examination couch; before she climbed on to it Hanna asked her to produce a specimen of urine in an enamel jug. This proved to be difficult, but she managed a few drops. Hanna boiled it up in a test tube held over a gas burner, and muttered, 'Just as I thought. Solid albumin.'

'Does that mean my kidneys aren't working properly?' Lily asked, and suddenly felt faint. Hanna helped her on to the couch and rang a call-bell.

Everything seemed to happen very quickly after that. A doctor arrived and checked Lily's blood pressure, palpated her abdomen, listened to the baby's heart and looked grave.

'You have a condition known as eclampsia, Mrs Redfern, and I think that the best course would be to get that baby out. Is there a way to contact your husband?'

As if in a dream Lily gave the doctor the name of the tool manufactory, and Hanna held a form for her to scrawl her own name at the bottom. Her clothes were removed and replaced with an operation gown. She was given an injection and told that she would be taken to the operating theatre, by which time she was feeling too sleepy to care. She felt herself being lifted on to a trolley that trundled along a corridor and turned a corner into a place that seemed to be all white tiles, white enamel fittings and people wearing white gowns and gloves. A man's voice said, 'Could start having fits any time,' while Hanna whispered, 'Don't worry, Lily, I'll be here all the time with you.'

'Breathe deeply in and out, Mrs Redfern,' said another man's voice. 'In and out, in and out, that's the way – in and out . . .' The words echoed in her head as something black and rubbery was put over her face, and somebody held her arms as she drifted obediently into oblivion . . .

'All right, Mrs Redfern, you can wake up now! Good girl, come on, it's all over and you've got a little baby boy,' said a man's voice, but the words had no meaning for Lily. *Who* had got a little baby boy? Hers wasn't due for another seven weeks or more. Something rubbery was taken out of her mouth, and she realised that she was parched with thirst.

'Here's water for you, Lily,' said Hanna's voice, and a cup with a spout on it was held to her lips. She drank the cold water greedily, and then – ugh, she felt sick. A kidney-shaped bowl was placed by her head as she vomited the water she'd drunk. Where on earth was she? What on earth had happened to her?

'It's all right, Lily, it's all right,' said Hanna. 'You've had a Caesarean operation, and you've got a baby boy. He's only tiny, and we've put him in a special little warm nursery.'

'Oh, is it born? Can I see it?' asked Lily, trying to sit up but finding that her tummy was very painful and swathed in bandages.

'Not just yet, Lily,' answered Hanna. 'You and he must both sleep for a while. You were on the verge of eclampsia, which can be very dangerous for both mother and baby, but we caught you in time. Thank heaven you came to see me when you did. Now I'm going to give you an injection to help you rest and sleep.'

Rest and sleep . . . rest and sleep. That was all she had to do. She fell into a painless doze until wakened by a voice she knew and loved.

'Darling Lily! We've got a little boy – you've given me a son, and I've just been to see him. He's a splendid little chap, nearly five pounds, the nurse said – oh, my own dearest Lily.'

'Alex. We'll call him Alex,' she murmured. 'Alex – after his father and grandfather and great-grandfather.' Her husband was holding her hand and kissing it. There were tears in his eyes.

'Thank you, Lily, my own dear wife – and I'm so thankful that you're all right.'

'We must thank Hanna, Alex – it was because of her . . . I came to see her because . . .' Lily's voice tailed away, and it was some time before Alex Redfern knew what had brought his wife to see a German Jewess on that twenty-eighth day of January, their son's birthday.

The next few weeks were somewhat bewildering for

Lily. While the other mothers breast-fed their babies, brought to them every four hours from the nursery, she was given a china pudding basin and shown how to express her milk into it by massaging her breasts and squeezing the drops from the nipple. She had to drink three pints of water every day, and after a few days a good milk supply spurted readily out into the basin, which was then taken by the nurses to give to baby Alex in a feeding bottle. At the end of ten days Lily was allowed up, her stitches were removed and she was discharged home with instructions to carry on expressing and bringing the milk daily to the hospital, where she was allowed to see and hold her baby, and a few days later to feed him herself from the breast, which made her feel more like a real mother. And then came the great day when baby Alex, now weighing over six pounds, was discharged home.

A new and demanding routine now claimed Lily's time and energy, for her little son needed her almost constant attention, twenty-four hours a day, seven days a week. She seemed to be forever changing and feeding him, and a series of sleepless nights forced her to move out of the matrimonial bed and into a spare room where the baby slept, howled and was fed during the hours of darkness without disturbing her husband, for he had to be at the tool manufactory each day from half-past eight in the morning until half-past five in the evening. He complained that he missed her warm presence beside him, and she missed his, but the baby had to come first. The lengthening days of February and March passed in a blur of tiredness, caring for the baby and getting meals on the table, washing and ironing. Grampy willingly went out shopping for her, queuing with housewives for the meagre rations from the grocer's and butcher's with which the Redferns were registered. The charwoman had been kept on and came in twice a week to sweep, dust, scrub and admire the baby.

Lily lost touch with the progress of the war, and was surprised to hear her husband remark to his father, 'Sounds as if the RAF and USAF gave Dresden a good pounding – knocked it flat.'

'Did you say Dresden?' she asked. 'Why should a beautiful old city like that be bombed now, when the war's going so well?'

Alex shrugged. 'There's also industry there, Lily, and a big communications network. And if it shortens the war by as much as a day . . .' He left the rest of the sentence unsaid, and Lily's thoughts went out to the mothers and babies, children and old people killed or injured in the merciless bombing – the wrecked homes, the broken water-mains, gas and electricity supplies; many would probably freeze to death in the bitter February frost. She shivered, but a cry from her son drew her at once to his cot, and her pity for Dresden took second place to his needs. Her husband continued to be morose and pensive, and eventually she asked him if the bombing of Dresden bothered him.

'Not unduly,' he replied. 'Let's just say that I'm not sorry I wasn't involved.'

As he probably *would* have been if he was still a bomber pilot, she thought, but did not say so, as she judged that he was thinking the same.

As spring came once again to London, bringing new greenness to the grass and golden daffodils in the parks, war-weary Londoners began to brighten and look ahead to the end of the war in Europe; Hitler was reported to have shot himself, and

Mussolini had been dispatched by his own countrymen.

One day towards the end of April Hanna Blumfeldt appeared at Elmgrove looking flushed and agitated.

'Lily, what news I have! Johannes has written to my father to say that when he went in search of his wife and daughter he found that they had been killed in a raid over Stuttgart in 1943 – and he says that he is therefore able to make an honourable proposal of marriage!'

Lily looked up from breast-feeding her baby. 'Hanna! So *that* was the reason why he was so – er – stand-offish! Because he considered himself still married, even though it had been annulled by her Church?'

'Yes, oh yes, Lily, it explains everything. Poor Johannes! He must be allowed time to grieve for them, and then – but I cannot say more about the death of an innocent woman and her child, except that now that he knows himself to be single and free of cr – other commitments—'

'I understand, Hanna, don't say any more. Let's just hope that he'll soon be back and able to tell you how he feels,' smiled Lily, stroking her baby's head as he sucked. She felt she ought not to encourage her friend before Edlinger actually appeared.

But romantic dreams had to be set aside when the British and American armies discovered the concentration camps. What had previously been just a terrible rumour was now revealed to be worse than anything imagined. People gasped in horrified unbelief at the newspaper reports and photographs, the announcers' shocked voices on the wireless.

'Grampy, have you seen this week's *Picture Post*?' asked Lily, looking around for her favourite weekly magazine.

'Er – no, my dear, I think it may not have been delivered this week.'

'Then we shall have to buy one. Are you going down to the newsagents this morning?'

'I doubt if they'll have any left, Lily. They don't print so many copies with this paper shortage.'

That afternoon Lily pushed baby Alex out in his pram, and passing the paper shop she went in and enquired about *Picture Post*.

'We delivered yours yes'day, Mrs Redfern,' said the woman behind the counter. 'It's awful this week, all the pages are taken up wiv them 'orrible camps. Maybe yer menfolk 'ave 'idden it from yer. My gal was at the pictures last night, an' it was on the Gaumont British News. She 'ad to leave the cinema wivout seein' the big picture, she felt that bad.'

Lily bought the last remaining copy of the magazine, and when she got home she settled the baby in his cot and then sat down to look at it. Her mouth dropped open in horror at the photographs of the dying and the dead, heaped up in great mounds. There were men in rags, limping along on stick-like legs; a woman held a dead baby to her withered breast; hard-faced SS guards of both sexes were burying bodies in a communal grave, watched by British and American soldiers, some of whom held handkerchiefs to their noses and mouths because of the stench of rotting flesh. And the first of these camps to be discovered was near a village called Belsen.

'I must go to Hanna,' Lily said. 'Keep an eye on Baby for me, Grampy. I must go to Hanna.'

What could she do but put her arms around her friend and weep with her? There were no words to convey the fate that had overtaken Hanna's maternal grandparents, along with other relatives and neighbours. And Belsen was not the only death camp: there was Buchenwald, Dachau, Ravensbruck and the gas chambers of Auschwitz and Treblinka, bearing witness to Hitler's plan to destroy a whole section of the human race – the Jews. Lily held Hanna in her arms, sharing the sorrow, the outrage at such a blot on the face of civilisation – not in some far-off past time, but now, in this day and age.

On 8 May 1945, henceforward to be known as VE Day, the end of the war in Europe, there were wild celebrations in the streets, cheering crowds singing and dancing in the exuberance of victory. Thousands of people gathered in front of Buckingham Palace, to cheer the King and Queen on the balcony with the two princesses, and joined by Mr Churchill, the great Prime Minister who had led the nation during its darkest days, and who, in his own words, had supplied the lion's roar.

The Redferns rejoiced that the war was over, but felt that excessive celebration was inappropriate, the revelation of the concentration camps being still fresh in their memories, and Alex absolutely refused to go out and join the cheering crowds who would stare at his face. It was Lily's idea to invite the Blumfeldts to a meal in the evening of that memorable Tuesday.

'They'll feel the same way as we do, Alex,' she said. 'Let's ask the Professor and Minna to come with Hanna, if she can get away. Then we'll have a nice evening of conversation between friends, and open a bottle of wine!'

513

The Blumfeldts gratefully accepted, and the Professor asked if they might bring another friend with them: Lieutenant Johannes Edlinger had just arrived in London! Lily was delighted, for it could only mean that the doctor was soon to become part of the family, a son-in-law.

And so the dinner turned out to be both a celebration of victory and of an engagement. The Redferns were told that the first thing Johannes did on his arrival in London was to seek out Hanna and ask her to marry him. Their happiness showed on their faces, for at last Edlinger was actually smiling, and Hanna's eyes were bright when she looked at him. The Redferns were invited to attend their wedding in June at the synagogue in Marlborough Place.

'Will you invite the Carters too, Hanna?' suggested Lily. 'You and I and Beatrice survived the bombing of St Mildred's – and you came to my rescue on that awful night.'

'And you saved the lives of my wife and son, Hanna,' added Alex Redfern seriously. 'And I've survived, thanks to Lily, and Heinrich and Minna are also survivors. God only knows what the future holds, and there's still the yellow peril to beat, but tonight we can celebrate. Come on, everybody, stand up and raise your glasses – what shall we drink to? Victory?'

'No, there is also defeat as well as victory in Europe, and so much misery,' said the Professor. 'Let us drink to peace in the world, that never again shall such crimes be committed by mankind on mankind.'

There was a slightly awkward pause, and Lily said softly, 'Let's drink to friendship – and long may we be friends. To friendship!'

'To friendship!' they all responded, clinking their glasses together. 'To peace in the world and lifelong friendship!'

Epilogue

1950

'Oooh, this is a bit of all right!' said Mrs Knowles. 'Sittin' in a nice garden in the sun, an' bein' waited on hand an' foot – whoops! Be careful with the pussycat, Alex, else she'll scratch yer!'

She was reclining in a deck chair at the back of Elmgrove with little Vera on her knee; the two-year-old wanted Grannie to go on bouncing her up and down, but Mabel was getting short of breath.

'Now then, you two, you're not to bother Grannie, she's our guest,' said Lily, though she looked fondly at her children. What a pleasure it was to have Mabel staying with them, to be able to fuss over her and make some amends for her unkindness and ingratitude in the past.

'They're not botherin' me, Lily, bless their little hearts. I only wish yer dad could see 'em! It's a funny thing, but I thought I'd be at a loose end when Daisy took over as matron, but it turns out I've got a lot more freedom to visit me grown-up Pinehurst children an' *their* children who all call me Grannie. They live all over the place, an' they give me such a welcome when I turn up!'

She smiled contentedly, a thin-faced woman in her late fifties with faded blue-grey eyes. 'Ol' Dr Jarman says me heart could conk out at any time, but I don't worry. I've been ever so lucky, Lily. I enjoyed me nursin' in the first war, an' when me Aunt Kate left me Pinehurst, it was a dream come true, 'cause I'd always wanted to look after children who'd had a bad start an' needed lovin'. An' your dear dad always understood that, an' let me do it.'

'It's not called the Waifs and Strays now, is it, Mabel?' queried Lily.

'No, since the end o' the war it's been the Church of England Children's Society – not that I ever called 'em Waifs an' Strays, poor mites. They was always known as the Pinehurst Children in Belhampton, an' now that my Tim and Daisy've taken 'em over, I know they'll be in safe hands. Oh, thanks, Lily dear, a nice cup o' tea! Now, come an' sit down an' tell me about yerself these days. D'yer think Alex has settled down at last?'

Lily rolled up her eyes but spoke affectionately about her husband. 'Pretty well, I think, Mabel. The children don't notice his face at all. They've never known him any other way, and our friends' children are the same. People in the street sometimes stare and whisper, but he's been easier to live with since he started his job at Roehampton. It's such a wonderful place, and of course he meets other men – and woman and children, too, sometimes – who need fitting with artificial limbs, breasts, eyes, noses – you name it, they do it.'

'Thank heaven for such places,' murmured Mabel.

'And for such men as Sir Archibald McIndoe. He's been knighted for his pioneer work in plastic surgery, not before time. Alex and I can never thank him enough – or Dr Wardley, who worked with him, and now he's a consultant in maxillofacial surgery at St Bartholomew's.'

'An' did yer say Alex is back to flyin' in his spare time, even though he's only got one eye?'

'Yes, he flies Tiger Moths at air shows, and loves every minute of it. Flying's in his blood, I suppose, though my heart's in my mouth every time he takes off!'

'A bit different from that wartime bombin', eh?'

'Yes. I think that will always haunt him, the innocent civilians who . . .' She shrugged.

'It's all in the past now, duck, i'n't it?' said Mabel. 'An' there can't ever be another war like that, not after they dropped that atom bomb on that place in Japan. I mean, no country'd survive after a few o' them, would they?'

'Let's hope you're right, Mabel, but Alex thinks this trouble in Korea could develop into an ugly confrontation between America and Russia, who don't trust each other any further than they can spit. And with us in the middle, it just doesn't bear thinking about.' Lily shuddered.

'Then we won't think about it, dear. We'll talk about somethin' else. I was ever so pleased to meet yer grandparents at the weddin', and be civil to each other. Yer can go on thinkin' the worst o' people for years an' years, an' then yer find they're no better or worse'n anybody else. An' it was me last chance, wasn't it?'

'Yes, poor Grandmama and Grandpapa died within a very short time of each other when we had that awfully cold winter in 1947. Dear old Grampy went soon after; all three of them were over eighty and had come through the war. What about the people I know at Belhampton, Mabel? And have you heard from your brother George lately?'

'Bless him, Georgie never was much of a letter writer, but I get the odd postcard now and again. You know he met a nice little widow in Vancouver and married her? Very happy, so he says, an' I'm glad o' that, Lily, 'cause he was too much under the thumb of his friend Davy, the one who wouldn't come over to fight for the old country – not that I blame him for that, he never owed England anythin' – but, well, a man needs a wife, 'specially when he's gettin' older.'

'And Geoffrey Westhouse is now the senior partner at Westhouses, I hear?'

'Yes, an' married to his Dinah, an' got two little boys. Dinah's a plain-lookin' girl with front teeth that stick out a bit, but she's very capable, an' won't stand for any orderin' around from Alice – no fear! An' she's very good to Geraldine, who's stuck at Cherry Trees 'cause she relies on her parents to help support Robert. He's seven now, a bright little lad. Shame she never married like Amelia, who lives up north now. There are lots o' changes at Belhampton since the war. Bever House has been bought by somebody who wants to turn it into a hotel, an' they've started by pullin' down them two big huts at the back!'

A faraway look came into Lily's eyes and her memory drifted back to those days and nights at RAFH Beversley.

She was roused from her reverie by the sound of children's eager voices.

'I think there's somebody at the front door, Lily,' said Mabel, and Alex shouted, 'It's Ruth and Esther come to see us, Mummy!'

'Oh, what a nice surprise!' Lily jumped up. 'Let's go and meet them, shall we?'

Their visitors greeted Lily and little Alex joyfully.

'Mabel, you must meet my very best friend,' said Lily. 'Anne Eddington and her little daughters. This is Ruth, she's four, and Esther's two. And as you can see, they're soon going to have another sister or brother!'

'Yes, John and I want a boy this time,' said a very pregnant lady in a deep, accented voice, making her stately way into the garden. Lily sat her down in a deck chair. 'And this is Mabel, Anne – my stepmother who's staying with us this week.'

'It is a great pleasure to meet you, Mrs Knowles, and to see the goodwill between yourself and Lily. It was not always so, but she has come to know and appreciate your worth since we worked together at St Mildred's. I told her that to speak ill of her step-mother would not bring her own mother back to life. And I was right!'

Lily blushed crimson. 'Thank you for repeating my foolish words from so long ago, Anne. Tact was never your strong point, was it?' She glanced awkwardly at Mabel, who gave her a broad, reassuring wink.

'Oddly enough, we were talkin' about the very same thing before yer joined us, Anne,' she said. 'I mean, the way yer can have a wrong idea about people, an' hang on to old grudges. You're not from this part o' the world, then?'

'I am an English Jew, with every loyalty to the country I have adopted as my own,' replied Anne, blushing in her turn. 'Lily always understood why I am the way I am, and our husbands are very good friends.'

'Well, that's nice,' smiled Mabel. 'And who are you, dear?' she asked the solemn little dark-eyed girl who had been listening. 'Is your name Esther?'

'No, I'm called Ruth,' the child answered promptly. 'My sister's Esther. What's your name?'

'You can call me Grannie if you like, dear.'

'But you're not my grannie. My grannie's called Minna, and Granddad's called Heinrich.'

'Is that a fact?' said Mabel. 'Well, you are a clever girl, aren't yer? How old are yer?'

'Four and a half. How old are you?'

'Ruth! You mustn't ask Mrs Knowles questions like that!' said her mother. 'Or she'll think you a very rude little girl.'

Lily simply could not resist temptation. 'No, Anne, not rude, just thoroughly tactless, like her mother. Yes, Ruth is her mother's daughter, through and through.'

The former Hanna Blumfeldt looked hurt. 'You would not believe that Lily and I are such close friends, Mabel. And if we live to be eighty, we shall still be close.'

'When we're in our eighties, it will be into the next century,' said Lily. 'And who can tell what the world will be like in another fifty years?'

'Well, I'll be pushin' up the daisies, that's for sure,' laughed Mabel. 'And as for these dear little souls, who knows? I reckon it's just as well we can't see into the future, don't you?'